"The Lord of the Grins"
by U.R.R. Jokin

(Mark Egginton to his friends...
if he had any...)

(...seriously... why else would
he spend ten years writing this
parody?)

Luna Press
PUBLISHING

...DID WE MENTION IT'S A PARODY?

First published by Luna Press Publishing, Edinburgh, 2016

www.lunapresspublishing.com

ISBN-13: 978-1-911143-06-2

In a world full of hate and sadness
Comes a man spreading joy and gladness.
For the love of your laughter
Is all that I am really after.

CONTENTS

THE FOLLOWSHIP OF THE NOSE RING

BEING THE FIRST VOLUME OF
THE LORD OF THE GRINS

OF THE FONDLING OF THE NOSE RING

Many years ago in the Third Stage of Muddy Earth, in a land called The Snore, there lived a people known as Halfbits. What are Halfbits? Halfbits need some explanation, since rising cholesterol levels have killed off most of them, and there are very few left now. They are — or rather were — a shy retiring folk who liked nothing better than to eat, drink and sleep, all of which they did very loudly.

Now the most famous Halfbit was one Bilious Braggins. Not only did he like to eat, drink and sleep, he also liked to party. It was at one such party, a Disney-themed night that he fell in with a crowd of Dwarves who worked as bailiffs for a local estate agency. They told him of an impending job they had procured, to evict a lonely dragon called Smog from the mountain kingdom of Errorbore, and asked if he would like to join their gang. At first Bilious declined their offer of as much gold as he could carry, but when they threw in as many dragon steaks as he could eat, he practically snatched their hands off. At the same party had been the owner of the estate agency, an old man called Alfred Grey who had come as the wizard chap from The Sword in The Stone. He had overheard the Dwarves talking to Bilious and thought he had better go along to keep an eye on things. Alfred was a well-known figure in Muddy Earth. Although he owned an estate agency in The Snore, he spent very little time there, for he had another job as a children's party entertainer, and that was the one he enjoyed the most. So Alfred decided to introduce himself to Bilious. He approached the slightly excited Halfbit with the drooling mouth, and gave him his calling card, which read thus:

"MIGHTY MAGICIAN AND CONJUROR FOR HIRE.
FIREWORKS AND BALLOON SCULPTURES
A SPECIALITY.
CALL MUDDY EARTH 0141 AND ASK FOR
THE GRAND ALF."

So that is how they all met and their adventure is told fully in the book called "The Question of Errorbore or The Halfbit, There or Thereabouts." I will only touch on their adventure here. The company encountered many perils on their journey, starting with a group of long-haired greasy rock trolls who rolled about and got stoned out of their minds. Next, they were kidnapped by the Dorks of the Musty Mountains. Bilious managed to escape, or better, he was pushed out of the way by a swarm of Dwarves trying to escape. He fell down a hole in the road and was just about to ring his claim-line when he found a piece of jewellery.

He then encountered Grumble, an old slimy creature who lived deep inside the mountain, in a cave, because he didn't like the way the modern world was changing. It was there that Bilious realised he had found a nose ring that Grumble had lost, and it was also there that he cheated in the riddle game by asking what he had got in his waistcoat pocket — knowing that Grumble didn't have any proper clothes and wouldn't know what a waistcoat was, let alone what pockets were.

Eventually they all escaped from the Dorks and continued on to the Forest of Murkywood. At the eaves of the forest they came across a nudist colony run by Bjorn the Bare, and were allowed to stay the night on condition of going natural. They did not at first like the idea, but when Bjorn said there was a feast waiting, Bilious was the first to whip off his clothes, soon followed by the others, The Grand Alf was the last to agree, saying, 'I do not uncloak for just anyone'.

The next morning before setting off, Bjorn told them of the dangers of the forest and not to leave the tourist trail, which of course they did in the search of some mushrooms the Dwarves said were magic. They fought off giant spiders — after the effects of eating them set in — and were captured by the King of the Silly Elves' soldiers, as they all stumbled about in some sort of catatonic blindness. Bilious did not get captured because Halfbits can eat anything they want without effect and because, at the last moment, he disappeared with the aid of his nose ring which he had discovered could make him invisible or totally uninteresting.

The Grand Alf was on one of his many previously booked gigs down south, and he had also a bit of bother to sort out with The Necrodancer of Gone Duller, so it looked like Bilious had to save the Dwarves all by himself. He accomplished this with the use of his magic ring, and with all the Elves being so blind drunk, the fact that the funny little people riding a pink Nelliphaunt were really the Dwarves escaping on the barrels they had drunk dry, did not seem to sink in until much later.

The group next encountered the men of Fake Town, a place left over from an old Follywood backdrop, inhabited mainly by actors, directors, shop dummies and The Master Technician. After bragging about what they were going to do to Smog for a couple of weeks, they were told to put up or shut up. This enraged the Dwarves so much that they tore off their false beards and wailed. They wailed so much that the noise awoke Smog, who by now had got wind of the eviction order. He came rushing down from the mountain, spreading fire, smoke and pollution everywhere. He burned Fake Town to the ground and melted many of the Fake men.

Now it so happened that the local heroic MP Lunchalot was away on a freebie dinner, so it fell to the studio's poet/rapper Bad the Boreman (so named because of his terrible rhymes) to kill Smog. He did this with a S.A.M, which was left over from the last Mission Implausible film, starring a dwarven detective in high heels called Stomp Clues.

With the dragon dead, the Dwarves took possession of No 1 Errorbore Towers, a crumbling old dwarf commune. This created a problem, as both the Dwarves and the Silly Elves had wanted to build a holiday theme park there, so inevitably there was a scrap. Bad the Boreman turned out to be the descendent of Gillian the Cross-dressing Queen of Dame. He turned up with the remnants of Fake Town's New Model Army and Thatfool arrived at the head of his Silly Elven Army. At the Battle of the Few Armies the Dwarves came off worst, as their leader, Throbin Oakenhead, was killed. It looked bad for the Dwarves until their cousins, the Iron Dwarves, led by their king Nine Iron, fought all the way to the doors of Errorbore Towers, where Nine Iron clubbed to death the Dork King Golfumble.

When all the dust had settled, everyone got a piece of the profits and they were happy — apart from the Dorks, who were all dead, so it was not known if they were dead happy or dead sad. What was known is that they weren't dead rich. The Dwarves laid Throbin in his tomb with Dorkfist in one hand, and his Achingbone in the other.

So it came time for Bilious to go home, saying farewell to his friends. He was accompanied home by The Grand Alf to the doors of Brag End only to find it being ransacked by his cousins, the Sackfull-Braggins. Bilious threw them out and settled down in his peaceful bachelor pad, and nothing much happened for many years.

THE BILIOUS' BIRTHDAY BASH

Many years later, Bilious was living peacefully in his bachelor pad. He was organising his 111th birthday party with his nephew Foodo, whom he had adopted when Foodo's father's aborted attempt to do away with his mother for an insurance scam resulted in them both dying — Doggo dropped the stone he'd tied to his wife through the bottom of their boat and then realised he couldn't swim. So Foodo, whose birthday it also was, ended up living with Bilious.

On the day of the party, a knock came on the door of Brag End. It was The Grand Alf who had been booked for the big birthday bash. When The Grand Alf saw Bilious, he was astounded. Although 60 years had passed, the Halfbit looked unchanged. Now there had been rumours about Bilious's looks in Halfbiton. Some said he was lucky and some said it was in his genes. But others said he spent his money on visits to Rubbermask Brown at Razscalpel who amongst the people of Muddy Earth was known as the wiz of the facelift biz.

At the party, Bilious told his usual stories till everyone started to fall asleep. When they awoke Bilious had disappeared, and was never seen again by any Halfbit in The Snore. Foodo returned to Brag End to find The Grand Alf waiting for him. He was told that Bilious had gone away and left everything to him, including the nose ring he'd won from Grumble. When Foodo opened the letter that had been left for him by Bilious, the nose ring dropped to the floor and rolled to The Grand Alf who picked it up and examined it closely. He let out a cry of horror, for written on the inside of the ring was, Made in Morbid by Sourone Inc.

'This is the Enemy's nose ring!' The Grand Alf told Foodo. 'How did Grumble get this?' He rushed off in a hurry, telling Foodo he had to go and consult the Magic Circle, and some time passed before he returned late one night. 'I have learned much, young Foodo, and it is not good,' he said solemnly. 'The nose ring you have belongs to the Lord of Dark Moods, Sourone himself!'

'Sourone? Who's he?' asked Foodo nervously.

'Sourone is the most evil of our kind. He was thrown out of the Magic Circle for practising the Dark Arts of Mumbo Jumbo and Hoodoo. It was in the Second Stage of Muddy Earth that he set about the conquest of the world by the use of a jewelry set he had taught the Elves to make, and then later stole from them in a heist. He gave these out to the Free Trade Peoples of Muddy Earth and ensnared them.'

In a deep voice, The Grand Alf then chanted the verse of old:

Three blings for the Elven kings under no roof
Seven for the Dwarf lords digging for coal.
Nine for Mortal Kings long of tooth
One for Sourone, damn his black soul.
One nose ring to fool them all
One nose ring to blind them
One nose ring to stun them all
And in a dark alley moider dem.
In the land of Morbid where your hope dies.

I've been told that the Nine have escaped from the high security prison in Alkaseltzer, and are roaming free.'

'The Nine? Who are they?' asked Foodo, trembling.

'They are extrememly old kings of men, but they are now stars of horror films. Ooh, they are dreadfully evil young Foodo, and terribly bad, for they never took acting lessons ...' continued Alf. 'They ride on great black bicycles and are named the Ring Cyclists, which is Nasal, in the language of the Dorks, for they are bogeymen of nightmare. They will come looking for the nose ring soon, for it draws them hither. You will have to leave, and soon. Go to Riverdwell, and take someone you can trust.' Suddenly he stopped, and gestured Foodo to keep quiet. Then he leapt towards the window, and pulled through it a startled Halfbit. 'Stan Gamble!' he roared. 'How much have you heard?'

'Oh,' said Stan, trembling, 'I heard a bit, sir, about Elves and their blings. Oh, I'd dearly love to see the elven blings, sir, and I heard you say Master Foodo had to leave. I couldn't help myself, I had to hear more. But I needed the toilet, so that's when I farted, which you heard. But if I hadn't, I bet you wouldn't have heard me.'

'Don't fool with me, Stan Gamble, or I'll turn you into

something fat and stupid!' The Grand Alf shouted.

'That wouldn't be hard,' muttered Foodo under his breath.

'No,' said The Grand Alf, 'I've a better idea for you, Stan Gamble. You'll go with Foodo to the house of Elbow the Halfman at Riverdwell. Go soon Foodo, before your birthday, and for safety's sake leave the name of Braggins behind. Go as Mr Undersized.'

As The Grand Alf left, he heard Stan Gamble say, 'I bet we'll never make it, the odds are against us.'

Stan Gamble was the son of Hamble Gamble, who had been Old Bilious Braggins' gardener. Bilious always politely called him Master Hamfist, but now Stan did the weeding at Brag End, when he wasn't in the betting shop. Grafter, as Hamfist was commonly called, got his nickname by being the only Halfbit to be working by ten o'clock in the morning, something virtually unheard of in The Snore. The Gambles' claim to fame was that they knew more about growing vegetables than anyone else in The Snore did. This wasn't hard because the clever farmers (which weren't many) grew hemp; the stupid farmers had been taken in by an outlandish scheme called GM crops.

THREE'S A CROWD AND TOM IS LOUD

As Foodo's birthday approached, he packed up his belongings, and sold Brag End to Lobbit and Hotfoot Sackfull-Braggins and their son Looter, who everyone despised. Helping Foodo with the sale were his young friends Meretricious Brandishmuck and Peregrinate Talk, otherwise known as Messy and Pipsqueak. Foodo had told those who asked that he was retiring to Crockhollow, the home for elderly halfbits, but Stan had blabbed to the two young friends and bet them they wouldn't get past the Bandyleg Bridge. Well of course, they did, and further — through Farmer Flogger's fields, and past the old florists owned by Old Man Wilbur, who had forgotten his glasses and mistook one of the Halfbits legs for lunch. Thankfully, he was put right by Old Tom Bombastic who came along just in time to save them, hopping and singing a song:

'OLD TOM MOANS LIKE A VERY OLD MAN
HIS JACKET'S TOO TIGHT AND HIS BOOTS ARE TAN
HE CAN'T SKIP FAR SINCE HE GOT FATTER
HIS BOOTS ARE TIGHT AND HE'S MAD AS A HATTER

TOM'S OFF HOME TO HIS PRETTY GOLDIGGER
SHE'S VERY NICE WITH REALLY GOOD FIGURE
DOWN BY A POND, THAT'S WHERE HE CAUGHT HER
SILLY OLD TOM AND THE GLIBBER-WOMANS
DAUGHTER

OLD TOM SMILES, BUT HE'S NOT HAPPY
GOLDIGGER'S BROODY SO HE HAS TO WEAR A NAPPY
THAT'S WHY HE WALKS A LITTLE BIT FUNNY
SO HE SKIPS ALONG LIKE A FRIGHTENED BUNNY'

Tom, whose real name was Iarwun Bas-tada, which means Odd Fatherless One, took them home to meet his pretty young wife Goldigger, who was known as The Glibber Woman's

Daughter. There they ate strange cakes and hallucinated until morning. Old Tom sent them on their way the next day, warning them to beware of the mists on the downs, as they could lose their way among the Burrow-mounds of the Soulkings of Can't-Hum. As they were leaving, Tom taught them a rhyme to sing in times of peril and made them sing it.

They set off in bright sunshine, but soon the mist crept in, and one by one they were taken, till only Foodo was left, wandering until he fell even more witless on the ground.

He was woken by a rumbling voice, rather like singing, but he could not make out the words. He was bathed in a strange light that made anything white seem brighter. He could even see the dandruff on his feet. He was lying on the floor of a tomb surrounded by handbags, and on the ceiling was a ball of many mirrors that cast back strange dancing lights. Along the floor groped a huge dark arm. Foodo shrank away, and pulling out his sword stabbed at the arm. There was a shriek of pain, and all the lights went out. Foodo was scared, and called out for help. It was then in the dark of the lair, that Foodo remembered the rhyme of Bombastic, which he sang in a loud and strong voice:

'PLEASE COME AND HELP US MR BOMBASTIC
WE THINK THAT YOU'RE SO REALLY FANTASTIC
YOU'RE SO CLEVER THAT YOU DON'T MISS A TRICK
WE NEED HELP AS WE'RE SO VERY THICK.'

Then came Tom Bombastic, who was out chasing butterflies and picking daisies and had heard his cries. Racing across the fields to the tombs, he sang:

'IS THIS THE WAY TO THE VALE OF RING-LOW
IT'S THERE I LOST MY ARMADILLO
THESE MUSHROOMS MAKE ME AN HAPPY FELLOW
DING DONG I AM MAD MY BRAIN IS MADE OF JELLO'

Tom flung open the big double doors marked "Fire Exit", and the light flooded in. He threw out the large boxes that had made the strange sound, and dismantled the mirrored ball so that no one else would be caught in this tomb. 'You have been very lucky,' he said, freeing the Halfbit. 'Not everyone escapes the

Barriwights!' Then he waved them good-bye and set them on the road to Free.

FREE FOR ALL

The town of Free was so named because the town council had come up with the grand idea not to charge you for anything if you had both your great-great-grandparents with you. It had been done for the sake of the tourism industry, as nobody would visit Free since it had got a zero rating in Hegone Roving's Places to visit in Muddy Earth. Many people thought even that was too good a rating for the dullest place outside of a dwarven funeral parlour.

At Free, they made their way to The Prattling Parrot. On the door of the inn was written "Rooms to Let", and underneath in small letters was "No Elves or Dwarves, by order of Barman Butterball, Innkeeper and Proprietor." They entered the smoky interior, and quickly found the innkeeper, a huge fat man.

'You'll have to excuse us good sirs, we're a little short staffed at the moment,' he said looking at Nod and Bod, his two Halfbit workers.

As Foodo gave him their names, Barman Butterball, looked at them strangely. Finishing the introductions, Foodo said, 'And I am Undersized.'

'I can see that, little master,' chuckled the innkeeper. 'Oh now, what does that remind me of? Never mind, I suppose it will come to me later. Once you're settled maybe you would like to join us in the bar. We've a karaoke on tonight.'

After they had unpacked they went along to the crowded bar. Now, beer of any type can loosen the tongue of any Halfbit and especially those as foolish as Messy and Pipsqueak. After only a couple of drinks, these two began telling stories about Bilious Braggins. Foodo began to worry, in case this reminded any of the audience about his family name. To make things worse, he was being stared at by a man with a strange look on his face. The story was coming perilously close to the mysterious disappearance of Bilious when the man came across and whispered in his ear, 'You'd better do something, and quick!'

13

So without thinking, up jumped Foodo and rushed to the stage. It was announced that Foodo would sing that well-known song by Elvish Paisley, "Heartburn Hotel," at which everyone cheered, because Butterball's catering was so bad that bottles of indigestion mixture were supplied free to all the tables. Foodo felt embarrassed as he sung and kept touching the nose ring in his pocket, when suddenly it slipped onto his finger. There was a blinding flash as Foodo stood on one of the stage lights, leaving everyone stunned and unable to see. Foodo took off the ring, jumped off the stage and did a runner, but was caught by the collar and spun round.

'You've got some explaining to do, Mr Braggins,' hissed the strange man at him.

By now, people were beginning to come round and complain. Some were saying that it was magic, and some were blaming Butterball for the dangerous state of his lighting. So, quickly, Foodo kicked in another one of the stage lights and pretended to be blinded like the rest of them.

After the commotion had died down, the Halfbits retired to their room, only to find Foodo's strange man waiting for them.

'What are you doing here, and what do you want?' Messy exclaimed.

Without moving a muscle in his face, neither smiling nor frowning, the stranger said, 'I have been sent to guide you.' Before he could explain further, there was a bang on the door. Hastily he hid under the bed, just before Butterball came in.

The fat barman looked worried. 'I'm sorry, young sirs,' he said breathlessly, 'but I can't think of more than one thing at a time, and if I've done harm I'm sorry.'

'What do you mean, Mr Butterball?' asked Messy.

'Well, it's this letter young sir. I was supposed to post it, but since the government has closed all the Sub-Post Offices, I forgot. It is addressed plain enough. Mr F. Braggins, Brag End, Halfbiton, The Snore.'

'What has that to do with me?' demanded Foodo.

'Well now, it's none of my business,' said Butterball, giving him a wink, 'but having your name sewn in your cloak, and "Property of Foodo Braggins" all over your travel bags might be a give-away. If you wanted to hide yourself, you should have been more careful. There have been people asking about you — Bill

Fony for one and that fellow in the bar, Stupor we call him, on account of that blank look on his face.'

At that, Stupor came out from under the bed, and said, 'Yes, and if you'd let me in earlier, I might have been able to stop these idiots from shouting, "Here we are, come and get us!"'

'You'd better give me that letter,' said Foodo.

Butterball, with a wary look at Stupor, gave the letter to Foodo. It was from The Grand Alf, and it read,

"LEAVE NOW! LEAVE YESTERDAY! DO NOT HANG AROUND! MAKE FOR FREE. YOU WILL MEET A FRIEND OF MINE THERE WHO WILL HELP YOU TO GET TO RIVERDWELL. YOU WILL KNOW HIM BY HIS EXPRESSION, OR LACK OF IT. HE IS CALLED BY SOME STUPOR. HIS REAL NAME IS PARAGON. HE IS ONE OF THE STRANGERS OF THE NORTH, AND THIS VERSE IS ABOUT HIM –

ALL THAT IS GOOD IS NOT CLEVER,
ALL WITH A SWORD ARE NOT BRAVE.
IF YOU FOLLOW THIS DIMWIT FOREVER
YOU'LL END IN AN EARLY GRAVE."

'How do we know he's the real Paragon?' said Stan Gamble suspiciously. 'I bet he's murdered the real one.'

'What odds would you give me on removing your head from your shoulders with one blow, Master Halfwit?' demanded the stranger.

Stan went suddenly quiet.

'I say to you, Foodo Braggins, I am Paragon son of Paramount, heir of Everdull's son Evenduller; and if I can get you to Riverdwell in one piece, I'll be lucky.'

That night, The Prattling Parrot was raided. All the Halfbits' beds were broken and the sheets were ripped, but the Ring Cyclists neither saw nor found their occupants. At dawn they fled empty-handed, while the Halfbits were still raiding the larder in the cellar. When Paragon found them, they had eaten half of Butterball's stock. Gathering them together, he ushered them upstairs, where they saw the devastation in their rooms. Messy and Pipsqueak were all for doing a runner without paying the bill, so they began packing their bags. Then in came Butterball. His face was like thunder, but when he saw the room he went purple.

'You've been raided, Butterball,' said Paragon. 'It was the Ring Cyclists.'

Butterball's face rapidly turned white. 'Save us!' he gasped.

'They come from Morbid,' said Paragon. 'Do you understand, Butterball? And we must leave, for they will come back.'

'And eat the rest of my larder?' asked the barman.

'Er, yes,' said Foodo quickly, and burped.

'They came for the Halfbits as well, and I must take them to safety,' Paragon said.

'Well, I wouldn't go off into the wild with a Stranger,' exclaimed Butterball, looking at Foodo.

'No, you're right, we'd better stay another night,' Foodo said.

Butterball looked horrified, and quickly said, 'There's none better than Stupor the Stranger to look after you on your journey.'

As someone had stolen their ponies, Paragon went in search of at least one replacement to carry the food the Halfbits had stashed behind The Prattling Parrot. Unfortunately, the only secondhand hoss-trader was Fony's Ponies, at which the greasy salesman proceeded to rob them. He sold them an old dwarven pit-pony which Stan named Still, mainly because it moved at two paces, crawl and stop.

And that was that. They left Butterball to clean up the mess, and for a long time afterwards he wondered why the Halfbits had not been killed, and how beings such as the Ring Cyclists, who were without substance, could have eaten all that food.

Once Stupor had led the Halfbits some miles away from Free, they asked him where they were going. 'We're heading for Wearytop,' he said. 'We'll rest there for the night.'

A PAIN IN THE NECK

They had not been at Wearytop for long before the Ring Cyclists struck. As they approached, Foodo had an irresistible urge to put on the nose ring. He could hear their voices chanting:

'BASH NOSE WITH BATTLEAXE
BASH NOSE WITH GINBOTTLE
BASH NOSE WITH GRAPPLINGHOOK
AARGH I BURNT MY HEAD WITH KRIMPINGTONGS
PLAY WITH THE RING! PLAY WITH THE RING!'

At last Foodo gave in, and as he put on the ring the Ring Cyclists came into view. They were terrifying, for their faces were all out of proportion. They had tiny little eyes and a little mouth, but their noses were massive. Some were crooked and some were broken. The Cyclist with the biggest one stepped forward, for he was the Lord of the Nasal, Witchy-king of Wagner, mightiest of the Ring Cyclists. Just as he got near to Foodo, Paragon attacked with a torch made of incense sticks, making the Ring Cyclist cough and splutter. Alas, the Lord of the Nasal stabbed at Foodo before they all fled.

All that Foodo could remember was the pain in his neck, and with his last bit of strength, he took off the ring.

When the others found him, he was shivering. 'What's wrong with him?' cried Messy, as Paragon examined Foodo.

Sticking out of his neck was a small pair of antique nasal scissors. When he attempted to pull them out, they dissolved at his touch.

Foodo did not make much of a recovery over the next few hours. As they made their way slowly towards Riverdwell, Paragon got more and more worried. He had tried everything. 'It is only a small wound, yet I have not the skill to heal it.'

'I bet he'll be dead before we get there,' said Stan. Just as he spoke, an Elf on a big white horse cantered down the lane. Paragon jumped out to stop him. The Elf leapt off the horse and

17

clasped his hand, saying, 'Inowfowndue Dulladan Imaygobyvan.'

'What are you doing here, Gloryfindem?'

'I had to turn up in one of these tales sooner or later,' he replied. 'Come, I will escort you to Riverdwell.'

Foodo looked up weakly at the Elf and said in greeting, 'Elven silly loonymen ohmygoshello.'

THE FRIGHT AT THE FORD

At the approach to the river crossing that led to the home of Elbow Halfman, they heard the unmistakable sounds of bicycle chains to their left and right.

'It's an ambush,' screamed Paragon.

Gloryfindem grabbed Foodo, put him on his horse and shouted, 'No no limp, Dashfellow,' which is Elvish for "Move your rump, Fastboy". At that, the great horse sped forward. Within minutes he had crossed the shallow river, and stood trembling on the other side.

The Ring Cyclists pulled to a halt, brakes screeching, waking Foodo from his slumber. As he looked up, the Halfbit could see that their front wheels were already in the water. He lifted his sword and said the Elvish invocation, 'Elderberry wine for all!'

It just so happened that this was the hour of the day when the Elves would open the flood gates to lessen the pressure on the High Dam, built at the end of the Second Stage by the great dwarven engineer Axen Schovel. Being the first dam built in Muddy Earth, it had been nicknamed A.S.1st Dam or simply AS One Dam. The resulting flow of water knocked the Ring Cyclists flying, and drowned their great bikes. They were now disabled, and their bikes over the years would be turned to rust.

As Foodo slipped from the horse into unconsciousness, he was caught by the strong arms of an Elf. He knew nothing more for days. When he awoke, he looked up into the face of The Grand Alf. 'Where am I?' he said.

'You are in the house of Master Elbow Halfman,' said The Grand Alf.

'Why is he called Halfman?'

'Elbow's ancestry is both Man and Elf. He is one of the Arfnarfs,' The Grand Alf replied.

Just then, Stan Gamble came running in and, when he saw Foodo awake, he whooped with joy. 'I've just won Mr Pipsqueak's best toe-pick! I bet him you'd come round today!' he said.

'Yet it was touch and go for a while, for you were pierced by

19

nasal shears belonging to the Lord of the Nasal, and they come from the dark city of Mucus Nasal,' said The Grand Alf. 'You were beginning to change; your nose was getting bigger. You would have become like them, but under their will, you would have been their slave. They would have tormented you with names like Beaky and Hooter. You had a lucky escape Foodo; for Master Elbow cured you with ancient remedies of ointment of menthol, from a jar he calls Vik.'

The next day, with Foodo feeling much better, the Halfbits decided to explore Riverdwell. In one room, marked "Dancing Room", rows of Elves were dancing with their legs high in the air. This, they were told, was a dance designed to keep your feet dry when crossing the river and it was called the Riverdance. Next door was the Praying Room. Inside a young Elf was kneeling before an altar and praying thus, 'Great Lady Vanhire give me happiness. Lord Manuel give me great joy. Great Lady Nivea give me peacefulness. Oh great Ill-Farter tell me, am I girl or boy?'

At that, they left quickly, and went to the last room, which was far larger than the others and was almost empty except for a little figure huddled in a corner by the fire. Suddenly, from a door in the other corner came a shadowy figure, and with a voice they all knew said, 'Get off my chair, you mangy moggy!' And there in the firelight stood Bilious Braggins.

Foodo rushed to greet his uncle and they all sat for what seemed like ages swapping stories, until they were interrupted by The Grand Alf, who told them that Foodo and Bilious were needed for a secret council, and whisked them both away.

THE COUNCIL OF ELBOW

At the council, they were greeted by Master Elbow, a strange person who had both elvish and mannish features. One ear was pointed and the other was round, one eyebrow was arched and the other was not. This created a lopsided look, which he countered by resting his face in one hand and his elbow on the table. Sitting with him, was an assortment of odd-looking people, who Elbow started to introduce. 'On my right, as you all know, is Paragon, son of Paramount. On my left is The Grand Alf.' They both rose and bowed. 'And here is Legless Greenteeth, champion dart player of the Murkywood Arms, son of The King of the Silly Elves, and lead guitarist in The Six Pistelves.'

'Pleeshed to meet you, hic!' said Legless, as he slipped off his stool.

'Sitting opposite him is Grimy son of Grubby of the line of Dunin the Coalking of Khaziboom.'

'At your service and your family's — as long as you have an open hearth,' Grimy added quickly.

'Next to him is Borrowit, a Man, and son of Denizen, The Stalwart of Minus Thrifty in the land of Gondour"

Borrowit nodded to Elbow. 'Honoured to meet such esteemed people,' he said.

Elbow replied, 'Yes quite right you are. Lastly, I've asked Gloryfindem along, because he's been feeling a bit left out lately. We are gathered here to deal with the problem of the Enemy's nose ring. I would ask you all to tell your stories.'

So Bilious told how he had found the nasal embellishment, which to most was a completely new story, mainly because he kept adding to it. The Grand Alf stopped him when he started bragging about how he killed the dragon, before beginning to explain why he was late and not able to meet Foodo at Halfbiton. 'I was delayed and held captive at Sourman's tower of Oldcrank, at the Citadel of Eyesonguard. I went there to consult him as the Head of the Magic Circle.'

THE TIRESOME OF EYESONGUARD

The Grand Alf told the council of his confrontation with Sourman. 'I rode to the tower that was built of old by the Neomenoreans, which is called Oldcrank, through the Ring of Eyesonguard, to the foot of the tower. I met him there, on his stairs. "What do you want, amateur?" he said, rather mockingly. Sourman had got quite bigheaded since he had been voted Muddy Earth's Greatest Magician by the Witty Council — the governing body for all acts in Muddy Earth. "I come seeking knowledge," I told him, trying to sound clever. "What wisdom can Sourman the Irate impart on the likes of you, a bumbling fool?". "I wish to know The Lore of the Jewellery Set," I said airily. "And what exactly has that got to do with you" he said, looking at me with a strange glint in his eyes. "Have you somehow managed to stumble upon one of its pieces?". He advanced towards me; I could see he was getting very agitated, and it was then I realised my mistake: I hadn't worn my running shoes that morning. My next mistake was even bigger: I didn't duck. When I awoke, he was standing over me; we were on the highest point of Oldcrank. He mocked me saying, "Here you will be imprisoned and forced to endlessly watch The Potty Harry movies. You will learn the error of your ways. I will break you, for I am no longer Sourman the Irate; I am Sourman the Seriously Pissed Off.". After the first film, called The Goblins on Fire, I was mad with despair; after The Philanderer is Stoned and The Bloody Halfprints, I had lost my will to live. I had to endure The Order by Phone-X twice and The Secants of the Cambers four times. The only glimmer of hope was when they showed me Hairy Pothead and the Prisoner is on a Razorban, but then the torture started again with The Deadly Shallows.

'I escaped by chance, for that day the Musty Mountains Gliding Club, called the Regal Eagles, were out practicing. One plane, called Winglord by its pilot Gary Weir, came straight out of the clouds and knocked me head over heels into the cockpit — I'm not sure who was most surprised. Once we got over the initial shock and swapped addresses and holiday photos, I asked him if he could take me to Halfbiton, for I was worried about young Foodo. He muttered something about thermals and that the nearest help I could get to was the land of Bovine. This left me wondering what underwear had to do with it; however, he set me down not far from their capital, named Udderas.

'I made my way slowly to Milkingshed, the hall of their King, and I greeted him in the manner of his people: "Where is you, Theocrat pal". He was not friendly, and had by his side the grotesque Grimly Worntwang. I asked for help but they would not give me one of their prized fighting Warbulls. Worntwang told me to go to the stables and find a horse, and that I could take any, for they were of no use to The Riders of Ridicule, who only rode Bulls into battle. I left then, and was rather lucky at the stables, for I found a horse with eight legs. I called him Slippery, which is Shinyflax to the Elves. I rode north with haste, to Halfbiton. My arrival there caused a riot. The stupid Halfbits thought I had kidnapped the three that were missing; they neither noticed or cared that a low life spud-planter like Gamble was also missing. They chased me out of town, so I made for Free.

'At The Prattling Parrot, there was a sign on the door saying, "No beer or food for a week. Waiting for supplies." At that, I knew you had been there. I rushed off, thinking I would catch you on the road to Riverdwell, but I forgot how slow and lazy Halfbits are and got to Wearytop before you. The Lord of the Nasal and his Ring Cyclists were also there before me so, outnumbered, I booby-trapped the hill with flares and grenades. I left a sign for Stupor hoping he would lead you away from trouble, but it was in the dark and I only got a D in Runes at school. Then I scarpered to here. That is my story and we know how Foodo arrived, so what do we do with the ring?'

'How do we know that this is the Nose-ring of Sourone?' said Borrowit.

'I have read the writing inscribed on it,' said The Grand Alf, and began to recite:

'BASH NOSE WITH GIN BOTTLE
BASH NOSE WITH BATTLEAXE
BASH NOSE WITH GRAPPLINGHOOK
ARGH I BURNT MY HAIR WITH KRIMPINGTONGS.'

'Never before has anyone spoken words of such rubbish in this house,' said Elbow.

'If we don't do something about this ring, then the Mumbo-Jumbo of Morbid will be spoken in every land of Muddy Earth,' replied the wizard.

'We still cannot be sure if this is the nose ring," said Grimy.

'Hic,' said Legless.

'Then let me tell you of the history of the Jewellry Set,' said The Grand Alf.

THE SECOND STAGE AND ALL THAT

'In the Second Stage of Muddy Earth, Sourone appeared to the Elves in the land of Fermentation, in the friendly guise of Hadanhaton. He promised them gifts of knowledge and to make them slight of hand. Now these Elves were artisans of great renown, unsurpassed in the brewing of ales and known as The Quaff-of-Mirthful. Their leader was Cellarbrewboy, son of Cupful, son of Freeholder — the creator of the potent Silvermarrywine, used when elves stopped hugging trees long enough to wed — and himself the son of the First King of the No-Older, Finewine. Sourone knew that Cellarbrewboy had invented the ring-pull on cans of beer, so he approached him with a business deal: he would teach the Elves how to make real rings and other shinies if they could be placed in certain cans for lucky winners to find; this would be financed and sponsored by Sourone Inc. The slogan for the jewellry-finding competition was to be:

FREE BEER FOR A YEAR
BUY ANY CAN OF ELVENBRU
BREWED IN TALKLAND FROM CONKERS
FIND THE TREASURE FOR YOUR PLEASURE.
(No purchase necessary)

The unlucky winners were Nine some Kings of Men and a few Dwarf Lords; however, Cellarbrewboy had made three extra earrings and had placed them strategically into cans so his friends could win too. When Sourone found out he went livid and wasn't very happy, declaring war and name-calling upon the peoples of Muddy Earth. He placed the ring through his nose and instantly the Men came under his control this wasn't very hard as they were all blind drunk, having got through most of the free beer. The Dwarves were uncontrollable; they had drunk all their beer and were partaking of the strange weed from The Snore, called Old Tipsy. It is told among the wise that the creator of the Dwarves, who they call Ollie the Hardy, made them indomitable to the will of others, for they had bodies and minds of stone — among those who knew, it meant stoned out of their mind.

War never ceased during that age: Sourone stole some of the pieces back in a jewellery heist, but he most wanted to get his hands on the three earrings: Nanny, Nelly and Willy. The war concluded in what is now called The Battle of the Last Abeyance, at the foot of Mount Gloom in the Land of Morbid. Sourone wrestled with Everdull, King of Men and Giddy-Lad, The Slightly High King of the No-Older; he was victorious but exhausted, having fought in a tag-team contest on his own. Then Evenduller took up his father's sword Nares (made by Telltale of Nod-Off) and cut the ring from Sourone's nose. Sourone was diminished for many years, thrown from the Magic Circle and banned by the Witty Council from practicing even street magic, he disappeared into what most thought was retirement.'

'Most of this is known by the wise, but for the witless among you I will continue the tale, for I was there,' said Elbow, looking at the mortals. 'As Evenduller took the ring, I counselled him to destroy it by throwing it into the Crack Of Gloom nearby, but he would not. He told me, "I take this as compensation for my father, as I can't be bothered suing,", then rode north from the battlefield. On the way home, he was ambushed by a group of Continuity Dorks, who didn't know the war was over. He bravely fled in panic and fell into the Great River Arduous, in full armour, he sunk like a brick; there he and the ring were lost from memory.'

'Then how can this be the same nose ring?' asked Borrowit.

'Whersh the toilet?' slurred Legless.

'I think I can carry on the story from here,' said The Grand Alf.

THE STOOL STRAIN

'It was on the River Arduous, nigh on the Gladdy fields — so named for its profundity of poppies cultivated by the local inhabitants — the ancient strain of Halfbits lived, which would one day become the Stools. One of these Halfbits was called Smear-Gob. He came from a wealthy family, but his side had been disinherited on some trumped-up charges. Now Smear-Gob liked fishing down by the river, but so did his rich cousin, Dear-Gob. When they were on the same bank Dear-Gob would brag about his new and expensive equipment, while Smear-Gob grumbled under his breath, so Dear-Gob called him Grumble. One day, Dear-Gob caught a whopper; he was jumping with joy and taunting Smear-Gob. It was too much to bear; he took the fish and beat his cousin to death with it, then took it home to cook it.

'When he got there, the fire was out and there was no wood, so he took his cookbook to see if there was anything else he could do with it. Under the heading "Sushi", he learned the joys of eating raw fish. As he prepared his meal, something popped out of the mouth of the fish: it was a large shiny nose ring. He had never owned anything so precious; he was so lucky, he thought it was his birthday. The next day he put the ring on his finger and went to town to show off how wealthy he was — that would teach them for disinheriting him. When he got there, people were ignoring him, and he suddenly realised that they either couldn't see him or couldn't be bothered with him. Oh what fun, he must have thought.

'During the next couple of months, Smear-Gob became a one-Halfbit crime-wave, until one night he went to town and it was empty. He thought it strange, but carried on with his nefarious ways. On his way home, laden with his night's work, he couldn't see where he was going and walked smack into the townsfolk. Now, they had seen a pile of their belongings floating up the road and thought it strange, so they followed it to Smear-Gob's hut. They rushed in only to see Smear-Gob surrounded by their missing valuables. They beat him, kicked him and threw him out of town — they got away with this because they did not have any Lib-Dems sitting on the town council fence.

'He wandered far and wide, until at last he made his way to the Musty Mountains, where he lived in a cavern way underground, keeping the ring for many years. Then one day, an abundance of greasy fish-oil made the nose ring slip from his finger and there, as we have already heard from Bilious Braggin, is where this item we see before us comes into our story.

'How do you know about Grumble?' asked Foodo

'Paragon and I went in search of him. He was found in the south, wandering witless in the Dread Mushlands. Paragon brought him back and I poured paraffin ever his body and threatened to stub out my pipe on him.'

'He blabbed good and proper,' said Paragon.

'They have him now in the woodland realm of King Thatfool, Lord of the Silly-Elves of Northern Murkywood.'

'Whash that?' said Legless, doing up his buttons on returning from the toilet. 'You (hic) mean, we did haff.'

'You don't mean he's escaped?' exclaimed Grimy. 'You can't trust Elves with anything.'

'I took pity on him, sho I took him to the Murkywood Arms for a few shlurps. He said he needed the toilet but, when he didn't return, I realised that he'd slipped out the back window.'

'Oh dear, the oldest trick in the book and you fell for it.'

Legless leapt up and said, 'Are you looking for a fight, Half-pint?'

'Now now,' cut in Elbow, 'time for fun later. What's done is done. We'll run into Grumble soon enough; the ring calls to him, and he does so love shiny bling. We must now hear why Borrowit has come so far.'

'I am Borrowit, son of Denizen, The Stalwart of Gondour. Allow me to tell you the story of my people. We are the last remnants of The Neomenoreans. When Neomanor was destroyed by Ill-Farter, due to the rebellion of Argh-Parazone, a part of the people called the Favourable escaped to Muddy Earth. They were led by Everdull, son of Alldull and his sons Evenduller and Anotherone. There they founded the Realms of Gondour in the South and Another in the North. Evenduller and Anotherone ruled in the south and they built the great cities of Minus Piffle, Ohgiveusalaugh and Minus Another. The High King Everdull reigned in the north and his seat was at Anumbass.

'For many years there was peace — this was due to Sourone being in an earlier enforced retirement. Too soon did we relax, for Sourone crept back through Passport Control, hidden in a false compartment aboard a caravan from Far Harass. Then a shadow fell on our people. Sourone had taken up his ring again and rebuilt his tower of Bad-Odour. In that time, The Lord of the Nasal took Minus Piffle and turned it into Minus Mucus or Mucus Nasal, which by some is called The Tower of the Gloom. Sourone laid Gondour under siege, he cut our supply routes and sightseeing tours so badly that you could not go anywhere without being attacked by Dorks on the take.

'In the year 2525, the last king, Ernest, rode from the gates of Minus Another, which by now was called Minus Thrifty, The Tower of Hardup, to do single combat against The Witchy-King. That is what he thought, until he ran into ten battalions of hungry Dorks. That night, those on duty at The Back Gates had a King-sized Man-and-Potato pie for supper. King Ernest left behind no heir, so his chief minister, The Stalwart Mardass, quickly moved into the palace; while his wife redecorated he promoted himself to Top-Dog-Till-The-King-Finds-His-Way-Home.

'My father is descended in unbroken line from Mardass, and as far as we are concerned the only King around is Elvish Paisley. As for Another, the kingdom of the North, we in Gondour know little and care less,' concluded Borrowit.

'I will be honoured to attempt to fill the empty space within your head in that respect,' replied Paragon. 'After Evenduller, the Eight King, Earbender had three sons who hated the sight of each other. Therefore, so as to show no favour, when he died he had the kingdom split into three. The names of these lands became known as Halfadrain, Ruder and Cardiac. Only in Halfadrain did the line of Evenduller survive.

'The last king of Ruder was killed in a road rage accident whilst driving his Boy-racer chariot, after making foul remarks and indecent gestures at a very large haywain. On seeing this, the driver of the haywain lost control and The King of Ruder ploughed into the swerving vehicle — it was wipeout time. The rulers of Cardiac had congenital heart problems and all died very early on in life. The last king died at the reins of his haywain, after being cut up by some purple-faced nutter in a flash Hot-rod chariot. The line in Halfadrain continued until the days of Halfashoe, the great grandson of Halfaleg II.

'At this time, The Witchy-King arose once more and captured Forlorn, the capital of Halfadrain. He drove out the remaining Dulledain and they wandered far and wide. Their king, Halfashoe, died trying to set up an ice-cream import business with The Icemen of Frozenwaste. Although Halfadrain no longer existed, the line of Evenduller continued through Halfashoe's son Halfanheart, who became the first Mainman of the Dulledain, of which I am the sixteenth,' concluded Paragon proudly.

Borrowit looked at Paragon with something akin to awe and said, 'How did you manage to say all that without moving your mouth?'

'Composure and the Botox injections I get from Rubbermask Brown at Razscalpel; after all, I am 87.'

'Anyway, enough of man's petty histories. We digress and time is moving on,' said The Grand Alf.

'Yes, and I'm hungry. I haven't eaten in well over fifteen minutes,' said Bilious, looking at Foodo for backup.

'Is the bar open yet?' asked Legless.

'Please be quiet,' said The Grand Alf to the Halfbits, who by now were rolling around the floor holding their rather substantial stomachs, acting as if their throats had been cut.

'Carry on Borrowit,' said The Grand Alf, exhaustingly.

'We are pushed to breaking point in Gondour. Soon Sourone will attack and we will be crushed. He has amassed huge Armies of foul Dorks and great Cave Thralls and he has allied himself with Men from Near and Far Harass, the Vile Eagerlings, the Variants of Klang and the slow but huge army of the Slothrons. Enemies beset us on all sides and I am the only warrior worth talking about in Minus Thrifty. We have shopkeepers, bank clerks and supermarket managers, ferocious they may be when being robbed of their wares by the local hoodlum, but put up against Dorks, they would run a league. Then there is my brother, the whimsical Faraway — he may as well be. He calls himself The Warrior Poet; it is because of him I am here.

'One night, after a heavy drinking session, I went to my bed late. At some time in the night, in what seemed like a dream, I saw a strange pale light and heard a voice calling out a rhyme:

SEEK FOR THE LINE UNBROKEN
IN DIMLADSBLISS HE DWELLS
THERE SHALL BE WISDOM WOKEN
WHEN DULLBOY OPENLY TELLS
NOW IS THE TIME TO HEARKEN
TO EVERY SINGLE STRAND
FOR WHAT EVENDULLERS HEIR SAYS THEN
NOT EVEN A FOOL COULD HAVE PLANNED

'At that point, I realised I was awake and the light was coming from the toilet, as was the voice. I got up angrily and charged into the toilet where I found Faraway reciting poetry. I smacked him round the head and told him none too politely to go to bed. In the morning, I was ashamed, so I set about trying to apologise. At breakfast, I asked him, though I was not particularly bothered, about the rhyme he had recited the previous night. He replied that he could not remember because he had been sleepwalking, but he thought it went so:

SEEK FOR THE CHAIR THAT IS BROKEN
IN DIMLADSBLISS IT DWELLS
THERE SHALL BE CURRIES EATEN
STRONGER THAN MORBID'S HELLS
YOU SHALL BE SHOWN A REASON
FOR THE TIME IS NEAR AT HAND
FOR EVENDULLERS CHAIR SHALL BREAK THEN
AND YOU WILL BE FORCED TO STAND

'So I come to seek a solution to the riddles. I have found the answer to the question of Evenduller's heir, but which of these rhymes is true and why this place is called Dimladsbliss, I do not know.' concluded Borrowit.

'The answer to your first riddle will become apparent soon,' said Elbow. 'The second riddle may come later; as for the question of the name of Dimladsbliss, that is easy. It is named in honour of Paragon's blissful love, for not only is this my home, it is also the home of my daughter who Paragon is besotted with. I had to bring up this daughter on my own, without a mother's tuition. Her mother, Celebrity ,went to the Uncrying Lands to escape the attentions of the Dork paparazzi, who had made her life unbearable. Celebrity is the daughter of Gadabout and Cellphone and our daughter is the living likeness of Lillian Tinnitus, who is Frighteningwail to the Elves. The name of my daughter is Olwen Undomesticated, The Lazy Everstatic, and she has agreed to marry Paragon.'

'Is she blind?' asked Grimy.

'Or drunk?' added Legless.

'Neither,' replied Elbow. 'She is dyslexic.'

'What do you mean?' asked Foodo.

'Paragon asked in a letter for their hands to be joined in marriage, but she thought it read, "Would you like to join the band I manage?". She answered yes and signed a contract. You will all meet Olwen later, at the feast in honour of Getting Rid.'

At that, the pointy ears of the Halfbits twitched and they momentarily forgot their hunger.

'I think it is time to discuss what to do with the nose ring,' said The Grand Alf.

'Let's hide down a deep mine,' said Grimy.

'No, let's see if it will dissolve in hard liquor,' said Legless.

'Lend me the ring,' cut in Borrowit eagerly, 'and I will return it when I have annihilated every living thing in Muddy Earth. I promise — cross my heart and hope to die.'

'No. It must be destroyed,' replied The Grand Alf.

'I have just the plan to kill two birds with one stone,' added Elbow.

'What?' they all answered in unison.

'One or all of you must take the ring to Morbid and throw it into the Crack of Gloom. This expedition will be led by Paragon, heir of Evenduller, who started this bloody mess,' replied Elbow.

Up to this point, Elbow had been avoiding eye contact with the others by staring at the floor. When he looked up, the Halfbits were hiding under their chairs, Legless and Grimy were heading for the toilet and The Grand Alf and Borrowit were doing a fair impersonation of Paragon, who still hadn't moved a muscle.

'Get back in here you miserable lot,' roared Elbow. 'Look, the ring can't stay here and neither can you.'

'Why not?' asked Paragon.

'Well ... erm ... um ... I do not have enough Halfbit, Dwarf, Man or Wizard food for you.'

'I am ok then,' said Legless cheerfully.

'We will run out of beer after the feast,' said Elbow quickly.

'Sod it, I am off with the rest. Where is the nearest inn from here?'

'There used to be one at Khaziboom,' offered Paragon, 'but it got closed down due to violence. The nearest is at Gadabouts in Lostlotion.'

'So,' began Elbow, hoping to steer the conversation back on track, 'who will take the ring to Mount Horridruin and cast it into the Black Chasm of Gloom?'

There was a period of silence.

'Someone has to, and don't look at me — my old war wound is playing up,' he said, showing off his appendix scar.

From the back of the room came a voice, 'I will take the bling, though you'll have to pay me,' said Foodo, who'd been sipping Legless' drink whilst he'd been on the toilet.

'Ok … What's your price?' asked Elbow suspiciously.

'I don't know. I'll have to think, though you do have a lot of lovely Elf maidens here. I know why Uncle Bilious looks so tired now — by the way, they do know how to cook, don't they?'

'Know how to cook?' replied Elbow, getting uppity. 'Some of them invented it, you stupid Halfbit!'

'So that's settled: Foodo is the Ringbreaker,' The Grand Alf informed those still awake.

'Bet he'll never get there on his own,' objected Stan Gamble.

'Undoubtedly Master Half-Wit,' said Elbow. 'I doubt he could go to the toilet without finding you there first. That is why you, the smelly Dwarf, the inebriated Elf, the Halfbits with hollow legs and the two Men with as much sense between them as a shop dummy, are going with Foodo. I will also send The Grand Alf, for this will be his greatest test, and getting you lot past the gates of Riverdwell will be a test in itself.'

That night the feast was held in honour of Getting Rid of the Guests. The Halfbits were shovelling food down their mouths, like famine conditions were going to be announced the next day. Grimy was wearing as much food as he had eaten and Legless was filling up his canteen, hip flask and prized brandy flavoured condom with any alcohol he could find. Paragon was chasing Olwen around her bedroom and The Grand Alf was sulking in his room because he was not given top of the bill status for the Entertainments. Borrowit had just collected his third helping of curried vegetarian beans, and was making his way back to the table he was sharing with Elbow.

As he arrived to sit down, Elbow said, 'I remember the last war like it was yesterday. Evenduller sat in that very same chair.'

As Borrowit sat down, the chair creaked once and then the legs gave way.

'Oh dear, I've been meaning to have that fixed,' said Elbow, looking down at Borrowit, whose face was covered in curry. 'You know, you Men are so heavy, you should try taking off some of that armour.'

Legless, who by now had filled up in more ways than one, came over, took one look at Borrowit and said, 'Whash wrong … can't handle the beer?'

It suddenly dawned on Elbow that this was the meaning of the second riddle, and said to Borrowit, 'That must be the reason why the riddle came to you! If you hadn't sat in that chair, I wouldn't have known how dangerous it was. Someone important could have been hurt.'

The next day, they packed the remainder of their things and got ready to say goodbye.

Foodo went to see his Uncle Bilious, who gave him his ancient blade, Stink, saying, 'This sword is magic. It will give off a strange smell when Dorks are about. I never could tell if it was me or the sword actually — you know how frightening these fights are young Foodo.' He also gave him a corset of Knitsteel, one of the hardest known substances in Muddy Earth.

Foodo took one look at the corset and said, 'I don't think it will suit me.'

'Funny you should say that,' laughed Bilious. 'That's exactly what the wife of Dunin IV said.'

Paragon had the sword Nares reforged, and he renamed it Andrex, the Issue of the West. At his side, Grimy had his axe, and Legless his bow and a spare set of darts. Messy and Pipsqueak had large steak knives, just in case anything stopped long enough to eat it and Stan carried the Tenderiser. Borrowit had the Horn and The Grand Alf had the sword Humdinger, the mate of Dorkfist, the sword that lay on the breast of Throbin

Oakenhead, in his tomb under Mount Errorbore — the sword Humdinger had been made in ancient days for King Turgid of Condom. So the Followship of the nose ring left Riverdwell and headed south into the wild.

THE RINGBREAKER SETS OUT

For many days they walked, until they reached the foot of the Musty Mountains.

'We must make for The Redherring Gate, which leads us to the far side of Cruel Carbuncle and, from there, we will take the Dimly Lit Stair into the valley of Mirrormire,' said The Grand Alf.

Grimy came and stood next to him and said, 'Long have I wanted to walk the land of my kin, though I have not been here; I have seen my great grandsires' photo albums. I know the names of these parts, under them lies Khaziboom, the Shallowshelf, now called the Dark Zit; Moribund in the language of the Elves. There stands Zanzibar, the Redherring, Cruel Carbuncle and there stands Silvermine and Cloddyhead, Celibate the White, and Fanatical the Grey, that we Dwarves call Ziggazagg and Bundesliga. Deep are the Waters of Khaki-zany, and cold is the spring of Nibble-kirsch.' There was immense pride in his voice. When he looked back to his comrades, they were half a league along the path to the Redherring Gate; he could just make out Paragon shouting, 'Come on Stumpy, keep up!'

Another half day saw them reach the Gate, which was of course locked. On the Gate was a sign that read thus:

> THIS GATE IS KEPT LOCKED OUTSIDE
> OF THE SKIING SEASON
> BY ORDER OF CARBUNCLE SKI LODGE
> PLEASE COME BACK IN 6 MONTHS.

'That's it then; we'll have to go back to Riverdwell,' said Legless hopefully.

'No we wont; there's another way,' replied The Grand Alf.

'Not Moribund,' said Paragon.

'It's the only way now, unless you wish to take the ring through the Glen of Bovine,' retorted The Grand Alf.

That night, they camped in a glade. They were attacked midway through the night by a group of roving Wags. These large wolves had been crossbred with hyenas to create a truly horrific species, which laughed its head off while it bit off yours. They sat at the edge of the glade, laughing and telling jokes.

'What is the smallest book in Muddy Earth?' asked one.

'The Halfbit Book of Diets,' came the answer.

'No, it's The Book of Dwarven Dating,' was the reply.

'What do you call a sober Elf?' asked one.

'I don't know,' answered another.

'Dead,' replied the first, echoed by howls of laughter.

All this banter enraged Legless. Now Legless was one of the best and quickest bowmen in Muddy Earth — best because he never missed, quickest because he fired two arrows at the same time, the reason being his double vision due to his attachment to various types of alcohol. Picking up his bow, he fired off a volley of arrows.

'180,' came the shout from Legless, as the nearest Wags dropped dead. Then the attack came, and the Wags leapt at the Followship.

At the same time, The Grand Alf rushed forward and shouted, 'Grenade!' and from his hand lobbed a phosphorus ball smack into the middle of the pack. The grenade lit the night sky with a flash. The Wags stood no chance and most were blown to smithereens. When the remainder had fled, The Grand Alf went to inspect his work. He turned to Paragon and pointed at a mangled Wag. 'You know what they call this, don't you?'

'No,' answered Paragon.

'Dead funny,' laughed The Grand Alf.

Legless joined them and, looking at the Wag, he said, 'I wonder what went through its head last.'

'It appears to be its rectum,' replied Paragon.

There were no further attacks, mainly because the Wags did not think the grenades funny and went off to find easier prey to laugh at. Lucky for them, it wasn't long before they ran into the local Labour Party.

During the night, fearing the glade was unsafe, they set out for Moribund. They reached the Doorway of Dunin just as the moonlight was failing. The companions settled down to watch The Grand Alf's pathetic attempt to find the handle. He began by explaining to them that Dwarf doors were magic, operated by electrickery and photosensible light. The doors had writing around them that were called Loonrunes. These could only be read by those who chewed carpets or howled at the moon. After what seemed like hours (mainly because it was), the clouds in the sky cleared enough to let a single moonbeam fall on the magic doorway.

Immediately, Grimy jumped up and ran to decipher the writing. 'It says here, "I Navvy made this Door. Cellarbrewboy of Fermentation scrawled the graffiti. Pay friend, and enter."'

'What does it mean?' asked Foodo.

'That's easy: you pay a friend to enter before you, in case of danger,' answered Grimy.

'So,' said Paragon, 'who's going first then?'

They all sat staring at each other, until it dawned on each of them that friends were in short supply on this trip. The quiet was broken as The Grand Alf suddenly roared with laughter.

After a few moments Paragon said, 'Are you going to let us in on your little joke?'

'The joke's on me; I'm an old fool!' laughed The Grand Alf, to which Borrowit applauded. The Grand Alf stopped laughing, gave Borrowit a withering look and said, 'The translation should read, "Pay, friend and enter". Has anyone got a Dwarf coin upon them?' asked The Grand Alf.

It just so happened that Grimy always kept a coin in his boot for good luck. Grimy handed the coin to The Grand Alf, who accepted it with a look of distaste. He then went in search of the slot to pay for the entry and found it nearby. Under the slot was a sign, which read thus:

UNDER NEW MANAGEMENT
ENTER AT OWN RISK
BEWARE OF DANGER
(DORKS, CAVE THRALLS AND BOUNCER)
MANAGER MORIBUND HERITAGE PARK.

The Grand Alf put the coin in the slot. At first it didn't work, so he stupidly put it in his mouth to wet it, the result being that he wasted his last meal. When he recovered, he tried once again to open the doors and this time they rumbled open.

The Followship stared into the inky darkness that was The Mines of Moribund. At Paragon's order, they collected their gear together and headed for the doorway. As they entered, the water in the lake behind them began to boil and a monster of nightmare and horror erupted, thrashing its way towards them. It had more limbs and teeth than a Synchronized Swimming Team. A long tentacle reached out and grabbed Foodo, pulling the Halfbit towards rows of ivory white choppers. The mouth of the Monster was contorted in a grimace that gave the impression of a sprayed on smile. The Followship attacked at once and rushed to Foodo's aid, with the Halfbits hacking at a tentacle and discussing whether to use garlic or spice with Calamari.

Borrowit shouted to Foodo, 'Throw the nose ring to me; it's far too important to lose.'

To which Foodo replied, 'What do you think I am: gullible or stupid?'

'I was rather hoping you'd be both,' came the reply.

Grimy was struggling with one of the tentacle, trying to get a good strike, and then, with one hit, he chopped it in half. Standing proudly admiring his work, he heard Foodo's voice scream to him, 'You've got the wrong one, stupid! Get over here!'

Grimy was perplexed, as there were tentacles all over the place, undulating in unison. Eventually he found the one curled around Foodo and started to attack it. After nearly decapitating Foodo, he managed to chop the tentacle off and then dragged the half-unconscious Halfbit to the safety of the doorway. The rest quickly followed them.

Outside, the Monster was not very happy. It was left with the choice to either leg it or continue its attack; the problem being, it was now practically armless. Alas, the Monster was also stupid so, with its remaining strength, it hit the doorway head on, tearing the doors off their hinges; this resulted in the whole of the entrance collapsing. Whether the Monster was crushed, or escaped into hiding for many years while attempting to re-arm itself, this story does not have a clue.

The Followship found themselves in total darkness; they were stuck inside, with no way to go but forward. From his side pouch The Grand Alf brought out a Cyalume Light-stick, which he snapped and attached to his staff.

The pale light bathed a world of chains and railtracks; scattered here and there were picks and shovels, the remnants of an industry that had imploded due to the greed of the mining Dwarves. On the wall was a tattered old poster showing an angry dwarf. In big letters the poster read thus:

STRIKE

MORE PAY +
MORE WOMEN TO SPEND IT ON
MORE FOOD +
MORE WOMEN TO COOK IT
MORE SEX +
MORE WOMEN TOO
MORE HO
MORE

The bottom part of the poster had long since crumbled into dust and was missing. They decided to continue along the tunnel that lay at the top of the stairs. The tunnel meandered for miles, twisting and turning until it opened into a large chamber. In the corner of the room was a large hole; this, it was deduced, was a latrine. As the companions sat and rested, they discussed what the plan of action was to be. Suddenly, a sound like that of waterfall grew to a crescendo and filled the chamber. Pipsqueak had desperately wanted a pee, and so had used the hole. Due to the unique acoustics of that area, the sound of Pipsqueak's ablutions had multiplied tenfold.

The Grand Alf came rushing over to where the startled Halfbit stood, and angrily said, 'You stupid half-brained Halfbit. I took you as a fool the moment I saw you. If you do that again, I'll throw you in.'

At that moment came a sound from below: tap tap CRACK, tap tap CRACK.

'That is the sound of a pick on a coalface or I'm not the son of a miner's daughter,' said Grimy hopefully. 'Maybe its my cousin Brawlin. He led a number of our most greediest people here, some years ago. He was a mighty warrior. It was said that he could start a fight in a room full of dead bodies.'

'Lets hope it is Brawlin and not some pissed off Dork,' said The Grand Alf, looking at Pipsqueak with fire in his eyes.

They rested there and Pipsqueak was made to stand guard all night. He imagined that he saw and heard all manner of things. Fearing to go anywhere near the hole again, he soiled himself. As Messy was the same size as he was, he swapped his trousers with his friend's spare pair. This would not have been a problem as most people would expect Messy to have dirty pants, besides the fact that Messy was too stupid to notice the switch anyway. Pipsqueak thought how clever he had been, until he put on Messy's stinking trousers. It was too late to do anything now he would have to try Foodo or Stan later on.

When it was time to wake his companions, he gently nudged them all, except The Grand Alf, who was sleeping like a log and snoring very loudly. He looked at him and thought, 'Make me stand guard all night, eh!' and gave him a swift kick up the backside.

The Grand Alf shot up. 'What? Where am I?' When his eyes registered everyone's faces, he sighed with relief and said, 'Thank goodness, I thought I was being booted out of The Muddy Earth Mud Wrestling Club,'

'Don't you mean again? I bet it wouldn't be the first time,' added Stan Gamble.

The Grand Alf stood up, gingerly rubbing his buttocks, muttering under his breath about sleeping on stone floors at his age.

When they were all ready, they set off down the tunnel, until they came to an intersection of three corridors. Above the left hand path, which descended into darkness, was a picture of a Dwarf with an axe stuck in his head. Above the centre way, which continued straight on, was a picture of a Dwarf with arrows stuck in his eyes. The right-hand one appeared to have no picture.

'Well, it looks like the right hand passage then,' said Paragon.

'Why?' asked Legless through a drunken haze.

'The big red neon arrow above the entrance might be a clue.'

'It might be a trap,' said Borrowit.

'Ok, we'll send the Dwarf down one of the other tunnels,' said The Grand Alf.

At that, Grimy broke The Muddy Earth Dwarf Sprinting Record as he headed down the neon lit tunnel. They caught up with him gasping for breath someway down the tunnel.

As he walked past the Dwarf, The Grand Alf threw in, 'It's a good job you didn't see the picture of the burned and mangled Dwarf head hidden behind that neon arrow.'

Grimy collapsed weeping on the floor.

For the rest of the day, the companions made their way through the tunnel, while Grimy heroically brought up the rear, in case of sneak attack. When they reached the end of the passageway, they emerged into a huge, dark and musty, many-pillared hall.

Stan took one look and didn't like what he saw. He turned to Foodo and said in his loudest whisper, 'It must have taken tens of thousands of Dwarves hundreds of years to make this hole so dirty. I bet, stuck in here, they didn't know about spring cleaning.'

Grimy turned and grasped the Halfbit by the throat. 'For your information Master Blabbermouth, this is no hole. This is Shallowshelf, the great city of the Dwarves. Once there was the light and warmth of a thousand coal fires here.'

'Pity you never built chimneys to go with them,' remarked The Grand Alf. 'Now put that purple-faced Halfbit down.'

'Why is it called Shallowshelf?' asked Pipsqueak.

'Unfortunately for us, we don't have any top shelves; everything is built at a low level, so that we can reach it,' replied Grimy, looking embarrassed.

'How did they build this massive cavern?' asked Messy.

'Oh, that's easy: we started at the top and worked our way down", answered Grimy proudly.

'Have you never heard of ladders?' asked Borrowit.

'Yes, of course; nasty horrible things that ruin your stockings.'

That was a rather strange thing to say, thought some of the others.

In one corner of the hall, they found a small space into which they entered. It was a burial chamber. On approaching the tomb in the centre, it was found to have writing on the lid:

BRAWLIN
SON OF FUMIN
LORD OF MORIBUND
Brawlinall Fumin Ushard Khaziboom-bum

Grimy was distraught. He wailed, gnashed his teeth and tore his false beard (which was getting shorter, the longer he stayed on this journey). 'He was dear to me; he was my kinsman and the bastard owed me money,' he cried.

Strewn around the floor of the tomb were the decaying remains of Dorks and Dwarves, united in their death throes. This was the result of a large battle and maybe the last game of Dwarf-throwing in Moribund. As they looked around for clues as to what had happened and hopefully the Scorecard, they came across a large, leather-bound book. The Grand Alf opened the book. On the inside cover was a label reading:

PROPERTY OF THE KHAZIBOOM CENTRAL LIBRARY
DATED 1981 OF THE THIRD STAGE

Stan whistled and said, 'I wouldn't like to be the person who signed that out. I bet there's a whopping big fine waiting to be awarded.'

The Grand Alf examined its content, 'It seems to be a record of the colony.' He turned a few more pages and read out, "'I battered that useless excuse of a beardless Dwarf offspring, Flaw, today. His was the job to bring the women; his excuse was there wasn't enough room on the wagon for them and his collection of false antique beards. How can we have a colony without women? Who is going to knit the steel?"' He looked further and selected another extract. "'Brawlin, Lord of Moribund, was shot in the backside with a poisoned arrow whilst searching for Dunins Wig in Mirrormire. No one could be found with the skill to suck out the poison. The Dork was killed but more came up The Slimyroad.'" Turning to the end of the book, through lack of patience and wanting to cheat, he read out the last few pages:

'"They have swarmed like flies over the bridge and have taken over the Canteen and Games Room. We are trapped. Rap music in the canteen, and we must get out. They are drumming." It ends there in the spidery script of a three year old,' explained The Grand Alf.

'That would be one of the Three Brethren in the community, Horace, Norris or Doris,' said Grimy.

Suddenly they heard a sound that sent them looking for earplugs THUD Bang THUD THUD Bang THUD, in a continuous dreary beat.

'Rap music in the Canteen,' said Grimy, shocked.

'We must get out,' moaned Legless who, being so old, only liked punk rock music.

'I bet we will never get out of here,' cried Stan.

And indeed, they were trapped, just like the numbskulls before them.

Paragon peered out of the door into the gloom. He could see the Dorks advancing. 'They have a Cave Thrall with them. Bar the entrance,' he said.

'No,' cut in The Grand Alf. 'Leave the back door open. The fastest of us may have to run for our lives, leaving the stumpy Dwarf to look after the fat Halfbits.'

At that came a huge pounding on the doors. The massive Cave Thrall was attempting to smash them down. It had got as far as planting its foot through the panel, creating a gap for a number of Dorks to gain entry. Stan saw this and smashed his Tenderiser into the big toe of the Thrall. The effect of this was firstly to squash said toe flatter than a pancake and, secondly, to send the Thrall screaming and knocking Dorks out of its way, all the way to the Hospithrall.

Meanwhile, the doors were holding, but the company had to fight the Dorks that had gotten into the chamber. One huge Dork made for Foodo, avoiding the other members of the Followship; it launched its oversized kebab skewer at him, which knocked him back against the wall, where he slid down to the floor unconscious. Paragon turned instantly and took off the Dork's head, after several attempts.

'Quick! Make for the Bridge of Khaziboom, I will try to hold them here,' said The Grand Alf, beginning to place stun grenades around the doors.

Paragon went to pick up the limp Foodo and was surprised as he staggered to his feet, saying, 'Its just a scratch, I will be OK.' Paragon thought that the kebab skewer would have passed through a wild boar but, looking at the fat Halfbit, he realised that Foodo could eat a wild boar on his own.

The Grand Alf caught up with his companions just as they approached the bridge. They headed across to the other side, with the wizard at the rear. Just as they were approaching the farthest edge, there came a loud roaring growl from behind them. Advancing towards them was a walking nightmare, covered in ash and surrounded by smoke; an image of living hell. Its mouth was lit by rows of fire and it looked like a volcano.

Legless took one look and wailed, 'Ai, a Labdog is come.' It was one of the Vollrauchen of old, last scion of Coughsmog, Lord of Labdogs.

'Unless you have a squeaky ball you had better go. You can't help me here,' cried The Grand Alf. 'The door to the Dimly Lit Dale is that way.'

'See you later then,' shouted back Paragon, as they all ran like postmen with rottweilers attached to their rear ends.

The Grand Alf advanced to meet the Labdog at the centre of the Bridge. He got there before the monster, with just enough time to place his last Heat Sensitive charge into the path of his adversary. Then he stood facing the beast and bellowed, 'Go back, Flame of Undone, foul spawn of Mortcough. I am a servant of the Secret Fire of Annex, and I'll kick your ass.'

As The Grand Alf edged back slightly, the Labdog pounced and landed smack on the charge. The heat from its mouth set off the explosives and the portion of bridge below it fell crashing into the abyss. With no foothold, the monster went with it.

The Grand Alf turned away from the carnage, but too late did he notice the dog's lead by his foot and, as it wrapped itself around his ankle, it dragged him down along with bridge and beast.

That was the last the company saw of him. They almost made out his last words as he tumbled into the abyss — something about dog fleas.

Paragon led them out towards the exit. On their way they ran into a group of Dorks who had heard that mixed grill was on the menu; unfortunately they also found out, albeit too late, that this food had a nasty bite. Once outside, in the bright clean air, the group collapsed exhausted and wept. This affected the Halfbits most. They wept freely, and loudly, for they knew that The Grand Alf was carrying most of the food in his pack. Paragon, who by now had been promoted to The Leader or Chief Blame Taker in the event of cock-ups, decided that they could not stop and rest, so he moved them on.

Grimy would go no further until he had beheld The Wonder of the Wig. This Wig was specially woven from Knitsteel, for The Father of his race and their first King, Dunin the Hairless. It was told in Dwarven legend that Dunin would come again to reclaim his Crowning Glory, and that it could be seen under the waters of Khaki-zany. Grimy only invited Foodo to look upon this wonder with him, as he thought the Elf might steal it to sell at the next inn for beer.

When Grimy and Foodo had rejoined the others, they set down The Slimy Road towards Lostlotion, travelling at the best speed they could.

After a few hours, the usually slow Halfbits wilted like boiled lettuce. Therefore, Paragon called another halt so they could dress their wounds, and wash their socks and smalls. Pipsqueak found this particularly handy, as he had been getting some very funny looks since leaving Moribund and only Messy would go anywhere near him. As the only First-Aider on the quest, Paragon decided that he had better inspect Foodo first.

'I think we should see what damage that Big Dork did to you, Foodo,' said Paragon.

'I am fine, no need for fuss,' replied Foodo shyly.

'Still, the weapons of the enemy are rarely clean and they don't wash their hands after going to the toilet. You could catch all sorts of diseases.' As he began to remove Foodo's shirt, Paragon exclaimed, 'I've been looking for one of them for Olwen!'

They all gathered round and saw the magnificent wonder that was The Corset of Knitsteel which once belonged to The Wife of Dunin IV.

Grimy came to Foodo with a strange glint in his eyes, and said to him, 'I didn't realise you were a cross-dresser.'

Foodo quickly put his shirt back on and a little distance between himself and the Dwarf.

After an hour or so, Paragon told them it was time to move

on, as it was starting to get dark. They knew that the Dorks of Moribund would hunt for them, for these Dorks did not like their food escaping. The Dorks of Moribund were renowned for eating the same food a number of times. The tracking of the Followship would also be made easier, because the metal-shod boots of Grimy left imprints a one-eyed novice tracker could find; added to this, the smell of Messy would bring every Dork for leagues down on their heads.

A few miles later, they came at last to the eaves of The Gilded Wood, and relative safety. They could now afford to go at a slower pace, which was just as well, as the Halfbits had started to moan incessantly. They complained about the lack of food, the lack of rest, the lack of food, the lack of blister cream and the total lack of anything to eat.

Paragon's patience was about to snap when Legless pointed to a nearby stream. 'This is The Nymphroving, of which the Silly Elves made songs long ages ago,' he explained.

'What, before breakfast?' whined Messy, holding his stomach.

'If you don't shut up, I'll cut your tongue out and feed you that,' roared Paragon.

Pipsqueak suddenly stopped and started to make a fire.

'What in Ill-Farter's name do you think you're doing?' screamed Paragon to the Halfbit.

'I was going to fry my piece,' said Pipsqueak, shakily.

'I give up. Doesn't anyone else want to be leader for a bit?' asked Paragon hopefully, but no answer came. 'Right then, we head on, and if I hear another squeak out of anyone about their hunger, they will be eating a knuckle sandwich.'

Pipsqueak was just about to ask what a knuckle sandwich tasted like, when Legless started to explain about their whereabouts. 'This stream is named after Nymphroving, the Elven-maid who the King loved. It is a sad story, for the Elves not only lost their King, but the moron took their greatest treasure with him too. You see, Sourone had put a curse on all the males of this realm, making them impotent. The Elves called on all their lore and knowledge to break it. With the aid of the three earrings - Nanny, Nelly and Willy - they created The Love Potion Lotion. Most of this was accomplished through the wisdom of Elbow, and the use of his Willy, however it was King Amlost who mixed the formula, and that is now forgotten. In his vain attempt to woo

Nymphroving, he took to sea with him the last bottle and only recipe; his ship sank and he was never seen again. I will sing The Song of Nymphroving and Amlost,

Amlost sailed upon the sea,
From shore to shiny shore.
Nymphroving chased the lads with glee
And hid from the stupid bore.

He sailed the sea by night or day,
A playacting sailor boy.
When he was home, she hid away.
When he set sail, she had great joy.

The Elven King did as he would like
And not as he was told.
He had a problem with his spike.
It would always tend to fold.

Nymphroving she did run away
With a band of travelling dancers.
Her mother knew not what to say.
For Amlost she had no answers.

Amlost went in search of her,
For love he would have given.
But her great love was for another
And had his bun in the oven.

Amlost took the secret lotion.
None knew it was with him.
His ship was lost upon the ocean,
Along with the King of Elvendim.

The Potent Potion of the Elves,
They shared it with no others.
The greedy bastards kept it to themselves
And hid it under covers.

The Elves now search forevermore
The secret of Lostlotion.
Things are not as were before,
Why that is, they have a notion.

Love potions they are weak or strong
And the most potent one of them all,
Went down with Amlost into song
And now the Elves don't walk so tall.'

With that, Legless stopped and could go on no longer as he could remember no more; he was very unpoetic for an Elf.

'Since they lost the Love Potion Lotion,' volunteered Paragon, 'the Elves of this Realm have been considered quite strange, so be careful.'

'What was so important about a potion?' asked Borrowit.

'The Potion gave back the vitality and vigour that Sourone had stolen,' explained Legless, 'and what's more it made them lusty in the bedchamber. They have tried to find the recipe of the potion, and continue to experiment, but so far they have met with failure. Yet, they persevere in their quest for the return of pleasure.'

'What was this Potion called?' enquired Foodo.

'It was known as Via-Grow,' replied Legless.

'Why Via-Grow?' asked Messy.

'Because via the potion, certain parts of their anatomy would grow,' answered Legless nervously.

'Would it make my brain grow bigger?' asked Pipsqueak.

'It worked wonders, not miracles,' laughed Paragon.

They continued on, until Paragon called them to a halt, 'We will soon be entering the woodland realm of Lostlotion. The Lord and Lady are Cellphone and Gadabout and their people are called The Gallivanthrim.'

They left the path and melted into the trees, all except Stan that is, who tripped over his own feet and landed in a holly bush. This made him squeal like a stuck pig.

From the tree above came a long arm. It shot out and grabbed the Halfbit by his leg, pulling him painfully from the bush. A voice, sweet and melodic, like the sound of wine being poured, said, 'Desist.'

Stan went limp and started to wet himself with fear. Three Elves appeared from the branches of the tree. The one holding Stan dropped him and he landed on his head, which made Foodo chuckle to Paragon, 'I bet that hurt.'

The Elf in charge introduced himself as Haldrear, the other two being his brothers Rummy and Origami, who he had brought along to play with when they had run out of Dork to hunt. Haldrear demanded to know who they were. Paragon stepped forward and began to introduce the Followship, while Legless was welcomed as the country cousin he was. That prompted him to ask at what time the pubs closed in Lostlotion and was overjoyed to learn that the licensing laws had been relaxed to celebrate the demise of Sourone, three thousand years before; he could now crawl out of the bar anytime he wanted to, that is if he was inclined to, which he wasn't. Borrowit and the Halfbits were treated with respect and some mild amusement. However, when Paragon told them of the Dwarf, the smiles on the faces of the Elves quickly disappeared.

Haldrear explained, 'Since the younger old days that are long ago for you, but not for us, Dwarves are banned from entering into Lostlotion. He cannot enter.'

Paragon looked perplexed, which was his usual demeanour anyway, and said to Haldrear, 'But Elbow of Riverdwell chose him to be the Dwarf rep on this Quest.'

'Only because there were no other Dwarves around at the time,' added Legless.

'Still,' pressed Paragon, 'he is one of the Followship and his axe has proved useful when looking for firewood.'

Haldrear turned and spoke with his brothers. There was lots of shaking of heads and a few fingers–across-the-throat gestures, but in the end they decided he should remain with the Followship. Certain conditions were attached to their decision: that he remained silent, that he took no holiday snaps, that he didn't get too near the sensitive noses of the Elves, and that he didn't breathe — this was found to be unreasonable, so it was changed to snore. So Haldrear led them off towards the centre of Lostlotion, leaving his brothers to play with themselves. The Elf took them back along the Slimyroad, until they reached a point where he stopped. 'This is Naff of Lotion and from here the dwarf must be bagged.'

'What do you mean, bagged?' asked Foodo

'It is the custom of our people that any of the Nowgrim who passes our borders must wear a bag over his head, so that they don't scare our womenfolk,' answered Haldrear.

Grimy looked upset by that. 'I am considered quite a catch where I live.'

'So is a trout,' added Legless.

Grimy was getting quite angry now and spluttered, 'That's fighting talk where I come from!'

'Good thing you moved then,' laughed Legless.

'You're not putting a bag over my head,' concluded Grimy, resting his hands on his axe. 'Which pointy eared tree-hugger wants to be picking his nose with his toes?'

Paragon stepped forward and, winking at the others said, 'Come friends, if the Dwarf must wear a bag then so must we. I will go first to show my solidarity with Grimy, my best friend.'

When they had all been bagged, Grimy grudgingly accepted his. Once he couldn't see them anymore, the others took their bags off.

They marched on for the rest of the day, occasionally and when they could be bothered, steering the Dwarf away from any tree or lamppost that got in the way.

Some time later they ran into a group of Elves who had paid to go on a hunting safari. They were currently tracking a company of Dorks that had stupidly crossed the border. The leader of the group had brought a message from the Lord and Lady of the Gallivanthrim. It seemed that they knew of the Dwarf, so they had sent the women and children to a holiday camp at Centre Parks. They allowed Grimy to take off his bag.

Black and blue and with a broken nose, he saw that the others didn't have a scratch on them, so he asked, 'How many times did they walk into a tree, trip over a root or fall into a hole?'

'None,' was the answer from several mouths at once.

Grimy couldn't understand that, so he put it down to Elvish jealousy of his rugged good looks. On examining his surroundings, he saw that he was standing by a large mound of rubble.

Haldrear said, 'You look upon what of old was Cretin Amlost. Here in ancient times was the house of the King. The

Elves of those days bulldozed it so that it didn't remind them, or any others, of their loss.' The last sentence was aimed at the sniggering dwarf. Haldrear decided that rather than punch the Dwarf and risk catching something unnameable, he could just wave the bag in front of his eyes. It worked, because Grimy's face took on a worried look and he mumbled his apologies in haste.

They marched on for a few hours, with Haldrear leading them down paths seldom trod by mortal feet, until at last they came to a huge clearing. They had arrived at the city of the Gallivanthrim, Careless Gallivant itself.

LOSTLOTION

Amidst a huge clearing sat Lostlotion, Fairground City of the Elves. Atop massive trees sat buildings with big, flashing neon lights above them. On the biggest tree, in the centre, was a huge structure with a sign that read, Cellphone's Casino. All around through the forest was a track-way, along which trundled a rollercoaster. Moving closer to the city, they came to the main gates and upon the gates was a sign that read thus:

WELCOME TO LOSTLOTION
LEISURE PARK AND FAIRGROUND
ALL PLEASURES CATERED FOR (EXCEPT THAT ONE).

'Come,' said Haldrear, 'here is Careless Gallivant. I will take you to meet our Lord and Lady.'

Through the centre of the great tree bearing the Casino, was an elevator into which they all entered. On the wall was a bank of buttons paired with the names of the different establishments next to them. The only one that Legless saw was for The Stagger Inn and he hoped that the greetings wouldn't go on for too long, as his tongue was starting to think it was a worn out flip-flop. Haldrear pushed a large button marked, Casino. The elevator slowly started to move. On its way to the top, it slowed to a crawl. A metallic voice complained, 'There are too many fat ugly Dwarves in the lift.'

Grimy looked around and said, 'There is only one Dwarf in the lift: me.'

The voice replied, 'One fat ugly dwarf is one too many. Please leave by the back door.'

Grimy looked out of the window of the elevator and saw that they were a few hundred feet up the tree. He was beginning to think that Elves didn't like Dwarves.

When they reached the top, the doors opened to reveal their hosts.

'I am Gadabout,' the Lady welcomed, 'and this is Cellphone,

which is Telephono in the language of the No-Older.'

To Grimy they looked tall and beautiful, but then, other than the Halfbits, everyone did to a Dwarf. The hair of Gadabout was as golden as the sun shining on a golden thingy, strangely similar to Colorall No5.

Cellphone, who had been partying all night, was wearing a tinsel wig. 'Welcome to the Fairground of Lostlotion. How r u gud ppl? It is gr8 2 c u,' said Cellphone, lapsing into the Qwerty text of The Haughty Elves. He caught himself, and continued, 'Welcome Paragon son of Paramount. It is thirty-eight of your years since we saw your smile in Careless Gallivant — the Botox injections have worked well. Forget your burden and rest for a while; you mortals do need your beauty sleep. Welcome Son of Thatfool; seldom do my kindred make the journey from the North, especially since they closed all the inns on the way here. It will be accounted among the marvels of our people that you made it this far.'

Legless looked quite drawn, and wasn't actually listening; his mind was on the ice-cold beer that awaited him in The Stagger Inn.

Cellphone turned to the Dwarf and said, 'Welcome Grimy, son of Grubby. Long it is since we fired your people from the Haunted House and Ghost Train; you frightened our young ones for a long time, but you know you went too far wearing those smiley politician masks. Maybe before you go we can renew the ties of old between our people and give the Nowgrim a contract to work on the Coconut Shy, as we have difficulties getting hold of coconuts these days.'

When the greetings had finished, Gadabout spoke again, 'The message we got from Riverdwell was that nine set out on this quest.'

Cellphone looked at the companions, 'Using both my hands and after a couple of attempts, I can only count eight of you. Did not The Grand Alf set forth on this quest also? I was hoping to greet him with you, for I much desired to see his stage act again. Where is he?'

Paragon looked pained as he told the story of The Bridge of Khaziboom. He told them of the fate of The Grand Alf. 'He fell in Moribund, locked in combat with an ancient evil,' and he would say no more.

'It was a Labdog of Mortcough,' explained Legless.

'Yea, verily,' moaned Grimy. 'It was on that accursed bridge that I saw the monster that haunts our very dreams, that which is known as Dunins Baying, the nightmare of the Nowgrim.'

Cellphone looked troubled. 'Long have we known that something evil had been woken by the Dwarves under Carbuncle, for we have spent many sleepless nights listening to the mad, incessant howling. We complained, of course, to the Environmental Elf, but he was virtually helpless as it was outside his jurisdiction. We sent several letters of which the first few came back unopened. It wasn't until the third one returned that we thought maybe our neighbours were pig ignorant, uneducated morons. I was at that point told that the Dwarves had been evicted by even thicker individuals. Things went quiet for a long time after the Dwarves were sacked from our employment. We had no knowledge of these others but the howling ceased. Now you tell me of this Brawlin; if we had known that the Dwarves had disturbed this evil again, then the Dwarf would be trying on his new concrete boots by now. I would also add that, at his end, The Grand Alf fell into folly.'

'No, he fell into a big hole,' said the small voice of Pipsqueak from the back.

'Amazing!' exclaimed Cellphone, staring in disbelief at the Halfbit. 'Who taught these things to speak?'

'Now, that would be Lingo of Longwinded,' said Pipsqueak proudly, 'who introduced us to Wyrdsome, the language of the big people; that would be about the 37th of Yowl, in the year 34723 of the Third Stage, in the Snore Reckoning. And then-'

'Do they always speak such rubbish?' cut in Cellphone. 'What possible use have they?'

'They are disposable Ringbreakers, cannon fodder, not much use for anything else at all really,' whispered Paragon.

'Yes, I can see one of these carries the nose ring,' said Gadabout.

Her gaze fell upon Foodo and he heard a voice within his mind, saying, 'Foodo of The Snore, you have come through many perils. Ill-Farter knows how you got here. We will meet later when the others are asleep for we have much to discuss.' Gadabout was Muddy Earth's top Psychic, Mind Reader, Fortune Teller and Spoon Bender. Foodo was instantly worried, as he had never been alone with a female before and thought he had better stick close to Stan.

The company was told to rest and wait, while their quarters were prepared. The Halfbits had one room, Paragon and Borrowit another, which left Grimy and Legless to share the last. Legless was not at all happy with this and complained about how loud the Dwarf snored. 'Your snoring would wake the dead,' he said.

Grimy retaliated by pointing out that Legless would be semi comatose by the time his head hit the pillow, and that if a herd of wild Nelliphaunt's wearing hobnail boots did the conga through the middle of the room, it wouldn't wake him. The argument descended into a childish squabble, so Paragon stepped in-between the two and said that he would sleep in the same room as the Dwarf.

They all went off to their quarters to take a bath and change their clothes, all except Grimy and Messy who said that they had already had one bath that year, and as they were wearing the same clothes as they had bathed in, then it stood to reason that they didn't need changing either. The two smelly companions were told that they could have no food, drink or sleep in Lostlotion until they had bathed. That sent Messy running to the baths, with Grimy dragging his feet after him. The sight (and smell) of them approaching the bathhouse sent the others running for cover. Whilst they bathed, the Elves washed and dried their clothes. They had taken it in turns to first fumigate, then disinfect and lastly boil, Grimy and Messy's kitbags.

After the companions had finished, they all met in the Stagger Inn for one or two drinks and to discuss their plans. They decided they would leave in a couple of days, head for the Falls of Raucous and then move on, past the two huge statues of Evenduller and Anotherone, called the Argonlamps. As for mode of transport, the Elves promised them some of the old canoes from the Log Ride. With their plans laid and their bladders full, they drifted back to their rooms.

As they walked, Foodo and Stan were waylaid by Gadabout.

'I have something special to show you,' she said to Foodo.

Now, Stan had noticed that at their first meeting she had held him long in her gaze. Stan thought he had better look after his master, as Foodo was very naïve that way and Gadabout may be a pervy Halfbit-fancier. Stan had, once or twice, been lucky enough to have fumbles with Dozy Hot-one, his intended; this made him a sex god compared to the celibate Foodo.

Gadabout led them to a room with nothing but a square mirror in. 'This is the Mirror of Gadabout,' she explained. 'Would you like to see its magic? It can educate you with things that were or things that may be; but beware, like all forms of media it can lie.' With that, she touched a button and chanted:

'MIRROR, MIRROR ON THE WALL
SHOW US WHAT IS ABOUT TO FALL.'

The mirror shimmered and a picture of a girl eating an apple appeared. Gadabout cursed and gave the mirror a good whack, saying, 'Wrong bloody channel again. This thing is knackered.' The image changed to one of Halfbiton.

Stan looked on in dismay. 'They've kicked the Grafter out of Blagshut Row and turned it into a casino! Why, there's Ed Randyman leading Dozy Hot-one up the garden path. Oh I've got to get home!'

'What do you think you will achieve by going home now?' asked Gadabout.

'Maybe I can stop Dozy from making the biggest mistake of her life, by going off with Ed Randyman instead of me,' moaned Stan.

'Doesn't sound a bad idea to me,' muttered Foodo under his breath.

Suddenly the image in the mirror changed to that of a great eye rimmed in red,with words above and below it. Around the top, it said Sourone Inc. TV, and below it in large letters, flashing, was the word Newsflash. A zombie-like newsreader appeared in its centre. 'Our great nation stands on the brink of war. Earlier today I interviewed the Chief Propaganda Minister. Here is what happened.' A hideous skull-faced man replaced him, with a caption that read, The Mouthpiece of Sourone. He began his diatribe with, "Know this, peoples of Muddy Earth, we in Morbid will not stand for this unwarranted aggression from Minus Thrifty and its deluded allies. We have signed a treaty with our good friend Sourman the Irate of Oldcrank and we will crush any opposition. Know also this, that war is bad for your Elves, and if the stunted Nowgrim get involved, they will be put in their

place, at the end of a shovel to feed the furnace of Bad-Odour".
The interview ended and the ghastly newsreader reappeared.
'Lastly, a reward will be given to anyone who has information on
Halfbits, one in particular by the name of Braggins. The Lord
Sourone wishes to honour him with his own plot of land at his
summer palace of Gravelands.' The transmission ended there
and the mirror returned to its natural state.

Gadabout looked at the shell-shocked Foodo and said, 'I
know what it is you saw, for I see it also; the Great Eye interrupts
the Shopping Channel constantly.' She then explained to Foodo
what the Great Eye was. 'Sourone has constructed a vast glass
dome atop the highest tower of Bad-Odour, and set within it
is the most powerful telescope ever invented; great Thralls toil
night and day to work its mechanisms. He watches constantly
for any who dare draw near to Morbid, and if the gaze of the
Great Eye falls upon you, then trouble will find you. Sourone sits
without rest, in the tower now known as the Hubble-bubble; he
has sat there so long his eye has become stuck to the telescope,
which is now known as the Eyepiece of Sourone. If you get
close to Morbid, you will see the Great Eye all rimmed in red, for
Sourone suffers from Glaucoma. Anything his Eye falls upon,
withers and is blighted; even the surrounding area of Morbid has
become a cesspit of bogs and marshes, the Dread Mushlands. As
Sourone's power has waxed, the blight has also grown. He sees
more clearly all within this blight, and it is also called The Nigh
of Sourone,'

Foodo was by now petrified, so he said to Gadabout, 'This is
all too much for me. Would you like the nose ring?'

Gadabout stared at Foodo and shakily said, 'Long have I desired
this thing, for with it we can remove the Curse of Sourone from
our males. We can return to nights of unbridled passion with our
drunken husbands; we can have lots of squealing children and
wash loads of dirty nappies.' At that point, Gadabout had a vision
of her naked husband and, turning to Foodo, she said, 'No, you
keep it. I will remain celibate and wash his dirty vests.' After she
recovered from the vision, she led them from the room. 'Now
you must get some rest, for you will be leaving soon.'

The next morning the Halfbits were first to the breakfast
table. As they started on their second helping, Legless and

Borrowit arrived from the bar area. Shortly afterwards Paragon appeared, at which the others started to snigger, asking him if he had managed to get any sleep. Paragon replied that he had slept deeply, undisturbed.

Legless however didn't believe him. 'How? It is not possible to sleep through that noise.'

'It was very easy, actually. When I went to bed last night, I walked into the room, went straight over to Grimy and kissed him, the result being he sat up all night watching me.'

Later, Grimy turned up for breakfast, glowering at everyone; he sat on a table on his own, all the time staring suspiciously at Paragon. Once the Halfbits had licked their plates clean, they did the same to the others, in what appeared to be a semi religious Halfbit-custom — one of the big folk had turned up in Halfbiton one day, claiming that he had invented automatic dishscrubbers and the maddened Halfbits nearly lynched him.

They packed their baggage and went to say goodbye to Cellphone and Gadabout. As promised, the Elves provided them with the canoes from the Log Ride; they also gave them Elvish weighbread, a heavy type of loaf that was quite filling, whose name was Alembaps. It was a type of concentrated pub grub and if you ate a piece and drank some water it tasted like a ploughman's lunch and a pint of beer.

Gadabout gave them also personal gifts. To Paragon she gave a shabby leather sheath saying, 'A sword drawn from this will never stain or break. It was left here by one of your ancestors.' Printed on one side was a note, "Retrieved from the body of Everdull, by his son Evenduller." She also gave him a large piece of gaudy costume jewellery made of green glass. 'Take now the name foretold of old for you, Alesser the Halfstoned of the house of Everdull.'

To Borrowit, Messy and Pipsqueak she gave souvenir belts of Lostlotion. To Legless, she gave one of the great fairground bows of the Gallivanthrim, the ones they used on the Shoot the Rubber Dorky. To Stan Gamble she gave a box with the letters G A on it, 'These letters are the first two in Gardener and Gadabout, but for you it could stand for Gamblers Anonymous. Inside is soil from our rubbish tip and nuts of the Malathion tree. Bury these nuts in your gardens and there will be no flies on you.'

She lastly turned to the Dwarf and said, 'I have no idea what to give a pintsized, smelly, grubby Dwarf. What is your desire?'

'Nothing, fair lady.'

'Are you sure there is nothing at all you need?'

'Quite sure.'

'Hear this, Elves of Lostlotion! Here we have Grimy the strangest of Dwarves. For any of you who say that all Dwarves are greedy, grabby and ungrateful, I say we have found our first non-materialistic Dwarf. We will not allow you alone to go from here without a gift. Name anything and it is yours.'

'Well ... if you insist, may I have, nay ... I need ... a strand of your hair.'

'What would you do with such a gift?' asked Gadabout, as she cut off three strands of hair and gave them to Grimy.

He took them, saying, 'I've had a piece of bacon stuck in my teeth since this morning at breakfast,' and started to floss with one. The other two would come in handy to tie and secure that shiny cutlery he had stolen from the dining area that morning.

Gadabout then turned to Foodo, 'Ringbreaker, I come to you last, for I had almost forgotten about you. I have prepared something you may need.' She handed him a small pocket-sized book, with the title File of Facts on the cover. 'This is the File of Gadabout; set within are spells to recite in time of trouble, also attached to the book is a handy little reading light, for there are many dark places in the land of Morbid.' Foodo took the book and bowed.

Lastly, she gave them all pin-on badges, which read I'VE BEEN TO LOSTLOTION. They all climbed into their canoes, raising their hands and waggling them in the Elvish manner of farewell and saying "Nomoreihere" to the Elves.

Foodo looked back longingly at the fairground, realising he had not been on the rollercoaster, nor would he ever. They travelled downriver away from Lostlotion; the water was sluggish and lapped against the canoe, and the rhythm of it sent Foodo to sleep. They drifted with the power of the river, assisted by paddles that the Elves had fitted from one of the other rides.

Some hours later, Foodo awoke with a stiff neck and the smell of cooking in his nostrils. He was lying in the bottom of the canoe, with Borrowit's large pack on his head. He sat up angrily. 'I hope you have saved some for me.'

Paragon looked at the Halfbit in surprise and replied, 'I gave it to Pipsqueak for you.'

Pipsqueak quickly stuffed his stolen rations into his mouth and hid the empty plate under Messy's bedroll. Then he stood up and, pointing at the sleeping Messy declared, 'I gathit ta Methy, ta gith ta Thido, burp.'

At that point Messy, who had been having a dirty dream (cleaning out the pigs at Brandishmuck Hall), rolled over onto the plate. The plate stuck onto his back and woke him up. Wondering what it was, he lifted his blanket and pulled it out just as the others turned to look at him. 'What is this?'

'It looks like Foodo's empty plate,' replied Paragon accusingly.

'That's typical of Foodo, always getting someone else to wash his dirty dishes,' said Messy, and flung the plate to Stan, adding, 'I bet it's your turn.' He then rolled over and went back to sleep.

At dawn they continued their journey through a dense, coniferous woodland. On the third day, the trees thinned out, leaving an area of deforestation caused by the Sourman Logging Company.

'This is the Browse Lands that lie between Southern Murkywood and the Embroil Mulch,' explained Paragon. 'You are looking across the land of Ridicule, Bovine of the Bulls-hitters, and soon we shall come to the mouth of the Limplot that flows from Fewgrown Forest into the Arduous.'

That night they stopped on a little island in the middle of the river.

Stan settled down next to Foodo, 'As we came downstream I saw something that made me think I was dreaming.'

'Was that before I kicked you for snoring or after I kicked you for snoring the first time, but before you were snoring the second time?'

'It's not funny, Mr Foodo,' retorted Stan, getting rather upset. 'I don't know if I was dreaming or not.'

'Well, what do you think it was then, Stan?'

'It looked like a log with eyes.'

By this time, everyone else was interested in Stan's dream too.

'It might have been a crocodile,' volunteered Messy.

'No, no. It sounds more like an alligator,' argued Pipsqueak.

'You wouldn't know the difference between an alligator and an alley cat.'

'Could it have been a very large ugly frog of the Lesser Spotted

Webberfeet Family?' asked Borrowit.

'It could have been an enormous fat ugly toad,' said Grimy.

'It can't have been, you're the only Dwarf around here,' laughed Legless.

'I think it sounds like an iguana,' said Messy cleverly.

'What does an iguana sound like?' asked Pipsqueak, with a puzzled look on his face. 'And did anyone else hear it?' he added, before disappearing under a pile of projectiles in the shape of boots.

'I know exactly what, or who, those eyes belong to,' explained Paragon, 'as I have seen them before and I can put a name to them. Grumble is on our trail, so we had better keep on our guard.'

On the eighth night of their journey, they travelled through the Hills of the Embroil Mulch, on their way to the Rapids of Stern Gamut. As they approached the rapids, the river flowed much swifter and the boats were drawn towards the rocks like Halfbits to food.

'Quickly,' shouted Paragon, 'we must make for the shore.'

Their legs pumped on the pedals to halt the boats; they pedalled for all they were worth, which meant the Halfbits did not do much. Slowly they turned towards the shoreline and managed to beach the canoes. As they clambered ashore, there was a twang of bowstrings from the opposite shore.

'Yuk,' said Legless in the tongue of the Silly Elves.

'Dorks!' said Stan. 'I can smell Grumble's doing in this.'

'Was that the log he was floating on last night?' asked Pipsqueak.

Just then, an arrow bounced off Foodo's corset. Grimy ducked for cover with an arrow stuck in his ginger beard, while a song of utter brutality came from the trees on the opposite shore:

'YOU'RE GONNA GET YOUR BLOODY HEADS
KICKED IN!'

As they sang, a huge shape lifted from behind the trees: a great flying reptile, a Fell Beast and relative of the amphibian Knockyless Monsta. It was a Terrorblacktail and sat atop this was the Lord of the Nasal. The Gobby Dorks below were wailing and gnashing their teeth — it looked bad for the Followship.

Legless stood, fixed two arrows to the Great Fairground Bow of Lostlotion, aimed and fired. The arrows soared through the air in a great arc; it was one of the greatest or luckiest shots of all time. With a loud pop, the suction caps at the ends of the arrows stuck to each eyeball of the winged beast, who was now temporarily blinded and spiralling out of control. The Gobby Dorks wailed in despair. Messy and Pipsqueak jumped for joy, ran to the water's edge and started chanting:

'YOU ONLY SING WHEN YOU'RE WINNING
SING WHEN YOU'RE WINNING
YOU ONLY SING WHEN YOU'RE WINNING!'

Then, with a loud crash accompanied by even louder screams, the beast plummeted into the Dorks. No more arrows came from the opposite shore, just screams of, 'MEDIC!'

The Followship slept huddled in their canoes, except for Grimy, who volunteered to keep watch while he kept one eye on Paragon. The next morning, the area was clouded in a thick fog.

'This should hide us from those Gobby Dorks,' said Stan. 'It must be the thickest pea-souper I have ever seen.'

The fog was a by-product of Sourman's industrialisation programme.

'We cannot attempt The Stern Gamut in this fog,' said Paragon.

'Why don't we get rid of these floating death-traps and set off to Minus Thrifty, then?' threw in Borrowit hopefully.

'Ah, poor Borrowit. Are you feeling homesick?' asked Legless, sarcastically.

'Are you sick of living, Elf?'

Paragon stepped between the two, thinking that Legless would soon be living up to his name and not because of his depleting hoard of alcohol. He told Legless that he needed his help and both legs would be advantageous on this mission. 'We must carry the canoes along the pathway that bypasses the Rapids of Stern Gamut. But first, by skill we must find it.'

As they departed, Borrowit said he would stay and guard the Halfbits. Foodo's heart sank as Borrowit came and put his arm around his shoulder, saying, 'We can't let anything happen to the ring … err … the Ringbreaker I mean.'

Sometime later, the scouting party reappeared.

'We have found a way to the lower level,' said Paragon.

'Was it the legendary tracking skills of Stupor or the keen eyes of the Elves that found the way?' asked Pipsqueak.

Grimy laughed. 'Neither. Can't you see the signpost over there that says, "This way to the Portage Point"?'

Legless gave the dwarf a look that meant he acknowledged Grimy had scored a point in their private war.

Paragon looked at the sky. 'There is not much time before the light fails. We must get the canoes up the trail.'

As they unpacked their boats, they divided the packs between the Halfbits and the dwarf.

Borrowit looked at the dwarf. 'This would be hard work even if the were all men.'

Legless laughed and said to Grimy, 'Don't let him speak down to you like that. Go and stand on that rock over there.'

Grimy did exactly that. As he climbed onto the rock, he immediately experienced vertigo, being more than a foot off the ground. Yet he came from a hardy people and, facing up to Borrowit, he bragged, 'I can carry the load of three men.'

Suddenly Grimy's pile of packs grew bigger, while Messy's grew equally smaller. 'I believe you,' said the Halfbit.

'So do I,' said Pipsqueak, as he tied his sleeping mat to Grimy's bulging backpack.

As this went on, Paragon, Borrowit and Legless pulled the log canoes from the water. To their surprise they found that attached to the undercarriage were the wheels used whilst on the track-way for the log ride. They made life a lot easier and it only took half the time they thought it would take to reach the landing site at the end of the rapids. They slept in the boats again that night. Grimy, the self-proclaimed Sturdy Dwarf, was snoring before his head hit the pillow, complaining and muttering in his sleep about pack animals and beasts of burden, but mostly about lazy Halfbits.

Paragon woke them early the next morning; he reported there had been no sight or sound of The Gobby Dorks that night.

'It's not surprising given the splash that the beast made,' said Legless. 'There can't be many left alive to report back to Sourone of its fall.'

'Is that why it's called a fell beast?' asked Pipsqueak. He received a whack to his head for his latest stupid question, and found himself once again in the horizontal position, picking himself off the ground as he was told to help with the loading of the canoes.

Once back in the water, they set off again on their quest. After a few hours they came to a ravine. From here the river narrowed and got faster, increasing the speed of the canoes. They sped through and shot out the other side, unable to avoid the unmistakable flash of the stealth tax speed cameras. The river carried them a little further until they reached the Gates of the Argonlamps, the mighty statues on either side of The Arduous. They had been built by Raymandaystill II, to guard the northern border of Gondour.

'Behold the Pylons of the Kings,' said Paragon. These were great images of Evenduller and Anotherone. In one hand they held huge spotlights, and in the other hand of Evenduller was an open scroll, reading:

ELECKTRICKERY BILL, FINAL NOTICE.

In the other hand of Anotherone was a scroll that read:

SMALL CLAIMS (DWARVEN SECTION)
NON-PAYMENT OF REPAIR BILL

'Many things have fallen into disrepair since the Kings were lost,' continued Paragon, trying to sound political.

Borrowit was about to get all leftwing, when it dawned on him that Paragon was right, or just right of centre.

They passed the ruined statues and emerged into the large lake of Non Hither. In the distance they could see the Tiltrock, also known as Tall Brandish; on either side of it sat Mons When, the hill of spying, and Mons Where, the hill of listening. Both these hills were used by the Neomanorealmen Order of Secret Intelligence (N.O.S.I.), to keep an eye on the Eye. That was the origin of the game, "I spy (with my little eye) on the Great Eye."

They made for the Western shore and landed on a spot leading to a large green lawn, where they unloaded their gear.

Pipsqueak looked around, felt and saw how serene and

pleasant it looked and said, 'I feel like I belong here. What's it called?'

'Pratt Garble,' replied Paragon.

With the canoes unloaded, they sat down to a small meal.

Paragon called them together, 'We have come to a point on our quest where we must decide what to do, whether to go with Borrowit and get paid a huge amount as mercenaries and die fighting impossible odds, or go with Foodo to certain pain and suffering or maybe death.'

Legless looked uncertain and asked Borrowit, 'Are there plenty of pubs in Minus Thrifty?'

'Do they have separate rooms?' asked Grimy, looking sideways at Paragon.

'Is it overflowing with food?' asked Messy and Pipsqueak.

Only Stan stood by Foodo. 'I placed a bet in Lostlotion that Mr Foodo would get to Horridruin and I'm going to make sure he does.'

'What were the odds?' asked Foodo.

'1,000,000 to 1,' replied Stan.

'You don't fancy taking the nose ring yourself, do you Stan? I quite fancy seeing Borrowit's horn collection,' said Foodo as he hurried towards Borrowit.

Stan grabbed Foodo by the collar and said, 'I bet that YOU would get there, and you are not going to spoil my chance of winning MY million.'

Foodo didn't know which way to turn or what to do. He looked at the others and said, 'It is a hard decision to make: it seems my only choice is death, death or even death.'

Pipsqueak was frantically counting his fingers and looked bemused. 'Sorry for appearing thick, but what is this third death?'

Foodo said nothing but just stared at Stan who was holding the Tenderiser quite firmly in both hands. He was in a quandary. 'Give me an hour and I will make my decision.' He hurried off to hide, thinking that once alone, he would be able to somehow talk himself out of this madness. He wondered why anyone would suffer pain, hunger and death on purpose, and for what? It wouldn't even push The Grafter's prized Marrow off the front page of The Daily Snore. As he wandered halfway up the hillside, he saw an old stonewall. He sat down on it and started contemplating his rapidly shortening future. He had been there for some time when a shifty looking Borrowit appeared.

'You know, you shouldn't be out here on your own. You could fall down a hole or be eaten by wild animals. No one would know what happened to you. It is a good thing that Borrowit is here to protect you.' As Foodo didn't answer, he continued. 'Why do we wander around in the wild? Come to Minus Thrifty. You can have all the food you want and lay aside this burden. If you lent the nose ring to me I could do the impossible. I could make daytime TV entertaining, make politicians tell the truth, I would make fast food taste better than flavoured cardboard, I could even make reality pop idol contestants talented, but most of all I would destroy all of Sourone's works.' Borrowit by now was losing control. 'Give me the ring Foodo, let me borrow it.'

'No you can't borrow it, Borrowit, for if you borrow it, Borrowit, you won't give it back.'

Borrowit looked confused, 'No, I only want to borrow it once not twice.'

'There will be no borrowing it at all,' said Foodo.

'So now you threaten me!'

'No, I am not threatening you. I am a lot smaller than you; how could I?'

'Yes you are and I could just take the ring if I wanted to, and I do.' With this last sentence, he lunged at Foodo.

The Halfbit was too streetwise and as Borrowit advanced towards him, he put his hand in his pocket and placed the ring on his finger. He disappeared before the big man got to him, leaving Borrowit to bounce his head off the wall like a mad bull. Borrowit staggered around, roaring and striking out blindly like a punch-drunk boxer who was haunted by bells. Foodo disappeared up the hill in more ways than one.

Behind him Borrowit screamed, 'Curse all Halfbits to dearth and harshness!' He then fell over a tree root and onto his face. He lay there for a while blubbing like a baby. When he rose, and thought about covering his backside, he shouted, 'Foodo come back! You misunderstood me! A malapropism took me, but it has passed!'

Foodo didn't answer, as he was far out of earshot and trying to put some distance between himself and Borrowit the Barmy. He soon came to the summit of the hill, upon which was a building. On the outside of it was a stairway leading up to a large stone chair called The Seat of Scenic, Mons When, or The Hill of the Spy of Neomanor. Foodo climbed the stairs, walked over to the seat and sat down. A pressure pad clicked underneath him and, from the top of the backrest, dropped a helmet-like device with frosted glass eyepieces. It lowered itself onto Foodo's head and as it came to rest, it switched itself on. Immediately his vision and hearing exploded into a 3D virtual reality with surround sound. A 3D map of Muddy Earth appeared in front of him. This was naturally aligned to the real world, therefore when Foodo moved his head to look at the land, he saw, by zooming in, things that were happening in that place. In the North, The Silly Elves were locked in combat with the Dorks of the Musty Mountains. South of them, the land of the Barings and the Hall of Bjorn were aflame. On the borders of Lostlotion, the Dorks were having barbecues. Turning slowly westwards, he saw the Riders of Ridicule being laughed at by the Wags. He then turned southwards, past Minus Thrifty and on to the Harbours of Harass, where the ships of the Corps of Umbrage sat in the dock. From there he turned eastwards, past the Dork infested ruins of Ohgiveusalaugh, past Minus Mucus and he looked upon Gorygorge, the Valley of Terrify in the Land of Morbid. Inch by inch his eyes moved towards Bad-Odour, until at last his gaze fell upon the uppermost tower. Therein sat Sourone and, as he became aware of Foodo's attention, slowly the Great Eye turned towards him. Foodo saw the red tunnel of the glaring gaze of The Eye fall upon Mons Where; slowly it crept nearer to him, groping.

From the Surround Sound came the evil voice of Sourone, 'Very soon I will come, I will come for you.' Then another voice, one he thought he should know, broke through. 'Take it off, take it off. And take your ass off the seat, fool!'

Foodo threw himself from the chair and onto the floor, just in time to feel the heat of the gaze fly over Mons When. He stood up and suddenly remembered the predicament he was in with Borrowit wanting to take the ring. He realised that he could no longer stay with the Followship — how many more of them would he have to fight off? No, the best thing was to go his own way, at least that way he could indulge in some intelligent conversation. The only problem was how.

The other members of the Followship had been left at the campsite, by the river. They had debated whether to go with Foodo to Morbid or with Borrowit to Minus Thrifty. Legless chose to go to Minus Thrifty, he had been told that even with rationing, fighting men got extra beer coupons, and anyway beer in Morbid was flat. Grimy and Messy had no wish of possibly going through another ordeal like bathing.

Paragon said, 'My road takes me to Minus Thrifty and my duty to my people.'

Pipsqueak got quite exited at that. 'Wow! Have you got a road named after you? Can I come with you to see it?'

Paragon then turned to ask Borrowit if he was taking Dewtea to Minus Thrifty as well, but Borrowit was nowhere to be seen.

'Where is he, and where is Foodo?' asked Stan. 'He's been gone a long time.'

Just then, a rather sheepish Borrowit appeared.

'Have you seen Foodo?' asked Paragon.

'Well, I did until he disappeared,' answered Borrowit.

'How … why did he disappear? asked Stan, worrying that Foodo had done a runner.

'I don't know. I've never seen anything like it. He vanished quicker than food off a Halfbit's plate.'

'He must have used the ring. Have you anything else you want to tell us?' said Paragon.

'Yes. Is there any food left? I'm starving.'

'We are not eating until we find Foodo.'

At that, the Halfbits ran off in a panic towards the woods shouting, 'Findo, Findo!' and 'Foodo Foodo, FOODO!'

'Damn, they will all be lost soon,' cried Paragon. 'Borrowit, go after the two young Halfbits and make sure they don't try eating anything bigger than themselves.' He set off after Stan, soon catching him with his longer stride pattern. As he passed the small, fat Halfbit, he shouted, 'Keep following this path, meet me at the top,' and then disappeared ahead.

Stan collapsed, having run over a league, the equivalent of the Halfbiton Marathon. He decided to go back to the campsite; while everyone was away, he could help himself to some extra grub. When he got there he found that some of the packs were missing and one of the canoes was paddling itself away from the shore. Stan put two and two together and, as usual, got the wrong answer: he didn't figure out that the canoe wasn't on autopilot. He ran towards the canoe thinking to save the food in it, but halfway there it dawned on him that thinking wasn't his best asset: he had forgotten he couldn't swim.

As his head disappeared under the water, Foodo, who was holding the canoe, thought, 'Well, that's one less to worry about.' As he turned away however, his gaze fell upon the very large pack of Grimy's that sat in the canoe; it hurt his back just thinking about carrying it. But, if he saved Stan, then he could do it for him! Foodo turned the canoe at once towards the frantically splashing Halfbit. The boat came to where Stan was feebly trying to doggy paddle. Stan went under again, only to resurface and crack his head on the canoe. At the same time, Foodo took off the ring and extended his arm over the side.

Stan's eyes were rolling around the back of his head, but he heard Foodo shouting, 'Take my hand!' With his vision all over the place, he could have sworn Foodo had turned into an octopus. He panicked and thrashed about in the water, squealing, 'Which hand?'

Foodo grabbed him and hauled him into the canoe, where he lay like a beached whale. After catching his breath, he told him, 'Let's pick up my cooking gear, then it's off to Morbid, Mr Foodo.' He returned to the shore, raided what he needed and re-embarked. 'Off we go; Morbid or bust.'

'I hope Stupor retains enough sanity to get the others to safety,' said Foodo. 'If I was like you, I'd bet we won't see them again.'

'I'll give you 5/1 that we will.'

They gained the opposite shore below Mons Where, taking their packs. Stan said words that can't be repeated here, and they headed over the Embroil Mulch and towards the Land of Shady.

THE TWO TOWNIES

BEING THE SECOND VOLUME OF
THE LORD OF THE GRINS

THE DEEP APERTURE OF BORROWIT

Paragon stood at the top of the hill, trying to read the story of the ground for any sign of footprints. This was made harder by the magnificent crazy paving that led to the huge patio area next to The Seat of Scenic. He climbed the stairs and inspected the chair; it was still smouldering from the gaze of Sourone. On the floor near the seat was one of Foodo's coat buttons — he recognized the Braggins family-crest of Crossed Knife and Fork, Surmounted by Pie of Porcus Piggus; he now knew that Foodo had been there. The Halfbit should have found his way back to the campsite by now, for it had been well over an hour since he had last eaten, and he would surely have been feeling faint. There was naught for him to do but go back down in search of Foodo.

Just as he set off, he heard from below the voices of Dorks screeching in their foul tongue. Above those noises rose suddenly the unmistakable Call of Retreat, sounded on the Ancestral Horn of the House of Howlin. Borrowit needed help. He stopped momentarily and thought, I will give him the address of my shrink, if we get home, and charged down the hill, screaming the family curse, 'Everdull, Everdull!'

When Paragon found Borrowit, he looked like a victim of a mad acupuncturist. He had more shafts in him than the Mines of Moribund. He knelt by him and saw that he was just about still alive.

Borrowit stirred, feeling the pain of many wounds; he looked up at Paragon and said, 'How bad is it?'

'I think I stubbed my toe coming down that hill, and we cannot find the Halfbits,' replied Paragon.

'Will you scratch my ear … I can't seem to move my right arm.'

'No wonder … there are at least three arrows holding it to this tree, but even if it was not so, I fear your arm is not long enough to reach your ear anymore.'

'Why?' asked a worried Borrowit.

'Well, see that tree, the third on the left, and the one with an arrow sticking from it?'

With failing eyesight, Borrowit squinted at the tree and replied, 'Yes … I can see it.'

'That arrow holds your ear to the tree, however it has done a beautiful job of piercing it, though it is a pity you haven't any suitable earrings,' explained Paragon. He looked around and could see only dead Dorks. 'What happened to the Halfbits?'

'Last time I checked, the Dorks were playing rugby with them.'

'They're a bit small for such a rough game, aren't they?'

'Not if you tie them correctly: they are about the same size as a ball.'

'Was Foodo with them, Borrowit?'

However, he never answered, nor did he ever speak again. Thus died Borrowit son of Denizen, of metal poisoning and an overdose of iron in his body.

Legless and Grimy appeared from the woods finding Paragon trying on Borrowit's boots. 'You had better help yourselves before the blood dries,' Paragon said.

'I'm having his flask,' said Legless, knowing that Borrowit had filled it with wine in Lostlotion.

Grimy was too small for any of the big man's gear, so he had to be content with the contents of Borrowit's pockets. 'Do you think anyone will notice if anything goes missing from him?'

'No, and we can always replace it with some of this Dork stuff,' replied Paragon.

Strewn around them were heaps of dead Dorks who had trampled each other in the attempt to claim a reward for catching a live Halfbit. Most of the dead were the normal run-of-the-mill Dorks; however, some were larger, man-sized, with thick heads. They bore on their shields a white clenched fist, with its middle finger extended and pointing upwards. On their helmets, they wore the letter S.

'S stands for Sourone,' said the semi-literate Dwarf, trying to sound cleverer than he was.

'No,' said Legless, as he drained Borrowits flask. 'Shourone doeshn't use Qwerty text.'

'Sourone will only use aliases and his people cannot even spell his name,' explained Paragon. 'Also the Dorks of Bad-Odour carry the sign of the Great Eye, so this S must be for Sourman, unless of course he was using his real name, Currynan.'

76

Now Grimy, who wasn't the sharpest tool in the box, asked, 'Is that pronounced Kurrynan or Surrynan? If it is the latter, then that can stand for S also.'

'It would shtill be written as a C you shtupid dwarf.'

'Who are you calling stupid, Elf? At least I don't look and talk like a big girl.'

They almost came to blows, but Paragon stepped between them. 'We have no time for this; we must take care of Borrowit's body.'

They carried him to the campsite, where they found a strange sight, for one of the canoes was missing. They placed Borrowit in one of the other boats, along with his remaining items — those that were of no use to his parasitic companions — the bent sword and broken horn. They pushed the log canoe off from the shore and watched it drift toward the Falls of Raucous.

Turning back to Prat Garble, Paragon knelt to read the signs on the ground. He noted also that two of the packs were missing, one of which was Grimy's, the one with the most food in it. 'If I read the signs correctly it means that Halfbits have been here, for only they would run off into the wild carrying virtually nothing but food. We know that Messy and Pipsqueak were taken by the Dorks; that means Foodo and Stan took the other canoe.'

'So we either take the last boat and follow the food … err … I mean Foodo, or see if we can rescue the two useless Halfbits,' recapped Grimy.

'Where Foodo and Stan are now, I cannot tell,' said Paragon. 'However we can follow the Dorks' trail blindfolded.'

The devastation left by the Dorks was like a scar on the land, with everything in their way trampled into the ground. Their only hope was that the Dorks would not acquire a taste for barbecued Halfbits. With that in mind they set off on the great chase. They followed the Dorks' trail northwards for the rest of the day and through the night, until they came across a pile of dead Dorks.

'There's been an almighty squabble here,' said Paragon. 'These are the smaller northern Dorks, not the same as the ones that used Borrowit for target practice.'

'It looks like they argued with their bigger brethren,' said Legless, 'maybe over whether to take the Halfbits to Sourone or Sourman. This won't be the last mangled Dork jigsaw puzzle we will encounter before the end of the trail.'

'Maybe they argued about the best way to cook a Halfbit, fried or boiled,' volunteered Grimy.

'Dorks don't cook their rations on the march, and they don't usually leave behind fresh meat. They must be in some hurry,' replied Legless.

'They have great need for speed,' added Paragon, 'for they have entered the land of Bovine and The Ruminates. The people of this land do not suffer strangers to wander at free will. We must be careful that we are not mistaken for Dorks ourselves.'

'In that case, I'm not as worried as the Dwarf should be.'

'If I were you, Elf,' replied Grimy, 'I'd be more worried about the amount of lumps my fists will make on your head. I will make you so ugly even the Dorks will wince.'

They carried on along the trail, now by the light of day. Along their way they found items discarded by the Dorks, wantonly throwing their litter across the beautiful countryside — beer cans and fast food containers led them on. League by league they went, with the Elf leading and the Dwarf straggling, moaning and retching, until Paragon called them to a halt.

'Stand still and don't move; footprints leave the trail here. They look like Pipsqueak's.'

'How can you tell which Halfbit they belong to?' asked Grimy.

'They are all over the place and there is no sense to them at all. Wait, look here!' Lying in the grass was a leaf-shaped badge, with I'VE BEEN TO LOSTLOTION written across it.

'Typical cheap and shoddy Elven workmanship. I bet the pin is broken,' said Grimy. Picking up the badge, he turned it over to examine it. Stamped across the back was, "By Appointment of His Majesty Throbin I, King Under the Influence". He quickly checked himself and said, 'I've never seen such wonderful craftsmanship. A fool is he that lost this magnificent item.'

'Well at least we know Pipsqueak is still alive then,' said Legless.

'I do not think he lost it,' explained Paragon. 'I think he may have thrown it away on purpose, because the pin is broken and may have kept pricking him. At least we now know that the Dorks did take the Halfbits and that at least one of them has the use of his legs.'

'The Dorks have not acquired a taste for Halfbit's haunch then; of that, we may be thankful,' added Grimy.

They pressed on, hopeful that they would draw nearer to the

Dorks. They travelled until it was dark and then debated whether to carry on during the night.

'They are far ahead,' Legless said. 'Maybe we would have caught them if we had not rested, or had to wait for Stumpy here to catch up. What is certain is that the Dorks haven't got any such hindrances, even though they must be carrying the lazy Halfbits.'

'I didn't know that Dorks had the strength or stamina to move at this speed,' said Grimy, looking angrily at the elf.

'Sourman must have given them Nandrelone,' assumed Paragon.

They continued the chase day and night; whenever they did stop and rest, out would come the Alembaps and they would sing or tell stories from the Older Days. One time, sitting around the campfire, Paragon told The Tale of Benny and Lillian or The Lay of Lection, The Release from Bandage. 'Benny son of Barry was a working class mortal,' he said, 'who fell in love with and married Lillian Tinnitus, the daughter of King Thingy and Mullein the May I. King Thingy sent Benny on a quest, saying, "If you wish to marry the daughter of the King of Elves, you must be in possession of a bottle of Silvermarrywine.". Thingy knew that Mortcough owned the last three bottles in the whole of the land known as Bellylard, if not the world, therefore sending him to certain death. The tale is long and full of sorrow, the death of King Thinrod Fellowgland not the least. With much help, Benny Chameleon returned out of darkness and wed with Lillian Tinnitus. Their child was Dear Helovachill, whose daughter Yelling married Herenditall, the son of Chewer, son of Hewer and Idiot Cerebellum, daughter of King Turgid of Condom. The sons of Yelling and Herenditall were Elbow the Halfman and Elroy. Elroy Tru Miniature was the first king of Neomanor and therefore my ancestor,' concluded Paragon proudly.

They drew straws for first watch and, as usual, Grimy fell for the trick of picking dead-man's watch. They slept only for a few hours until, gathering their gear, they continued the chase. It wasn't long before Legless stopped, saying that he could see little people far off.

'So it's little people now,' said Grimy. 'I suppose it's a change from pink Nelliphaunt's.'

Paragon asked Legless to describe the people he saw. 'What do they look like?'

79

'They are bizarre, brightly dressed men sitting atop great bulls, three to each bull. The sun glints off some form of strange armour.'

'But who are they?' asked Grimy.

'They are the people of Bovine, The Ruminates or Riders of Ridicule,' explained Paragon. 'They are not like we Dulledain, being not of Neomanorealmen descent. They do not write their histories in books, rather they drink and sing many bragging songs about the team they support. What is known is that Err the Wrong led them from the North, where their kin the Badlads of Vale and the Borings still dwell.'

'Whose side are they on?' enquired Grimy.

'We will soon find out, for they are drawing near,' answered Legless.

What started as a dull noise on the edge of their hearing, grew in a crescendo, until the thunderous sound of hooves beating the ground could be felt near at hand. Over the hill came some of the most preposterous looking individuals in Muddy Earth, with some wearing various types of cooking utensils on their heads, and others yellow braided wigs. Most wore armour of sorts, being mainly breastplates of the Oven Door type; all carried shields that looked strangely like dustbin lids. They all rode on bulls, which were steered by a driver (not always the one seated at the front), by the use of ropes tied to the horns.

As they passed the place where the three companions were hidden, Paragon leapt up and shouted, 'Hail Riders of Bovine! We are new here, and from the North!'

Some of the astonished riders fell off, but the rest wheeled and surrounded the three. Their leader, a tall skinny fellow, was dressed in an outrageous manner. He wore a bright luminous green silk shirt and red leather trousers; his footwear was silver knee-length platform boots. 'Who and what are you?' asked the leader.

'I am Stupor the Stranger of the North, Dork hunter extraordinaire.'

'Your look is indeed strange and you dress so dully, almost as dull as the Dorks. You even smell like them.'.

'I beg your pardon for our attire, for we had need for speed and had no time to change. We have chased a group of Dorks for days, yet they have outrun us.'

'No wonder, dragging a Dwarf along, and with no magnificent steeds like ours to ride.'

'What a load of bullocks,' snorted Grimy.

The tall rider jumped from his steed and strode towards Grimy. 'Stand up and tell me your name Dwarf or we will be playing the Bonceloss game with you.'

The rest of the riders banged their shields and chanted in their own language:

'HEADA OFFA, HEADA OFFA
WEASEEA HARMA DRAMA!'

'I need your name, Bulls-hitter, because I promise you won't forget mine,' replied Grimy.

'Then know this, Dwarf, I am named Earmore, son of Earnaught. I am The Third Master of Ridicule and you stand in Bovine, not some dark underground northern hovel. Here I call the shots.'

'He stands not in Bovine alone, but also in a very large cowpat,' said Legless, looking at the sticky mess Grimy was standing in.

'It is said by our most ancient lore, that this stuff is good for growing things in, is that correct Lord Earmore?' asked Paragon.

Before he could answer and anyone could stop him, Grimy was rolling in it, singing and whooping:

'I WANT TO BE FIVE FEET TALL
BE THE BIGGEST DWARF IN MY HALL
I AM SICK OF LOOKING UP
AT EVEN THE YOUNGEST ELVEN PUP.'

Nobody had the heart to tell him it did not work on Dwarves, but Legless said, 'At least he won't smell any worse.'

Earmore looked at the companions and wondered what he had run into. 'You still haven't told me what you are doing in the land of Bovine, and who sent you here.'

'I come and go as I please,' said Stupor proudly, 'and take orders from no one. Neither do I need an excuse to hunt the servants of Sourone or Sourman in any land, for I am Paragon son of Paramount, and I am called Alesser the Halfstoned, Dulladan, The Heir of Evenduller, Everdull's son of Gondour.'

'I thought you said your name was The Stupid Stranger,' said Earmore.

'That's Stupor The Stranger. It is what they call me in Free.'

'Well, it is so confusing. You have more names than my whole war band, so I will name you, in our language, Stult, if I can,'said Earmore.

Paragon nodded. 'You asked why we are here: I can tell you that the Dorks we follow stole two of our companions. Pray tell if you have seen any Dork band recently. They would have been carrying two small people, even smaller than Stumpy here,' said Paragon, pointing at the Dwarf. 'They would be the size of large, round, overfed children.'

'We separated the heads of a group of ugly Dorks from their fashion-less bodies. We burned their dirty retro clothing, but saw no children,' said Earmore sadly.

'We didn't say children,' cut in Grimy. 'Our companions were Halfbits.'

One of the riders standing nearby roared with laughter, 'Come, Lord Earmore, leave these mad wanderers to their delusions — at least one of them is drunk,' he said looking at Legless. 'We all know that Hole-biters are tales invented to scare children into eating their greens. I can recall my mother telling me that if I didn't eat my food, then Halfbits would appear by magic and eat everything I was given, forever. How stupid is that?'

'You have obviously never met any Halfbits then,' commented Grimy.

'I've never met The Man in the Moon either,' replied the rider.

'I have,' said Legless. 'Marvellous chap.'

'My lord, this is madness,' said the now irate rider.

'Shutta ur Blabba, Earphone!' said Earmore, in the language of the Ruminates. He turned to Paragon. 'My lord, will you not tell me of your errand, so I will know whether to aid you or not?'

Paragon paused for a moment to consider the gaudy, foolish looking rider; ridiculous as he may be, he was not evil. Eventually, he told Earmore of their journey. 'I set off from Dimladsbliss as one of nine. With me went Denizen's son, Borrowit of Minus Thrifty, who wanted me to go to that city to help him fight against Sourone. My other companions' quest cannot be spoken of here, but it was of vital importance to our leader, The Grand Alf.'

'The Grand Alf Greymane is known to us in Bovine,' said

Earmore. 'He has spent many a season here as top of the bill, though I fear he is less than wanted, now that Worntwang has taken over the running of all business in Milkingshed. Since Greymane's last flying visit, things have gone bad for us with our neighbour Sourman. Earlier this month a band of Dorks from Eyesonguard attacked and killed the King's son, Theologian. I wish Greymane were here, for we have need of sensible counsel.'

'Alas, The Grand Alf has given his last performance. He bombed out on the Bridge of Khaziboom, and is no more.'

'Your tale goes from bad to worse!'

'There is more,' continued Paragon. 'After escaping from Moribund we fled to Lostlotion, where Gadabout and Cellphone gave us aid. From there we travelled down the river Arduous to the Falls of Raucous and there upon Mons When. The Dorks you slew used Borrowit as a pin cushion.'

'This is sad news indeed. When did this happen?'

'It has been four days since we sent him up the creek without a paddle,' answered Paragon forlornly.

'Four days!' cried Earmore. 'From the Falls of Raucous to here? That is a marvel to have come so far. How did you do that with a Dwarf as a companion?'

'That was the easy part, for when we set off, we had three options: follow our other companions, follow the Dorks or go to Minus Thrifty. As we had no clear idea where our other companions had gone, that left the Dorks or the City; as Grimy has an aversion to civilization in the form of baths, we decided for the Dorks. He ran for the first day like he was trying to escape death itself.'

Earmore nodded. 'Now that I know your tale in full, I must return to the hall in Udderas to report all to King Theocrat, my uncle. I will aid you as I can.' A bull was brought forward and given to the three companions. 'Hassleful is his name, it took many strong riders before he was broken, he is strong enough to take the weight of three grown men. You should be okay, as the girly Elf does not weigh much, so that should make up for the fat Dwarf's excess midriff. Beware as you go, for Sourman has loosed his Dorks and some of them are Wag-Riders. They have set up camp in The Glen of Bovine. Also, look out for Sourman himself: he walks this land, trying, some say in his jealousy, to mimic The Grand Alf, so beware if you see an old man,' he added.

'Thank you for your aid and your Enemy Intel Report,' Paragon said.

'You can still change your mind and come with us. Think what great things could be achieved by the Heir of Everdull and the Sons of Err.'

'No, friend Earmore, we must find our companions, first.'

They climbed onto their snorting mount, waved goodbye and held on for dear life, as the bull bolted back along the trail towards their destination. The bull was tireless as it thudded along and they marvelled at its energy. Some time later they came to a pile of burnt Dorks, surrounded by a heap of ripped clothing, armour, swords and helmets. A spear was thrust through the middle of the pile, and had a Dork's head stuck on its spike; nailed to the forehead was the message, FASHION VICTIM. They examined the burnt remains for clues.

Paragon prodded at the pile and a large charred bone fell at his feet. 'That reminds me, Grimy, you can stand down from cooking supper tonight.'

Legless looked at the carcasses and asked whether anyone had found anything belonging to the Halfbits.

'I can find no trace, which is good, for I also feel that, if any of the fat Halfbits had been on this pyre, then it would still be burning,' answered Paragon.

They set camp and decided to light a fire. Paragon instructed them not to go too near the forest. 'Pick up only dead branches.'

'Why did Cellphone warn us about going into Fewgrown Forest?' asked Legless.

''Tis a strange thing when a Woodland Elf asks a man about the mystery of Fewgrown,' replied Paragon.

'Yes, but you have been around a bit, while I have been on a pub-crawl since before you were born. Yet I do remember some old drinking songs about the Fonodrim, that are also known as Rents.'

'Fewgrown is old, last of the great forests of the older days.'

Once they had gathered enough wood to last the night, they settled down around the campfire. Grimy asked Paragon about the origins of Sourman, and where had he come from.

'Sourman and The Grand Alf are kin, as is Rubbermask. They are the Wiztari and they appeared in Muddy Earth around the year 1000 of the Third Stage. Their real names none now know, but when they first appeared they were called, Currynan, Mythroving and Highwindmill. Rubbermask opened a plastic surgery and bird sanctuary at Razscalpel. The Grand Alf stayed nowhere long, being a travelling entertainer; he took his act to the people, to give them pleasure. However Sourman is a different matter. He has fallen from the high mission that he and the Five Wiztari were sent here for, and he has turned Oldcrank into a pale copy of Bad-Odour.'

'You said five Wiztari,' cut in Grimy, 'yet you have only named three.'

'The other two were sent from the Uncrying Lands into the east; their names were Avatar and Palindrome. They were worshipped by the cults in the East, and each became a Dog God.'

Just then, Grimy gasped and pointed towards the edge of the campsite. Where the light from the fire was weakest, stood an old man. Paragon saw him and asked him to join them, offering him a flagon of wine, which Legless was less than happy with. As Paragon advanced to meet him, the old man disappeared. In the far distance, the snorting of a bull could be heard.

'That old man looked a bit past it for a cattle rustler, don't you think?' asked Grimy.

'I think it was Sourman — don't you remember the warning of Earmore,? He told us to beware of the old man, and now he has run off with our pack animals,' said Paragon angrily.

'Never mind,' said Legless, 'we still have the dwarf.Let us get some sleep, we may have a long walk tomorrow, and Grimy needs his rest.'

THE UGLY EYES

Pipsqueak was having a nightmare. He could see himself running around madly, as if looking for something. That, however, was not the cause of his worry, for it was normal for him to act in such fashion. He was shouting "Findo" or "Foodo" at the top of his voice and he got the horrid feeling that he would not be fed until he found what he was searching for. He charged on through the dark dream, while thorny bushes clung to him and snagged his clothing. Running became difficult; he fought his way through the last bush and into a clearing. There, he was confronted by what looked like a group of large gingerbread men. He rushed forward hungrily. Yet, as he drew near, he saw that something was amiss: they were nothing like the sweet smiling cookies he stole off his granny's table. Instead, they had yellow fangs that dripped with blood, and their ugly, evil eyes glowed red with hate.

He awoke with a start and the first thing he realized was that he could not move his arms, as they were bound together in front of him. The second realisation told him that he was lying on the ground next to Messy. He could not see his friend, but unless there was a cesspit nearby, he could smell him. He turned over and saw the monsters of his nightmare, but these Dorks looked even uglier than the gingerbread men of his dream.

The recent events started to come back to him. He had been with Messy, looking for Foodo, and they had been told that there would be no food until he was found. They had charged off in a maddened frenzy. He knew not how long for, or how far they had run, but it seemed like forever — at least a good few hundred yards. They had not seen the Dorks nor had they been seen, until they had ran into each other. If the Halfbits seemed the most surprised, the Dorks were the most disgruntled, many complaining about the size of the portions they each expected to get. As the Dorks grappled with the Halfbits, Messy ate at least a dozen fingers before he realised that their assailants were not going to kill them. None of the Dorks had drawn their scimitars, but seemed content enough to tie them up and play some form of catching game, with them as ball.

Just as one group of Dorks had scored, Borrowit came crashing through the very same bushes that he and Messy had emerged from moments before. He had stopped, seen the Dorks and said something unprintable. He'd raised his horn and sounded the only call he had ever mastered: retreat. Before the last note had cleared, the Dorks answered with the sound of strings; bowstrings. The last thing Pipsqueak remembered of Borrowit was the big man seated against the tree, playing with his horn. From there on he remembered nothing, as he passed out from fear or lack of food.

Now he was lying on the cold ground. He struggled to see if he could free himself, but his movements were noted by one of the brutish Dorks.

'You're not going anywhere, you little bog crawler,' said the Dork, showing him a wicked, curved dagger. 'If I see you move again, I'll stick you with my toothpick. My orders are not to kill you, but they said nothing about removing your teeth one by one. Damn those Eyesonguarders. Mukluk's a bonkbag sag plushdog Sourman's bog gob-bosh skab,' he added in the Bleak Speech of Morbid, before walking away.

Pipsqueak was terrified and went rigid — how was he going to eat without any teeth? He listened as the Dorks argued. There were many voices, but he could make out some of the more distinct ones.

One voice said, 'Let's kill them.'

Another argued, 'Let's have some fun first; let's play a bit.'

A third voice said, 'Let's kill them, then play with them, before we eat them.'

'Dung eater!' replied the first voice. 'Don't you know it's bad manners to play with your food? Let's chop off their legs, then their arms, then their heads, then after eating them, we will kill them.'

Pipsqueak suddenly realized he was becoming so fluent in understanding Dorkish logic that he thought he must be part Dork himself.

A new voice entered the fray. 'Orders are they not be killed; they are not to be harmed, nor are they to be searched or starved.'

Pipsqueak nearly whooped with delight and had to bite his thumbs to keep quiet.

'We are from the mines and we haven't got any orders,' replied the first voice again. 'These little rats and their friends killed our Kapitan; we want revenge!'

'Then you're going to have to look for their friends because I, Mukluk, am in charge here and I say they go to Sourman at Eyesonguard.'

A snivelling, slimy voice cut in, 'Beware, Old Red Eye will sort out the traitor Sourman, and then the name of Mukluk may come to the attention of the master. I, Grizzlyneck, say they should go to Slugbooze.'

'Don't you threaten me or I'll be feeding you to your own dogs,' roared Mukluk.

'We'll see about that!'

Pipsqueak sneaked a look at the adversaries. Facing each other were two Dorks: the one he took to be Mukluk was a large thick-headed individual, with a face like an old boot; Grizzlyneck was of the smaller breed, with long, apish arms. It appeared that most of the Dorks surrounding Mukluk were of Grizzlyneck's tribe. Suddenly, from out of Pipsqueak's view, sprang some of Mukluk's bulky Ugly Eyes, with large scimitars in hand. Grizzlyneck's band jabbered and postured as they cleverly backed down.

What followed was a minor skirmish, which left a number of Grizzlyneck's followers no longer needing helmets. One of the dead Dorks fell with the sword still in his hand, the huge blade slicing the air as it thudded into the ground inches from Pipsqueak's head. Luckily the Halfbit had been picking wax from his ear at the time, exposing the bonding between his wrists, allowing the blade to only slice the rope.

The skirmish was over before it had got chance to start. Grizzlyneck had melted into the background leaving Mukluk with the mastery of the war band. The large dork barked orders to his thickheaded followers, and it looked like they were breaking camp.

Pipsqueak could see a mass of bodies in a frenzy, thrashing at everything in sight; he had to admit, these Dorks were very good at breaking things. When they had finished, Mukluk ordered them to get the Halfbits to their feet and it was only then that Pipsqueak realised that Messy was either very tired or unconscious. There was nothing he could do about it, for bearing down on him was a large, squinting, Ugly Eye Dork. The monstrous brute grabbed him by the front of the jacket and, as he did so, the badge of Lostlotion came undone and stuck deep into the clawed hand of the Dork. Now, whether his howl had been caused by the pin of the brooch or perhaps because the holy Elven badge had burned the Dork, Pipsqueak knew not. The badge, dripping with dark Dork blood, was thrown away by the angry Ugly Eye. Not wanting to lose the only thing of worth he owned, Pipsqueak ran to pick it up but, before he had gone more than a few paces, the huge Dork slammed a fist into the back of his head, sending what little sense he had spinning. He felt himself being lifted off the ground and thrown over the shoulder of a Dork — he did not know why but he felt pity for the one carrying Messy. He was carried that way for some hours, before he was thrown on the ground next to his kin.

Messy, now awake, was anxiously looking around for anything to stop the death pangs he felt coming from his stomach. 'Have I missed breakfast?'

The nearest Dork, cuffed Messy across the ear and said, 'The only thing that will break fast is your jaw, if you don't stop flapping it.' The Dork thought this quite clever and acknowledged the laughs of some of his comrades.

The merriment was suddenly cut short by a wail from somewhere along the line. The Halfbits could only make out snatches of what the Dorks were jabbering about, but it seemed that one of the Bully Boys had been spotted.

Mukluk ordered the guards to attention, picked up the Halfbits once again, and led the warband at speed towards the nearby forest. They reached it sometime later, and stopped at its edge to make camp. The Dorks who had been carrying Messy and Pipsqueak put on their lipstick, tall wigs and sequin frocks and went off to entertain the troops, replaced by two big Ugly Eyes.

Mukluk ordered the newcomers to guard the Halfbits, saying, 'If we are attacked by the dirty Wanskins, and they break through, kill them.'

One of the guards, a more than averagely stupid Dork, called Slugbash asked, 'Kill what, the Wanskins or the Halfbits?'

'The Halfbits, you stupid moron!' roared Mukluk.

'You did say Wanskins, didn't you?' asked Slugbush.

'Yes. WANSKINS!'

'I'm glad that's what you said,' replied the Dork, relieved.

After Mukluk left, Slugbash sat down and complained about the hunger in his stomach, as he kept looking over at the Halfbits.

The other Dork noticed this and said, 'I wouldn't touch them — at least one of them has gone off judging by the smell of it.'

Slugbash grunted. 'To think it was only last week we ate that minstrel, that singer in the wandering band called Verse. Now, he did taste good!'

'I got his foot. What did you get?'

'I got myself a bit of sweet arm and knee.'

They spent most of the night on a knoll, huddled against a large tree. They could hear the snorts of many large animals coming from the outer darkness. Every now and then, an apparition of doom would come thundering out of the gloom, and relieve a Dork of its miserable existence.

Slugbash stood and roared. 'We're being picked off like sitting Dorks. Let's teach these Bully Boys a lesson. If we rush, we can have Bully Beef for supper instead of maggoty flesh.'

Mukluk appeared and shouted at him, 'Get down! If you don't hide that ugly head, we'll be having you for our next meal. Haven't you learned anything? These Wanskins eat lots of carrots and have excellent night vision.'

Just then, from another part of the camp, came the sounds of weapons clashing followed by screams and wails. It seemed that some of the riders had crept up on the camp and dispatched a number of Dorks to whatever hell awaited their dull souls. Mukluk charged off followed by the guards, to find out what the trouble was.

Messy and Pipsqueak watched them disappear with unbridled hope and joy before they too, set off crawling towards the wood. They had gone no more than a few feet when they were confronted by a pair of dirty, smelly, hairy legs. They looked up straight into the sneering face of Grizzlyneck.

'I've got a little trip planned for you two, a guided tour of Bad-Odour, and allow me to introduce your tour guide,' he said, tapping himself on the chest. He grabbed the two Halfbits by their collars and dragged them towards the forest. By a trick of fate, the moon emerged from behind the clouds, sending a beam that bounced off Grizzlyneck's baldpate. A nearby rider, suddenly confronted with the illuminated Dork, let loose an arrow which struck Grizzlyneck in the rear end. The Dork howled with pain and dropped the Halfbits, as he limped towards the tree line. As the Dork reached the woods, the rider caught up with him. The Halfbits remained completely still, as they watched a man on the bull throw his spear and skewer the Dork to a nearby tree.

'That's a pierce of good luck,' said Messy to Pipsqueak.

By now the whole camp was in uproar. The riders had attacked and were showing the Dorks the error of their ways. The Dorks were clearly losing this argument by many points. The Halfbits turned towards the trees and disappeared within.

TREEBRED

'This is Fewgrown Forest, isn't it?' asked Pipsqueak. 'Weren't we warned about coming in here?'

'You can always go back and ask those nice Dorks to escort you back to Lostlotion if you want,' answered Messy.

'What do you think I am, stupid or mad?'

'Are those the only two options you're giving me?'

Somewhere, deep in the forest, they could hear the sounds of animals fighting; from a branch over their heads, an owl hooted, while the darkness of the place closed in on them.

'I'm scared,' said Pipsqueak. 'It's as dark and musty here as the Smells of Muckborough. Did you know they haven't been cleaned since my great, great grandsire, Old Geriatric died?'

They moved through the undergrowth with the speed of a startled ground sloth and by midday they had wandered a fair distance into the forest. As they struggled on, they came to a less dense area; far off, a shaft of sunlight broke through the canopy. They made for it, and an hour later they reached the place where the sunbeam hit the forest floor. They collapsed exhausted on the rich moss, basking in the warm sunshine. Soon the Halfbits became drowsy and, moments later, the sound of snoring echoed through the forest.

Messy woke sometime later and shook Pipsqueak. 'Did you have a good sleep?'

'I slept like a log.'

'I've never heard a log make the noise you made.'

'Of course not; a log is just a piece of stupid, dead wood.'

'WHAT!?' boomed an incredibly loud voice. 'Until I heard you speak I may have agreed with you, but I have spoken with planks that sound more intelligent. Turn around and let me see whether you look as stupid as you sound.'

The Halfbits turned to face a giant, greenish-coloured being.

'Wow,' said Pipsqueak, 'I've never seen a green man before.'

'I am not a man; I am a Rent,' said the big fellow, slowly and very loudly.

92

'Arent,' said Pipsqueak, mishearing, misunderstanding and mispronouncing what he had heard.

'Don't argue with me, you little runt, or I will knock you senseless,' roared the annoyed Rent.

'You're too late,' cut in Messy. 'Somebody beat you to it.'

'Anyway, what are you, strange creatures?'

'That's easy; we are Halfbits,' said Messy proudly.

'Half of what bits?'

'Halfbits of The Snore.'

'What bit is half a snore?' asked the confused Rent.

'Everything west of the Three Farting Stone,' said Pipsqueak, trying to sound world-wise.

'You've lost me,' said the bemused Rent.

'It is on the East-West road, just outside Passwater,' exclaimed Pipsqueak.

The Rent was by now totally unaware of what the Halfbits were talking about. 'Whatever you are, you don't seem to fit into any of the old songs.' Then he began to recite:

'I WILL TELL YOU THE STORY OF ALL CREATION.
TO START THERE WERE FOUR.
THREE WERE PEOPLES
ELF THE FIRST BORN, BOTTLE IN HAND
DWARF THE MINER, THEIR MALES FRUSTRATED
RENT THE FULLGROWN, GENETICALLY MODIFIED
MAN THE BUTCHER, MURDERER OF ANIMALS

HUM TI TUM

HEDGEHOG THE FLATTENED, FOX THE HUNTED
WHALE IN DANGER, SEAL PUP BATTERED
LAMB THE SLAUGHTERED, PIG THE BUTCHERED
BEAR THE BAITED, HOUND ILL-TREATED

HMM!

'I do not really think I want to go on with that song, however I will add in a new verse the next time I sing it. How about, "Half-Witted Halfbits, Speakers Of Nonsense"? Yes, that sounds like you.'

Messy was beginning to warm to the big fellow. 'What are we to call you? Do you have a name?'

'A name, yes, I have several. Fewgrown I am to some, for we have no children, but most call me Treebred.'

'Are you a tree then?'

'Well ... sort of tree-ish.'

'Are you a cucumber tree?' asked Pipsqueak.

'No! There is no such thing,' replied Treebred.

'Then what is that?' continued Pipsqueak, pointing to something poking out of the holly, which was the clothing of Treebred.

'Ahem, hmm,' said the Rent, turning away to the sound of a zip closing. With his modesty restored, Treebred explained to the halfbits what a Rent was. 'We Rents were created by Val Halla Chemicalengineering, to protect the trees from exploitation of the Junk Mail Companies. We were created from bits of leftover DNA belonging to the Children of Ill-Farter, Genetically Modified Trees and scraps of vegetables off the dinner plate. Now that you know my name, what am I to call you two? Let me guess, is it Silly and Smelly or Thinknot and Stinkpot in the Silly Elven tongue?'

Messy looked up at the Holly Green Giant and introduced himself formally. 'My name is Meretricious Brandishmuck and I am also called Messy.'

'And I am called Peregrinate Talk; Pipsqueak to most.'

'Very appropriate names, but what brings you to this part of Muddy Earth? And to be more precise, what are you doing in my Tautoloomin Tumblemovin Tumbletauto Nomeani — oh I am sorry, that is what it is called in Old Rentish — what would you call it?'

'Wood,' replied Pipsqueak.

'Yes, wood would be quicker to say.'

'It is even quicker if you say it onl- AAArgh!'

He never completed the sentence because Messy had punched him on the nose, 'Don't you dare say it.'

Eventually they told Treebred the story of their quest and how they had escaped from the Dorks of Eyesonguard.

'Hmm ... this is grave news. The Grand Alf dead you say, and as for Sourman I have long suspected he was up to something. He has sent these Barroom Brawl (he made a noise like he was clearing his throat) Dorks to fell trees in my wood, I must do something about that, but first we must go to the Rent-Mooch.'

'What's a Rent-Mooch?' asked Messy.

'A Rent-Mooch is where I meet the rest of my kindred, we talk and drink, drink and talk, then talk some more — it is a bit like your parliament — we will discuss what to do about Sourman, then change our minds a few times. We will go via my ancient home, Dwellinghole.' The Rent picked up the two Halfbits and strode off into the heart of the wood.

Many hours later, they arrived at their destination. Treebred showed them to his living quarters, asking if they fancied a drink. He went to a metal receptacle in the corner of the room, and lifted the lid. The room was bathed in a rich green light. The Halfbits were given a large jug each; Treebred told them that the drink would keep them green and glowing for a long time. It did not take long before they were dizzy, and they spent the rest of the night with their heads spinning, telling tales of their adventures. The next morning the Halfbits looked ill. Therefore, when Treebred came in, and with a booming voice asked if the young Halfbits were hung-over, Messy held his head and shushed at the Rent.

'What in all the fires of Morbid was that brew you gave us last night?' asked Pipsqueak.

'I get cans of it from the local stream, The Rentwet; some of the local population have been leaving them for years, no doubt as offerings. Come, I will show you.'

As they passed the metal receptacle in Treebred's living room, Messy read the faint words clear Wa, and asked Treebred what it meant.

'I think it means clear water, but some of the letters rubbed off.' Treebred carried them the short distance to the stream. In a pool at its side was a jumble of the metal cans.

Messy moved to the edge of the pool and tried to read the lettering on the cans. What was obvious was that they belonged to Sourone Inc.

'What type of water is it?' asked Pipsqueak.

'I don't know, but what does Nuclear Waste mean?' he replied, as the hair on his feet turned green and he grew two inches.

Pipsqueak looked on in amazement as he felt either his head expand or his brain shrink.

'Don't worry my merry little Halfbits; the effects soon wear off,' said Treebred, through his second mouth. 'Now we must be off to the Rent-Mooch,' he added. Treebred scooped them up once more and hurried off towards Dinglederry, the mooching place of the Rents.

By the time they got there, the mutations had died down. However they had grown somewhat taller and Pipsqueak had picked up the annoying habit of catching passing flies with his tongue.

The Mooch-Place was a hollow in the centre of Fewgrown, around which now stood the other Rents, an assortment of multi-limbed GM mutations. Treebred put the Halfbits down outside the circle, telling them to rest awhile, for the mooch would take some time. After a couple of hours of strange noises and booms of hot air escaping, Treebred returned to tell his charges of their progress.

'The Parliament of Rents has discussed the problem of the Dorks felling trees. It was sent to a sub-committee and then to a quango. The report has now come back via a special commission: the result is, because when found, you had neither axe nor chainsaw, we think you are not Dorks,' said Treebred proudly.

'What?' burst out Messy. 'It has taken you hours to figure that out? We told you that when you found us!'

'Did you now; you don't say.'

'He did say! I heard him,' said Pipsqueak.

'Well, urm, hum rum tumpty tum,' sang Treebred as he slid off back to the mooch. More explosions of wind and sounds of trumpeting followed. The booms of Treebred could be heard above the others quite clearly. This went on for the rest of the day, until the Rent reappeared accompanied by a large, rotund individual.

The Halfbits, bored by the long wait, were playing "I Spy". Pipsqueak was in and Messy was guessing.

'I spy with my little eye something beginning with T,' said Pipsqueak.

'Tree,' replied a very bored Messy.

'No.'

Knowing how Pipsqueak's brain worked, or didn't to be more precise, Messy answered, 'Two Trees.'

'No.'

'Three Trees, Ten Trees.'

'No,' giggled Pipsqueak.

'The Trees, Them Trees or Those Trees,' said Messy, getting slightly irate.

'No.'

'I give up, what is it?' asked Messy.

'The Sky,' answered Pipsqueak triumphantly, as Messy reintroduced him to the delicacies of the knuckle sandwich.

'Ho ho, my pleasant young Halfbits, are you enjoying your game?' asked Treebred, interrupting them.

'I am,' replied Messy.

'I was, but I don't think Messy likes losing,' said Pipsqueak, through a fat lip.

'It looks as if you are getting bored and tired, so I have brought along one of our younger Rents. He has had his fill of drinking, err, I mean talking. I will leave you with him. He will take you to his dwelling nearby,' said Treebred, before returning to the mooch and leaving the Halfbits with the Rolly Green Giant.

'Hello little ones, my name is Bagolard,' he said, 'which is Quickbulk in your language, though that is but a nickname. I was so named by another Rent when I lost my footing and rolled past him, downhill. Come, I will take you to my home,' said Bagolard, as he picked them up and headed off into the wood. By the time they arrived at Bagolard's abode, the Halfbits were fast asleep, so the Rent placed them in a bed, once he had made room for them by shifting the shrubs along.

During the next few days, the Halfbits ate and slept most of the time. Messy wanted Bagolard to elaborate further on what a Rent actually was, and he duly obliged. 'What you've missed out, are the vegetables. Now, take me for instance: I am part cabbage, Treebred is part turnip, but we are still mostly tree. I am Sycamore and Treebred is Yew, so you could say I am Sycacabbage and Treebred is Yewturn.'

Sometime during that day, there was a large explosion of air, resulting in a mini mushroom shaped green cloud that bent the trees in the local vicinity. As the gust died down, it was followed by a stench of stale beer and rotting vegetables.

'Wow, what a bender that was,' said Bagolard.

Moments later Treebred came staggering through the trees. 'Phoar Phew Phooey,' he said in Old Rentish. Behind him were the rest of the Rents, most in a sorry state. 'We have come to a decision: we are going to Eyesonguard to sort out Sourman.'

'It's about time; we've been bored out of our minds for three days,' said Messy. Then he looked sideways at his dimwit kin, 'Well, I have.'

'What took you so long?' asked Pipsqueak, ignoring his friend's jibe.

'Err, hmm, well, that's difficult to explain. I will let Bagolard tell you as we go,' said Treebred and strode off to the head of a growing number of Rents.

Bagolard laughed, 'It is quite simple really: the first day they greet each other, get the troublesome bother out of the way, then drink and congratulate each other's cleverness for the next few days, until they run out of things to say or drink.'

By now the whole of the forest seemed to be on the march, and the Halfbits could make out the Battle Song of the Rents:

'WE REND AND RENT WITH BOOM OF BUM
TA TUM TI TUM TI TUM TI TUM

TA RA RA BOOM DAY'

Bagolard caught up to Treebred and handed him the halfbits.

Pipsqueak, who was getting quite excited, said to the older Rent, 'Sourman had better watch out; I wooden like to be him when this lot catches him.'

THE WHITE RINGER

Grimy was the first of the three companions to wake — the small bird that was trying to make a nest in his brown beard made sure of that. He leapt up, startling the bird, which flew off, leaving Grimy to clear stuff out of his eye. The Dwarf looked a right mess, not only did he have an eyeful of dirt, but also a beard full of twigs. He took off the latter and changed it for his ginger one, quickly hiding the ragged article in his pack for fear that the others saw that he wore a chin wig. However, the fuss he had made earlier had already woken the other two, and they were now yawning and stretching. Paragon asked the Dwarf why he hadn't started breakfast yet.

If you remember,' said Grimy indignantly, 'the old thief stole most of our baggage because someone forgot to unpack the animal last night. However, I have a few old sausages left and will soon have them sizzling in a pan over the fire.'

'Great, that brings a whole new meaning to the words, small fry, Stumpy,' said Legless.

'At least they are more substantial fare than those damn fairy cakes you Elves pass off as food,' retorted Grimy.

As the Elf and Dwarf pulled faces and gesticulated at each other, Paragon looked for clues about the visitation from the old cattle thief of the previous night. Looking at the ground where he knew the fellow had been standing, he said to the others, 'There is a strange story here; the old rascal has left no mark on the ground.'

'Do you think he was an illusion?' asked Legless.

'We know how used to them you are and he may have been an illusion, if only you had seen him, but we also saw him.'

'Do you think it was a spirit then?' asked Grimy.

'It wasn't like any spirit I have ever seen, ' said Legless.

'Don't you mean drank?'

Legless gave the dwarf the required answer, using the Elven sign language of the two-fingered salute, meaning go away rapidly.

Oblivious to the bickering of his companions, Paragon said, 'I have heard that Sourman is a master of Tekromancy. I think it may have been a Hollowgram.'

'What's a Hollowgram?' asked Grimy.

'It is a projected, see-through, false image'

'Oh I see, like a politician.'

'More or less,' agreed Paragon, then continued searching the area near the forest, followed by his companions. It wasn't long before he came across the unmistakable footprints of the two fat Halfbits.

They followed the tracks until they came to a point where the Halfbits' footprints disappeared and were replaced by larger ones.

'Unless the Halfbits have grown somewhat,' said Paragon, 'then someone passed this way, who surely has trouble finding the right boot size.'

They continued on the trail of what they had nicknamed Bigfoot for a short while until, a few miles on, Legless stopped them suddenly. Now, having run out of anything alcoholic many days before, the fabled Elven eyesight had returned — either that or he had remembered where he had put his Bigoculars (a marvellous Elven invention for seeing things far off). In the distance, he had spotted an old man, moving amongst the trees. He motioned the others to look.

'It is Sourman,' said Paragon.

'The Cattle Thief?' enquired Grimy.

'No, the Wizard.'

'Are there two of them then?' asked the confused Dwarf.

As they discussed him, the old man drew nearer. When he was close by, they could see the odd flash of white underneath the cloak he was wearing. In a short time, he was standing before them.

'Good day, friends,' said the old man. 'This is a strange sight: Elf and Dwarf within smelling distance of each other, and a man, no doubt acting as referee. What are you doing in Fewgrown? Looking for some Halfbits, are we?'

'Where are they, Sourman?' said Grimy as he advanced on the wizard. 'If you have hurt them, my axe will give you the shortest haircut you will ever have.'

The old fellow threw back his cloak and hood with the

blinding flash of an old stage trick, however there was too much powder in the flash pan and it flew all over the three companions. They looked like they had been caught in a minor explosion: their hair standing on end and singed, their faces blackened by soot.

As they stood there stunned, the old man instantly apologised. 'Oh, I am sorry. It's never done that before. Cannot think what went wrong.'

With the spots that were dancing before his eyes receding, Legless looked upon a familiar face. 'Mythroving!'

They all stood there, gawping at the old wizard, until Paragon said, 'I was blind, but now I see, Grand Alf. Yet you are all in white and look like Sourman.'

'That is because I have taken Sourman's place as head of The Order of Wiztari, and in truth these are Sourman's robes, which he left behind after the last meeting of The Witty Council at Lostlotion. I arrived there, shortly after you had left.'

'But how did you get there? We thought you dead. What happened with the Labdog of Mortcough?'

'The Black Chasm of Moribund was deep and seemed to go on forever,' began The Grand Alf. 'As I fell I was engulfed in the foul smoke of the beast. His lead was wrapped around my ankle and I could not shake him loose — he dragged me down with him. Yet, I was not without precautions, for if you had noticed, my pack was bigger than most, not with food as the Halfbits imagined; no. I still had the parachute lent to me by the Regal Eagles and it proved enough … just. We fell into a lake, and I clung to his back as he doggy-paddled to safety. I left him there, on that deathly shore, exhausted. I ran for my life up the Endless Escalator. As I neared the top of Ziggazagg, I heard him as he dogged my steps, rushing up the stairs after me. When I reached the top, I stood by a window at the top of the mountain. He ran at me then, with all the speed he could muster. I waited until the last possible moment and stepped aside. He flew past me into the void beyond — and I must say it was quite funny watching him trying to fly without wings, though I am sure he thought he had them for some reason. He bounced off the mountainside and came to rest halfway down. I leaned out to look at him: he was looking a bit flat.

'Of that fall I was glad, however I was still wet and my robes were starting to freeze. I was in a quandary: I could not stay where I was, but to go down the mountain meant freezing to death. I could not even use the one-way escalator as it rolled endlessly upwards. Therefore, I set off down the mountain, running as fast as anyone who is thousands of years old can. It was not long before I started to slow, but I knew I was in trouble when I could no longer put one foot in front of the other. Hypothermia set in and I started to hallucinate. At some point I must have fallen backwards, for all I could see were the stars, wheeling in their dance of the upper air. When all feeling had gone from my body, I imagined myself floating, lifted up, for in truth I was. I had been found quite soon, by the Musty Mountains Rescue Team, led by my old friend Gary Weir. He had witnessed the fall of the Labdog and my exit from the mountain.

'I was taken to Lostlotion, where they healed my frostbite, and I once again felt the warmth of life coursing through my veins. However, I was not wholly cured for, as you can see, the extreme cold affected me so that the colour of my hair has retained its frosted look. In Lostlotion I found not only healing, but also promotion. When our Order found out about Sourman's treachery, he was dismissed. I have taken his place at the head of The Order of Wiztari. I am no longer Alfred Grey — I changed my name by deed poll - I am now Alfred Whitehead, though my stage name will remain the same. During my stay in Lostlotion, I consulted the Mirror and spoke with Gadabout. She had messages for all of you.

'Firstly, here is Paragon's:

"THERE IS A PATH THAT WILL LEAD TO THE SEA.
GO THAT WAY TO SET THE DEAD-HEADS FREE.
CAREFUL MY FRIEND FOR THAT WAY IS DARK.
REMEMBER THIS WILL BE NO WALK IN THE PARK.
YOU WILL NEED HELP FROM YOUR DULLEDAIN KIN,
TO HAVE ANY CHANCE OF THIS WAR TO WIN."

To Legless, she sends this message:

"LEGLESS GREENTEETH ASLEEP UNDER TREE,
YOU HAD BETTER WAKE UP FOR YOU NEED A PEE.
IF YOU LIE THERE MUCH LONGER

102

YOUR PANTS WILL BE WET,
FOR AS OLD AS YOU ARE
YOU'RE NOT POTTY TRAINED YET."'

'Did she send any word to me?' asked the Dwarf.

'Yes, she sent these words, "To Grimy, son of Grubby, The Right Flosser:

WHEREVER YOU GO, MY CUTLERY GOES WITH YOU,
BUT HAVE A CARE WHERE YOU LAY
YOUR THIEVING HAND AND MAKE FREE."'

'Kismet Bazookas,' the Dwarf shouted gleefully which, translated from Khushidul the language of the Dwarves, means She loves me, and he rolled around the floor in an ecstatic way.

They headed out of the forest, and in a short time emerged at its edge.

'We have work to do,' said The Grand Alf and, with that, put two fingers to his mouth and gave the famous Wiztle.

In the distance appeared a swift eight-legged horse, which shone like a shiny thing painted with luminous silver paint. With it came Hassleful, snorting and proud.

'I have never seen such a horse,' said Legless.

'Nor will you ever again, for he is one of the Meanders, Lord of Hoss'. He was left in Udderas by Oddone, God of The Scandium's.'

They were soon mounted and ready to go.

'Where are we heading?' asked Paragon.

'We go to Milkingshead. Things are moving fast and Theocrat must be warned. Sourman's army is crawling like maggots from Eyesonguard. War is afoot, battle is at hand, and he has a head start. Already his fingers stretch towards Bovine.'

With the anatomy lesson over, they sped off towards Udderas.

They rode day and night, stopping to rest for a few hours and rising early to greet the dawn and its chorus of birds that so annoyed Grimy. They continued their journey until mounting a rise and looked down on the green plain that surrounded Udderas. Their town was built upon a hill, occupied by the thatched houses of the Ruminates and at its highest point was a long, barn-like structure.

'Behold, Udderas and Milkingshed, the Hall of the Olden King,' said the Grand Alf. 'There dwells Theocrat, son of Thegnguy, King of the Muck of Bovine. Be careful; leave the talking to me. Say nothing, lest they run us out of town, fearing we are touched by madness.'

They rode to the gates where they were met by guards, wearing the ceremonial silver-plated kitchen armour of Ridicule.

'Passpots,' said one of the guards.

'What?' asked The Grand Alf.

'Passpots,' replied the officious guard. 'You can't just waltz in here dressed like that. You dress like the folk from Mundane, city of the South, so you need a pass to excuse you from the wearing of pots or pans.'

Grimy was about to introduce the guard to his own piece of ironwork, when The Grand Alf whipped out four sheets of paper and gave them to the guard. Written on them was his shopping list.

'Oh, well that's OK then,' said the man, who was reading them upside down. He clicked his fingers and one of the other guards stepped forward. 'This man will guide you to the Doors of Theocrat. Good day to you.'

As they followed the guide, Paragon asked The Grand Alf how he had managed to fool the guard.

'Many of these morons can't write, so it figures that a lot cannot read. The fool at the gate didn't want to look stupid to his comrades, so he pretended.'

'When they arrived at their destination, the guide banged on

104

the doors, before doing a runner, glancing backwards, worryingly, until he disappeared.

The doors flew open and a purple-faced individual emerged, roaring, 'All beware, your death is near!' He stopped, looking rather startled by the sight of the strangers who stood in front of him. 'Ah, your pardon, we are plagued by youngsters playing some game called, Knock a Bore Run, though why it is called that, I don't know.' He seemed to calm down and the heat disappeared from his face. He was a big fellow, bald, and dressed all in black. He strode forward, fiddled with his black eye protectors and then introduced himself in some strange dialect. 'I am Harmer, Da Doorman of Theocrat, ya can't take yuzz pieces in here, and I gotta frisk ya.'

They started to whip out their weapons and lay them aside. Legless and Grimy gave up bow and axe, knives, scissors and nail clippers; however, Paragon didn't think he should have to do anything, by order of the local yokel, be he king or not.

Harmer stuck out his chest, cracked his knuckles and pulled out his cosh, saying, 'Theocrat is da Boss of dis joint. He pays da dough.'

Paragon gulped and said, 'This is no ordinary sword; it is Andrex, remade from the shards of Nares, The Sword That Had Brokered. I do not wish to put it aside.'

'Ya should be more worried about da broken skull of Paragon, than some secondhand sword,' said the big guy menacingly.

'Now, now friends, lets not squabble,' said The Grand Alf amiably. 'Here is my sword Humdinger, it is far older and of higher lineage than his battered old family heirloom.'

With the others urging him, Paragon relented and placed his weapon with the others.

'Good, now we can get on with what we came here for,' continued The Grand Alf, moving to enter the hall.

Harmer moved to block his way, saying, 'Dat Kendo quarterstaff has gotta stay put Master Wizard. It's a well known fact dat da hand of a wizard on his staff can cause trouble.'

The Grand Alf hunched over, shrinking about three inches, and said, 'It is but for support. I am an old man whose fighting days are over. I have a war disability! See, here is my doctor's report,' he added, pulling out another piece of paper. This one had the recipe for jam tart on it, for most of the people who knew him also knew of his fondness for tarts.

Harmer stared at the paper momentarily then, feeling sorry for the bent old wizard, and not wanting to, by his inability to read, appear stupid, he stepped aside and ushered them through the doors.

They walked the length of the barn, and halted in front of the Porcelain Throne of Bovine. Sat on the throne was an old man in a camouflage onesie; around his forehead was a diamante necklace, obviously too small to go over his head. The once yellow, braided wig he wore was now so old and bleached by washing, that it appeared white. He looked every bit the King of Ridicule. Behind the throne stood the Big-Boned Lady Earwax and, sat beside the King was the weedy, pasty-faced Grimly Worntwang.

'Greetings, Theocrat son of Thegnguy. I come to give counsel and aid in your struggle against the hoards of Sourman,' said the Grand Alf.

'There will be no whores in this house,' said the Lady Earwax strenuously.

'Peace lady. Let the King have his say,' said Worntwang expectantly.

The King looked upon The Grand Alf and said, 'Have you, Greymane? Or maybe you simply wish to cause a war. It seems to me fights break out wherever you go, setting neighbour against neighbour. Do not be surprised if you get no welcome here, Master Warhawk.'

'Oh, well said my lord,' the smarmy Grimly Worntwang said, as he stood clapping the King. Turning to The Grand Alf he added, 'With unerring accuracy, here you are again, just in time to gloat at our latest misfortune. My lord's son, Theologian, has been killed as Sourone's Dorks move against the world of men. You chose this time to turn up and denounce our great friend and ally, Sourman the Magnificent. As for aid, where is it? Surely you do not think you can stop Sourone with a fat Dwarf, a girly Elf and a stunned man? With you at their head, conjuror, illusionist and trickster, how will you do that — with sleight of hand?'

The Grand Alf grew to his full height, and threw back his cloak. He raised his staff then brought it down with force on Worntwang's head. For the mealy-mouthed moaner, the sun went in and the stars came out. 'Oh dear, looks like I was slightly heavy-handed there,' said the wizard. He turned then, facing Theocrat, and pulled out a pocket watch on a chain. He started to swing this from side to side, as he intoned to the King, 'Look into my eyes,' and, 'You are very sleepy.' Theocrat slumped on the throne. 'When I count to three, you will awake and once more rule the roost. One, two, three!' said The Grand Alf, and clicked his fingers.

The king leapt up, flapping his arms and making clucking noises. They chased him around the barn, eventually coaxing him down from the rafters with a handful of corn. When they got him back on the throne The Grand Alf tried again, this time choosing his words carefully. The wizard did manage to revive the King who, from that moment on, walked in a very strange way.

'It is time to look upon what is left of your kingdom, after Worntwang's mismanagement.' The King raised himself to his feet, and The Grand Alf shouted, 'Open the doors! The Lord of the Muck is abroad.'

Together, they walked out into the fresh, dung-laden air.

'I feel like I have slept for years,' said Theocrat, 'for I cannot remember any of it.'

'Nay lord, by drugs and mesmerism is your memory blank. Worntwang was given them by Sourman.'

'To what purpose?'

'Sourman promised Worntwang something very precious to Bovine, if he did this thing.'

Looking back, Theocrat saw Earwax. 'Not my Mothergrand-daughterneice!'

'No Theocrat, he wanted some other things.'

'No! Not Earmore. I knew Worntwang didn't have a woman, but I put that down to his ugliness,' said the King.

The Grand Alf shook his head. 'He wanted the bulls of Bovine. Sourman promised him the fast food franchise for this area. Worntwang was going to set himself up as the Burgerking of Bovine. He is Sourman's spy. He has locked up Earmore, for he wished no resistance from Bovine against the army of Sourman. And he has almost succeeded, for Eyesonguard is ready for war and it will not be long before they make minced meat out of you. Escape is the only option: take your people to Thelma's Keep, and make your stand there.'

'Before we do anything, we must decide what to do with Worntwang. Harmer, release the Lord Earmore and bring Worntwang to me.'

Sometime later the big doorman came back, dragging the quite clearly shaken Grimly Worntwang. With him came Earmore, holding the King's sword, Heavygrip.

'My Lord,' said Earmore, 'I bring Grimly son of Gammy, and in his possession he had your ancient blade, which he was attempting to sell on the open market.'

'He's lying,' whined Worntwang, 'the one on sale in Ye Olde eBay Shoppe was a replica! I bought it from a theatrical used goods agency called m.'

'Well,' thought Theocrat, 'two swords will be better than one. We will need all the weapons we can lay our hands on for you, along with all the Riders of Ridicule, go to war Master Worntwang.'

'But ... my lord, surely you are not going to send faithful Grimly to war? Who will make sure your eggs are not too runny at breakfast? Who will comb the food from your beard and who, after your toilet, will wip-'

'That's enough of that,' interjected The Grand Alf. 'See how this spineless worm tries to wriggle out of his fate. Worntwang, if you wish to crawl back to your real master, Sourman, I am sure he will reward your failure. However, if you wish to really serve the King, come with us, for he and all his household go to Thelma's Keep.'

A look of sheer horror came over Worntwang's face. He started to shake uncontrollably, caught between fear of The Grand Alf's sleight of hand, and the thought of dying in some horrible way. His mind raced as he imagined himself mutilated, mangled and ripped to pieces by the Dorks. He could not help himself as he puked at the feet of the King. Eventually, he rose to his feet and bolted.

Earmore moved to chase him, but Theocrat motioned him to stop. 'Gutless in more ways than one. Let him go — Sourman can have him. We have no time to waste on that wastrel. Our time is as short as a Dwarf's watchstrap as it is, and we must prepare and recuperate as best we can, for soon we ride to Thelma's Keep.'

THELMA'S KEEP

They spent a short time in Udderas, planning the movement of its people and stores. A farewell dinner and dance were organised for the evening. Grimy enjoyed the food, however, having never danced with a female before, soon discovered that he had two left feet and two black eyes. Legless left early, sick of telling the big hairy brutes of Bovine that he didn't want to dance with them. Paragon was chased all night by the big buxom milkmaid, Earwax; he even tried to tell her that he loved another.

The hard of hearing Lady of Bovine replied, 'Yes, quite right, you should love your mother. My mother, Theoddwine, died of consumption when I was young.'

'Consumption of what?' asked Grimy, who had wandered close.

'What?' asked Earwax.

'Consumption of what?' roared Grimy, through cupped hands.

'There is no need to shout. I can hear you quite well. She died of consumption of alcohol.'

Still shouting, Grimy said, 'Do you mean, her liver packed in?' then gave Legless a knowing grin.

'No, she was nowhere near the river. Her chariot driver had one too many and crashed,' she answered, before going in search of Paragon, who had used the Dwarf's inquiry as a chance to escape.

They enjoyed what was left of the night's entertainment, knowing that soon they would make for Thelma's Keep.

When they rose on that bright morning, they reclaimed their armour from the kitchens, which the cooks had used the night before for preparing the feast, before riding forth to war.

They had travelled for two days, when they came upon a lone rider. He was a bald fellow, and was known by the name of Curly. The man moved forward and asked for Earmore, yet it was Theocrat who advanced.

'Your king is here and you see before you the last riding of the Beerswiggers.'

'Then lord, you had better run for your lives,' said the exhausted rider. 'There are some serious kick-ass Dorks heading this way. They broke through the defences of Shirkingbad whilst he was asleep, and he has taken the remnants of his force to Thelma's Keep.'

The Grand Alf looked at Theocrat, turned, then did what to all present looked like a runner. As he disappeared into the distance, he shouted back over his shoulder to Paragon, 'Ride to Thelma's Keep! Look after Lord Muck and wait for me at Thelma's Grate!'

They journeyed fast, always knowing that a great host followed on their heels. In the night, the sky was ablaze with the evildoings of an army of mad pyromaniacs. It was not long before they reached Thelma's Ditch and eventually the gate. It was there that they found the many men that Shirkingbad had left to guard it.

The leader of these men was an old warrior called Gumling the Bald. He enquired if they had seen anything of Shirkingbad and the riders of Worstfold, then went on to report on the defences of the keep. 'My lord, we have a few thousand. Some are men and some are mere boys. The boys do not know one end of a spear from another, whilst the Old Guard have forgotten what the point of a spear is.'

The King and the men of Udderas rode into the keep and took their place on the battlements of the Weeping Wall. It was so named for, in the past, enemies had broken themselves on it and therefore, when the women of the slain had come to collect their dead husbands and sons, all that could be heard was their anguish. Yet, the army that made its way towards them now was the strongest that had ever come to test itself against the stronghold.

From the vantage point high on the wall, Legless watched the huge force moving towards them. To Grimy, who had just found a box to stand on, the Elf said, 'I wish that some of my kindred were here on this wall tonight.'

'Why?' asked Grimy.

'It is the custom of the Silly Elves to drink in honour of fallen comrades — the more the merrier is our motto.'

'Before the end of this night, you will wish for more of my

kindred, to dig us out of the crap we have fallen in,' replied the Dwarf.

The Dorks attacked in the middle of the night, aided by the moronic Wildmen of Dunceland. Upon the wall, Earmore and Paragon drew straws to see who would lead the counterattack. Earmore won and, with a shout of "Guffwhine for The Muck", he leapt forward into the fray. He was followed by Paragon, who answered with, "Andrex for the Dulledain". The Dorks fled before them, unable to cope with the flashing of the weapons of these mighty men. Yet the odds were overwhelming, and soon they had to retreat. As they gained the safety of the keep, they closed the gates and barred them against the army of vicious Dorks, but in so doing they trapped Harmer the Doorman outside. The last they saw of the great man was a vision of him trying to frisk the Dorks, and shouting, 'You can't come in here without a tie on!'

The first waves carried the usual siege equipment of ladders and grappling hooks; others were equipped with the mad inventions of Sourman's Lab. The machines were dragged into range — massive catapults that threw Dorks on the ends of parachutes over the walls. Many shot over too quick to open their chutes and splattered against the mountain; others fell short, their bodies sliding down the walls like blackcurrant jelly, and the ones that did succeed were met by Grimy shouting the Dwarven battle cry, "Backoff Khazi mayonnaise!" as he brained them with his axe. Legless shot some as they flew over, yet many climbed the ladders and fought with the Ruminates on the walls. They clashed for most of the night, and the battle raged on, swaying back and forth.

At some point Paragon noticed a group of Dorks wheeling a large wagon towards the wall. Hooked on to the back of this wagon, with tubes linking them, was another cylindrical one. They parked both of them at the base of the wall. Large groups of Dorks queued to enter them, whilst others used pumps and machinery that were attached. Paragon called for Legless; when the Elf joined him, he asked if he could read what was written on the wagons. The Elf informed him that the largest was called Latrine and the cylindrical one was called Methane Gas. Only Sourman knew the true meaning of these words; they were lost to the men on the walls — they were about to find out in the most shocking way though. From their vantage point, Paragon, Legless and Theocrat watched as the Dorks poured oil over the two wagons, set fire to them and retreated to a safe distance. In less than a minute, the carriage named Methane Gas exploded, making a right mess of the wall. When the dust settled, a great hole had appeared in the stonework. Clinging to the area was a stinking green fog that stung the eyes, and burned the throats of anyone who got too close.

Years later, those who survived the battle would tell of the awful stench — the first time an enemy used Gas Warfare.

The gas did not linger and, as it dissipated, the Dorks poured through the gap created by the explosion. The defenders retreated under the onslaught, up the stairs and into the higher level and another set of battlements. They locked the gates and put the statue of Thelma Heavyhand wielding her rolling pin up against them. When it came to call the roll, they found that Earmore, Grimy and Gumling, along with a number of men, could not be accounted for. Paragon went to the inner hall to find the King.

Theocrat was hiding in a wardrobe and would not come out. 'I wish I had never listened to Grand Alf Warhawk,' wailed the king. 'I could be tucked up in bed now with a cup of cocoa. In the morning, I am going to do a runner with as many men as possible. Go and find the best escape route — there's a good chap.'

Paragon turned, leaving the King quaking in his platform boots. He went to the battlements to look at the positioning of the Dorkish troops. Most of the causeway was clear, but all around the front of the walls was packed with large Dorks. Some of these noticed him spying on them and jeered him, shouting, 'Where's your sulking king?' Paragon answered, 'The King awaits the light of day. He will come to inspect the lawn you have damaged, then you will feel his anger.'

They laughed and answered, 'What of the lawn? We are the Farting Ugly Eyes; we go where we please, and we fear nothing!' With that they turned, pulled down their britches and mooned him.

Paragon listened as they hollered their guttural song:

'WE ARE THE FARTING UGLY EYES,

BIG FAT BELLIES AND WOBBLY THIGHS.
WE TALK TO EACH OTHER BY BUTTOCK SIGHS,
FOR WE ARE THE FARTING UGLY EYES.'

They all broke wind at the same time and a great cloud of
methane gathered by the gate. One of the Dorks raced toward it
with a box of matches.

Luckily for Paragon, some of the matches must have been wet,
for the gas didn't immediately light up. Having seen the effect of
this gas earlier, he legged it back up the stairs. No sooner had he
retreated from the wall than the gateway blew in. Now, it may be
that some power of old descended that moment for, as the Dorks
moved forward to enter, they were blocked by the tottering form
of Thelma Heavyhand. They halted, and squealed as the massive
statue fell forward, flattening many that had forced their way in
through the shattered gates. Yet the statue did not stop there, for
Thelma continued to roll, killing hundreds as she went.

Whilst all this was happening, Paragon, a reluctant Theocrat
and the remainder of the Riders of Ridicule had mounted up
and were following the statue as it rolled down the causeway and
into the main body of the Dorkish army. They fought their way
to the ditch and it was there that they would have made their
last stand. Yet, as they looked out they saw that a huge multi-
coloured forest had grown overnight, and coming over the hill
nearby was The White Ringer.

The Grand Alf had caught up with Shirkingbad and the
Riders of Worstfold, convincing them that the worst of the
fighting was over, and was now leading them into the fray. The
Dorks, caught between the rolling pin of Thelma and the fresh
troops of Worstfold, fled into the trees. Of that army, not even a
rumour was ever heard again. However, soon after, a local trade
in Dork-skull potplants, candleholders and ashtrays flourished.

THE ROUTE AND TWIG TO EYESONGUARD

Whilst Theocrat and Paragon patted each other on the back, The Grand Alf and Shirkingbad enjoyed a huge cigar each, and congratulated one another. From a nearby ditch came the bedraggled figures of Gumling the Bald, Earmore son of Earnaught and, as usual, lagging behind, came the bloody Dwarf. The meeting of the friends produced much bragging and tales of one-upmanship. The Grand Alf separated the Elf and Dwarf, at the point where they had killed half the Dork army each. All present were amazed to see the wood that had appeared in the valley.

'Surely this is the mythical Headwood of Woodwoods,' said Theocrat.

The Grand Alf laughed theatrically. 'If you want to know more, then follow me to Eyesonguard.'

'To Eyesonguard? We are not strong enough to attack Sourman,' replied Theocrat, as his knees started to knock again. 'I am getting too old for this. I need a rest!'

'OK. For those of you who go with me to Eyesonguard, you had better slope off to your beds for a few hours,' said the Grand Alf, and he too went off to hit the pillow.

Whilst the Eyesonguard party bluffed its way, the remainder set about piling the bodies of the fallen Riders of Ridicule into two mounds, one for the Bestfold and the other for the Worstfold — these became known, in later years, as Thelma's Breasts. This task had been given to Shirkingbad but as usual, he had got someone else to do it, in this case the Wildmen of Dunceland. These were the last remnants of the people who once inhabited the valleys of Airhead Nitwit; never the cleverest branch of man, they had fallen for the old casual worker, paid in dung-wattle trick. They buried Harmer in a lone grave: he had died whilst trying to deprive a few hundred Dorks of their weaponry.

After their rest, the company that formed the Eyesonguard mission gathered before the Headwood. When all were ready, The Grand Alf led them in. Some time later, as they struggled through the tightly packed wood, Grimy, who had got steadily more vocal with his complaints, yelped in pain. They stopped and looked back at him. He was bedraggled, demoralised, and looked like he had been hit by every branch that he had passed.

'These trees don't like Dwarves,' he moaned.

'Nobody likes Dwarves; why should the trees?' said Legless, in a matter-of-fact sort of way.

That was the end for Grimy. He snapped and his dirty pudgy hand went for his axe. As quickly as he moved, he was thrashed by a handful of branches. He fell backwards off Hassleful and sprawled in a heap on the forest floor. When he rose, he was livid. He stood with axe in hand, ready to face his tormentors.

'Master Dwarf, I suggest you put your axe away before the trees stop playing and get serious,' instructed The Grand Alf.

'Playing?' sputtered Grimy. 'Well, if this is a game, it looks like it's my turn next,' he added as he advanced on the nearest tree. At that moment, a large green arm reached through the canopy and pulled the Dwarf's false beard off. This sent him racing towards his pack with his hands covering his face; by the time he had found his spare chin-wig and cleaned out the bird's nest, the others had set off again, and he was too embarrassed to face them. When he caught up with them, he climbed back on Hassleful and faced backwards. He remained in that position for the rest of the journey, muttering under his breath about how he wished he were back in the caverns he had hidden in during the Battle at Thelma's Keep.

Legless overheard the dwarf talking of wondrous sights and asked him, 'Were you bashed on the head and hallucinating?'

'No! And I hadn't been drinking any Elf-brew either. I saw some of the most marvellous sights; the walls shone with strange kaleidoscopic lights of rainbow hue and those sparkling prisms of light burned into my mind. Oh, great are the Glitzy Caverns of Aglowlong.'

Legless looked at the Dwarf and thought what a great opportunity it would be to pull his stumpy leg. 'Are you sure you hadn't taken any strange substances? he said mockingly, and laughed towards the others whilst making circular motions with his finger around the temple area. At that moment, as they left the tree line, the chuckling of Legless died in his throat. He gasped as he looked back and, pointing into the trees, he said with a voice that quavered, 'I can see large eyes staring at us.'

'Now who's been smoking the wacky-baccy?' laughed Grimy, as a large brown multi-limbed and many-eyed Rent, that had obviously started life as a potato, waltzed past, looking like someone had mixed up all the body parts.

'What in the hell is that?' cried Theocrat.

'No need to worry,' answered The Grand Alf. 'It is only one of the Rents; they are the Tree-Hordesmen. They are able to wake the slow lazy trees to full life, and make them move great distances in a very short time.'

'Do you think they could do the same to Dwarves?' asked Legless hopefully.

Grimy gave the Elf a withering look. 'It would take more than a horde of Rents to wake a drunken Elf.'

They continued their bickering, until they came to a freshly built mound.

'There was a great battle here,' explained The Grand Alf. 'Theologian was ambushed by battalions of Dork engineers. They had been sent here to build a bridge over the Iron River; however, having only digging tools to fight with, they killed very few of the Ruminates, and chased off the rest. This will be forever known as The Battle of the Forks of Iron. I came upon the remnants of a rather large force, half of which I sent with Glumbod of Worstfold, to join up with Shirkingbad. The other half formed the burial party, and then rode under their leader Effinghel, to protect Udderas.'

The party rode on past the burial mound and on towards Oldcrank. After a few hours they came upon a pillar, on top of which was set the familiar white hand and its welcoming gesture — they knew that they were close to their destination. A few miles on, they emerged from the mist to a scene of utter desolation. Where once had been the Oldcrank National Park, with its orchards and landscaped gardens, picnic tables and children's play area, there was now only destruction. It appeared as if some strip-mining lunatic had scooped a great hole into the ground. Yet now the waters of a great lake filled those holes that Sourman had delved to house his minions — the army that marched from this hole was long gone, and was now plant food. Sourman's servants and workers, who had stayed behind, had died like rats in a trap. Rising from the centre of this artificial lake

116

stood the Tower of Oldcrank, which in Silly Elven means Mount Fanatic or, translated into the Ancient language of Muck, meant Conning Man.

They rode toward the gateway and came to a halt before its splintered gates for, sat by the roadside,were, what looked for the entire world like two fat children gorging themselves on a pile of plunder which towered a good few feet above them. One of these creatures witnessed the approach of the King and his companions, and rose unsteadily to his feet and greeted them.

'Welcome to Eyesonguard,' said the green-haired Halfbit, 'We are the Gatekeepers. Meretricious, son of Salacious am I, and this,' he said, giving his companion a kick, 'is Peregrinate son of Perambulate. The Lord Sourman is in his tower clobbering Worntwang. We were told to wait here and greet the King of Bulls-Hitters as best we could.'

'And what have you got to say about the blisters on my feet, and not to mention the crick in my back, you ever-eating, evanescent emigrants?' roared Grimy. 'What's more, how about sharing some of that food you are attempting to hide?'

'Damn the food; how many bottles of wine have they got stashed?' said Legless, advancing on the pile of plunder.

'OK, you can have the plonk, but we're keeping this,' said Messy as he grabbed the big barrel of Largebottom Leaf. The halfbits then proceeded to roll a spliff each, light them and blow smoke rings into the air.

'This is amazing,' said Theocrat. 'Our tales of the Hole-Biters never spoke of smoke.'

'The reason for that is simple, my lord,' explained Messy. 'It is a pastime we have enjoyed for only a few hundred years. It was Tootbad Holeblower of Largebottom in the Southfarting who first discovered the real use of the weed, which would be in the year 35235 of the Snore reckoning. How Old Tipsy, as we named him, came to be smoking anything and everything that grew in his garden is still a mystery to us.'

'Beware Theocrat,' warned The Grand Alf, 'these halfwits will bore you to tears with the non-events of their petty histories and stories of their in-bred families, letting you know which nobody they are related to; they will babble on in the middle of battle, only stopping to put food in their mouths. Just ignore them and they will soon find someone else to annoy.' The wizard then drew his hand across his mouth in the Elvish sign language, which meant in the Haughty Elvish, Zip It. He then said to Messy, 'Where is Treebred?'

'He is over there, tormenting Sourman,' answered Messy, pointing north.

'Come Theocrat, and learn how Eyesonguard has been rent asunder,' said the wizard.

As they moved off, Theocrat turned to Messy. 'Farewell, Master Hole-Biter. When we meet again, you can finish your story about Tootbad, the Dope and his narcotic pipe-lore.'

Pipsqueak stirred and said, 'Who is the old fellow with the pan on his head?'

'That, my good friend, is Theocrat, the King of Ridicule,' replied Messy.

'He does look a bit daft, doesn't he?' laughed Pipsqueak.

'At least he only looks it,' replied Messy sarcastically.

LOTSA EATS

As the King and the wizard left, Paragon, Legless and Grimy joined the Halfbits for food and wine.

'Where did you find all this marvellous fare?' asked Paragon.

'There is a lot more than this. Our little pile is but a snack,' answered Messy, pointing to the five foot high mound.

'And where is this wondrous store-room, you munching midgets?' asked Grimy.

'Come,' replied Messy, standing up, 'I will show you.'

The Halfbit led them along the wall, then through a gap in it, up some stairs and down a corridor, until they reached a door marked:

SOURMAN'S STORES
Incorporating
WORNTWANG'S WARES

They entered a large room, packed to the roof with heavy-laden shelves.

'All this is fresh,' explained Messy, 'and must have been delivered by the last haywain convoy from The Snore. Here are barrels of Old Wino; also barrels of Soothing Tar, Old Tipsy and Largebottom Leaf from the Southfarting. There is food-stuff here that wouldn't go amiss on a Halfbit's table at third breakfast. You won't find any Dorkish fast food here.'

'What's wrong with fast food?' asked Grimy.

'I think they call it fast food, because you put it in one end and it shoots out the other,' explained Pipsqueak, who had proof of this thanks to Messy's constant demonstrations.

They ate their fill, then waited another hour for the Halfbits to eat theirs. Eventually they settled down for a smoke, at which point Paragon took the opportunity to ask the Halfbits for their story.

Messy and Pipsqueak told the three runners of their capture and of Borrowit's death, the journey with the Dorks and their escape, the finding of Treebred and the Rent attack on Eyesonguard; how Treebred and his people had dismantled the stronghold of Sourman, like children knocking building blocks over in a tantrum. Sourman had fled from the advance of the verdant vandals, and was now trapped in his tower. From there he was loosing his vile chemical warfare on the Rents. He could be seen lobbing glass bottles of flaming oil at some of the Rents that got too close — he had already turned a few Ash's to ashes and roasted a number of Chestnuts. When Treebred and the Rents witnessed this Bonfire of the Calamities, they flew into a rage. They surrounded Oldcrank like brown berserkers within a green gale. They threw anything they could lay their hands on at the tower. This consisted mostly of wreckage and floating bits of rubbish; so mad were they that a Rent named Beachball was bounced off the tower repeatedly. Eventually Treebred called a stop to the assault. They realised their efforts were in vain when it was discovered that the tower was made of the second hardest substance in Muddy Earth; the first being the enamel on a Halfbit's tooth. The Rents pulled back to a safe distance, which wasn't really that far, as Sourman hadn't been very good at ball games in his youth, and his throwing arm was a bit weak.

'As we settled back for a rest,' said Messy, 'a horse came speeding up the road in a flash of brilliant light — well, it was a number of flashes really, because the rider, who was dressed all in white, was heard to mutter "Damn", as he had set off the local stealth-tax cameras. The horse came instantly to a halt in front of us, sending the rider in a graceful arc through the air, ending with him landing in a crumpled heap on the floor. Then, with a voice we recognised, he said to Pipsqueak, "Don't just stand there you damn fool; help me up and show me where that Master of the Mixed Veg, Treebred, is drinking." Now, Treebred heard the commotion, and came through the gateway holding a can of his favourite brew. He took The Grand Alf away to a mini-mooch. The Rent was heard to say as he was leaving, "It's a good thing you turned up: I can't do any more damage and that damn wizard won't come down. The boys and I had so looked forward to a few games of Whip the Wizard, but he doesn't appear as playful without his thuggish Dorks to back him up". They were away for only a short time. When the Grand Alf had left, Treebred told us that the wizard had asked to borrow the Shorns, a slower, dull-witted type of Rent, with long whip-like branches that can remove the head of a Dork with one swipe. Treebred said he had promised The Grand Alf his Shorn-Horde. That night the land seemed to slide past us. We could see dark shapes moving, as they came in and out of focus. We put out our Old Tipsy roll-ups because we thought we were having a bad trip. From the distance, we heard the Tree-ish marching song that goes:

ONE TWO THREE FOUR,
WE'RE THE SHORNS, WE'RE OFF TO WAR.

FIVE SIX SEVEN EIGHT,
WE'LL KILL THEM DORKS AT THELMA'S GRATE.

'The morning after, the sound of a cowbell was heard from the road and a thin, frightened, wasted specimen of a man, who was clinging to a heifer, came into view. When he saw us he grinned, dismounted from his perch clumsily, and advanced in a threatening way. Alas, his grin soon changed to a look of horror and fright as Treebred appeared behind us. Pipsqueak told him, "Have you met our big brother?". The man attempted to do a runner, but Treebred plucked him up in mid-ride, into the air. For a few seconds his legs kept pumping, until he realised he had travelled as far as a hamster on a wheel. Then he went limp and started to whine. He told us his name was Grimly, son of Gammy, and that he was a special envoy and ambassador for King Theocrat.

'Because he was the wisest, bravest and most honourable man in Bovine, he had been sent to discuss peace terms with Sourman. "Yes, The Grand Alf has been and told us to expect you, Worntwang," said Treebred. He lifted the weedy looking man further into the air, and turned towards Oldcrank. As Worntwang saw the ruins, his face turned deathly white. Treebred said to him, "Would you like to swim or to fly to your Master?" "I don't know how to swim," whined the much shaken man. "You don't know how to fly either, so I will give you a bit of help," replied Treebred. He waded out towards the tower, hoisted the violently struggling man higher, and catapulted him through the nearest opening. From the hole that had once been a window for Sourman's laboratory, came the sound of bottles smashing.

It looked like Treebred had done serious damage to Sourman's Weapons of Glass Destruction. That was the last we saw of Worntwang. Afterwards, Treebred came and told us of this storeroom, and to wait at the gate to greet some very important guests.'

As Messy finished his story, Pipsqueak looked confused and, turning to Paragon, asked, 'That's what's puzzling me. Have the VIPs turned up yet, and do you know who they will be?' The familiar feeling of dizziness came over Pipsqueak, and it suddenly went dark, except for the stars.

SOURMAN'S SPEECH

Messy picked Pipsqueak off the floor, as the companions went in search of The Grand Alf and Theocrat. When they found them, the wizard informed all those present that higher authority, namely The Magic Circle, had sent him to serve an eviction order and a writ upon Sourman, for him to appear before The Witty Council. To enforce that order, they had been chosen as representatives of the Free Trade Peoples of Muddy Earth, to go and witness this event.

'Won't that be dangerous?' asked Messy. 'He can fire-bomb you from his window, and they say he can put a dissimulate spell on you.'

'What they say is true,' replied The Grand Alf. 'Sourman is a Master Liar, The King of Counterfeits and The Duke of Deceit. Do not believe a word he says.'

As they approached the tower, they noticed that the Rents had hardly scratched its surface.

'What is this hard rock?' wondered Legless.

'It's a type of music!' said Pipsqueak proudly. 'Even I know that!'

The others ignored him, much to his chagrin, and listened to Grimy explain that it was made of basalt, a type of hard lava.

'Ugh, I can't stand bugs,' commented Pipsqueak inanely.

The Grand Alf pushed the Halfbit to one side, saying, 'If you can't say anything of significance, then stop your foolish talk, you foolish Talk.'

'Did you hear that echo? That basalt has marvellous acoustics,' continued Pipsqueak.

'Shut up, you mindless midget and go stand over there,' roared The Grand Alf, pointing to a dry area. The Wizard approached the main door of the tower, which happened to sit below the balcony of Sourman's Laboratory.

On the door was a sign that read thus:

NO SALESMEN (Unless you have any NOSE RINGS).

The Grand Alf rang the doorbell and high in the tower a siren wailed. The dreadful noise was accompanied by a flashing red light. Yet, after a few moments, both were cut off. Then a bandaged head appeared over the balcony, looking down on them.

'Oh — it's you lot. What do you morons want?'

'Watch your tongue, Worntwang, or I will turn you into something nasty,' said The Grand Alf, realising only after he had said it, that Sourman had beaten him to it. 'Where is Sourman?'

'He is not here. He is on holiday in Far Harass.'

'We don't have time for these lies. Bring out The Once White Wizard — we want words with him.'

At that, Worntwang disappeared and they all stood there, staring at the opening for what seemed an age. After twiddling their thumbs and scratching their bums for some time, they began to think that Sourman the Surpassed would not appear.

Suddenly, the vanquished wizard emerged onto the balcony. He looked down and flashed a huge cheesy grin, as false as Grimy's beard. In a smarmy voice he said, 'Ah! My good friends, I knew that you would come to save me. I have been besieged by a huge Dork army for over a year. You do not know how much I wanted you to come to my aid, for only you, Theocrat, greatest of living kings, could hope to match the power of Sourone. If it wasn't for the friendly Forest of Fewgrown, there would still be Dorks at my door, instead I look out and see my bestest bosom buddies, whom I think of as the greatest in Muddy Earth.'

The King and his entourage stood transfixed, unable to speak, for whilst they had been listening, Worntwang had released a nerve gas that Sourman had invented for Politicians. This gas, coupled with the hypnotic voice of Soporific Sourman, had the effect of making those present believe any lie.

Grimy looked at the stunned faces of his companions, and wondered why, apart from it being Paragon's normal demeanour, the others stood there slack-jawed. Now, the reason Grimy was unaffected by it was that his chin-wig was woven using special carbon fibre and was acting as a filter. He suddenly shouted, 'This wizard's words have affected your heads. We haven't come to Oldcrank for this cheery cheat to pull our legs.'

'Who in the hell spoke to you, you stunted ugly toad?' vented Sourman the Sham. 'This has nothing to do with the race of Truculent Troglodytes. Keep quiet whilst I speak to my good friend Theocrat.' He turned then and addressed the King. 'Well, Theo old pal, whadya say? Do you wanna shake hands on it? Let bygones be bygones?'

While the wizard was trying to trick his way out of his predicament, the winds of fate blew against him. Said wind came in a form that smelt of rotting veg, from the West, where Treebred and his Rents stood. This cleared much of the Nerve Gas away, stirring the companions to hold their noses.

The first to speak was Earmore. 'This old liar is truly amazing. With one hand he offers a slap on the back and with the other he holds a knife.'

Theocrat added quickly, 'The only thing I want to shake is your throat. That will give us all some peace.'

Sourman was livid, and spluttered with uncontrollable rage. 'Dogs and dolts, that's all The Sons of Err are. Go back to your hovel, Theocrat Bulls-Hitter. Why I bothered to offer you my great skills is beyond me. I won't waste any more time on you or those tiny whelps you keep hidden. Good riddance!' He turned to walk away, but found he couldn't move his feet. He looked down and saw that they were caught fast in some form of sticky tree resin — or at least that's what he hoped it was.

It was at that point that The Grand Alf decided it was time to issue the eviction order. 'You must come down, Sourman, and give me the key to the front door of Oldcrank.'

'There is no way I am coming down there at the moment,' answered Sourman, struggling to free his feet.

'In that case, I have been authorised by the Witty Council to strike your name from the Magic Circle,'

Just as The Grand Alf finished speaking, an object came flying out of the window, narrowly missing the heads of Sourman and Theocrat, and landed at Pipsqueak's feet. The inquisitive Halfbit bent to pick up the strange object, but stopped suddenly at The Grand Alf's command. 'Do not touch that, Halfwit,' said the wizard, snatching it from the ground. He didn't even look at it, and instead put it straight into his pocket. He then turned to the others. 'Come, we will leave Sourman and Worntwang to starve to death, or kill each other from cabin fever.'

They left with the sound of Sourman screaming for Worntwang to help him out of his boots.

At the splintered gates, they came across Treebred. 'So, Sourman didn't want to come out to play then?' asked the Rent.

'Sourman is a bit stiff and not much into playing games.'

'He will be very stiff soon,' laughed the Rent, 'especially when they run out of their meagre rations.'

'What was it you left for them?'

'I left that up to the Halfbits; they understand food better than any other living thing.'

'Well, what was it?' The Grand Alf asked Pipsqueak.

'I left a load of fish,' he answered proudly.

'Were they cured?'

'I didn't know they were ill.'

'You stupid Halfbit! Where did you get them from?'

'They were floating upside down in that beautiful green lake over there,' he answered, pointing to a sign that read, TOILET FOR RENT.

'That water is polluted,' said The Grand Alf. He looked skywards at the blazing sun, and added, 'They are not going to last long.'

'I did leave quite a lot for only two of them,' said Pipsqueak, to the usual accompaniment of stars in his eyes and ringing in his ears.

They said their farewells to Treebred then, and mounted to leave.

As Grimy attempted to climb on the back of Hassleful, his weapon came loose and fell at the feet of the Rent. Treebred raised one of his three eyebrows, looked down at the Dwarf and said, 'That is one hell of a chopper for such a little fellow, and I hope you are not planning to use it around here.'

Grimy picked up his weapon, tucked it away and ran after the others, with the odd embarrassed glance backwards.

They rode most of the day, heading for Udderas, only stopping to rest for the night. Most of the travellers were so tired that they slept instantly.

Pipsqueak however, could not settle, but had things on his mind. This was quite unusual for Halfbits, who, with single-minded brains, only thought of ways to quell the constant ache

126

in their substantial guts. Yet tonight Pipsqueak was thinking of the shiny object that the wizard had secreted away into the pocket of his robes. The Halfbit thought that he must see it again and find out what its use was, so he waited until everyone was asleep. Accompanied by the sound of various grunts, whistles and snorts, he made his move. Slowly he crept towards where The Grand Alf lay sleeping. The wizard's mouth was open and he was snoring loudly. The pint-sized pickpocket found the wizard's robes and started to rummage through its pockets. The first thing he found was an old ring that was inset with a piece of red glass; he threw it to one side, thinking it was the type of junk sold in Lostlotion. The next thing he pulled out was a set of Elven-Maid playing cards and, after a while, he threw them to one side as well. Finally, out it came, the shiny bright object. He held it lovingly, and crept back to his bed. He sat there for some time inspecting it. The object was oblong, with buttons at one end, and a square piece of deep black glass at the other. Pipsqueak decided to press one of the buttons but, when he did, nothing happened, so he pressed another, then another and another. He was just about to give up, thinking it was broken, when the dark glass burst into life. Like a searing red flame it lit up the campsite; but it was not the light that woke the others, it was the scream from Pipsqueak.

The Grand Alf jumped up and found the Halfbit sitting, staring stupidly at the glass, his fingers twitching madly on the buttons. As the wizard approached Pipsqueak, he heard a metallic voice coming from the object, saying, 'Go and get the wizard, thou moron, or I will shrivel thine already useless pea-brain to naught.'

The Grand Alf grabbed the object, and pressed the off switch. He then cuffed the stunned Halfbit around the ear, and said, 'What did he ask you, and what did you tell him?'

'He asked me why I had called him, so I told him I hadn't called him anything. He then asked me if I was stupid, and I told him I did not know anyone called Stuart Pid, but that my name was Pipsqueak. He then got angry and asked what type of brainless Dork I was. I told him I was not a Dork, and that I was a Halfbit. I think he must have misheard me, because he kept calling me halfwit. He then said to me that he wanted to speak to the useless, snivelling wizard, so I told him you were asleep and you would get even more grumpy if I woke you,' replied Pipsqueak.

The Grand Alf gave the Halfbit a look that meant, 'Shut up — you are in mortal danger", but Pipsqueak just prattled on.

'He also said to tell the pathetic wizard that this Numpty is not for him and that he will send a dispatch wing-rider for it. I was about to ask what The Grand Alf would do with a Numpty, when you switched off the shiny thing.' Pipsqueak found out almost immediately what the wizard would do with a Numpty, as the Halfbit adopted his now familiar horizontal position.

'Did the Halfbit spill the beans?' asked Paragon.

'No, luckily. The stupidest of us stumbled over the link between Oldcrank and Bad-Odour; even Sourone was confused in conversation with Peregrinate Talk, and will think of nothing else but the Halfbit, trying to fathom what the hell he was on about. As for the link, will you take The Seeing-Phone of Oldcrank and keep it safe? Beware though, for it is highly dangerous.'

'Not to everyone. The P.I.N. is an heirloom of my house, for surely this is The PAL.HAND.T.V of Everdull.'

As they spoke, the massive shadow of a flying beast passed over them.

'Nasal!' cried the wizard. 'No time to lose. I will take Pipsqueak to Minus Thrifty while you go back to Thelma's Keep.' He grabbed the Halfbit and leapt onto the back of his eight-legged horse, shouting, 'On Shinyflax, we are on!'

The horse surged forward with a speed that could only be matched by a spoon in the hand of a hungry Halfbit.

As the land became a blur, Pipsqueak could hear the wizard singing a rhyme:

> 'BIG SCREENS AND LOUD RINGS
> WITH POLYTONES THREE.
> HOW GOOD IS IT TO HAVE AT HAND
> A THING WITH WHICH TO SEE.
> SEVEN STYLES OF SEVEN PHONES
> WITH ONE IT'S TARIFF FREE.'

The Halfbit asked the wizard what he was mumbling about.

'It is part of the Ode of Load and would be of no interest to the peasants of The Snore.'

128

'We have rhymes in Halfbiton,' replied Pipsqueak, and then proceeded to chant his verse:

'THERE ONCE WAS A WIZARD CHAP
WHO BETWEEN HIS EARS HAD QUITE A GAP.
A TERRIBLE BORE,
WHO MADE US ALL SNORE,
AND WHOSE STAGE ACT WAS UTTERLY CRAP!'

If they had not been travelling so fast, The Grand Alf would have launched the Halfbit. However, when Pipsqueak, oblivious of the danger, continued questioning the wizard, The Grand Alf could not resist showing off and being a know-it-all.

'So, what was that about Seven Styles of Phones you were singing of?'

'The Seven Phones are The PAL.HAND.T.V of the Kings of Neomanor. The name means That With Which To Communicate From Afar, and the Seeing-Phone of Oldcrank was but one of them.'

'Are they a product of Sourone Inc.?'

'No, they were made by The No-Older and came from Eldorado via Worseness. They were given to the Elf-Wannabes among the Neomanoreans, who were not in the service of Argh-Parazone, enabling them to talk to the Elves of the Uncrying Lands. The Seeing-Phones were brought to Muddy Earth by Everdull, after the Downsizing of Neomanor, which is called in that tongue of old, The Alackabath, or Atollslanted, for those caught on the island had a wash, whether they wanted it or not.'

'And of what use were the Phones to men in Muddy Earth?'

'The people of old would talk to each other over huge distances for serious matters of great import, and maybe ordering the odd pizza. There were Phones at Minus Another, Minus Piffle and at Oldcrank. The Master Phone was in the broadcasting room of The Old Time Music Hall, under The Dome of Stardom in Ohgiveusalaugh. The other three were in the North, so no one gave a damn about them. Sourone must have stolen The Piffle-Phone, and with The Mumbo-Jumbo of Morbid he has spoken his twaddle and ensnared Sourman.'

As the wizard told the tale, Pipsqueak watched the land go by and asked for the first, but not the last time, 'Are we there yet?'

THE TAKING OF SMEAR-GOB

It was a number of days after they had stolen most of the company's rations and run off into the wild that Foodo and Stan suddenly realised what a mistake they had made. Though Halfbits are domesticated and work well in kitchens, they are not very good at outdoor pursuits like fell-walking and mountaineering. Therefore, as they stood atop a cliff looking down, they smelt the air drifting up from below them, for it was heavy with the stench of the creeping cesspit that was The Dread Mushlands, that ever-expanding rotten morass also known as The Nigh of Sourone. They wondered how the hell they were going to climb up and down all these mountains, when the highest either of them had climbed on their own was on a chair to reach the top shelf of Butterballs' larder. They set camp and Foodo asked Stan, already knowing the answer, what was on the menu.

'Well, Mr Foodo, there's Alembas or Alembas; there's Alembas with Alembas, or the specialty of the house, warm Alembas.'

'How have you managed that?' asked a surprised Foodo.

'Easy,' replied Stan, as he pulled out a mangled mess from his pocket.

'I think I will leave it.'

'Suit yourself,' said Stan as he munched on the unsavoury looking lump, adding, 'though I wish this was the real thing and we were sat in The Skivey Brush Tavern in Passwater. Come to think of it, any tavern in The Snore would do, though some parts I have seen have very strange kinds of Halfbits. Some of them look and even act different from us intelligent Halfbits of Halfbiton. Why is that, Mr Foodo?'

'No Stan, it is only the Shallowhinds that are clever. The Hardfoots are the stupidest and the Stools are the dirtiest. We Braggins are Shallowhinds, which is why we are the only Halfbits in Halfbiton that can write in words of more than one syllable.'

'So, what's a Silly Bull then?'

'Exactly.'

'What, are we Gambles then?' asked an excited Stan.

130

'I think your family is a mixture of Hardfoot and Stool, which would make you a Footstool or a Hardstool,' replied Foodo, letting Stan make what he could of the information.

'Then why are they called Shallowhinds, Hardfoots and Stools?'

'It is said that the Shallowhinds are so named because, being the shortest, their backsides are closest to the ground. The Hardfoots are the workers in field and town, like farmers and builders, and lastly the Stools are so named because they come from the bottom of Halfbit society.'

They left it at that and went to sleep, with Stan realising why, as a spud-planter, he was always covered in muck. They woke the next morning, ate and packed, then contemplated the drop from the cliff.

'We could always parashoot down using our blankets,' said Stan, pulling them out of the packs again; however, on closer inspection, they found them to be full of holes where the hungry Halfbits had tried eating them in their sleep. As Stan despondently packed them away again, he noticed something that he had bought in Lostlotion nestling in the bottom of his pack. They were the famous B'ungees of the Elves: magic rope that stretched and returned to its original form when not in use. Stan had acquired them in the hope of curing his uncle, known as Andy the Groper, of his affliction, and had thirty of them. 'I'm a nincompoop,' he said.

Foodo did not argue with that.

'We'll link these together, hook them onto our belts, and climb down.'

'Ok, you try it first,' suggested Foodo, unconvinced that he wouldn't be finishing this journey on his own.

Stan set off slowly down the cliff. However, being the son of Hamfist the Clumsy, it was not long before he slipped.

All Foodo saw was Stan disappearing downwards, screaming "Maaassterrr", and as he shot back upwards past him, Foodo could see the fear etched across his companion's face, along with his breakfast. After a number of these bounces, a shaken Stan came to a halt, gibbering, at the bottom of the cliff. Foodo climbed down the weighted rope and bounced off Stan's stomach, landing gracefully on the ground. He unhooked the B'ungee from the belt of his friend, resulting in Stan bouncing on the ground and the B'ungee shooting skywards. With no weight to hold it, the rope loosed itself from the rock it was looped around and came tumbling down on Stan's head.

'Well, that worked out fine, didn't it?' said Foodo, as he helped the rubber-legged Stan to his feet. 'At least we haven't left an easy way for Grumble to follow us down.'

'Speak for yourself; my way down wasn't easy the first time or the fifth.'

Later, as they tried to pick their way through the land below The Embroil Mulch, their path became more arduous. The rain had made the muddy stone slippery and the local health and safety executive hadn't posted any hazard signs. They decided, after a long day's struggle, to shelter from the rain in a group of rocks, one of which had fallen against a large boulder. They huddled close for warmth, but not too close, for they knew that some misguided people would misread brotherly love and comradeship in adversity as something entirely different. Therefore, they spoke of manly things that dominated their male world like, being nagged and cheated on by their best friends. Stan started to worry about Dozy Hot-one; after all, Foodo was quite rich.

However, their musing was cut short by Foodo, as he said, 'What's that?' pointing towards the cliff face close to where they had not long since descended.

Walking down a nice gentle path, only yards away, was a skinny, wretched creature. The two companions kept very quiet and perfectly still, apart from Stan's usual stomach rumbling and odd outburst of gas from his rear. They listened as the creature moved slowly along the path, muttering, 'Bloody weather, grumble. I can remember when we had proper summers, grumble. I blame the aerosols.' As it moved closer, it slipped occasionally on the slick mud. At one point they heard it say, 'Careful Pernicious. We knows you wants The Treasure, but if we fall and break our necks, we can't sue the local council; it's been hung for years by Sourone.' It moved a few more yards until it was immediately above, then slipped and landed smack in front of them.

Quick as a fat lazy Halfbit could be, Stan was on it. They struggled for a few seconds, until he had used up his third wind and the decrepit creature had got the better of him.

Foodo decided that two Halfbits must be the equal of an age-old pensioner, so he joined in the fray. It was touch-and-go for a while, until he drew his sword and stuck it under the creature's nose. 'You have met Stink before. You know its smell. Make one more move and you will wish you had never heard the name Braggins.'

The creature released Stan and started to whine, 'Oh we does, we does, grumble, and in my day the elderly were treated with more respect. Muggings of old people were virtually unheard of. Shame on you, grumble. I blame the teachers.'

Foodo looked at the shrivelled old thing and thought of what his future had in store for him: being treated like a second-class citizen, being patronized and ignored, and made to feel like you were of no use anymore. Foodo was aghast with dismay; he did not want to end up looking as old and shrivelled as a sun-bed addict, with a face like an old, worn leather bag. 'We cannot kill him. Just tie him up,' he said to Stan, who took out the Elvish Elastic band known as B'ungee, and tied up the slimy creature.

Almost instantly he began to whine in a high-pitched voice, 'The band. It squeezes it tight. Take it off,' he pleaded. Then something strange happened: the wrinkled old face contorted into a mask of pure hatred, he looked at Stan and, with an equally nasty evil voice, said to him, 'You heard him Fatso — take it off him or I will brain you.'

Stan looked at Foodo in amazement. 'What's he talking about?' said the surprised Halfbit.

'Don't you understand plain speech, stupid? You either take this thing off him, or I will come over there and bounce you, Fatso,' replied the creature.

'But it is on you; who else are you talking about?'

'Him!' said the evil voice, pointing to someone standing beside him.

Stan was utterly confused, which was not that hard a thing to do, but he tried very hard to see something that was simply not there and ended up giving up and saying, 'Who?'

The creature became very animated and started to leap from one spot to another, alternately saying, 'Him, Me ,Him, Me, And Us.'

'He's out of his mind, Mr Foodo.'

'I think not. I believe that, rather than being out of his mind, he has someone else in there with him. I think he is one of those Schizofrantics.'

'What's a Schizofrantic?'

'It is someone who has dual personalities, like two different people sharing the same head,' replied Foodo.

'Oh, I see; like Dozy Hot-one at the end of the month,' said Stan.

'Well, not exactly,' answered Foodo, giving up. He then turned his attention to the creature. 'I know who you are and that you have followed us a long way, Grumble. If I release you, then you both must promise to be good and not try to escape; that means Smear-Gob as well.'

The evil face disappeared, and was replaced by the relaxed look of the more amiable personage. From the creature came the softer voice of Smear-Gob, saying, 'He has gone, so Smear-Gob will promise for The Pernicious, but Smear-Gob must swear on IT.'

'What's IT?' asked Foodo suspiciously.

'That which was and is; the thing which caused The Pernicious to be, My Treasure!' exclaimed Smear-Gob.

'Then swear your oath, Smear-Gob Treasure Seeker, for surely the treasure you seek is the treasure I assuredly carry, and if you don't promise to help us, I will leave you tied up here.'

'No, no, no,' wailed Smear-Gob. 'I promise, He promises, We promise and the rest of us do too,' he whined.

'Ok Stan, release him.'

'Are you sure, Mr Foodo? Shouldn't we at least crush one of his feet, so he can't follow us?' replied Stan, holding the Tenderiser in anticipation.

'No, we may need him to guide us to Morbid,' said Foodo, turning to Smear-Gob. 'Do you know the way to The Back Gates?'

'Why, what do you want to go there for?' asked the old fellow.

'I need to get into Morbid. Do you know the way?'

There was a hiss as he sucked air through his broken dentures, then Grumble reappeared. 'What would such nice innocent Halfbits want in that dead land? There is nothing to eat there. I've been before, but he hasn't,' he said, pointing to himself.

'Ah, umm, we are on a special errand to gather some fungus

that can only be found there. It is to save a dying elven princess,' said Foodo, none too convincingly.

'What's she dying of and what's this fun-gas stuff?' asked a suspicious Grumble.

'She is dying of boredom, for she has no part in this story, and has become morose. The fungus are mushrooms that are magic,' replied Foodo, trying to sound a bit more convincing.

'That's a different matter then. Follow Smear-Gob; he knows the way to The Back Gates,' said Grumble and, with that, off they went with Smear-Gob leading the way.

THE PATHWAY THROUGH THE MUSHLANDS

They followed their guide down from the lowlands of The Embroil Mulch, to the start of the Morass that was The Dread Mushlands. Grumble led them to his secret path, which he had found whilst escaping from Morbid some years before. By the side of the path was an old weather-beaten plaque. If they could have read the bleak speech of Morbid, they would have realised it said:

THIS PATH WAS CONSTRUCTED BY
THE 10th Bn DORK ENGINEERS TO AID
THE ESCAPE OF THE GRUMBLE CREATURE.

BY ORDER OF SOURONE THE MERCIFUL.

They travelled this path for most of the day until, worn out and tired, they stopped to rest and have their meal. Stan brought out the Alembas and asked Smear-Gob what food he had with him.

Grumble said, 'Oh I've got a joint of beef, a roast chicken and a cherry cream pie hidden in my raggy loincloth. Other than that, there are lots of juicy slimy things to eat around here, if only we had some garlic,' he answered sarcastically, whilst popping a few snails into his mouth.

'You can try some of our food if you want,' said Foodo.

'What have you got?' asked Grumble, slavering expectantly.

'Alembas.'

'Oh, I can't eat any of that damn Elvish Weighbread; it's far too heavy for my constitution, and I need more roughage at my age.' With that, Grumble stuck his face into a nice soggy mud pile.

They slept then, being so tired, oblivious to what Grumble was doing. When they awoke some time later, he was back, his face covered in green slime. The Halfbits looked at him in disgust. Foodo asked Stan how much food they had left, worrying that
136

the last thing on the menu may be Green Slime. They were already on half rations and, for the first time in years, Foodo's waist measured less than his age.

Their passage through the boggy marshes was not something either of them recalled with any joy. The stench of the marsh gas was only slightly worse than being next to Messy in the little boy's room. What made it even worse was that at least they could escape the smell of Messy from time to time. They walked for days through the stinking mess, and the marsh gas that bubbled up through the slimy pools stung their eyes. They did not know it at the time, but the gas also had hallucinatory side-effects. It wasn't long before they were seeing all sorts of amazing things; the best of these, they later agreed, was a show of The Battle of Daggerbag, put on by The Underwater Re-enactment Society. It was on the last night of their journey through the marshes that Stan awoke in the middle of the night and overheard a strange conversation between Grumble and Smear-Gob.

'Smear-Gob promised to be good,' said Smear-Gob.

'Yes you did, didn't you, but I didn't, did I,' said Grumble.

'No, Pernicious, you didn't.'

'Then I will throttle them and take back The Treasure from the Braggins.'

'Yes, do-in Fatso, but not the nice one.'

'Especially him; he's a Braggins. The whole family are thieves.'

'But how are we going to do it? There are more of them than us, and they have a smelly sword,' moaned Smear-Gob.

'What are you snivelling about? There are only two of them and there are two of us. Besides, we have our friend to help us. She is getting sick of her usual tidbits,' replied Grumble forcefully.

'Oh no! I don't like creepy-crawly things; you know I don't.'

'What are you talking about? That is exactly what we are. We are going that way, whether you like it or not. I want my Treasure back,' grumbled Grumble, as he looked at Foodo with an evil glint in his eyes.

That was enough for Stan; he had heard as much as he could take. He jumped up, stretched, scratched his rear end, and added to the stink of the marshes whilst mentally taking note to bring some Imodium capsules on the next trip. Trying to make as if he had not heard the conversation between Smear-Gob and

Grumble, Stan said, 'Oh my goodness, is that the time? We should be moving on. What do you say, Grumble?'

'I have never seen anything as lazy as you Snorings,' he replied.

Foodo woke feeling refreshed, and said to the old fellow, 'Well, tomorrow should see us at our destination. It is good of you to get us there, Smear-Gob.'

Grumble just smiled back at the Halfbits, and thought to himself, you won't think it's so good when you get there, and gestured for them to follow him into the last dark of the night.

THE BACK GATES ARE BEING REPAIRED
(Go Around The Front)

They staggered out of The Mushlands along a dusty track that of old had been called The Spring Field. Before them was Morbid. To their west was The Effete De'Ath or The Mountains of Slum Shady. To their north were the peaks of Airhead Livid. These were the walls of Morbid, built on the orders of Sourone in ages past. In those early days, the owner of Sourone Inc. had grand ideas of adventure playgrounds and theme parks, like water skiing on the shark infested inland sea, which had since become dead and was now known as The Sea of Mourning. The problems had started when he gave the plans to build Morbid to low budget Dwarven landscape gardeners from the east. They had read them upside down and back to front. The original idea was for the open arms of the mountains to invite in the stupid Dulledain, using Morbid as a giant sheep-pen. Therefore, that was how Foodo and Stan found themselves before Morbid, looking at The Back Gates.

'Well, what now Mr Foodo?' asked Stan.

'I don't really know, I hadn't given much thought to anything past this point, and I didn't reckon on the gates being so big or so closed,' replied Foodo.

Grumble's eyes rolled skywards and he muttered under his breath for help from whatever divinity still cared that he existed.

'What we need is a diversion so that, when the guard comes out to investigate, we can sneak past him,' said Stan, feeling proud of his scheme.

'You stupid fat Halfbit, what about the thousands on the other side of the gates? Are you just going to waltz by them, passing the time of day? You cannot get in this way!' said Grumble.

'Then why didn't you tell us that before we got here?' asked Stan angrily.

'Because Smear-Gob likes the view from here stupid, and I wanted to find out why you needed to get into Morbid. Well I know now: you are going to sell The Treasure to him in exchange for food!'

'What in Muddy Earth makes you think that?' exclaimed Foodo.

'It is no good denying it; I've heard the fat one in his sleep, talking of the millions he will get once he has you inside Morbid.'

Foodo started to laugh and said, 'I think you've got hold of the wrong end of the stick. Stan placed a bet with the elves in Lostlotion, at a million to one, that he would get me to the end of our mission.'

'Then I cannot make up my minds as to which is the most stupid — Fatso or the Elves. What possible thing of worth would a dense dung distributor have in his possession to cover such a bet?'

'My family heirloom has been left with the Elves of Lostlotion. It is one of the most valuable items in all The Snore,' replied Stan proudly, but what this fabled thing was he would not elaborate.

'So Grumble, if we cannot get in this way, do you know of any other way?' asked Foodo hopefully.

'Well, you could always go all the way Northeast or Southeast around these big mountains, and go in the front way. You lazy fat Halfbits might get there by this time next year,' replied Grumble. The thought of that made the Halfbits quite faint.

'Are you sure there aren't any shortcuts?' asked Foodo hopefully.

'It is funny you mention that; there is a nice gentle path that meanders through the mountains.'

Stan was instantly suspicious. It wasn't his working class distaste of double-barrel names that made him distrust Smear-Gob Grumble — it was the double-crossing twin aspects of the creatures mind, which Stan had named Soppy and Stroppy, that worried him. Yet Foodo had decided to trust the wretch, so Stan tried to keep quiet.

'Tell us why you didn't mention this pathway before,' said Foodo.

'I have only been that way twice, and he's only been once before,' replied Grumble, pointing once more to his other self.

'We were lucky to find it, weren't we Pernicious?' added Smear-Gob

'I found it, not you. Without me you would still be lost, idiot. I found it when we escaped from him. My secret path out of The

140

Gorygorge and past The Tower of The Soundless Silly Whatsits, through the nice, small, cosy and not very dangerous tunnel. After that, we gets to the staircase; very easy going down, very hard going up. Then at the bottom is Minus Mucus, The Tower of the Gloom, that was once Evenduller's city of Minus Piffle. We must go past The Gloomy Tower, then up my secret way,' explained Grumble.

Stan wasn't very happy. 'This secret path that only you know about, who built it then? Are you sure that Sourone or his legions of foul Dorks don't know of it? Surely it is patrolled by them?'

'Not bloody likely,' muttered Grumble under his breath.

'What did you say?' asked Stan.

'Only nightly,' he replied through clenched dentures.

'Why not during the day?' asked Foodo. But Grumble would say no more, for the name of that high place was Critter Ungodly and, if the Dorks heard it mentioned, they would wet themselves. They turned southwards and once again followed Grumble into the unknown.

THE ROBBING OF STEWED HERBS

After a couple of days, they came to a dense wooded area that of old was called Piffling, a small insignificant sub-realm of Gondour. For the rest of the day, they continued into the wood, until they came to a suitable place, within a clearing, to stop for the night. They couldn't agree who would sleep first and who would prepare the meal, or who would attempt to hunt for fresh rations. Foodo decided that the only way to do things was democratically, so a vote was rigged by Foodo (who was of the ruling class). He wrote out his name in Elvish on three pieces of paper, knowing that the other two weren't versed in that language. He placed them upside down and asked Stan to pick out the name of the person who wouldn't be cooking.

'What does it say, Mr Foodo?' asked Stan.

'It says I am not cooking, Stan. Your turn Grumble; let's see who isn't hunting for food.'

Grumble picked one and showed it to Foodo.

'Looks like my lucky day: I am not hunting either,' laughed Foodo as he went through the motions of picking his name out for who would get first rest. 'That leaves you two, to find out who is doing what.'

Immediately, Stan and Grumble started to argue.

'I am not cooking. I haven't cooked anything for a very long time. If I catch anything, let's eat it raw; saves time and washing up,' said Grumble hopefully.

As Foodo dropped off to sleep, the last thing he remembered hearing was Stan telling Grumble to go look for something to eat, and Grumble replying sarcastically, 'Oh I'll just pop down to the corner shop, or the local butchers. There's bound to be plenty of them around here.' Then he turned and disappeared into the undergrowth, moaning about the price of fish.

Almost an hour later Grumble reappeared, looking quite pleased with himself. 'It is a good thing you have an experienced hunter with you, or maybe you would die of starvation,' he said, rather smugly, as he dropped two small, skinned and ready-to-cook animals, along with a sack, at Stan's feet.

'What are they? I hope they're not rats.'

'Of course not stupid; they are robbits.'

'What's a robbit?'

'Did I say robbit? Oh dear, just a slip of the tongue. I really meant rabbit,' replied Grumble quickly.

'Well, whatever they are, I may just spit-roast them over the fire,' said Stan.

'What bloody fire?'

'That fire.' He pointed proudly at the small fire he had managed to start.

'Argh, you stupid Halfbit — it will bring the men to us. Put it out!' screamed Grumble.

'There are no men around here; we're at least a hundred miles away from Minus Thrifty,' said Stan, before adding, 'Here, you haven't seen any, have you?'

'No, no, not even the slightest glimpse of one. Umm, I just remembered something I had forgotten about. Won't be long,' said Grumble, as he slinked off into the undergrowth.

Oh well, more for us, thought Stan. 'What I could do with a Gorge Fourmen griddle now. However, I think, instead of wasting all those juices by roasting, I will stew them.' As the water was boiling, he chopped up the meat and popped it into the pan. Inside the sack that Grumble had brought were what Stan later described as vegitaters. These were a variety of edible roots. He chopped them up and added them to the pan, then sat back and waited for them to cook. Now, if Stan had paid more attention to the writing on that sack, he would have seen that it read:

ONE MAN RATION PACK.
PROPERTY OF THE STRANGERS OF PIFFLING.
Run out date 3019TS.

However, Stan's mind was, as usual, was fixed on the food; some proper food at last, and not that damn boring Alembas. An hour or so later, with Stan already having had two helpings, he woke Foodo and gave him a bowl of stew.

'Bloody hell, where did this come from, Stan?'

'Grumble brought the ingredients back from somewhere,' answered Stan, pointing to some indiscriminate place.

'Strange; I had Grumble marked as a fisher, not a hunter.'

'Funny, I had him and his friend down as a villain and a nutter,' replied Stan.

'Well, never mind; we have some hot food for a change. What is in this marvellous stew?'

'Robbits ... sorry, that's what Grumble called them. I mean, they are rabbits. There are also some vegitaters, which came in that sack.' He pointed at the empty bag.

'Let me see that sack a moment,' said Foodo. Stan passed it to him. Foodo laid it out flat in front of him and read the words written on it. 'Oh bloody hell! Quick, put out the fire and collect your gear; we are moving.'

Yet fate was against them that hour, for Halfbits cannot do anything quickly unless it has to do with eating and, before Foodo's last words had time to sink in, they heard a voice nearby.

'This is where that awful smell is coming from, over here. We'll soon have the little sneak thief caught like a rat in a trap.'

Seconds later, a group of tall men stepped into the campsite. They were dressed in green tights and shirts, with ankle boots and jerkins of dull brown. Upon their heads were pointy hats, in which were feathers of a variety of different birds. Their leader took one look at Foodo, who was still holding the sack in his hand, and said 'Ah ha! Caught red-handed. Where is your pet rat creature, the one who was seen stealing those very rations?'

'It looks like he's set us up and done a runner,' replied Stan angrily.

'A likely story from partners in crime. If you are trying to protect your accomplice, it will go bad for you. Tell us where he is and why you have taken to pilfering in Piffling,' ordered the man.

'We're just poor travellers on a mission out of Dimladsbliss. We were sent by Elbow Halfman. I am Foodo, son of Doggo, and my companion is Stanwitless, son of Hamfist. We are but two of a larger band known as the Followship. We left the others at Prat Garble, near The Falls of Raucous, for they were going to Minus Thrifty with Paragon and Borrowit, the two men of our company.'

'Borrowit, the son of Lord Denizen, was The Eye Wardship of the Sight Tower and our Captious Generic. We haven't missed his picky, heavy-handed upper-class mentality lately, I can tell you. How came one so high-minded to be travelling with such rustic simpletons?' asked the leader.

'Here now, Mr Foodo, are we going to let some fellow in tights talk to us like that?'

The leader looked at Stan dangerously. 'I can see clearly why you are called Stanwitless. Before you spoke, I only thought you looked simple.' He turned to Foodo and said, 'We will finish our conversation later. I have news of a large army of Slothrons nearby. We go to ambush this ambling army of Harass. I will leave you in the capable hands of Madlunge and Damnodd.'

The Halfbits were told to pack their gear away and Stan complained, saying, 'The pan is still half-full of stewed herbivore.' Much to his horror, Damnodd confiscated the pan and its contents and placed them into a container from his pack. 'I was going to finish that off,' moaned Stan.

'You are lucky that I'm not taking the other half back. This is stolen property and evidence of theft by you and your little rat friend,' replied Damnodd.

'It wasn't us that stole the food, and we know not where our companion is. We certainly didn't want to draw attention to ourselves,' said Foodo.

'Then which idiot made the fire using damp rotting wood?' asked Madlunge.

Stan looked sheepish and muttered, 'Wait until I get my hands on that Smear-Gob Grumble; I will do in the pair of them.'

'So there are two of those little rats running around out there?' asked Damnodd.

'No, there's only one of them: he's a schizofrantic and thinks he is two men,' replied Foodo.

'Oh, I see. I've known a few of our men like that, especially after a few beers on a night out at the tavern.'

As they packed, the sound of fighting grew louder and nearer. They moved from the open ground to a higher position. It was not long before the battle was being waged only yards from where they had been camping. The Strangers of Piffling, led by their tall leader, were routing the men of Harass. This was the first that either of the Halfbits had seen of the men of the South. They were dressed in baggy pantaloons, curly-toed boots, and turbans over spiky helmets. However, the strangest thing about them was their orange skin. Damnodd told them that, in

Minus Thrifty, it was believed that, in ancient days, the people of Harass could only sleep during the day under open skies. Therefore they invented strange boxes that collected and stored sunlight, so when the sun went down, they switched them on and slept on them; they called them Sunbeds. Just as he finished explaining, there was a loud crash and a massive form came into view, knocking woodland down as if it were grass. The big, grey, baggy-legged beast was clearly distressed.

Damnodd and Madlunge gathered the Halfbits together, and Madlunge said, 'Beware! Keep down; it is a Mumikill they have with them. When these beasts are upset, they go wild and trample everything in sight.'

'What in Muddy Earth has upset that one?' asked Foodo.

'The Slothrons only use the female of these beasts, for they are normally heavier and used to carrying things. Because of the shortage of water, they all wash in the same hole, man and beast alike. This makes the beasts think that the Slothrons are their offspring. When their offspring are in danger, the Mumikill goes mad,' explained Damnodd. The Strangers by now had destroyed or chased off most of the southerners.

Stan said to Foodo, 'Wait until I tell The Grafter that I've seen a Nelliphaunt.'

'That's if we ever get back,' replied Foodo.

'Oh, I bet we will; I'll make sure we do. That bet I made in Lostlotion is doubled if we make it back. That will make me two million, and I will be the richest gardener in the whole Snore,' said Stan gleefully.

THE WINSOME OF THE WEST

They rested then, awaiting the return of The Piffling Strangers. It was not long before Stan was snoring. He had not slept normally since taking up with Grumble. The absurd dream of Grumble stealing the Alembas would not leave him. He awoke some time later, halfway through the recurrent nightmare of Grumble the Crumble, throwing all the food down a ravine. Ridiculous, he thought. Grumble could not touch anything of Elvish origin; the B'ungee rope had proved that. Besides, Stan always slept holding onto his pack like an octopus.

Looking around, he suddenly realised that the warriors had returned, and were now sat listening to their leader question Foodo.

'You have told me much, yet not all. In Minus Thrifty there is a prophecy; now... how does it go ... oh yes:

WHEN THE HALFBIT IS FORCED TO STAND,
THEN EVENDULLERS BLAME SHALL BE TAKEN.

That is part of it, if I 'member aright, I think. So, tell me who is going to take the blame,'

'I have taken the blame, for I am being paid to; yet, if any should take the blame, then it should be Paragon, son of Paramount,' answered Foodo solemnly.

'Why, what makes him more special than the heir to The Lordship of Minus Thrifty, and a descendent of The House of Howlin, Stalwarts of Gondour?' asked the tall leader, with pride in his voice.

'Paragon is the heir of Everdull's son, Evenduller. He is descended from The Kings of Neomanor, that was Worseness, and in whose veins runs the blood of Benny and Lillian; kin of King Thingy Greatmangle was he and Elude Singular Lord of the Thousand Cafes, in Manygrowth of Doorhehath; husband also to Mullein the May I who, in the day before days, descended upon Larda with the mighty I-know, Spirits of Great Potency and Solvers of Soduko. To prove this, he carries Nares, The Sword That Had Brokered, which has been re-forged, and named Andrex.'

'Are you trying to prove something? Sounds like just another one of those plastic princelings we get from time to time, all claiming to be descended from some long lost love child of some king or other. As for his sword, how do we know it isn't fake, a replica? You can get anything from Ye Olde EBay Shoppe these days.'

'If Borrowit were here, he would tell you it isn't a scam. He would tell you it was true.'

'Yes, we come to Borrowit: your close companion. Your trusted, faithful ally,' said the man.

'I wouldn't put it exactly like that.'

'So, you weren't on friendly terms when you parted?'

'Well actually, he was crying like a baby when I left. I am almost positive he didn't want me to leave.'

'Then I suppose that it would upset you slightly to know that your best friend is deceased,.'

Thinking back to the slopes of Mons When, it was all Foodo could do to stop himself saying, "Well I wouldn't put it exactly like that." What he did say was, 'Oh dear. Really? How did it happen?'

'If you don't know, how do you expect me to? You saw him alive long after me,' replied the man accusingly.

'I wouldn't say he was full of the joys of spring, but he was quite animated when last I saw him. How do you know that he is dead?'

'I had just left one of the many taverns dotted along the wharves of Ohgiveusalaugh, when I noticed what appeared to be a log floating nearby, upon the waters of the Arduous. I would have left it, thinking it of no import, but I saw the moonlight glint off something metallic. I strode out from the shoreline, until I got close enough to recognise the stench of rotting flesh. As I drew near to the log, I noticed that it was hollowed out in the form of a boat. Within the boat were the remains of a man of Minus Thrifty and, for some strange reason he was wearing Dork boots on the wrong feet. An uncanny feeling came over me, so as to make me think I knew the bloated face of the decaying man. It was then that I saw it: The Horn of the House of Howlin that Varlet, Stalwart of Gondour, took from the fabled cattle of O'Roamin. It was broken into two pieces, yet I knew it and by it I realised that I was looking upon the badly bloated body of Borrowit the Brave. Upon closer inspection, I noticed the maggots and that he looked and smelled somewhat similar to one of his famous morning-after-the-pub crawls.'

'Yes, that does sound a bit dead to me,' admitted Foodo.

'I took the horn and gave it to The Stalwart, who is the father of my brother, for I am Faraway, the more charming and intelligent younger son.'

'Well, I am glad to meet one sane member of the family. I hope your father hasn't got Borrowit's fiery mood.'

'Oh, my father has his moments and can get quite hot under the collar when he is upset. You will notice that when you meet him in Minus Thrifty.'

'But we are not going to Minus Thrifty, Faraway.'

'Oh, don't worry — it isn't really that far,' said Damnodd.

So they set out southwards. Faraway fell in alongside Foodo and Stan. 'I think you had a problem with my brother, and I suspect it may lie with Evenduller's Blame. Though our family is not of the high lineage of Evenduller, Borrowit was always a social climber who thought he was the big fish. Still, he would have thought himself strong enough to handle the Blame,'

'He was told at The Council of Elbow that not even The King in Hiding should take The Blame of Everdull,' replied Foodo.

'By who?' asked Faraway.

'The Grand Alf.'

'The Grey Pillock; the one we call Mythroving, which the dwarves call Thickone, and in the South is named Imkantdo?'

'Yes, that is the fellow. We called him Habba-ra-ka-Dabblin in the Commingle Speak; yet no name is of use to someone who is dead.'

'What? Mythroving is dead?.'

'Yes, as dead as a dodo. A once wiz. An elapsed enchanter and a malodorous magician.'

'Well, there is no news like bad news. Are you sure that he is dead?'

'I saw him fall into a bottomless pit of never-ending nothingness.'

'A bit like the Liberals then!' said Faraway, adding, 'Come to think of it now, I remember well the stories Mythroving told of the thing taken from the nose of Sourone. Is this the same as Evenduller's Blame? Was it the cause of Borrowit's dilemma? What this thing is I know not, but surely a nose-hair clipping wasn't the weapon of the enemy. It must surely have been more than a hairy, bogey thing.'

Foodo was beginning to get worried; Faraway was getting too close to the mark. He remembered well the reaction of Borrowit the Barmy, and wanted no repetition, so he kept quiet. However, he was heartened when Faraway declared an oath, that he wouldn't touch anything from the nose of Sourone, even with a bargepole; even if it was the most powerful weapon in Muddy Earth.

'Phew, if only you knew,' Foodo muttered to himself.

They walked on then through the fairly fair land of Piffling, until some miles later they came to a stream. Faraway stopped and turned to the Halfbits in a matter-of-fact sort of way. 'We have a custom that none should see the hidden way to our hideout, so you can choose to have one of the following: have your eye's poked out with a sharp stick, get your eyelids sewn together or have hot lead poured over your eyeballs.'

'Are they all the options?' asked a worried Stan.

'Yes, that's about it, I am afraid, unless you know of any other ways of blinding someone that doesn't involve tearing out the eyeballs from their sockets,' said Damnodd, advancing with a strange look on his face.

'Well, as you come to mention it, the very clever and intelligent Elves of Lostlotion have a marvellous and ingenious way, called Bagging. They put a bag over your head so you cannot see the way,' said Foodo quickly.

'I am not putting a bag on my head for anyone,' replied Damnodd.

Foodo knew, at that point, that he was amongst The Dulledain. 'No, you put the bags on our heads so we cannot see,' he explained.

'Oh, I see; so you cannot see,' said Damnodd, thinking himself clever.

'Yes that is about the long and short of it,' replied Foodo, in exasperation.

The Halfbits were bagged and they continued on the last part of their trek. After a number of miles, they stopped again. In the background they could hear an argument brewing.

'Why don't you admit we are lost?' said Madlunge.

'You said, turn down the path to the left,' argued Damnodd.

'No, I said keep going past the path on the left. Anyway, any fool knows all you have to do is follow the stream.'

'Shhh,' came the loud reply from many lips.

The Halfbits were bundled back down the path they had just trodden. Eventually, they reached their destination and were de-bagged. When their eyes grew accustomed to the light, they saw that they were standing behind a massive sheet of thick, toughened glass, on the outside of which ran a waterfall. A rainbow effect could be seen as the sun shone through the glass and the water.

'This is The Window of the Sunglass, Hotness Anneal. No outsiders have ever before seen its magnificence,' said Faraway, in a dreamy, faraway type of voice.

'I bet they haven't, without any eyes,' whispered Stan to Foodo.

Inside the hideout, which was formed from a large cavern, were beds, tables and stores. They all rested and ate. As they did this, they talked at length and the Halfbits told their story. However, they made a few adjustments concerning Borrowit's part, almost to the point where he single-handedly defeated The Labdog of Mortcough.

'That sounds like my brother Borrowit the Brave,' said a proud Faraway.

Stan recalled to himself how Borrowit had fled like the wind, throwing the Halfbits behind him.

'Still I think that my brother would have been slightly apprehensive about entering into Careless Gallivant and the perils of Gadabout's Fairground. We in Minus Thrifty have long held in fear and awe The Wych-Lady of Lostlotion, the land that was named of old, Laurelandhardirealm,' said Faraway.

'I don't know of any dangers from Lostlotion. We all had a marvelous time there. The problem with Borrowit ...' At that point, Stan trailed off, realising that, having drank too much, he was blabbing.

However, Faraway pressed him, saying, 'So the problem with Borrowit was, maybe he thought it was dangerous to have too much fun and that they may become bewitched and idle, forsaking their quest. Is this what you meant?'

Foodo thought to himself that it wouldn't be much fun for Faraway finding out the truth about how dangerous Borrowit had been.

Stan however, didn't pick up on this and said, 'No sir, your brother thought the rides were too dangerous and didn't want to show he was scared of them. Besides, he wasn't interested in relaxing and having a good time. The only thing he was interested in was Sourone's Nose-ring.' Foodo gulped and started to choke. Stan turned to him and said, 'You shouldn't try eating and speaking at the same time.'

When his throat cleared, Foodo replied angrily to Stan, 'Yes, and I told you to stick to eating and refrain from speaking, at any time.'

'Ha, ha, ha, ha, ha,' came the fanatical laughter of the fatuous Faraway, his face contorted into a grimace as he leered at Foodo. 'Ha, ha, ha! Heh, heh, heh!' He continued his inane cackling. 'So, my big bad brother Borrowit, father's favourite, the greatest warrior in Muddy Earth, could not even take a nose ring off a diminutive dimwit! And now, here you are, and I have a chance to go one better than my big-headed brother. A chance, at last, for Faraway to qualify in the eyes of his father as a real warrior.' His eyes were rolling and he began to stagger like a drunk towards them. Either by luck or fate he tripped over his sword scabbard and went flying into the wall. He slid down the wall and sat holding his head, looking anything but a warrior. He started to chuckle, a very different sound than before. 'I am glad I do not have a bargepole to test myself with, yet I think I would have stayed true. We men of Minus Thrifty are Oath-Boasters and do not make promises lightly, unless it involves housework. Mind you, it is a good thing that I did not say, I wouldn't touch anything from the nose of Sourone, even with a wicked curved dagger,' he said, whipping one out.

The Halfbits edged backwards, until their backs were touching the cavern wall.

'It is ok. I am fine now. Come and sit down; you are safe.'.

Foodo wasn't convinced. During Faraway's fleeting moment of madness, he had looked awfully like Borrowit the Barmy.

'Come Foodo; sit. I have no wish for power, no plans of

domination, I would be no good at the head of an army. In fact, like most second-born aristocracy, at most things I am useless. Well, that is what Madame X calls me anyway. So, where will you go from here? I was going to take you to Minus Thrifty by way of Ohgiveusalaugh.'

'Oh, Mr Foodo, by rights I don't think we should go there,' said a very intuitive Stan.

'Quite right, Stan. To go anywhere near there now, well, that would be a stupid idea,' said Foodo. He turned to Faraway then and said, 'I must go to Morbid, through the Gorygorge, to the Mountain of Murk and throw the nose ring into the Crack of Gloom, and I do not know how the bloody hell to get there.'

'I would have told you to follow The Mellow Brick Road, but all roads east have fallen into disrepair. The Dorks have robbed most of the stones to build their hovels and the fast food chain of Muckdorkalds. East, you must go, you say, so rest now, for whatever way you find, I have a feeling that things are going to get very sticky from here on.'

They were woken later that night. Foodo looked up into the face of Faraway as he bent over the Halfbit. There was a strange look in his eyes, and he was winking at him. Foodo began to feel worried, but was mightily relieved when he spoke.

'Don't move; I have lost my contact lens.' He rummaged about for a while. 'Ah there it is! Come Foodo, there is a puzzle to solve.'

Foodo thought it was a strange time to wake someone, just to do jigsaws. Faraway led them to a ledge, from which they looked out and saw afar the moon going down behind the snowy top of old Mindofruin. Looking down, they saw a deep pool.

Faraway pointed. 'Do you see there, that slimy creature? What do you reckon it is?'

Before Foodo could answer, a man emerged from behind a bush where he had been hidden; in his hand was a bow.

'I have been watching it for four hours. I reckon it is one of them Squiggle things, or even a Fingkisser of Wurkymood,' said the man, who was named Ambored.

'Don't you mean a squirrel and kingfisher of Murkywood?' asked Foodo.

'Yes, that's wattle I said, wangle it?'

Foodo gave a confused look towards Faraway, who whispered in his ear, 'Ambored gets his words mixed up because he was dropped on his head when he was born.'

'That was unlucky,' replied Foodo quietly.

'He was lucky that his father couldn't find anything higher than the bedroom window to drop him from.'

'Can I shout at it with abode and narrow?' said Ambored.

'He wants to shoot the thing. Shall we let him?' asked Faraway.

Stan could hardly stop himself from leaping in the air and shouting, "YES", and would have done so, if he had not clumsily fallen backwards and rolled back down the path. Back at the top, Foodo begged them not to shoot.

'So, this is the rat thing which was seen stealing the rations?'

asked Faraway.

'He is in my narrow joint; can I shout, for surly coming unbounded to this place is deaf?' said Ambored.

'If Mythroving were here, he would say not to kill this creature. Apparently, he had the strange notion that this thing had some bit part to play before the end. It may be important, or it may not but, at the moment, the least he can do is to be my unofficial tour guide,' said Foodo.

'You mean this thing knows its way around here? Does it know then its way into Morbid? If so, how? The only ways out of Morbid are in the belly of a Dork or to be let out, and I don't see a kebab skewer sticking out of that thing's mouth. That can only mean Sourone let him go for a reason. Therefore we cannot let this spy come and go as he pleases,' said Faraway, with a worried look on his face.

'Let me go down and see if he falls for the old pals' act.'

Now, when The Strangers of Piffling had captured the Halfbits, Grumble had thought himself pretty smart, which was until Smear-Gob reminded him that the Halfbits still had The Treasure and that maybe the men would find out what it was. It was then that all hell had broken loose. The creature had started to punch itself; the left arm giving kidney punches and the right arm doing serious damage to the nose, all the while arguing with itself.

'You should have warned them about the men,' said Grumble.

'You shouldn't have been seen stealing the rations,' said Smear-Gob.

'Argh,' screamed Grumble.

'Ugh,' moaned Smear-Gob.

'It's all your fault anyway. If you hadn't lost the ring in the first place, none of this would have happened.'

'You were wearing it last, not me.'

This had carried on for some time, until the creature had collapsed from exhaustion. Then Grumble had shouted, 'Stop!' As it lay there panting, Grumble had said, 'Why are you beating yourself up over a few silly mistakes? I accept your apology and that's that; we'll hear no more about it.'

Therefore, it had been decided to follow the trail left by the men. When they disappeared behind the waterfall, Grumble had found the pool around the corner and decided to hide there, waiting for them to come back out. He had discovered to his delight that, apart from the odd yellow-coloured submersible and titanic shipwreck, complete with film crew, he was on his own with a multitude of marine life. The downside of this was, there was no equipment around to catch the fish with, due to the politicians killing off the fishing trade, and so bare hands would have to do. It was at that point that the Strangers of Piffling had found him.

As Foodo crept nearer to Grumble, he could hear him complaining to himself.

'All alone again, grumble. Nobody loves us. Horrible Halfbits find friends with food and don't worry about starving Smear-Gob.' As he mumbled away, his hand suddenly darted into the water. When he withdrew it equally as quick, he had caught a fish. He proceeded to bash it against the rocks. Once it was dead, he sank his filed-down dentures into its flesh, taking a huge mouthful. 'Umm, yummy. Battered Cod, scrummy tuck,' said Smear-Gob, to which Grumble said threateningly, 'You had better save me some of that or there will be trouble.'

As the creature munched on its supper, Foodo shouted its name from the shadows. This frightened the wretch, causing it to gag on a mouthful.

'You stupid Halfbit, don't you know not to creep up and scare old folk, grumble? You could have given us heart attacks, grumble. I blame the television.' said Grumble.

'It is me, Foodo.'

'Never heard of you,' said Smear-Gob petulantly, to which Grumble added, 'Got bored with your new friends have we? Or have they just run out of food, so you come running to The Great Grumble to save your skins again? Bah, I blame the additives.'

'Erm, yeah, something like that. Now come with me, for there are men here that don't know of the hunting ban, and you will only be safe with me.'

'Why is that? So that I can hide behind your fat belly?' said Grumble, but he followed Foodo all the same.

Halfway up the slope, Grumble smelled a rat, or to be more precise, Ambored's stinking leathers, which were in fact held together by rat gut. However, before Grumble could bolt, the big man flung him into a sack and tied it up. Grumble wriggled and cursed furiously but, after several minutes, he went limp and quiet. Ambored picked up the sack and slung it over his shoulder, causing Grumble to grunt.

The bag was carried back to the cavern, where they were met by Faraway, who told Ambored to empty the sack. 'Let us see what this creature really is.'

'I hope you haven't hurt him,' said Foodo, getting worried.

Stan, on the other hand, thought it would be nice if these big brutes had broken something, so it couldn't follow them anymore.

The men untied the sack and dumped Grumble out onto the floor. He looked in a state of shock, and cowered away from Faraway and the others standing over him.

'What are you doing here?' asked Faraway sternly.

Grumble looked around and pointed at Ambored. 'The big ugly one dragged me here.'

'Don't try being clever with me.'

'Why, do you want me to act stupid like that fat Halfbit?' said Grumble, pointing at Stan.

'Do you not know that it is against the law to fish in this pool?'

'Well excuuuuse me, if I thought that being beaten half to death and mistreated this way was the penalty for forgetting your rod license, I would have had it renewed. I blame the government.'

'It was very foolish of you to come to this place, and you are very lucky not to have met a premature end,' said Faraway.

Stan said to Damnodd, 'We are unlucky that you missed an opportunity that has been long overdue.'

Grumble was looking a little bit less sure of his situation and started to shake. 'It wasn't my fault. Don't kill me; kill Smear-Gob.'

'If Foodo hadn't been here, you would already be fish-food.' said Faraway.

At that, Stroppy disappeared, to be replaced by Soppy, who proceeded to lick Foodo's feet, saying, 'Yes, isn't the Master marvelous,' whilst fawning all over him.

Faraway grabbed the wretched creature and, nose to nose, stared him out.

At the same time, Stan was longing to punch Grumble's lights out.

'Where are you taking them, and no lying,' Faraway asked Smear-Gob.

'That is no secret; we are going to Morbid. Why they want to go, I don't know. Ask them,' replied Smear-Gob, pointing at the Halfbits.

'Which way are you taking them?'

'That way,' answered Smear-Gob Grumble, pointing in opposite directions.

Foodo interjected at that moment, seeing that Faraway was beginning to lose his temper with the wretched thing. He told him of their journey to The Back Gates and of the hidden path above Minus Piffle.

'Minus Mucus, you mean!'

'I am not sure; it is Grumble who knows the way.'

'That path is known as Critter Ungodly.' At the mention of that name, Grumble started to shake and Smear-Gob squeaked. As his eyes rolled in their sockets and his raggy loin cloth got damp, Faraway continued. 'It is the dwelling place of some ancient evil, whose hunger for food can only be matched by a naughty Halfbit child who has been sent to bed without supper.'

'Well, if you know of a better way, pray tell me, for we Halfbits will do anything for an easy life. We cannot get through The Back Gates and the front way is too far away, Faraway. I must trust Grumble to sneak us in safely.'

'But can you safely trust that sneak? I am not sure. There is something in the way that his eyes hide the truth.'

'That'll be the cataract. He is nearly 600 years old, you know,' replied Foodo.

'We will soon part company Foodo, son of Doggo, so my parting advice would be for you to keep an eye on that two-faced trickster and his sidekick. Beware of him,' said Faraway.

'I bet that will be my job then, sir. As you know, I have no love for that dubious double-dealer,' said Stan.

'Well, Master Stanwitless, you had better not live up to your name, or we will all be in the crap.'

ALONG THE CRAP ROADS & ON TO
THE STAIRCASE OF CRITTER UNGODLY

They left Faraway's camp early the next morning, full of praise for the generosity of the men of Piffling. The store master had luckily managed to issue most of his out-of-date stock to the Halfbits — it was a matter of legend that Halfbits have an iron constitution and are almost immune to food poisoning. Grumble was also returned to them, with tales of mistreatment and crimes against The Green Eaves Convention, which incidentally only The Elves of Ohsillyland had signed in the days before Bellyland was destroyed by the tumults of The Wars of The First Stage, when Mortcough still walked the halls of Hangbad beneath Thatgotridofhim.

Their journey along the Crap-roads was largely uneventful, until they got to the junction of the four roads. They came across a piece of what would be called post-modern sculpture, but was really an old masterpiece that had been attacked by a bad renovator. That so-called artist was a Dorkish Expressionist called Damnanit Hurts. The statue that had been cut in half — Stan had named it a Narfdork, due to the pathetic attempt by the artist to replace the shattered half of the statue with the image of a demented Dork. The resulting renovation looked like it had been done by an ape on drugs.

They turned away from the monstrosity, travelling eastward along the road. Many hours later, they arrived within sight of Minus Mucus, The Tower of Gloom. Everywhere they looked was rotting and green. The floodlights that lit the walls lining each side of the road were mouldy and caked in verdigris; this gave off a catarrh-coloured glow that reflected back at them in evil-green. The lights flickered in a pulsating, hypnotic way, so that Foodo felt strangely drawn to the big city. As they drew closer, they could make out the billboards advertising various restaurants and fast food outlets, such as Muckdorkalds. These began to play on his mind. Then he saw a sign, proclaiming:

ALL YOU CAN EAT,
FOR JUST ONE NOSE RING.

Seeing that, Foodo took off running towards the city gates. It took all of Stan and Grumble's strength to pull him away, and the struggle was quite violent. Grumble's dentures went flying and Stan's cloak was ripped off, along with his souvenir badge. They only just managed to drag Foodo behind the cover of a pile of large boulders situated at the bottom of The Staircase, before the great shutters that protected the entrance to the city clanked and screamed, as the motors that winched them kicked into gear. Slowly, they rolled up, revealing an image of death-incarnate. Sat atop a new shiny black mountain bike was The Witchy-King of Wagner, Lord of the Ring Cyclists. As he peddled forwards, they saw an army of dread emerge behind him. Battalions of Big Brutal Barbaric Men of the South, hordes of Horrible Half-Dorks and a deluge of Demonic Dorks trudged out of Minus Mucus, following The Morgue Lord. As he drew level with their hiding place, they heard a sharp hissing sound from the direction of The Witchy-King, and he came to a grinding halt.

The huge army stopped and groaned. The Lord of the Nasal dismounted and stood with his arms crossed, looking around and tapping his feet with displeasure. From the ranks of the army scuttled a small Dork engineer, puncture repair kit in hand. He began work on the front tyre, nervously looking up at the Nasal. He pulled out the cause of the puncture and, without looking at it, threw the badge reading, I'VE BEEN TO LOSTLOTION, at the boulders where the three Halfbits were hidden.

The badge struck Grumble between the eyes, so that Foodo had to quickly clamp his hand over the creature's mouth, as he let loose a string of unprintable four-letter words.

With the tyre fixed, The Morgue Lord took one last look around, sniffed the air suspiciously, then mounted his bike and pedalled off down the road with his minions in tow.

When the last of them had passed, Grumble grabbed Foodo's arm and pulled him towards The Staircase. 'Quick, quick, no time to waste.'

Stan was instantly on guard. 'Here, what's your hurry? They have all gone now and we need rest and food.'

'Stupid fat Halfbit, you always want to rest and eat. But what if they have only gone for a route march and come back?

'They are not coming back; they are off to cause trouble somewhere, and you know it. '

'Yes, and for that reason Stan, we must go. The Big Boy's battle is about to begin, so there isn't much time left. The one consolation is that the Crap-roads will slow them down a bit,' said Foodo. He moved towards the foot of The Staircase, not noticing Grumble grinning evilly at Stan.

The climb up several flights of stairs nearly did in the Halfbits. Nothing in their lives before had ever prepared them for this.

When they got to the top of The Spiral Staircase, Grumble urged them on, lying through his broken dentures, telling them how well they were doing. 'Now we have got that out of the way, we can go up The Sloping Stairs. They are longer, but much easier and, when we get to the top of those, Fatso can stuff his face and snore.'

'Not another stack of stairs. What comes after them?' moaned Stan.

'Wouldn't you like to know, Fatso,' mumbled Grumble under his breath.

'Come again?'

'You will know if you move faster,' answered Grumble with a smile.

Some hours later, after a gruelling climb, they reached the top. Stan, who was standing on a ledge, was the first to see what the next part of the journey had in store for them. He looked down the trail, into The Land of Morbid. 'Damn, bloody hell.' Then he turned and dragged Grumble by the throat up the last few steps. 'What the hell is that?' pointing to a tower with his other hand. 'I thought you said this way is secret. Is that apart from whoever lives there? How are we going to get past that?'

'I got past it twice, and even Smear-Gob got past it once. It is nothing more than a glorified guard-hut. There aren't many Dorks there; they will be needed for the war. They told Smear-Gob, that's why it is guarded by See-See TV. It is called by the Dorks, The Tower of The Silly Soundless Whatsits. The Whatsits are always broken or the Dorks are always asleep on duty. Trust Grumble, you won't have to worry about getting past that tower.'

'You seem very confident of that, Grumble. Why is that?' asked Foodo.

'That's easy: you are not going far that way.'

'What?'

'Err ... That way is far easier, you will see,' said Grumble quickly, adding, 'Trust us.'

But Stan didn't, and didn't want to.

They ate some food and rested, before setting off again into what, for the Halfbits, was the unknown. They travelled only a short way before they began to smell a filthy stench. It was the unholy stink of death, murder, and dead flesh. It was the unmistakable smell of Fast Food. As they came to the entrance of a tunnel, Grumble knew what it was, but didn't say its name. It was called Tore Ungodly, Sheblob's Larder.

'It smells awful, like dead Dork. I wonder how many have died in there. I can't go in. Isn't there another way?' asked Foodo.

'You know there is. We can always go back, fight our way through that big army and go the long way,' replied Grumble.

The Halfbits looked at each other, held their noses, and advanced into the darkness of the tunnel.

SHEBLOB`S LARDER

Grumble went in first, into the pitch black hole, into the kind of darkness that he had become so used to in the caverns of The Musty Mountains. He had then scarpered, leaving the Halfbits to discover that Grumble the Glib had gone in the gloom.

'Smear-gob!' shouted Foodo.

'Grumble, where are you? I swear I'm gonna kick you if you don't show yourself,' shouted Stan. 'He's tricked us, Mr Foodo. He wants us to fall down dark holes and die in here. He wants to take The Treasure off your dead body, but he's going to have to do it over mine,' said Stan.

'Well bless me, Stan Gamble, I don't know what I would do if you weren't here.'

'Your pack wouldn't be so light for a start.'

'Light! That's it! In my pack is Gadabout's Gift. The File of Facts has a light with it,' exclaimed Foodo. He took off his pack, and rummaged for the File of Gadabout. When he felt the cold silver metal of the front cover, he flicked open the fastening. The light was on the end of a flexible arm. Foodo found its switch and pushed it to the "ON" position. The passageway was lit for a few yards in front of them, so they edged forward slowly, oblivious of the attention that was been paid to them by an unseen foe. By the time they found out, it was too late.

Sheblob was suddenly in the tunnel before the Halfbits. She moved slowly in their direction, a great bulk of fat on spindly legs.

Foodo and Stan backed away, horrified.

'Quick, Mr Foodo, what does The File say about great big overweight, one-eyed spiders? There must be a spell somewhere in there!'

Foodo flicked the pages quickly until he got to S. 'Sperm Whale, Sphinx ... ah, here we go — Spiders,' He read out the invocation:

'AHA HERENDITALL ELATION ANATHEMA'

The instructions were to then turn the light to face the cover of The File, and thus Foodo did. The light reflected back off the polished silver in a powerful beam that burned into the eyes of the monster. Sheblob retreated down a side passage and the Halfbits made a dash for it. There is only one thing that will make a Halfbit run faster than they would for their supper, and that is if something is threatening to make them the supper. They knew not what they had stumbled upon, but Faraway's warnings scared the hell out of them.

That day went down in Halfbit folklore, for no Halfbit had ever, nor ever would, run that fast again. They had good reason to do so, for their pursuer was Sheblob the Large, last of the kin of Ungodliaunt. She was a vast monster, not unlike a waste disposal unit on legs, the only living creature in Muddy Earth to eat more than a Halfbit could. She ate almost anything that came her way. The only thing she hadn't eaten was Grumble — the effort wouldn't have been worth it — and he had promised her some Northern delicacy in exchange. Over the years, she had grown fat and bloated on fast food, and nothing came faster than the food from the Tower. The authorities had orders to catapult any Dork that had displeased The Hierarchy from the Tower. They usually ended up at the mouth of Sheblob's Larder, crumpled and bleeding. She called this Dentmucky Flied Goblin. Her favourite, however, was Dorkburgers and Hotdorks from Muckdorkalds.

Her hunger that day was for moist, miniature munches though, and no illuminated insect was going to stop her. As the Halfbits sped off down the wrong tunnel, Sheblob, with all the cunning of an overweight predator, took a shortcut to ambush her prey.

With Foodo being lighter, and his pack even more so, he soon put some distance between himself and the gasping Gamble.

Stan saw Foodo disappearing around a corner, with the light some distance ahead, and he shouted for the quicker Halfbit to slow down and wait for him.

Foodo, who was running flat out, was almost at the exit. He turned, and was about to shout, "No way" when he tripped over the long, outstretched leg of Sheblob. He went flying one way and the file the other, just as Stan turned the corner.

Sheblob emerged from her hiding place, snatched the Halfbit from the floor with one limb, and clubbed him unconscious with another.

In one flash, Stan saw his chance of winning millions, and his family heirloom, disappearing fast; that was, unless he did something quick, and that was almost impossible for a dull-witted, spud-planting Halfbit. However, this Halfbit had motives to motivate him. Sword in hand, he advanced on Sheblob, who was now leaving the tunnel.

When he was halfway there, something hit him from behind; it was Grumble. The wretched thing had been following closely, though he hadn't taken into account the light of the Halfbits and was still half blind from it, but he didn't want anything else spoiling his plan of finding The Treasure in Sheblob's leftovers. Stan staggered under the added few pounds that amounted to the weight of the skinny, shrivelled Smear-Gob. He was desperately trying to dislodge the creature, who was now strangling him with his bony forearm. He could hear Grumble's voice rasping in his ear, 'Who's the daddy now, Fatso?'

The creature's breath was hot on Stan's face and he decided, whatever happened after this, he would advise Grumble to see someone about his halitosis problem. Still, there was something else important to worry about now: Sheblob had disappeared with Foodo. Stan knew it was time for the last resort; he would use the ancient art of Halfbit self-defence called Plaipossum. This consisted of going rigid, toppling over and pretending to be dead.

Poor Grumble broke the fall of the fat Halfbit and his pack. The air gushed out of him, along with his dentures, and he let go of Stan instantly to rub his bony ribcage.

Stan struggled to his feet and watched him groveling on the ground, gasping for air.

When Grumble saw Stan, sword in hand, he quickly jumped to it. He stood, facing the Halfbit, looking for ways to grab the slow, fat fool's sword-arm but, when Stan started swinging wildly at him, he scrambled away, screeching and cursing about the lack of buses on this route. As he disappeared back into the gloom, he muttered, 'I will get you, fatso.'

Stan didn't chase after him, and instead headed after Sheblob, picking up the File with its light on the way.

THE ODDS AGAINST STANWITLESS

As Stan emerged from the tunnel, he saw Foodo lying on the ground, covered in some form of white glutinous substance. Sheblob loomed over him. From a gland in her huge, quivering body she was squeezing out the liquid that covered Foodo. Over the centuries of her existence, she had evolved ways of ridding her vast body of the by-products of Fast-Food. The gland oozed pure cholesterol and toxic trans-fats.

Stan still had the bet on his mind as he charged. On his first attack, he bounced off the thick, flabby, spongy hide of the creature.

Sheblob was overjoyed; firstly, the size of the rations, it seemed, had just doubled; secondly, the food had come to her, so she didn't even have to waste time and energy hunting it down. She wasn't bothered about the bag of bones; there was more meat on a Dork's dagger. She advanced on him, limbs swinging.

Stan dodged as best he could, looking desperately for any opening. A couple of times, he managed to jab his sword, hilt deep, into the layers of fat. These were like mere pinpricks to Sheblob for, in truth, his sword was only a dagger. Besides, it still would have taken him all day to carve up this monster, even if he had been Hewin Fallen's son, Chewin, the wielder of the sword Gorefang, which was once Anglehell, that was forged in the dim past by Hellhol, the Dark Elf of Nab Elfmutha, with which he slew the dragon Glaring, and gained the epitaph, "Chewin Chewinbar Glaring a Daggerin" (that story is told in The Harm I Kin Hewin). As Stan was starting to feel the pace, he suddenly remembered The File. He opened it and, as if by fate, it fell open on the spell for one-eyed insects. Only knowing the rudiments of written language (which Old Bilious Braggins had taught him, so that he could run to the betting shop for him), it was a struggle for him, trying to invoke the spell. On the third attempt, he somehow managed it:

'ON ELECTRIC LIGHT MODE,

A MANY PLATED DIODE.
THE NARROW SILVER LASER
FOR TURNING INTO PHASER.'

The light burned with a power never seen before. A small section of the silver cover extended outwards, exposing a magnifying glass. Then the metal arm holding the reading light moved into position between the silver cover and the lense. A piercing ray of pure light exploded from The File. As Stan moved the beam, it sheared through one of Sheblob's legs. The power within The File was beginning to grow, and Stan felt it throbbing. The light shot out in a succession of increasingly powerful bursts. One burst lanced Sheblob's body, burning through years of gluttony.

She screamed in agony as bits of blubber fell quivering from her. Not since that time she had tried to excrete the by-products of an armour-plated Dork she had once eaten, had she felt such pain. She wasn't used to her food biting back. She advanced, crippled, yet still determined.

Stan held out The File, as if to shield himself from the anticipated blows.

Sheblob was almost on top of the illuminated irritant and, as she looked down at the Halfbit, she stared down at her doom. Light burst from The File and exploded into her eye, giving her a major dose of bad corrective laser eye surgery. In excruciating agony, and totally blind, she retreated, knowing that she was beaten, her monstrous mauling days over. She lurched off to retire to The Slum Shady Mountain Home for Infirm Insects.

Stan hurried over to where Foodo lay covered in the white, congealed mess. Trying to free his companion was making him dizzy, but not on account of the effort or the lack of food. What he didn't know was that the strange, pasty glue's toxicity was coma inducing. He prodded Foodo. 'It's OK; the monster has gone now. You don't have to keep playing dead.' Foodo didn't move though, not a flicker. 'Come on, this is not the time for some extra sleep.' He was beginning to get worried now. He started to shake him and slapped his face several times. He even tried holding his nose closed and shaving off one of his eyebrows, but zilch. So Stan tried his last desperate trick. 'It is supper time, Mr Foodo. If you don't want yours, can I have it?' When Foodo didn't move, he knew he must be dead, like really dead.

Stan started to panic, and desperately tried to remember whether his bet was that he would get Foodo, or just the nose ring, to Horridruin. He knew he had now probably lost the return bet; however, he could still pick up the reward and payment for being The Nose Ring-breaker. So, looking at the positives, Grumble was gone — one less hungry mouth to feed — and a bonus payday. Well that's that.

So it was that Stanwitless Gamble took the nose ring of Sourone from the body of Foodo, son of Doggo, and headed along the tunnel towards the tower and the land of Morbid. He had not got very far when he heard the guttural sounds of several Dorks. 'Oh damn, that's all I need,' he cursed, sure that the Dorks would discover him. As the voices drew nearer, he suddenly remembered the nose ring's power. He slipped it from the toilet-chain that Foodo had so recently been wearing around his neck, and put it on his finger. Instantly, his mind reeled, and his thoughts went back to the first time The Grafter had caught him smoking Old Tipsy. With him being underage and still only a tweenager, The Grafter's idea of a cure was for Stan to smoke ten massive joints. After five he was sick; after ten, his world was spinning and everything had gone hazy. What he saw now, was very similar to that.

When he had adjusted to the strange sights on the periphery of his vision, like the Dorks marching past him in slow motion, he realised that the fight with Sheblob must have knocked some of the wax out of his ears, because he could quite clearly hear the Dorks somewhere down the tunnel as they met their compatriots. Their Kapitans greeted each other warmly.

'Hey, Growbag, you damn malingerer; found some way out of the fighting, have you?' said the first.

'Don't you take that tone with me, you bloody war-dodger. How's that comfortable penthouse of yours, Shagbag?'

Before they could come to blows, one of the other Dorks shouted, 'Hey, hey, look: a pie.'

Stan wondered what the hell they were talking about, so he crept back down the tunnel to take a look. Standing around Foodo were a number of Dorks, all jabbering.

'Shut up, you horrible lot. Your squeakings will bring her back,' said Shagbag.

'Shut up yourself,' retorted Growbag. 'This is one of her pies she isn't coming back for. Haven't you noticed all the flesh around here? Looks like someone's done a bad plastic surgery job on Queen Lardass.'

'Right then lads, lift it up; we're taking this back to the tower.'

'Whoa there a minute, Shag. I know this is only a little pie, but why can't some of my lads have a slice?' said Growbag, to loud applause.

'Morons! Orders from Slugbooze say anything found alive on this path is to be sent to Bad-Odour.'

'Haven't they got enough food? What do they want with a dead meat-pie anyway?'

'You idiot, he isn't dead; he's just stunned. Sheblob likes her food to be playful and warm,' Shagbag said with a sneering voice.

With that, the Dorks lifted Foodo and carried him off towards the tower. Stan's brain went skew-whiff; the odds had just doubled again. He couldn't believe it: he had left a fortune just lying in the road.

Growbag looked weary. 'Well, you've got this one, but what about the Big Warrior Surgeon who skewered Sheblob? He must still be running around out here. I think you should sort that problem out, or you might end up as Wag-meal.'

The Dorks carrying Foodo had now reached the tower and Stan, as usual, was lagging behind. He reached the gates just in time to have them shut them in his face, quicker than if he was a political canvasser. He wondered whether it would be worth the risk trying to save Foodo now. The odds were clearly stacked against him. However, he was a hopeless gambler, and he was still unsure if the Elves would actually honour the bet if the Foodo factor was missing. So Stan's mind was made up: he would try to free his friend, Foodo.

THE RETINUE OF THE KING

BEING THE THIRD VOLUME OF
THE LORD OF THE GRINS

Pipsqueak awoke, looked back at The Grand Alf, and said, 'Are we there yet?'

'No! Go back to sleep and don't annoy me again, or I'll be angry with you.'

'You can't be, because I'm not angry at the moment.'

The Grand Alf swore under his breath, and asked Ill-Farter for patience.

Pipsqueak, oblivious of his danger, prattled on. 'How will we know when we are there then?'

The Grand Alf, trying to keep his rising anger at bay, replied, 'You will know, Peregrinate Talk, when you develop a splitting headache.'

'Oh, are we going to an inn? I'd love a good drink right now.'

'No! I'm going to use your head to knock on the gates with, if you don't SHUT UP!'

Pipsqueak now finally got the message and dozed off again, mumbling nonsense even in his sleep. About an hour later, the Halfbit woke to the sound of conversation.

'Here are ten coins of the realm, my good Wingold,' said The Grand Alf.

Pipsqueak saw the wizard passing some money to a large man.

'Ah yes, now I remember you Mythroving. Since you know the seven secret handshakes, I will let you pass.' Then he noticed the Halfbit, 'What in Muddy Earth is that? It looks like a stunted dwarf, or could it be another of your lovechildren that you are trying to foster out?' 'SHUSH! Wingold, that's our secret!' exclaimed the wizard, looking around nervously.

Pipsqueak heard the metallic sound of more coins passing hands.

'Oops, sorry, and thank ye lord,' replied the gratefully richer soldier of Minus Thrifty.

'This is a valueless Halfwit of the North,' said The Grand Alf, grateful to change the subject.

'What have you brought him for? Surely it is big, strong,

powerful warriors, like our lord's son, Borrowit, that we need now, right?'

Pipsqueak may have been dozy from sleep, or just naturally dozy, and he certainly wasn't the sharpest tool in the box, but he normally knew when someone was being less than complimentary. 'Well, I'm more of a warrior than Borrowit. The only thing strong and powerful about him now is probably the smell. What's more, I am a Halfbit, not a man, and of more value than your perishing Borrowit.'

'What's the halfwit on about? Is he as mentally deficient as he is vertically?' laughed Wingold.

'That story will be told before the Stool of The Stalwart,' replied The Grand Alf. 'We don't have much time, for trouble draws near.'

'Well, tell us something new. We sussed that out the moment you turned up,' said Wingold.

'Then I say to you and your compatriots get ready for war; sharpen your swords and your axes. If you haven't any, a dagger will do. Failing that, get out your butter knives. If you can't fight, you can make sandwiches, for soon there will be other Halfbits here and they are a hungry folk.'

This gave rise later to the story that hordes of ferocious Halfbits would be turning up to fight for Minus Thrifty, because someone had told them that the Dorks would beat them to the food.

They rode in through the main gate and wound their way through the winding maze of streets that spiralled their way to the upper levels.

After twenty minutes or so, Pipsqueak asked, 'Where are we going Grand Alf? Are you lost?'

'No, you halfwit; we are heading for the second gate. It is hard to find. Part of the defence of the city is its maze of streets.'

'I think the whole city is amazing.'

'Keep quiet! I am trying to remember which turn to take.' He choose to turn right. This led to a street with a gateway at the end.

'Do all Gondourians look the same?' asked a more than usually puzzled Pipsqueak.

'No! Stop asking stupid questions. They are all different, just like Halfbits.'

'Well, that must be Wingold's twin at the gate then,' replied the Halfbit. The expected rebuff died on the wizard's lips when he saw who was greeting him.

'Sorry,' said Wingold. 'I forgot to tell you, the War Department have changed all the road signs.'

'What the hell for? The Dorks are more stupid than Halfbits and can't read road signs!'

'The Lord Denizen said it was to confuse the Great Harbinger of Doom himself.'

'Who? Sourone or The Witchy-King?'

'Neither, Lord Mythroving. He said it was some old conjuring charlatan from the North, calling himself The Grand Alf,' explained the sentry.

'Oh, I didn't know you were so famous down South,' said Pipsqueak to the wizard.

'What do you KNOW ABOUT ANYTHING? And have you ever thought about how you are going to eat without teeth?' said the wizard, eyes flashing with anger. Turning back to Wingold, he asked, 'Ok then, what's the direction code to get to the top?'

'Just keep turning left, right, left, right, left, and in a week you will get to The Citydwell of Denizen; or you could just take that cable car there.' He pointed at a square wooden and glass box, ten feet in front of them.

'That wasn't here the last time I was in Minus Thrifty. Where has it come from?' asked the wizard.

'Duh, that's obvious — it came down that metal rope from up there,' said Pipsqueak, pointing to the upper levels, trying to sound clever.

The Halfbit, not for the first time, found himself in the horizontal position, with a ringing sound in his ears he had become so familiar with. As such, he didn't hear Wingold's explanation that the cable car had been installed by King Drain Ironyloot's Department of Dodgy Dwarven Developers, who had stolen it from their own ski lodge on Carbuncle, therefore having to replace it before the start of the new season. Having "fallen" off Shinyflax, Pipsqueak was now staggering around. He stumbled toward the cable car, intent on discovering the delights of the interior.

The wizard leapt from his horse with all the speed and agility of someone with a thousand year old arthritis problem. He gained the vehicle just as Pipsqueak began insanely pressing buttons and pulling levers, all the time saying, 'Oh, I wonder what that one does.' Too late to be stopped, Pipsqueak hit the start button and the cable car shot upwards at full speed.

The Halfbit was looking out of the window, delighted. 'Ooh, look at that, and come and see this!'

The Grand Alf wasn't interested though, as he was frantically trying to reset the controls. Failing miserably, he decided to take the scientific approach and coolly smashed the control panel with Humdinger. The car started to slow, but not quickly enough. It smashed into the buffers, throwing the occupants onto the landing platform at the feet of the Guard Attendants. These Guards had been specially picked and wore the ceremonial uniform that had descended from the bodyguard of The Six Sea-Kings, otherwise known as The VI Kings. These were Tar-Anonymous I, Erik I, Kilocycle and Kilohertz. For some reason, the last two were never included on The Roll of Kings; they were Pop I, and Tugboat Will I. The Grand Alf stood up, dislodging shards of glass from his beard.

'Oh dear, look what you have done. You'll be in trouble now.' Pipsqueak said, seeing the damaged cable car.

The Grand Alf's eyes flashed dangerously at the Halfbit as he dragged him by the collar towards the Citydwell.

In the middle of the courtyard, Pipsqueak caught sight of a strange tree. 'Why has someone thrown an old plastic Yowltide Tree into that smelly pond?'

'You pint-sized pillock — that is the last known replica of Nimbus the Fake, copied from the images of Galoretinsel and Teleperspex. The only reason it is in such a state is that it is the King's responsibility to pay for its upkeep. It is said that, if the King ever comes back, then he will find a new one. Now that reminds me, don't mention anything about a King or the nose ring to Denizen; he has been known to explode in a boiling rage at the thought of being demoted. So don't utter the names of Paragon or Foodo.'

'Is Foodo going to be a king?'

'Don't be so damn stupid.'

'Well you said don't mention a king.'

'I was talking about The Nose Ring and Foodo, and The King and Paragon,' said The Grand Alf, through clenched teeth.

'What? Stupor, a king? He couldn't fit a crown under that hood. Plus, he's far too scruffy. What's he going to be: King of the Road?' replied Pipsqueak.

The Grand Alf was at least a little more convinced that the secret was safe with the Halfbit, and decided to trust to luck. They walked to The Sliding Doors of Citydwell, which opened by means of Elektrickery and entered into a vast hall that had rows of large, identical gold coloured plastic statues on either side. When Pipsqueak drew nearer, he could see that someone had written names in silver spraypaint over the name of Ozkha. If he had been able to read, he would have made out names like Tarragon Fullastuf and Minustan the Pale. There were a further two with the names Erik and Ernie, while the last statues in the line had no names against them. When they reached the head of the hall, they found an old man there, sat on a footstool. The stool was positioned in front of a magnificent carven throne, upon which was a placard that read, POSITION VACANT.

The Grand Alf spoke then, and said to the old man, 'Hail Stalwart and Governor of Gondour, Denizen, son of Egalitarian. I come to counter the dark tide.'

The old man looked at the wizard and said, 'By the dark floorboards of my drawing room, how are we going to counter the tide without my Borrowit? With nothing more than a useless half-pint that stood by whilst the greatest warrior of this Stage died.'

'For your information, the word is Halfbit, not half-pint or halfwit,' said the disgruntled Pipsqueak.. 'And what's more, Borrowit wasn't anywhere near as good as Stupor. He could kill ten Dorks at a time with his king-sized sword.'

The Grand Alf growled and cuffed the Halfbit, then turned to The Stalwart. 'Verily, this is one of the twits, Pipsqueak; the other is being held at arms-length by Theocrat of Bovine. He is, as he says, a Halfbit and one of the party that left Dimladsbliss, and he witnessed the death of your son.'

The Stalwart looked at Pipsqueak. 'How could a runt like you have survived, when a big strong man like my son couldn't?'

'A Halfbit can be killed by one arrow; your son had about one hundred stuck in him. It was a good thing Borrowit was so large, or both us Halfbits couldn't have hidden behind his big butt. The problem with all his body piercings though, was that he got so heavy that he fell on top of us as we tried to make a quick exit.' The Halfbit then strode forward, towards the old man, who was holding the bits of Borrowit's broken bugle. 'I would like to honour my debt to you and your son, by helping to somehow repair the damage.' He started to fumble in his pockets. Now, the only thing slightly magical about Halfbits is the amount of rubbish they can fit in their pockets, which is another reason why, all those years ago, Grumble had stood no chance of guessing what Bilious had in his pockets. The first thing out of Pipsqueak's pocket was some sticky tape, which he held up to The Stalwart proudly. Denizen glared at the Halfbit, so he quickly put it away and pulled out some glue. The Stalwart's face turned red, then purple, leaving the Halfbit under no illusion that repairing the bugle wasn't on Denizen's mind. Pipsqueak quickly said to him, 'Well, the only other thing I have is my sword.'

The Stalwart looked at the thing Pipsqueak was holding, and began to laugh. 'What would I want with that? I've got a drawer full of them. I even have some antique ones like that. Tell me, where did you find it?'

Pipsqueak looked a bit sheepish, and mumbled something about it falling into his pocket when he had been freed from the Burrow-mound of The Soul-Kings of Cant-Hum, by Tom Bombastic.

'Are you trying to say that you have met Iarwun Bas-tada? That is a tall tale to weave.'   'It is true, Denizen,' explained The Grand Alf. 'They were caught by a Barriwhite,'

'Well, if you wish to pay me back in some way, then you can enter into my service, bonding yourself and your children's children to be my servants.'

'Ok,' answered Pipsqueak, turning to the wizard and whispering that he had gotten off easy, as he had no children, so his grandkids were safe. Then he turned to Denizen, 'You've got a deal, but just a couple of questions first: do I get extra rations now that I am a warrior, and why do you sit on that tiny footstool when there is a big, comfy, king-sized chair up there?' The thud of The Grand Alf's staff against his head was barely registered by the Halfbit, as he was preoccupied with the sudden appearance of the constellation of Manofmacaroni, complete with shiny helm and all, dancing before his eyes.

The Grand Alf dragged the limp halfbit, who now had a king-sized headache, towards the doors, and out to the accommodation that had been prepared for them.

When he awoke the next morning, he heard The Grand Alf as he left room saying, 'I'm in a hurry, and seeing as you have had a long rest, you can check on Shinyflax. These beastly people are wise enough to be good to me, but horses are a different matter. They are more skilled at cooking them than looking after them.'

With the wizard gone, he rose and ate the breakfast that had been left for him. When he had finished, he ate The Grand Alf's leftovers, then went in search of anything else edible. As he left his quarters, he ran into a dishevelled, scruffy, ill-shaven soldier, who obviously hadn't managed to make roll call that morning.

The man introduced himself with alcohol-laden breath. 'My name is Beerygrog, son of Barrelborn. Are you Perryangin the half-pint,' he said, licking his lips at the thought of anything drink-related.

'That's Peregrinate the Halfbit,' replied Pipsqueak warily.

'Yeah, well, whatever. I've been sent to give you a guided tour. Where would you like to start?'

'I would like to see something of interest.'

'There is an interesting inn around the corner.'

'Well, I meant something of more interest to Halfbits, like food.'

'There's an inn around the corner that sells food.'

'I was hoping that there would be more than one place to get food.'

'Why didn't you say? There are plenty of interesting inns that sell food. So, it's a pub crawl then!' said an overjoyed Beerygrog. 'Erm, um, you've got some money, I hope. I don't get paid until tomorrow.'

Pipsqueak had been given some coins of the realm by The Grand Alf, in an attempt to keep him out of his way. So he decided it would be worth taking the soldier with him, as he seemed to know so many of the inn places. They walked the little way to the first inn, called The Guard and Fence. Beerygrog told him that this was his regiment's watering hole.

The big soldier approached the bar and spoke to the Tender. 'Greetings, Gutrot. I have special permission from The Stalwart to be here. We have a new recruit and I have to teach him the regimental customs and drinking songs.'

'What'll you have then?' growled Gutrot.

Beerygrog looked at the money he had been handed by Pipsqueak and, thinking hard of the best way to make it last and keep the greedy Halfbit happy, he replied, 'Two pints of lager and a packet of crisps, please.'

'What flavour?'

Pipsqueak, who was sat next to the soldier, answered with a more than usual perplexed look on his face, 'Well, I was hoping for a really strong, lager flavour actually.'

'Not the beer. The crisps, blockhead!' shouted Gutrot.

Pipsqueak had only ever had Snore crisps, and they only came in one flavour: Muddy Earth. This was due to the Halfbits' total lack of knowledge concerning hygiene and their habit of cooking spuds without washing them. So, he asked for his favourite.

'We ain't got any. We've got Fried Rat, Boiled Rat, Smoky BarBQ Rat, Rat or Two i.e., Spicy Rat, or cheese and onion.'

Beerygrog pulled a face and said, 'Ugh! Cheese and onion; that's disgusting. Give me some Fried Rat, please.'

Once they had been served, they settled down at one of the tables and started to tell each their stories. Pipsqueak told the tale of his life, which would have been considered a tale of someone else by anyone who actually knew him.

Beerygrog then told of his life as a soldier of Gondour. 'We are elite Special Forces, and have been raised to fight as shock troops in the forefront of battle. Our job is to steal ammunition,' said the proud man.

'What's the name of your unit?' asked the Halfbit.

'We are the 180th Target Force of the Bullseye Brigade. Our nickname is The Arrowcatchers.'

Pipsqueak nearly choked on his beer. Even a stupid Halfbit like him knew what that meant, and he began formulating ideas for how to get a job in the palace kitchens.

After visiting a few more inns, Pipsqueak's mouth started to flap as he got carried away with the sense of his own importance. Before long, he was telling people he was the son of the Halfbit head honcho. From this, word went out into the city that a Halfbit prince was going to call upon hordes of Halfbits from the North. It was said that each Halfbit could eat three times his own body weight and that the Dork army would be no match

180

for these peckish parasites, and would be eaten alive. The people cheered when Lord Pipsqueak passed by them, and dubbed him Ennui Phewenough, the Halfbit Prattling.

Finally, inside their umpteenth inn, Beerygrog rose unsteadily, and said something about being on guard in thirty minutes.

Pipsqueak excused the scruffy man, and jokingly said, 'It will take you more than half an hour to sort yourself out.'

'You're mistaken, friend; I am already that amount late. I should be guarding The Warning Woodpile by now.'

'What's so important about a bonfire?'

'This one is an intruder alert to warn our allies, the Ruminates, of any imminent attack,' slurred the big man.

'Won't the Ruminates know when they are being attacked by Nimmynants, whatever they are?'

It wouldn't be the last time that the Halfbit would leave a Gondourian unable to understand his prattle. All Beerygrog could say as he left was, 'You may want to seek out my son, Beerguild; he is training to be an innkeeper at The School Inn for bartenders. He will be in The Old Gitshouse by now, in the lowest circle of Minus Thrifty. It is at the rear end, near the sewers and is known as The Cellardrain Path. However, be careful if it rains. We call it The Damptights Street when the sewers overflow.'

It was along that street where, sometime later, Pipsqueak ran into the son of Beerygrog. He was standing by the wayside with a gang of hooded youths. When he approached their location, they stepped out to block his path. Taking him for a kid from out of town, they looked him up and down. The first thing they noticed was his total lack of branded name footwear, so they demanded his dinner money. Nothing could have been more fatal for the gang of yobs than the thought of losing food was to a Halfbit. Pipsqueak flew into berserker mode. Pieces of hoodies went flying every which way, followed by the cowards wearing them. The Halfbit then cornered the slowest of them, who instantly wet himself and started babbling about human rights. The lad also added that he would call the law, who would turn up and arrest him for having the nerve to stand up for himself. Pipsqueak demanded the name of the miscreant. In between the odd sob, he named himself Beerguild, son of Beerygrog of The Blahguards. 'Then today is your lucky day, for I am Pipsqueak the

Halfbit and I know your father. It was he that suggested I would find you here.'

'Oh no, this is getting worse. My father will really know I've been playing truant once you've blabbed to him. I'll be put in front of The Joyfineall Court, where I'll have to go through all those phony hard luck stories of my poor life again. My mother left me and my drunken dad for a wife-beating, cheating, gambling, no-good loser, but she thought he was OK because he was young, tall and good looking.' Beerguild gave a strained sob, whilst peeking between his hands to see what effect this was having on Pipsqueak.

The Halfbit, who came from a large, extended family (and unfortunately still knew most of them), began to feel sorry for the lad and started to cry along with him. Before long, they were leaning on each other and sharing in each other's woes.

'Last Yowltide I didn't get the latest designer gear,' wailed the brat.

'Why not?'

'My father bought me a home brew kit instead.'

'My hamster died last year,' bawled Pipsqueak.

'How?' asked the sobbing lad.

'I ran out of snacks one night.'

After about half an hour, they were chatting like close friends. Pipsqueak had decided to forgive the young lad, while Beerguild thought to himself, there's a mug born every day. However, he decided that there may still be some advantage to tagging along with this stranger. So he invited him to watch the arrival of the Outlandish Overlords with him at the Main Gate.

They arrived just in time to see Forgon the Flat, Lord of Lostdeknack, leading a few hundred farmers carrying ploughs. They were desperately hoping someone in Minus Thrifty could turn the tools into weapons. The men were strong and proud though, and were all too glad to help fight Dorks, rather than their battle-axe wives. Next came the men of Ringlow Dial, marching with their lord's son, Defonnin. From the land of Morefood and the Blacktooth Male came Droolman and his sons, Droolin and Devourin, accompanied by five hundred bow-legged men. From Fallonass, the Landslang, came Gollygosh, leading a line of scantily clad men. From Lamexcuse came a few Ill-men, and a sick note from their captain. Some Fish-wives arrived too, turning the ether blue with their cursing. Then came Hurlyouin the Hairy, with a few hundred men wearing green galoshes. Last of all came the magnificent site of The Lord of the Dolt Amlost Shipyards: Himhadrill son of Dadhadrill. He was leading the troops of Horse and Foot, carrying before them their banner of The Ship and Swan Public House. It was told that Himhadrill was descended from Himrestalot, a Neomanorealmen Boat-Builder and a wandering Silly-Elf Maiden, who had been lost. She was named Missfellas.

When the last men had entered the city, the gates closed and a sign was fixed on it, reading, AWAY ON HOLIDAY. PLEASE CALL BACK IN A FEW MONTHS. As the gates clanged shut, Pipsqueak's heart sank. He was trapped, and it hadn't taken long for him to realise this. The Halfbit and the young lad parted company at that point, and Pipsqueak found his way back to the room he was sharing with The Grand Alf.

When he arrived, the place was empty and dark. He stumbled around the room and banged his head on the table which resulted in him being stunned more than usual. He fell backwards onto the floor, and remained still.

About an hour or so later, The Grand Alf returned. He promptly entered the room, tripped over the Halfbit and fell flat on his face. He leapt up, roaring and shouting, found the light, and shone it onto the face of the snoring Halfbit. He grabbed the dozy Pipsqueak who, by now, was quickly wakening. 'You stupid Halfbit, why aren't you sleeping on a bed?'

Looking around the now lit room, Pipsqueak said, 'It's on the wrong side of the table.'

'Then why didn't you move it?'

'Oh, that table is too big and heavy for me to move on my own.'

'Not the table; the bed, you moronic midget.'

'Why move the bed? It's the table that's in the wrong place,' replied Pipsqueak.

'Then why not go around it, fool?'

'I couldn't see it in the dark, and I didn't know where the light was.'

'It was on the table, where we left it,' said The Grand Alf, who was beginning to foam at the mouth.

'Yeah, but if I had moved the table, then I still wouldn't have

183

found the light,' said Pipsqueak, thinking himself awfully clever. The Halfbit saw a familiar set of dancing lights, and darkness descended as he settled back into his sleeping position.

THE PARTING OF THE GREY MATTER

The Grand Alf and Pipsqueak disappeared into the distance, leaving behind Paragon, Legless, Grimy and Messy.

'Well, where to now?' asked Grimy.

'Anywhere there's an inn, I'd say,' answered Legless hopefully.

'We are going to Minus Thrifty, by way of Udderas. We go to war with The Riders of Ridicule,' said Paragon.

'Then Ill-Farter help us,' said a worried Legless.

They gathered their gear and joined the Ruminates as they set off towards Udderas.

A few miles down the road, a rider with a rather large backside charged to the front of the column shouting, 'My Lord, there are men on horses behind our rear,'

'Strange, young Fulrear, how you managed to see past yours,' joked Theocrat.

'Nay Lord, I heard them in the distance complaining of the smell,' replied the young rider, unabashed.

'That cannot be, for the Dwarf and the Halfbit are up at the front,' laughed Legless.

'What smell? I can't smell anything,' said Messy.

'Well, aren't you the lucky one,' said Paragon.

By now the riders had drawn close, and Earmore shouted back into the darkness, 'Stop! Who rides through The Muck of Bovine?'

'The Muck of Bovine; so that's the smell,' said the stranger. 'My name is Halbadass Dulladan, Stranger of the North. My companions and I, are looking for Paragon, son of Paramount. We heard he was up to his neck in The Muck,'

'And you would be almost right,' said Paragon, as he looked at Messy sat next to him. Paragon dismounted, and the two Dulledain stood talking to each other.

Halbadass told Paragon how many of The Dulledain had stayed at home, giving excuses like headache, sore throat and runny nose.

'Well how many came then?'

'Oh, quite a few.'

'How many, Halbadass?'

'A few more than I expected,' said Halbadass unconvincingly.

'How many is a few?' exclaimed The Mainman of The Dulledain forcefully.

'Well, only a very few, to be precise; about thirty. However, we have brought the Elven Bothers, Ellovaman and Ellovabovva. They are always looking for a fight.'

'Well, I suppose thirty is better than none.'

'Not if the strength of their arms match the strength of their wit,' whispered Theocrat to Earmore.

They continued their journey, with Paragon riding alongside Halbadass and the Elven Bothers. Ellovabovva passed on a message from his father, Elbow. 'If you need to be quick, take the shortcut, along The Road of the Dead-heads'

'I don't think I will be quick to take that road,' said a worried Paragon.

Later that night, they reached The Wornbog. There they ate and slept, none more so than Messy.

In the morning, he was woken by Grimy and Legless.

'Wake up, sludgerat and get out of your sty,' said the Elves. 'My word, getting you small brothers up takes some doing.'

Scratching his green, matted hair, Messy yawned and asked where Paragon was.

'He is in the Chamber of the Bog,' replied Grimy. 'He went there last night to sit and think, or something like that. With him went Halbadass.'

The three of them set off to find the others. On the road they ran into Theocrat and Earmore, who were arguing about the pros and cons of pan lids as cheek guards. The King informed them of The Weaponsmake of Udderas, where the Ruminates were turning everything they could lay their hands on into weapons. Many a chef or housewife would find their sharpest knife tied to a mop or brush handle in the days to come. Messy offered up his steak knife, which by now was one of the most dangerous weapons in Muddy Earth, for it was so dirty that it would give either food or blood poisoning.

'Glibly will I take it. Arise now, Espouse of the Muck of

Bovine, and be rare with good fortune,' said Theocrat, desperately trying to avoid touching Messy or his knife. The King then asked Earmore and the others of the whereabouts of Paragon.

The Stranger of the North reappeared at that moment. 'I have troubles of the mind, and have seen things that are scary. I feared so much that I have had to change my person.'

'Was the Old Tipsy that strong?' asked Earmore.

'I have heard, Theocrat, that you go to Dunharrowing. When will you get there?' asked Paragon.

'Three-and-a-half bit days until we arrive, then you will see the full Bluster of Bovine.'

'Three-and-a-half-bit days. That is slow going.'.

'We have to stop every night to get drunk on mead, just to keep the courage up,' replied The Lord of the Muck.

'Then me and my lot must be off. We need more haste. We will take a shortcut through The Road of the Dead-heads.'

'The Road of the Dead-heads! You fool,' exclaimed Theocrat, to the unanimous agreement of The Dulledain. 'That is no place for living men,'

'Alas Paragon, I hoped we could party on our way to war. If you take that dark path, I fear you will never read the Sunny Gazette again,' said Earmore.

'Fear no more, Earmore; I have a spare copy I keep for my toilet. I will drink your mead and sing your blustery battle-songs with you again, even if I have to fight through the whole army of Morbid to get to your toga party.'

The Heir of Evenduller and his retinue parted company then with the Ruminates, and went their way. The Riders of Ridicule took the Halfbit Meretricious Brandishmuck with them, for none of Paragon's retinue had the space or the will to carry the smelly creature.

As the Ruminates thundered off into the distance, Paragon and his companions turned back to The Tower of the Bog. Legless commented to Paragon that he looked a bit worse for wear, and added that he was surprised not to get an invite to The Strangers' reunion party. He also enquired as to the name of the brew that had given him such a hangover.

'Nay, I'm sorry my boozing buddy, but t'was not the drink that drained my dashing good looks.'

'The only thing dashing about your looks is the speed with which they left you, and I fear The Old Tipsy has addled your brains, my plastered pal.'

'I have spoken to Sourone on the Seeing Phone.'

'You looked into that cursed Phone of Visisee! The Grand Alf was scared to even text Sourone,' said Grimy.

'Yes, but you forget, friend Grimy, this is The Seeing Phone of Everdull,' said Paragon. 'Its operation manual is one of the heirlooms of my family, and it is genetically encoded to my D.N.A through my bloodline. It has hidden areas of access that can only be gained through interfacing with The Ring of Barry, here worn on my finger. Neither Sourman nor Sourone could use its full potential. So I mocked The Lord of The Dank Tower in my disguise of an Ancient King of Another Realm. I texted him saying that, if he was lonely sometime, then he could give me a ring. Then I asked him if he nose of any way to clean old gold. It was at that point I showed myself by Visilink. I could see that he was in a red rage, so I smiled and showed him Andrex the Reformed Sword, then waved and smiled again, asking him if his phone did this, and switched it off.'

'That will make him really mad.'

'Yes, and in his insane rage, he will make big mistakes. I made him think I was in Minus Thrifty.'

'Then he will attack right away.'

'The Dwarf isn't as stupid as he looks,' said Legless.

'You'll look stupid without any teeth, Elf,' Grimy replied hotly.

Paragon once again had to step between the two companions. 'We must take the shortcut along The Road of the Dead-heads, for I have received information by WAP alert that Sourone has already planned a sneak attack from the South. Elbow sent word with his sons to remember the words of Maltbreath the Beerseer who, when drunk once said,

THE DEAD-HEADS AWAKEN,
FOR THE TIME WILL COME FOR THE
OAFBREEDERS TO STAND BEFORE
THE STONE OF HEDWRECK,
AND SWEAR AT THE HEIR OF HIM
WHO PUT THE ROTTEN CURSE ON THEM.

188

So who wants to show me how brave they are, by following me through The Hating Valley?' finished Paragon, as he headed along the path which led to the door.

'I will follow you, for I don't fear The Bogeyman,' said Legless, as he sneered at the distressed Dwarf.

Now Dwarves lived most of their lives in the deep, dark places of the world yet, even so, they lived in fear of spooky spectres. Grimy had no wish to meet The Phalanx of the Phantasmagoria, but he also had no wish to be seen as more frightened than the girly Elf. So he squeaked at the top of his voice, 'I'm not scared either. You won't find a more fearless Dwarf this side of Muddy Earth.'

'You wouldn't find a fearless Dwarf anywhere in Muddy Earth,' laughed Legless, as he disappeared down the hole.

Finding himself standing alone, Grimy dashed after the others, shouting, 'Hey, wait for me.' As he entered, he heard a steady knocking sound, growing louder. He only realised some time later that the sound was in fact being made by the armour around his knee area.

So began the journey to The Hill of Hedwreck and their meeting with The Dead-heads. Of that journey, Grimy could only remember the knocking sounds, the need to change his undergarments, and the sound of shuffling, mumbling and moaning that followed close behind them. The smell of decay was ever-present, but he was oblivious to it, for he smelt just as bad.

Only once did any of the retinue look back; it was Legless, searching for a bottle of Ruminate Rum in his rucksack, who saw the shambling swarm that had been following them. He almost put the bottle back, but decided to take a big swig anyway. Turning to the Dwarf, he said, 'Don't look now, but we have the whole army of The Deathless Dead-heads following us.'

A look of absolute horror crossed Grimy's face, as he realised that he had used up the last of his clean underwear from Lostlotion.

Some hours later, they reached The Hill of Hedwreck. Sat atop the hill was the stone that Evenduller had brought from Arghmeanyloss and the wreck of Neomanor. Upon that stone had the son of Everdull cursed the men of that place, with the words, 'Go rot in Hell', for they had drunk into the night and overslept, therefore missing the early call for the Dork-bash that had led to the end of The Second Stage and the umpteenth downfall of Sourone, The Dank Lord of Bad-Odour.

Paragon strode to the top of the hill and, turning to the horde, he said, 'Why have you come, Oafbreeders?'

'We have nothing better to do,' came a shout from the back.

'We wanted to see what you were doing before we ate you,' said a voice from somewhere nearer, which set Grimy's knees knocking again.

'Where is your king? It is to him I would speak,' said Paragon.

There was an uneasy murmuring from the crowd, followed shortly by a loud hissing, as a rotting old man with a rusty crown on his head stepped forward. 'I was the King, but they blamed me for our predicament. I forgot to set the alarm, so they stripped me of my title. Now I am King-shorn of The Dead-heads.'

'How would you like to lead your men again? Join me, and I will release you from the curse of starring in B-movies and computer games like Residue Evil,' said Paragon.

The King contemplated this, for he was indeed sick of being dismembered and shot in the Dawn, Day, Night and One Hour After Breakfast, of the Dead-heads series of films. He had even been one of the principal dancers in Jack Michaelson's video of his huge hit, Stiller. He and all The Dead-heads could only find work as zombie extras, and were getting sick of being typecast but, because they weren't members of the union, they didn't have a leg to stand on. 'Who are you to promise us release from our rotten curse?' asked the King.

'I am Paragon, son of Paramount, Alesser Heir of Everdull's son, Evenduller.'

'Suppose you'll have to do then, seeing as there is nothing better. Where is the fight to be?' said the King.

'We go to Pellagra upon Arduous, and when that place is clean of the disease of Sourone, I will release you,' replied Paragon.

'Well, what are we waiting for? Come on lads,' shouted The Once and Future King. At that they arose as one and, picking up various limbs that had fallen off, they followed Paragon down the hill.

Legless turned to him and said, 'I hope these rotters don't lose their heads when it comes to a fight,'

'I'd be more worried if when we got there they turned out to be armless,' replied Ellovabovva.

So they started for Gondour, and the war. As they went, the battle song of The Dead-heads could be heard throughout the valleys:

'WE ARE THE MANY MOULDY MEN.
WE APPEAR ON SCREEN, NOW AND THEN.
WE STAR IN FILMS WITHOUT A PLOT,
WHILE OUR BODIES SLOWLY ROT.

WE'D LOVE TO GO AWAY TO WAR,
BECAUSE WE MISSED ONE ONCE BEFORE.
THAT'S WHY WE ARE A BLOODY MESS.
WE'D LIKE OUR SORROW TO BE LESS.

THINGS COULD NOT BE REALLY WORSE,
BECAUSE OF IDIOT BOY'S ROTTEN CURSE.
WE MET THE FOOL UPON THE HILL,
AND ALL WE HAD TO DO WAS KILL.

FAIL, FAIL AND FALL APART,
TILL YOUR BREATH SMELLS LIKE A FART.
WAIT AROUND WITH LITTLE HOPE,
FOR THE RETURNING OF THE DOPE.'

THE BLUSTER OF BOVINE

Theocrat, King of the Muck, along with his company, returned smugly from the defeat of Sourman, and came to Dunharrowing. He was met there by Dunghere, Chief of the Harrowingdull, who told the King of how The Grand Alf, upon Shinyflax, had passed through the town quicker than fast food through a Dork, shouting something about mustard and bovine.

'I found that somewhat offensive, as we don't eat beef. Then came a thing that filled us with dread and gloom; it blotted out the very light from our lives,' said Dunghere.

'Oh no! Tory Blur hasn't returned again, has he?' asked Theocrat.

'No, something with even bigger wings than his ears flew over Milkingshed, screeching and wailing, leaving men crying in pain,' replied Dunghere.

'Sounds like Slimon Cowhell is working for Sourone Inc. TV's Flop Idol, and sent the latest winner to harass us.'

'Yes, my lord, maybe it is so; yet we ran and hid like frightened rabbits at the start of the hunting season,' said the chief.

'Well, you can no longer malinger here. Tell your womenfolk they will live hand-to-mouth for the next few months. Go to your kitchens and retrieve your weapons and armour, for we ride to war.'

They rode on, heading for Old Dunharrowing. Word had gone before them to the four corners of Bovine, that there was to be a bluster. A bluster usually took the form of a massive festival, where the King paid for all the mead. The idea behind this was that all the men would drink until they were drunk. They would then sing many bragging songs and be unable to back down from the fight the following day. This process would be repeated many times on the way to a battle. When they arrived at Old Dunharrowing, it was full of Bulls-Hitters singing songs of heroic deeds that only existed in their own minds. When they saw the King, everyone cheered. The Ruminates raised their glasses, mostly empty, as the King and his potty party wound its way through the camp, for they were hoping for a refill.

'Ale, Theocrat King, ale,' came the hopeful cry.

So, as he made his way along, The King of The Muck drank-in the love of his people, and they drank for the love of it.

As they wound their way up to Old Dunharrowing, Messy noticed the strange statues lining the route. They looked for all the world like some first-year art student's attempt at sculpture, using a claw hammer and screwdriver. One of the Ruminates told him that they had been given as a gift by a drunken dung wattle called Truly Hummings. They had been hidden away from Udderas because people said they were sick of the sight of them, and therefore named them The Puking-Men.

When they reached the top, they came to a wide-open grass area, which men called The Flippantfield. To the south lay The Sarcornistori, to the north stood The Ironysaga, and facing them was the darkness of The Dimmerberk, The Hateful Mountain. On either side of the road that led up the slopes of the mountain, were lines of uncarved stone pillars. This was due to Truly Hummings' screwdriver snapping before he could get to work on them. If any dared that road, it would take them to The Door of the Dimdolt.

When they eventually arrived at their destination, they were met by a sour-faced Lady Earwax.

'Hail, Mothergrand-daughterniece. Why the long face?' said Theocrat.

'Who's got a wider wrong face?' asked Earwax angrily.

'Wait, you've got it wrong,' replied Theocrat, a little louder this time.

'There you go, saying I'm the wrong weight now. No wonder that prat Paragon made excuses and left; even after I had begged him to stay.'

'How long ago did he leave?'

'Yes, it was wrong of him to leave,' said the sour-faced Milkmaid of Bovine.

'Which way did he go?' shouted Earmore.

'Ok, there's no need to shout. He went that way.' She pointed to a sign with a skull on it. 'He said something about parts of him being dead-red. I thought it a weak excuse; however, he doesn't look like he is used to riding bulls much.'

Who does, apart from these nutters? thought Messy.

'So he has taken The Road of the Dead-heads', said Earmore.

'Who are the Dead-heads, and where does that path lead?' asked Messy.

Earwax looked perplexed. 'Who mentioned red-heads, and who cares if their baths leak?'

As they unpacked and headed for their tents, Theocrat took the Halfbit to one side and explained. 'The path leads to The Dimdolt, then through The Hated Valley. Little is known of where it emerges, for no living man can, or has, entered and come out alive. It is said that, when my ancestors, The Earingers, led by Braggo and his son Bolder, arrived out of the grim north, they found the entrance with a shut-sign on it. Sat beside it was an old man, who told them, 'THIS PLACE IS SHUT. BUSINESS IS DEAD, UNTIL ONE COMES TO OPEN IT AGAIN. KEEP OUT'. Bolder asked the old man when it would be reopening. The old fellow was just about to answer when a huge boulder fell off the rock face and squashed him. "That's unlucky" said Braggo. "It's more than unlucky — we were just getting chatty when the conversation went flat. It's a bloody disaster" said Bolder, as he saw the mess oozing from under the boulder. It is told that, later, when Braggo celebrated the building of Milkingshed, he drunkenly said that he would brave the door; yet it was his son who was bolder and went one step further than his bragging father. He ventured through that hated door and was never seen again.'

'Then why would Paragon take such a dangerous path?' asked Messy.

'Who knows the destiny of The Heir of Evenduller? Yet maybe it was the lesser of two evils.' said Theocrat, with his back to Earwax.

At that moment, the sounds of a scuffle carried to them from outside the tent. The Officer of the Guard stumbled through the tent flap. 'Sorry, my lord, but there is an Erring-rider of Gondour here. He wishes to speak to you.'

Reluctantly, Theocrat said, 'Let the dull one in.'

As the big fellow entered, Messy gasped, for the man bore more than a passing resemblance to Borrowit. This was probably due to the Neomenorean habit of inbreeding.

The rider knelt before Theocrat and presented a blood-coloured candle.

194

'The Red Tallow!'

'I am Heregone, fastest rider of Gondour. This candle, once lit, represents the span of time left for Minus Thrifty. The Lord Denizen asks for your aid.'

'Ah well, first we must consult the Unified Nationalities to make sure we don't break some non-article something or other.'

'That's best known to you, Lord, but if you debate too long then Minus Thrifty will fall and Sourone will march on Udderas unopposed. And Lord, if our great city falls, what chance has your cowshed of standing against the wrath of The Dank Lord of Bad-odour?'

'Go tell Denizen that Lord Muck of the Bulls-hitters will be at his gates in the same time it takes the Postal Services to deliver a letter; or it takes a check to clear at the bank; or to get an appointment at the hospital to get my hip replaced.'

'Three questions Lord: is the letter first class or second? Is that a working week or a calendar week at the bank? And are you talking of the N.H.S or private treatment for your hip? For the difference in time may find the Sweaty Eagerlings and Dorks already ensconced in the best bars of Minus Thrifty,' said the Erring-rider.

'Then be glad that you have asked aid of the best barroom brawlers from Bovine. However, now it is time to rest. Get some sleep, Messy; I will need you alert in the morning,' said Theocrat.

'Are we following Paragon down the Road of the Dead-heads?' asked the smelly Halfbit.

'Not bloody likely! And what's all this WE about?' laughed Theocrat.

Messy was starting to get the idea he was surplus to requirements and went to bed with growing fears of abandonment.

The next day, whilst on route to Udderas, Messy rode up to the King on the small bullock he had been assigned, called Skidda. That name had been given name due to its inability to stop. Theocrat, who was riding his white mount, S'nomanure, the Blocked-up Bull of Bovine, saw the young Halfbit fly past him before eventually slamming on the brakes and shouting, 'Whoa! Everyone just hold on there a minute. I get the feeling I'm not wanted on this trip,' he said, looking pointedly at Theocrat.

'Wad bade du fink dat?' replied the King, holding his nose and backing off slightly.

'Well, how come everyone apart from you, me, Earmore and Earwax, sit three to a bull, and you went out of your way to find me Skidda of the Muck?'

The King Retreated a few yards more and breathed a sigh of relief. 'Well, it's like this, old chap: no-one has the room or the will to carry extra baggage. We are going to Mundane City, in the south, and that is a long way to hold one's breath. So you will, for certain, stay with the Lady Earwax and hold the Dork horde at bay without us.'

Earwax rode forward and said to Messy, 'If you are coming with me, then there is a change of gear in my pack; though, why the King talks of curtain draw-cords for bay windows, I know not, for they will not help in the defence of Udderas.'

So Messy rode with the big-boned milkmaid of Milkingshed, back to Udderas.

On arrival at the city of the Ruminates, Messy sat alone watching the Riders of Ridicule ready their gear for war. So it was, after some considerable time, and with only the flies to keep him company, that Messy noticed a rather large, formidable warrior looking at him. The man was so big he had two oven doors for chest armour. Instead of a pan on his head, he wore a small cauldron, which had two holes drilled in the front for vision, and its handle serving as a chinstrap. The back legs of the cauldron had been filed down, yet the front two stood proud like horns. Messy was more than a little worried when the walking cooking-range continued to stare at him. Before long though, he was distracted by the movement of the riders mounting and readying to leave. He sat disconsolately, watching as Theocrat and Earmore led the Riders of Ridicule out of the gates of Udderas. As rows and rows of the great bulls passed Messy, dread fell over him, as he feared that he would see out the war shovelling dung and making dairy products. He didn't want an epithet like the famous Dullborer Talk. He was just imagining his tomb, with the words "Messy the Cheesemaker" engraved on its entrance, when he was hoisted up and bodily dumped in the front seat of the war-bull belonging to the strange, large warrior.

From inside the helmet came a deep, echoing voice. 'So you want to go to war with Lord Muck, do you?'

'Yes, I'd rather go to war than shift dung.'.

'Then you shouldn't eat so much, little one. You will come with me to Mundane. There are few rations, so you won't have that problem this time,' said the large warrior.

Messy thought that the warrior had misheard him. 'What's your name, mister?'

The warrior replied in an even deeper voice, 'I'm no one's sister. What makes you say that? Would you like to see my hairy legs to prove it?'

Messy thought he was slightly mad and quickly replied, 'No thanks sir, though seeing as I don't know your name, I will call you Deaf-helm.'

'Yes, Death-helm; I like that name.'

So it was that Messy went to war on Deaf-helm's large bull, Fulofwind. They rode through the night, passing the now smouldering bonfires atop the hills of Raidon, Callanhide, Mistimin and Herelast.

Looking to the hills, Earmore shouted worriedly, 'Hurry! Ride fast! We don't want to miss last orders at The Cairn and Rose.'

NOTE: So, at this moment, let us recap. The Grand Alf and Pipsqueak have arrived in Gondour. Legless, Grimy, Paragon and his growing retinue are on their way to Gondour. The Ruminates are drinking their way to Gondour, and the massive army of Morbid is marauding its way towards Gondour's capital of Minus Thrifty via Ohgivusalaugh. The only ones going the opposite way are Foodo and Stan, and definitely not via Ohgivusalaugh. This part of the war was later to be known as The Surge to Gondour.

THE SURGE TO GONDOUR

Pipsqueak was rudely awakened by The Grand Alf as he prodded him with a bony finger, saying 'Get up, you lazy little lump.'

'But it's not ten; we Halfbits never get up before the sun had a chance to get warm,' said the annoyed Pipsqueak.

'There's a war on, in case that has slipped your mushy brain. Do you want to wake one morning and find that the Dorks have beaten you to breakfast?'

'They won't find much of that here,' said Pipsqueak, looking at what seemed like prison food to him.

'Well you had better eat it. Denizen wants you, and you won't be getting any more until much later,' replied The Grand Alf.

'It couldn't get any less,' whined Pipsqueak.

After the greedy and exceedingly hungry Halfbit had made the measly meal disappear in the blink of an eye, before then trying to eat the patterns off the curtains, he found himself being led to the hall of The Stalwart. Upon their arrival, they found Denizen sitting on his stool.

'I've been giving some thought to what job you could do; it has been said that you are good for nothing,' he said, glancing at The Grand Alf. 'However, my cook has asked to visit his dying mother in some strange place called Asfahawayasikan so, Peregrinate, can you find your way around a kitchen?'

The Halfbit stood dumbstruck, mouth open, silently giving thanks to whichever minor vassal of Ill-farter had been so bored that day that it was looking after the multitude of mindless needs of the Halfbit race. As he thought of all that food, his stomach rumbled so loudly that Denizen asked the guards to check whether the attack had started.

So it was that Pipsqueak became the only happy person in Minus Thrifty. His sole hours of duty were for the three meals that the tall people ate. He was very glad they didn't observe the Halfbit custom of having seven; not that that stopped him from doing so.

Later on that day, during his break, he was out walking along the battlements towards The Guard and Fence with Beerygrog when, from far-off, they heard a screech that froze even the alcohol in the soldiers' veins. Upon looking up, they saw the great Terrorblacktail Flying Beasts, which had taken the place of the old mountain bikes for The Ring Cyclists. The beasts and their masters were chasing a group of horsemen, as a shout went up from the wall, 'Beware! Flying Ring Cyclists! The Nasal Airs are chasing our lord's son. He is Faraway, but will he make it back to the gate?'

Things were looking bad for the horsemen when suddenly a huge flash lit up the darkened skies. The Grand Alf, riding on Shinyflax, was firing signal flares that scared and confused the beasts. Thus, the men and their saviour made it safely back to Minus Thrifty. Beerygrog and Pipsqueak went down to the gate to greet the returning warriors. When Pipsqueak approached The Grand Alf, Faraway was amazed, and asked what a Halfbit was doing in the tower, especially now they were short of food, adding that he had seen exactly how much they could put away in a single sitting.

'He is employed as your father's cook,' said the wizard, wondering how Faraway knew so much about Halfbits. Faraway, meanwhile, was thinking about how he was going to explain how he knew so much about Halfbits.

Some time later, they sat in the main hall, listening to Faraway tell of his adventures, in which he portrayed himself as a heroic figure, leading his men from the front in a great battle against the Harrassdim.

'My men fought hard and bravely, so I gave them the night off and allowed them into town, and I bought the first round of drinks in The Cairn and Rose. However, I have another matter to discuss: this is not the first Halfbit I have seen lately.'

'Oh, have you been to The Snore?' asked Pipsqueak.

'Be quiet!' barked The Grand Alf. Then he asked, 'When exactly was the last time you saw a Halfbit, Faraway?'

'I was coming to that. You see I, well, sort of, kind of, ran into three of them a couple of days ago,' replied Faraway quietly.

The Grand Alf relaxed visibly and took a mouthful of wine whilst Faraway continued.

'They were called Foodo, Stan and Smear-gob Grumble.'

Wine exploded from the wizard's mouth, as he spluttered,

'Grumble! What was that miscreant doing with them, and which way did they go?'

'They took the path to Critter Ungodly.'

'Didn't you warn them about Sheblob?' asked The Grand Alf incredulously.

'To tell you the truth, I was more worried about the creature they had with them.'

'This is terrible.'

Denizen, who had been sitting patiently listening, asked, 'Why were these three heading to Morbid?'

Faraway and The Grand Alf looked at each other with more than a hint of guilt.

'You tell him,' said The Grand Alf.

'No way. It's your baby. You tell him,' replied Faraway.

'It's your story.'

'Will someone please tell me what is going on?' said Denizen.

With a slight quiver in his voice, Faraway said, 'They were sort of popping off to Mount Gloom to destroy The Blame of Evenduller.'

'What? You let two stupid Halfbits and a mad cretin, run off to Morbid with Sourone's Nose-rinG?' roared The Stalwart.

'They weren't all as stupid as this one,' said The Grand Alf, pointing at Pipsqueak. Then he thought to himself about how the Gambles weren't blessed with much between the ears.

'This is worse than terrible, Mythroving. It's a catastrophe,' said Denizen.

'He's not casting it off for free; the Elves are paying him,' said Pipsqueak, as another lump appeared on his head.

'Why did you let them go? Your brother would not have done so. He would have remembered my birthday. You should have gone to Riverdwell instead,' whined Denizen.

'Well, pin your ears back Daddy-o. Firstly, Borrowit wanted to go to Riverdwell so he could ogle at the Elf-maids,' said Faraway.

'So?'

'Secondly, you not only allowed him; you sent him.'

'So, what's your point?'

'Thirdly, and more importantly, big brave Borrowit tried to take The Blame for himself and failed miserably. So, the reason Borrowit is fish food and I'm not is because I am Faraway, the more clever, the more good looking, and charming member of the family. Oh, and did I mention I'm more lucky?' laughed Faraway.

'Well, let's hope the army of Morbid is full of their women or your attempts at retaking Ohgivusalaugh will get pretty hot,' said Denizen.

So it was that Faraway found himself with a return ticket to the Gondourian city of Ohgivusalaugh, where indeed things did get very hot. From the walls of Minus Thrifty they could see and hear the results of the large green methane explosions all through the night. The next day, The Grand Alf came back, leading the Ambulwains, their blue lights flashing and full of gassed soldiers. He met The Stalwart at the gates.

'I hope that bloody useless son of mine hasn't come back,' said Denizen.

'No, I left him to contend with The Witchy-king,' replied The Grand Alf.

'Oh, so that's the reason you volunteered to bring the sick back. You know the prophecy as well as I:

TO KILL THE WITCHY-KING, IF YOU CAN,
MAKE REALLY SURE YOU'RE NOT A MAN.

So you left my son to die there at the hands of that monster.'

'Who sent him there?' replied the wizard to the scowling Stalwart.

Some time later, tattered remnants of the Gondourian army staggered back to Minus Thrifty, chased by the army of Morbid and The Nasal Airways. Once The Grand Alf was sure it was safe, and that The Witchy-king wasn't about, he led The Knights of Dolt Amlost to rescue as many as they could, again with the wizard firing flares from his staff to chase off the Terrorblacktails. They all returned safely with Himhadrill carrying the body of Faraway, who had been shot with a poisoned peashooter. The Prince of the Dolt Amlost, Shipyard, took Faraway to The Left Tower, only to find that everyone else had also done so with their wounded. With plenty of complaining, he brought Faraway to Denizen, who was now in The Right Tower.

'Lord, your son has broken my back. For a lift does this tower have great need,' said Himhadrill.

Minus Thrifty was now surrounded by the enemy. It wasn't long before the great Thralls wheeled huge machines of warfare into position and massive towers appeared. Sourone was a master of psychological warfare, and soon the towering loudspeakers began belting out Great Balls of Fire by Very Wee Slewit. After some hours, the music changed to Somebody to Lob by Squeam, as the Dork Delivery Department sent parcels to wives and mothers by first class mail ahead of schedule.

That day, as Faraway lay dying, and his father sat skiving, Pipsqueak stood outside, wondering how long he could carry on claiming rations for these two non-combatants. The Halfbit approached The Stalwart and said, 'Don't worry, Lord; he is young and strong. Hopefully he will recover soon.' He did this with his fingers crossed behind his back. 'Have you thought of asking The Grand Alf if he has any Anti-venom?'

'Don't mention that fool's name to me. That idiot has dropped us all in it. Sourone's pierced nose will once again have an adornment. He can read our minds and seeks to ruin us, for he has my bank details and password access for the Hinternet. The House of the Stalwarts has failed. Sourone has left us no money and no means to pay our mortgage. Neither of my sons can help, as they are now on incapacity benefits,' moaned Denizen.

'But Borrowit is dead, lord,' said Pipsqueak.

'Well, how incapacitating is that?' said Denizen, as a group of captains, with thoughts of a military coup on their minds, approached.

'The first circle of the city is burning. The people need you,' said their leader.

'The first circle ... Isn't that where the bureaucrats stopped us demolishing the slums for a Hypermarket? Come back in a day or two. Until then, follow The Grey Pillock.'

'But lord, men are deserting; they cannot stand the heat,' said the captain.

'Oh, if only men spent more time in the kitchen. Why run? We will all be cooking soon. Go to your stoves, for I go to my pie. No burial for Denizen and Faraway; only the long marinating awaits us. We will die like Ernest, the King of old, he became a man and potato pie,' said Denizen. He then dismissed Pipsqueak. 'Goodbye, Peregrinate, son of Perambulate. Your servings were short, and I release you to eat what little remains. Go and die as quietly as your people are able to. Before you do though, send in my minions.'

Pipsqueak knew that death wasn't far away for him either, as he'd eaten most of the rations anyway and his stomach was already thinking that his throat had been cut. Pipsqueak knew he had better speak to The Grand Alf about what had just happened so, after half-an-hour in the larder, he set out to find the wizard.

As he left, he saw Denizen and a group of men carrying Faraway up The Silage Street to The Path Dining. Pipsqueak ran for all of twenty seconds; a great feat for a Halfbit. Halfway there, he bumped into Beerygrog, who was malingering under the pretence of guarding some obscure inn from invasion. Pipsqueak told of his plight, and said that Beerygrog must fight to save Faraway. Beerygrog's survival instincts kicked in, offering lame excuses about death to those who left their posts. Pipsqueak told the big man that The Grand Alf had promised to turn all the wine into water if he didn't help. At that, Beerygrog broke the land-speed record for a man in an iron suit. Pipsqueak followed as best he could, but ran straight into the fight of the century.

During The Surge to Gondour, many of the Dorks had been killed trying to beat down the gates. However, the enemy considered this to be but a small loss, for they were just testing how good the Gondour Guards.com security services were. Then came Grind, named after The Ancient Rammer of the Underworld, aiming itself at the gates accompanied by a deafening beating of drums. The defence at the gates was the thickest, which meant, because they lacked a good leader, the gates were virtually defenceless. Grind crept slowly forward, impervious to damage. Those who aimed it died in the most horrendous ways: blood pumped from their ears and their heads exploded, for the men who guarded the gates sang every insipid boy band song known to them over megaphones. Many Dorks and Thralls fled, fearing for their sanity. But, for every stupid Dork that fled, two more idiotic ones took their place. So it was that Grind crept onward until, at last, it was before the very gates of Minus Thrifty.

A huge figure came forward then, dressed in black and sat upon a shiny new black mountain bike. Grind banged loudly against the gates. Each time it did, The Lord of the Nasal uttered the words of Arcane Musical Power, "Take That," and the wielders of Grind replied in response, "And Ram It". Three times he spoke these words, until the gates, that were known as Bill and Gareth, lay in ruins.

In through the wreckage strode The Morgue Lord, and then instantly tried to find an excuse not to be there, for only one person greeted him: The Grand Alf, astride Shinyflax. The wizard could not for all his efforts make the damned horse move. No matter how much he tried spurring him to flee quickly back to the city, Shinyflax wouldn't budge. The horse had found some tasty grass growing between the cobblestones and so was oblivious to the oncoming threat. The Grand Alf, stuck in a predicament, pulled out a tour guide hat and said, 'Tickets please. No ticket, no entry.'

The Witchy-king, who had no class or manners, replied, 'You old fart; you're on my time now. Dost thou not know a deadlock when thou sees it?'

With that, they held their swords aloft ... and nothing happened. Motionless was the battlefield, expectant for the fight of the century. Then, from a distance, came a sound like the horns that were used during government-banned hunting parties. Theocrat and Bovine had arrived just in time for a real ding-dong.

THE RIDE OF THE RUMINATES

In the dark, Messy had found a place to sleep near some trees. He awoke to a dull thudding, that he at first took to be a hangover, only to realise some inconsiderate moron was playing bongos.

A large figure loomed out of the darkness before the Halfbit. It was staggering in a way that could only mean that whoever, or whatever, it was must have been drinking all night. The figure stopped inches from him and he heard the sound of a zip being opened.

Messy leapt to his feet, shouting, 'Whoa! Just hold on a minute. I'm not a urinal, and what the hell is going on? Are those Dork drums I can hear?' He saw now it was Effinghel who stood before him who, having followed the smell, thought that he had found the camp latrine. Confronted now by the skunk-like Halfbit, he realised why he had made that mistake.

Putting some distance between them, Effinghel answered, 'No, master hole-biter; you hear the Wussies, The Mild Men of the Suds. They live in Drudgadan Forest.' After Effinghel had relieved himself of the night's excess, he staggered back to the camp, with the Halfbit in tow.

Upon reaching the open space of the campfire, Messy noticed Theocrat and Earmore talking to a short, squat character who looked like a badly carved garden gnome. Then Messy remembered The Puking Men statues, and realised that the mad artist hadn't done that bad a job after all. The small man was naked, apart from a strange grass skirt, from which he was picking bits and putting them in a smoking pipe. From his position, Messy heard their talk.

The small man said, 'No, big Bulls-hitter; me no a scrappa-do. Only wishi-washi. No like Grunge. Hate Dork clothes. Me helps yuz.'

'Well, you're not much good to us unless you can gut a Dork with this,' said Earmore, as The Martial Marshal of the Ridicule held up a spud-peeler tied to the end of a broom handle. 'What else can you do for us?' he added.

'Weeze havva looky point upa-der,' replied the little man, pointing to the mountain top. 'We seea Dem Drudge Bustas a-comin, but now only seea Dorks swarmin dem howsez offa dem Stoned Men. Lotsa Dorks, more dan youza little party man. Den der is more on road. Ambush for youza set.'

Earmore asked him if he had passed any form of maths exam that qualified him to count past his fingers and his toes.

The little old fellow wasn't happy. 'Mild men are Mild, free and easy man, but not stupid. I am Big Outahedsman Ghon-bludi-Ghon, son of Ha-bludi-Ha. Me do a-countin for tribe. Weeze a-countin revolooshons for dem Woodi-washi masheens, weeze knowa dema kick yu ina yu ass,' said Ghon.

'But we need to hurry. Mundane is already burning,' said Earmore.

'Ah but Ghon-bludi-Ghon knowa secret way. Dis road hassa no toll or dem speedi camras. Road is forgot; wassa dumpawain servis road from stonedig wurks. Mild men showa dat road. Yousa kill Grungy-Dork. Mild men go back to scrub in the Mild Suds.'

So it was that Ghon-bludi-Ghon led The Riders of Ridicule through The Stonedway Valley. During the night the Ruminates crept and hid bravely from the Dorks.

At one point, a rider turned to Theocrat and said, 'Lord, my name is Windfarta. I live in the Mould of Bovine. I am used to bad smells. There is a change in the air here. Something smells like rotting flesh.'

Messy tried to hide further inside Deafhelm's large cloak as Theocrat sniffed the air and said, 'I think you may be right.'

They rode on, approaching the now brightly lit Minus Thrifty, until they eventually came to a crest overlooking the Besieging Bad Barmy Army of Bad-odour.

Theocrat turned to his men, and taking a swig of mead, he laughed and made small of the huge army. 'Take the last of your mead. Drink to courage. No dork can stand before a boozer of Bovine.' He continued:

'DERIDE, DERIDE, RIDERS OF THEOCRAT.
PELL-MELL INVOKE. IRE AND LAUGHTER
DREAR SHALL BE BROKEN. SNEERS SHALL BE STUNTED.
A WORD DAY. A REHASH DAY. ERE THE FUN RISES.

DERIDE NOW, DERIDE NOW. DERIDE FOR GONDOUR.'

At that, he grabbed a trumpet from Gruflaf, his band-leader, and struck up a powerful note which, upon hearing, the Ruminates took up and expanded into The Ride of the Valhalacries. The Ruminates sped down the hill towards the cringing Dorks, with Effinghel's herd on the right and Grimbod's on the left. Earmore was in the centre, bravely behind Theocrat, as The Lord of the Muck sped down the hill, like O'roamin on Naffnag, straight into the army of Morbid.

THE PELL-MELL BATTLE IN THE FIELDS

It wasn't just a Dork-boss or a Big-headed Bigot that lorded it up over the cringing slave army of Morbid; it was The Morgue-lord. However, fortune, in the form of the Ruminates, gave him an excuse to avoid a hair-pulling, eye-scratching and name-calling episode with the old codger conjuror. Besides, he'd heard that the wizard had a few phosphorus grenades up his sleeve, and he certainly didn't like bright lights, as they hurt his eyes. So, when Theocrat and his band of bawdy Bovine Bulls-hitters turned up, he was almost glad. He would have smiled and laughed if he could remember how. That smile would not have lasted long, for the Ruminates slammed into the Dorks at breakneck speed.

The Dorks ran just to keep ahead. This caused absolute panic, as the charge of the great bulls scattered Dorks like tramps at a speed-dating party. Then Theocrat espied the Slothron Supremo and charged into him and his bodyguard. He slew them all before they had a chance to even stir. The remaining Slothrons, who had been rudely awoken by the clamour, made their excuses before fleeing, complaining that they were only going to rise for a victory parade.

As Theocrat smugly congratulated himself, he saw looks of horror cross the faces of his men while it got suddenly darker. A shadow blotted out what little light there was, as someone's big brother had turned up, in the shape of The Witchy-king, riding the Nasal Airways. The Terrorblacktail descended, screeching, looking for its next meal, deciding a bullburger would do, and it had its eyes on a king-sized whopper. Theocrat, with his back to the pouncing predator, was last to actually notice it. All he saw was the Ruminates charge off towards a more important battle against the young guard of Sourone's Slothrons, consisting of that nemesis of the nursery, Kid Caramel, the Champion of Gone Duller, also known as The Slack Eagerling.

So Theocrat found himself alone, facing Sourone's bully-boy Witchy-king of Wagner, Lord of the Ring-cyclists, Morgue-lord, Nasal and part-time Scream extra. The Witchy-king and
208

his steed pounced on the lone figures, knocking the bull onto the King. One rather stupid rider stood before his king, for he had misheard the bugle call for honourable speedy retreat. It had been the bull Fulofwind who, relieving himself of the burden of a bad breakfast, had blocked out the sound of the call.

It was Deafhelm who stood before The Witchy-king and said, 'Get thee gone, thou foolish Dweeberlike, Lord of Craziones. If thou touch the King, I will spike thee.' At that, he showed the Lord of the Nasal a meat-skewer tied to a broom handle.

A hollow laugh echoed from inside the hollow head of the Nasal, and a dead voice said, 'Oh man, you Bulls-hitters are so crazy, man. Like, haven't you heard that no man can kill me?'

'Who's a crazy man? I am Earwax, Earnaught's daughter,' replied the rider, taking off their helmet.

The Witchy-king took one look at the big-boned Milk-maid of Bovine and said, 'Oh damn, this is so heavy, man,' then proceeded to pull out a scroll upon which was written The Prophecy of Gloryfindem. 'Ah, no mention of male or female. Is it man or mankind? Or just not Dwarf or Elf?'

Messy, who was lurking nearby, crept forward and stuck his Neomanorealmen steak-knife into the Nasal in the place where once he would have had something to sit on. At the same time he shouted, 'What does it say about Halfbits with magic blades?'

The Witchy-king looked down at Messy and screamed, 'Halfbit, you smell like a rat!' He turned back to Earwax, just as she rammed her weapon into his hollow mouth.

'I told you, the name is Earwax. Who the hell is Norman?'

The Lord of the Nasal started to shake uncontrollably and to dissolve. He shrieked, 'I'm melting. I'm melting. Who would have thought a girl could do this to me?'

'Apparently some born-again Elf did?' replied Messy, rolling up the scroll for some later use. Then he went and stood over the fallen king, who was lying underneath his great war-bull.

Theocrat recognised the smell of the Halfbit even before he saw him. 'What are you doing here, master hole-biter? I left you to look after my little niece,' said the King.

The thought of the Big-boned Buxom Milkmaid of Bovine passed through Messy's mind and he turned just in time to see her fainting. He thought about how she had destroyed one of the most powerful creatures in Muddy Earth; that is, after

Sourone, The Grand Alf, Gadabout, Elbow and Sourman. Oh, he thought, is that Sourman before or after The Grand Alf's visit to Oldcrank? Come to think of it, would The Grand Alf have been powerful enough before his near-death experience and had his name changed by deed poll? His head was beginning to swim as he heard his name being called through the haze.

'Hey, don't just stand there; give me a hand up!' shouted the King.

Messy looked around desperately for the King's hands, only to realise that S'nomanure had almost completely covered him when he had collapsed during the attack. 'I'm sorry, my lord, but your bull has crushed you. The only thing showing is your head.'

'Oh, I wondered what that dead feeling was in my little toe. I am afraid I'm getting a little dizzy, master Messy. Tell me, how goes the war?'

'The Dorks panicked and fled all over the battlefield, and The Witchy-king is about as powerful as a Halfbit's will to diet,' replied Messy.

'Good. I did not wish to fail. We have gained a victory here that is worthy of praise. I feared going to the burial grounds as the weakest link in the family. As I lie here now, I can quit whilst I am ahead.' He then closed his eyes and apparently died, killed by the weight of expectation though, in later songs this was changed to excrement for, at the last, S'nomanure had lost a few years of built-up fibre in fright.

Messy lay on the ground, afflicted by the same bad breath of The Witchy-king as Earwax was. The last thing he remembered was Earmore riding up, and Theocrat waking.

The King said, with his last words, 'Ah, Earmore, late as usual.' Then he truly did die.

Earmore leapt from his bull, knelt beside him and gently, almost tenderly, ripped the crown from Theocrat's head. Making sure there were no dents in it, he placed The Gold-plated Bronze Basin of Bovine on his head and shouted, 'Ale Earmore, The King of the Muck.'

This had the desired effect of bringing back the brave Bulls-hitters of Bovine, who had bolted at the approach of the big bad Witchy-king. When all were gathered, the new king surveyed the mounds of the slain. There, like a mountain amongst the foothills, was Earwax, his sister. The new king was distraught;

one state funeral in the family was enough, but having to pay for two was too much. He wept, and cried out, 'Earwax, Earwax; for once in your life, could you not have heard the instructions? You were told to defend Udderas, not be defiant to the upper class. This is going to cost a fortune.' At that, Earmore climbed back aboard his bull and shouted, 'Debt, debt; ride to ruin and the bank's lending.'

They charged off then on a Nellifant safari, leaving Messy behind, for he had been hidden by the Big-boned Buxom Earwax. Regaining his feet, he stood with his Steak-knife in hand, which was still smouldering on account of the Magic Muck of the Mucus from the Gluteus Maximus of the Morgue-lord. The acidic anti-matter that clung to the blade burnt the metal to a crisp. Thus passed the knife that was crafted for some rich person's dinner service in Worseness; that had inhabited the land of Anotherone, poor northern relation of Gondour. However, the Smith Brothers, who had made this blade, would have been glad that its last cut was no mere piece of murdered cattle, and that the serrated edge had held true. Men came and took the King away on a stretcher made of capes and broom handles. Plenty more also came with lifting equipment and a tent, fashioned into a cradle, enabling them to shift Earwax. The men who had not been quick enough to scarper from the onslaught of the beast were separated from the Dorks and laid to rest in a mound, away from the heroes. In another mound they laid S'nomanure, where he had keeled over in fright, and upon it set a stone which read:

FIBREFUL SERVANT THAT ENDED KING'S TENURE.
LIGHTSTOOLS BULLOCK SHIFT S'NOMANURE.

It was said that the grass grew green and plentiful on the mound of S'nomanure for many years, due to the high quality of the compost.

Messy followed the stretcher-bearers at a distance they deemed safe. He heard them discussing him, saying, 'Poor little blighter's soiled himself,' said one of them.

'So would I. Didn't you see all those big horrible things lying all over the place?' replied his friend.

'Yes. I wonder why the Ruminates don't allow more of their

women to fight then.'

Himhadrill, Prince of Dolt Amlost, rode towards them and, seeing their burden, asked, 'Is that a woman?' Then, beholding her greatness, added, 'I hope they have more like this one. Are there any more?'

'No, lord; only this one and, according to the Halfbit, she is the Lady Earwax, sister of Earmore,' replied the stretcher-bearer.

'Is she dead?' asked Himhadrill.

'No, lord. Cans't thou not hear her snoring?'

'I thought that was one of those great Nelliphants advancing onto the battlefield. Take her to the city,' replied the prince, and he then rode off to join the Nelliphant safari.

Across that battlefield advanced the Mumikills and, out of Ohgivusalaugh, came another force, led by Coughsmog the Second, the Lafintenant of The Morgue-lord. With him came Eagerlings in taxis, the noisy Variants of Klang, marching to the music of heavy metallic instruments, the sleepy Slothrons in their ceremonial, scarlet, silk pyjamas and, from Far Harras, came the semi-slave Half-thralls with wide-eyes and red toupees. Then, from the walls of Minus Thrifty, came the cry from the men of The Corrective Lazy Eye Treatment Regiment, 'The Corps of Umbrage! The Corps of Umbrage!' for, coming up the Arduos, were the Bark Ships of the South.

So it was that the defenders of Gondour found themselves attacked from all fronts (oh, and all sides as well). The retreat was sounded, sending all friendly troops flying to the city (that is, without wings, for the sake of any future discussion forums).

This was too much for Earmore to bear. He decided that, with nothing left to lose, and being close to bankruptcy — what, with the bill for the ale that his uncle had left him to settle, two state funerals and a coronation to pay for — he decided to go for broke and make a stand against the rising tide of invasion. He turned to his men and shouted:

'OUT OF DEBT, IN THE BLACK
AND THE BASE RATE RISING,
I CAME SINKING IN THE SCUM,
MY SWORD FOR SELLING.
FOR HOPE OF LENDING,
I RIDE TO DEARTH'S MENDING.

He faced the new threat and raised a number of fingers in dismissal. His face however, changed in surprise, for the flag flying from the mast of the lead ship was not the Scull and Crossbow of The Pirates of Perchance, but the White Plastic Yowl Tree of the line of Nimbus the Fake, the family emblem of Everdull.

And so came Paragon, son of Paramount, having led the army of The Dead-heads to free the slaves of Umbrage just in time, before that dread army fell apart. The slaves had manned the ships, setting out for Gondour's port of Fargon. On route, Paragon had devised a plan to add to his small army of slaves. They had stopped at Laidabedin, waking it's dozy inhabitants, and then on to Lamexcuse, promising them a free booze cruise as they went. Halfway up the Arduos, the locals realised they had been tricked when Grimy and Legless started handing out captured weapons. Cries of "I don't like fighting. I want to go home," and "I want my mummy," had filled the air. Many had wept openly, saying, "We are going to miss Big Sister." Others, enraged, had suggested fisticuffs.

Then forward had stepped Paragon, between Legless and Grimy. Fierce they had looked and full of fire, for Legless had found the rum ration.

Paragon had said, 'Any man who fights for me will get a share in the land of their birth, a house with a low mortgage rate, and a job in the soon-to-be-formed King's Reconstruction Company, with a franchise from a favoured friend, set up by myself and headed by Chief Executive Grimy. Or you can stay on these ships that are rigged to explode one minute after I leave them.' So it was that Paragon's army found itself flung into the fray and having to fight its way valiantly through the terrified fleeing army of Morbid.

In the middle of the battlefield, Paragon found Earmore pitching his marquee for the After Battle Booze-up Bash. When Earmore caught sight of his friend, he said, 'Blooming heck, I never thought I'd see you again.'

'I told you I wouldn't miss this party for anything.'

'Well you are more than welcome, yet you seem to have found
213

a vast amount of hangers-on. I don't think there is enough mead for them all.'

'No need to worry, friend Earmore, for I have a supply ship that I liberated from the Ethanol region, just south of Ginhir.'

'Looks like you got here just in time. May much lush and sozzle befall us,' said the new king of Bovine.

The Party was well underway and the film crews from Follywood had already started work on the new film called Carrion Ringing, when some Eagerlings who had hung around too long tried to gatecrash the party. This ended with The Battle of the Bouncers of Bovine, as they battered the battle-worn battalions of Bad-Odour. With their beating ended The Battle of the Pell-mell in the Fields.

THE PYROMANIAC DENIZEN

When The Witchy-King had decided it prudent to run away and fight another day, Pipsqueak had been mighty glad, for he had hidden bravely during the boring standoff between the two prolixing protagonists and now emerged, shouting, 'Grand Alf, Denizen's gone mad.'

'That didn't take long. What have you said to him?'

'No, no; it's Faraway. Denizen says he is going to roast him alive. He has gone to the catacombs and plans to turn them into vast ovens. He has told men to make a pie; he means to cook himself and Faraway, and burn the city at the same time,' replied Pipsqueak, waving his arms in the air.

'I smell the work of the enemy in this. Come, follow me,' said The Grand Alf, as he set off at a fast snail's pace. Having got more than thirty yards and not heard the usual prattle from the silly Halfbit, he turned to see said Halfbit standing with his nose in the air, sniffing, with a puzzled look on his face. The Grand Alf growled, walked back and cuffed him around the ear. Picking up the staggering Pipsqueak, the wizard set off again for The Daft Binin and The Tombs of the Dead-stupid.

As The Grand Alf rode, they met Himhadrill, and the wizard was glad to abdicate responsibility for the seemingly bad way the battle was going. As they approached The Daft Binin, they came upon a scuffle, involving Beerygrog and the servants of Denizen. It seemed that The Stalwart had began confiscating all things inflammable, including Beerygrog's favourite tipple: rum, whiskey, brandy, etc. The soldier had been driven mad by the lack of them. Now, with it being at least an hour since his last drink, he attacked the servants, who dropped two of the barrels, causing them to shatter and stain the floor with red rum. Beerygrog leapt over chairs and other obstacles to lap up the liquid, whilst the servants retreated, shouting 'Drunkard' and 'Toper.'

As the Grand Alf arrived, so did Denizen, who was complaining about the noise, 'It is enough to wake the dead.'

To which The Grand Alf answered, 'What about your son?

He is faraway from being dead.'

Pipsqueak tugged at the wizard's robes and said, 'No, no; I saw him lying in one of the tombs.'

'My son is in there basting in a sauce of brandy and wine, but soon he will be burned black, for I intend to ruin the victory feast of the Dorks,' replied Denizen as he flung open the doors; therein lay Faraway, on a banqueting table.

The room was full of barrels and bottles of spirits. It was clear that Denizen was intending to release a conflagration upon the people of Minus Thrifty. The rivers of fire coming down from on high would certainly give meaning to the saying, in the heat of battle. Denizen, who was soaked in alcohol, came staggering towards where the wizard was standing.

There followed a few seconds of pushy-shovey between two old men, before The Grand Alf stopped and said, 'Seeing as you are inebriated, in the spirit of fair play, I will give you the first shot.' With that, he stuck out his chin.

Pipsqueak once again tugged at the wizard's cloak, and piped up, 'He's already had a few shots, if you ask me. And what type of drink is Fair Play?'

Once again, the Halfbit was ignored and, as Denizen staggered forward, he slipped on the wet floor and fell forward, face first. As The Stalwart lay grovelling on the floor, the wizard rushed past him and into the room, towards the Faraway pie. Pulling back the pastry, he dragged the limp body of Faraway free.

Denizen staggered back into the room, crying, 'Don't wake him; the meal is prepared! Why should we not die together as main meal and side order?'

'Authority is not given to you, Stalwart of Gondour, to order the manner or method of your servings! Come, there is much fighting to be done, and I may still be able to save your image for any future governing post in the forthcoming elections.'

At that point, Denizen laughed uncontrollably. Standing on a table, he produced a P.A.L. hand T.V. Chortling and, chuckling, said, 'I have read all the latest WAP reports and have had visions, by Brood-band, of the ships that now sail towards us from Umbrage. The choice was to either stand and fry, or run away and call them names from a safe distance. As all paths of flight are now closed, I will burn this city to the ground, leaving nothing for the invading Dorks or this Stranger of the North you've been trying to keep secret. Did you really think an imbecile Halfwit could keep his flapping mouth closed long enough to think about what was coming out of it?'

Pipsqueak asked what a Nimby was and how to seal one; that couldn't be ignored and the halbit took his usual prone position.

Denizen rambled on. 'So you seek to supplant me in some military coup, I who am the rightful ruler born of The House of Howlin and Stalwart to the line of Anotherone? Replace me with some wandering tramp from the bankrupt house of Evenduller on our throne? And I suppose there is absolutely no profit in this for you. Long has it been known of your desire to be appointed Entertainments Minister, therefore attaining top-billing at any future Royal Variety Shows.'

'Well, seeing as you won't step down, the only thing left to tell you, in my capacity as the next king's best friend, is that he was going to sack you anyway. He thought you were getting on a bit and losing your marbles, to which your present actions can only add weight,' retorted The Grand Alf.

Denizen flew into a fiery rage and, blood boiling, he charged towards the ignition barrel with torch in hand. However, halfway there, he tripped over Pipsqueak, causing him to go crashing into some spare brandy bottles which broke, drenching him in fluid. Denizen erupted in flames, and so he ended, not as The Pie of Denizen, but as a flambé fool.

The Grand Alf turned to Beerygrog and the servants of Denizen. 'You must work together now, for this cretinous cremation has caused much dust and ashes, which will need to be cleaned. Furthermore, this firebomb needs to be dismantled and the alcohol dispersed, preferably to its owners.'

'I'd like to volunteer for that,' said Beerygrog and Pipsqueak simultaneously.

'No, I need you two to help me carry Faraway to The Houses of Squealing,' said the wizard.

So, with heavy hearts, and an even heavier burden, they left, wishing they had more pockets to stuff bottles into. Yet, even as they set out, a great shrieking wail could be heard, more powerful than a failed reality show contestant. The Grand Alf, realising this to be the demise of The Witchy-king, grinned and said, 'Well, that's one problem I won't have to solve.'

'It's a good thing then, seeing as you had run out of insults to throw at that fellow you were so scared of,' said Pipsqueak.

If The Grand Alf hadn't had his hands full just then, the Halfbit would have suffered from the usual disorientation that followed any sentence that made the wizard growl.

They deposited Faraway with The Neomanorealmen Healing Squadrons, whose nickname was No Health Saved. Leaving Beerygrog to stand some form of guard, the wizard went to see how the battle was going. He dragged the reluctant Halfbit with him, who continued to moan about the lack of real food in frontline rations.

THE HOUSES OF SQUEALING

The work party of many men struggled to fit Theocrat and Earwax into what the locals called The Ghostpital. The doors were made to admit large, tall Neomanoreans. The problem was that Earwax was just plain large all over and, when S'nomanure had fallen on Theocrat, the beast had created one of the tallest Kings of Bovine ever. This led to his later nickname of Theoflat Hedskew.

Messy followed some way behind, at the insistence of the stretcher-bearers. After a tiring climb of almost thirty steps, the Halfbit started to weaken. This was not feigned, nor was it because of his natural lazy way. Having been bereft of a sense of smell through many years of overexposure to himself, he had been completely unprepared for the gasp of grave-gas that had issued from The Witchy-king when the Halfbit had rammed his little knife into the nether regions of that foul being. The smell had truly been more evil than the stash of used underwear hidden in his bottom drawer at home.

It seemed that it also had a delayed effect, for now he staggered blindly up the stairs with little remaining sense of the little sense that had been bestowed upon him. Luckily, or unluckily some might say, he ran into Pipsqueak, who proceeded to babble on and prattle about everything of insignificance that had befallen him since they had parted, all while his friend deteriorated before him. If it hadn't been for young Beerguild rushing up the stairs and falling over the two Halfbits, then Messy may well have been bored to death, long before he expired.

The Gondourian did a double take at the sight of the two Halfbits, then squeezed his nose and said, 'Phew, what's that smell? Is he dead? Are you taking him to be buried or fumigated?'

'Oh, he's just pretending to be asleep. He always does this when he doesn't want to listen to my marvellous stories,' replied Pipsqueak. With that, he gave his friend a shove. 'Hey, say hello to my new friend, Beerguild.' This only caused Messy to keel over and lie flat at the feet of the young lad.

'If he's not dead, then that's a good impression. I think I'd better get some help. Wait here and I'll get a shambulance,' said Beerguild as he turned and ran away, gasping with relief.

Sometime later, The Grand Alf appeared, pulling a Red Tree City Dustcart, and wearing a mask and boiler suit. 'I've been told that a smelly Halfbit may have passed away,' said the old wizard.

'No, he is still here; the smelly Halfbit in question is Messy,' replied Pipsqueak, pointing to a pile of dirty clothes propped against the wall.

'Indeed it is,' said The Grand Alf. 'We had better move him to the Citydwell. If he stays here much longer, it will cause a panic, for the people may take him for a small Dork or, worse than that, the plague returning.' The wizard was sure glad he'd talked Elbow into allowing these Halfbits on the journey, for here was another good reason to keep him away from the main battle.

Faraway, Earwax and Messy were placed in special beds in The Houses of Squealing. Faraway's bed was brought to him from the old Stalwart's room. Although big, it was not quite king-sized. Earwax, who was used to sleeping in the cowshed, had to make do with a hammock that had been made from two sails spliced together. Messy was placed in a cot from the nursery ward, because the nurse thought he was a child that needed its nappy changed. They were looked after well enough, seeing as there were no doctors anymore, since the practice had died out when the last of the Doc-kings vanished. Now there were only nurses, medics and first-aiders of the Paint Ones Shambulance units, whose abilities ranged from issuing plasters for stomachache or leprosy, to a poultice for heart attack or head-loss, whichever was worse at the time. So the medical staff at The Houses of Squealing was virtually helpless when it came to the biological and germ warfare of The Bleak Shroud.

The patients were left in the care of an old battle-axe matron called Irewrath, and her able assistant, Annie. Sister Annie was a huge brute of a woman and it was unfairly said that she was part Cave Thrall; her favourite medical implement was a club. Many had gone to surgery to have the odd stitch or two and never recovered from the tender care of Sister Annie Stetick and her club.

Irewrath would, from time to time, come up with a piece of nonsense only the very old understood, and would constantly mix up the Doc-kings with the Sea-kings. She said on one occasion, bemoaning the loss of royalty, 'I wish we had a king again. I remember reading about all those days off: public holidays, street parties, birthday parades, hmmm ...' she mused. Then, out of the blue, she said, 'The hands of a king are the hands of a sealer.'

'What the hell has tarring a boat got to do with this?' said The Grand Alf, pointing at the three grey, pallid patients.

'Oh ... er ... um ... tar is good for blocking the airways, so as to stop the noxious gases from causing damage,' replied the none-too-sure matron.

'Well, apart from the fact that blocking-up the airways after the attack would be useless, it would also stop them from being able to breathe at all,' said the perplexed wizard.

Earmore and Himhadrill left Paragon standing outside the city, for the stranger was used to living in a tent, or wrapped up in his old blanket. Lately, his only experience of living within four walls was at Elbow's Last Hobo House at Riverdwell. Meanwhile, The Chief Bulls-Hitter and The Prince of Dolt Amlost went in search of The Stalwart.

They found where the old king had been laid in state on two tables, and Earmore asked for the whereabouts of his sister, adding, 'For surely thou canst not lose something that big?'

Himhadrill answered, 'She has been taken to the Houses of Squealing, and now lies amongst the soon-to-be-dead.'

Earmore's heart was for that moment uplifted, for his outgoings now did not look so bad. Overjoyed, he left with Himhadrill for The Houses of Squealing. When they arrived, they found the malingering magician, who was only too pleased to tell the long tale of the three sick incumbents.

Now, when Himhadrill learned of the deceased Denizen and of the seriously ill Faraway, it passed through his mind just how closely he was related to the House of Howlin; after all, a prince was quite senior. His dreams were dispersed by the sudden appearance of Paragon.

'Is this the way to the throne room?'

Two guards were stationed at the door or, to be precise, one-and-a-half, for it was Beerygrog and Pipsqueak who advanced on what they perceived to be a scruffy intruder.

'The way to the back door of the kitchens is that way. I'm sure you can scrounge some scraps there,' said Beerygrog smugly, as he pointed somewhere indiscriminately.

The smile was wiped away by Pipsqueak who, having now caught a proper glimpse of the stranger's face, rushed forward and shouted, 'Stupor, how the hell did you get here? Did you stowaway on those ships that arrived earlier?'

'Sorry, Peregrinate Talk, I don't have time to tell you of my heroic and courageous exploits at this moment in time.'

'I wouldn't let common folk talk to me like that if I were king. I would have a magnificent name like Himhadrill the Highbrow,' said The Prince of Dolt Amlost.

'Himhadrill the Highfaluting, he means,' whispered Beerygrog to Pipsqueak.

'Well, seeing as that is not very likely, I will be known as The Lesser Half-stoned EverYakYak, The Respewer.' With that, he opened his cape and cloak, and there was the lump of green Elvish glass that Gadabout had given him; this was rumoured to be the base of a smashed bottle of Silvermarrywine. 'Stupor I was called before you were born, and that shall be the name of my house; in the posh lingo, it shall be Tallconcealer,' said Paragon, staring blankly at Himhadrill.

'That is posh. Most people call their house something simple, like Brag-end,' said Pipsqueak.

Even Beerygrog stared at the stupid Halfwit.

Paragon cuffed him as he entered the room, then inquired as to the nature of the sickness infecting the problem patients. The Grand Alf explained that all three had fallen foul of the fetid breath of a foul fell being. Pipsqueak had just climbed off the floor again, just in time to be knocked back down again after asking if The Witchy-king had been sent-off by a referee for two fouls, or two dives. Paragon was then taken to the three sick patients and, as the most medically trained person present, he examined them with all the skill he had acquired over the years. He had, after all, stood watching at the elbow of Elbow Halfman whilst he doctored everything at Riverdwell, including the accounts for The Elbow Elfy Living Company, which sold tap water to stupid humans. Paragon turned to Irewrath and asked if the patients had been given anything for their pain.

The staggering Pipsqueak, who had once again managed to

render himself upright, asked, 'Why, is it worth much? If so, I could be rich soon.'

At that point, Beerygrog thought it best to drag his friend outside; besides, he hadn't had a drink for at least half-an-hour.

The matron assured Paragon., 'Sister Annie has made sure they feel nothing. They may have a slight headache or a small fracture around the frontal lobe, some loss of memory, or brain damage, but nothing a bread-and-cow-manure poultice, and a small dance vigorously waving a stick wouldn't put right.'

Paragon was shocked to his core, for it was well known that, due to the blockade, the people of Minus Thrifty had eaten their last cow a long time ago; as such, surely the manure was well out of date by now. He held back his anger and asked the matron if there was any Mentholas in the Houses of Squealing.

'I don't know that word, and have never heard it spoken before. I think I had better ask The Herbal Verbal Master; he is always telling us that he is much more clever than we lowborn normal folk are,' said Irewrath.

'It is also called Klingfoil, after the silver leaf which it is wrapped in,' said Paragon.

'Oh, I know of that. I never knew it had any other use than for the freshening of the breath after the smoking of the weed. In fact, I have remarked many times how annoying it is when it gets stuck to one's clothes or the sole of one's shoe,' replied Irewrath.

'Well, if you value your position and love the perks that go with it, then go and scour the city for some freshly wrapped Mentholas,' said Paragon irately.

'And if she cannot find any in this starving city, I will take her by paths now open, to the massive Amalgamated Dulledain Shopping Area superstore (ADSA) in Lostheknack,' offered The Grand Alf.

So Irewrath went in search of the virtually impossible, and Paragon set about pretending to know what he was doing next.

Sometime later, a smug, superior looking old man entered the room and, whilst peering through spectacles that perched upon the end of his long, thin nose, he said, 'Which peasant asked for Klingfoil? Or, as we nobles call it, Mentholas? Or, to those of us with superior intellect, who know the tongue of Valliknownbinon-'

At that, he was cut off by Paragon. 'I speak Spindrawlin, Qwerty and Old Adunacake, and I don't care if you call it Klingfoil or Aspear Arrowmintion, just as long as you have some!'

The Herbal Verbal Master looked shocked and distressed. 'B ... b ... but, that tongue was only spoken by the highest of the high, and descended to us from the Elves of Vallinotknown in the Uncrying Lands. It was used only by the King at court, his in-bred close kin, and in small print, for dodgy legal documents.'

'Do I look like a shyster?' asked Paragon.

'No lord, but you don't look like a king either.'

'You lot are hardly experts on kings. When was the last time you saw one? And on that note, what should they look like?'

'Well, sort of old with a beard; a bit like him, but with a crown," said The Herbal Verbal Master, pointing at The Grand Alf.

'If that's your problem, then let me tell you that I am eighty-seven-and-a-bit years old, and know a brilliant plastic surgeon. I have a magnificent barber too and, as for a crown, I bought one from The Olde Ebay Shoppe last week.'

'Oh dear; I seem to have gotten mixed-up somewhat. Do I take it that you are the hero all Minus Thrifty is talking about? The person who came to the rescue of our city and destroyed our enemies?'

'Yes, your king has returned,' answered The Grand Alf proudly.

'That's funny; the reports said that you were either a large, manlike woman or a small, smelly midget,' replied Herby (as he shall now be called, due to the author's pen-nib breaking from the effort of writing his name out in full all the time).

'No, that is these two of which you speak; they had but a small part in the battle,' said Paragon, pointing to Messy and Earwax.

'Small part?! They killed the Witchy-king, something the Magnificent Marauding Mythroving couldn't do; so pray tell me, who did you kill, Lord Paragon?' replied Herby, as the wizard made an excuse about needing to go to the toilet.

'That is no secret: I killed Dorks and Thralls, and more Dorks and Thralls; and, in the extended version of my memoirs, you will learn that I also killed Coughsmog the Second, the Laffintenant of Minus Mucus,' said Paragon proudly.

'Oh, did you now? Can you describe him for us?'

'He was in fancy dress; it was hard to tell if he was a Dork who worshipped The Nasal or a Nasal trying to avoid war crimes by hiding amongst the Dorks,' said Paragon.

'So you don't know what race he belonged to then?' asked Herby.

'No, not exactly but, when you find someone who can, will you let us all know?'

'I can see that you are not only a great storyteller, but you are also a warrior of wisdom. So, lord, you will understand that we hold no stores of the thing wrapped in Klingfoil. We issued the last of it years ago to our ancient allies, The Y'hangkey, for their wars in Hererack and Aftermathistan. It would be no good in a place of sick men who ask only for final cigarettes, and they should have asked long ago for something in place of that, which in truth makes men sick. Yet, its only virtue seems to be for sweetening the breath, when talking to good-looking ladies at court or, if you believe in old wives' tales, or trivial verses like Irewrath does, you could place some store on this.' He then began to recite:

'WHEN THE BAD BREATH BLOWS
DOWN THE WITCHY-KING'S NOSE,
WHICH SMELLS OF GRAVE GAS,
COME MENTHOLAS! COME MENTHOLAS!
LIFE TO THE GASPING,
IN THE KING'S HAND GRASPING.'

At that point, Beerguild burst in with a six-packet wrapped in Klingfoil. 'It is not new; it was found behind shelving, and is two weeks past its sell-by date. I hope it will help,' said the young lad who, upon seeing the prostate Faraway, burst into wails and gnawing of teeth, fearing that his father would soon be out of work again, as he so often was.

Paragon said, 'Fear not; it is exactly what I need.' He then took two pieces, unwrapped them and, popping them in his mouth, began to chew. Those close by, followed by everyone else in the room, gradually began to feel the lessening in strength of Paragon's halitosis. All in that room would later report how the sudden freshness in the air was sweeter than any top brand air freshener. And so the mouth of Paragon became refreshed.

After a couple of minutes of chewing, Herby asked if what

Paragon was doing was actually helping the sick patients.

'Of course, I am but waiting for the right consistency; then I take one last chew and take it from my mouth,' said Paragon, demonstrating. 'After that, I pull a small piece from the whole and roll it into a ball, open Faraway's mouth, place the ball beneath his tongue ... like so ... and close his mouth again. Then I hold his nose and, after a few seconds, he will begin to chew, and the vapours start to work on his sickness. See, he stirs.' Faraway started to gag and choke. 'And now, I must perform The Mindkick Hindmover.' He lifted Faraway and stood him in the centre of the room. Next, he gave him a swift kick in the butt and the small piece of chewy stuff came shooting out of the new Stalwart's mouth.

'Good Lord! I say,' spluttered Faraway, looking at Paragon.

'I'll try to be,' replied The Stranger. He turned to The Grand Alf and Himhadrill and, looking at Messy and Earwax, the Buxom Milkmaid of Bovine, said, 'Now, we must look at these other one-and-a-half patients.'

'Yes, lord' replied Himhadrill, and saw Faraway looking questioningly at him. 'Yes, Faraway; unfortunately for us, a king has returned.' Faraway looked sceptical.

Irewrath was overheard saying to Sister Annie, 'See, I told you: the Ands of a king are the Ands of a healer.'

The Grand Alf gave her a withering look, but that just made her rush off even quicker, so she could tell everyone who could, or would, listen about how she had discovered a king-sized secret.

Paragon moved to where Earwax lay. 'Here is a groaning heart in a heavy body. Alas, she has fought a foe beyond the strength and size of even her great bulk. She is a fair-sized maiden; what has made her so, I can only guess. Do you think, Earmore, maybe it is food she has found joy in and, as yet, not loved any man, save her uncle, who gave her control of running the household and the keys to the larder?'

'Why ask me? I'm not to blame for her bad condition. She was OK when we left. Come to think of it, she was OK until you came along. That was when she started to act differently, washing the cow dung from her fingernails, and even combing the straw from her hairy legs.'

'She was damn well bored!' said The Grand Alf. 'While you were out being the big playboy, she was changing incontinence

226

pants. The only man in her life was a decrepit old one and the cretinous Worntwang. The moment she saw a new face, no matter how boring it was, she was besotted.'

'Well, we must be thankful for small mercies: she could have met the Dwarf first.'

'That would have saved me the trouble of having to practically fight her off at Dunharrowing,' said Paragon.

'Well, can you fix her?' asked Earmore.

'Yes, and no. I can mend the damage of the Bad Breath, but I will never manage the manoeuvre I showed you earlier. Plus, I have no wish to be the first face she sees. You are her brother, so you will be safe.'

So Earmore was instructed in the finer points of medical care and what do when Paragon gave the order. Then Paragon took the Mentholas and said, 'She is a maid made manly in size, so I must use two-thirds of what is left for her.'

Pipsqueak, who had crept back into the room, said mournfully, 'But that will mean you've used three-thirds, and there won't be any left for Messy.' The Halfbit was chased from the room by The Grand Alf.

Paragon placed the Mentholas into the Earwax's mouth and he held her nose until she choked. At that point, he ran off, shouting, 'NOW!' from a safe distance.

Earmore chopped the rope holding the large hammock to the wall.

Earwax crashed to the floor, making the room shake, and dislodging the gum. At last she awoke and said in a groggy voice, 'I've just had the strangest dream; I dreamt I was in another place and that I killed a Witchy-thing by melting it. I knew I was dreaming, for those red shoes would never have fit me really. Oh, where's that smelly dog that bit the Witchy-things bottom? No, wait, that's wrong; it was the smelly Halfbit Messy, wasn't it?'

'It's good to see you wake in prime health,' said The Grand Alf.

'What is it with you lot, always talking about my weight? I know I'm hefty,' said Earwax angrily.

They all made a quick exit and found Paragon already administering his medication to Messy. They arrived just in time to hear him muttering a curse against greedy Halfbits. 'He swallowed it before I could do anything,' said Paragon.

At that moment, Messy sat bolt upright and said, 'I hope there's more for breakfast than that.'

The others laughed and left Messy and Pipsqueak talking about nothing in particular — well, at least nothing anyone outside of The Snore would want to know about. Shortly after, it was announced that the King had left the building.

THE LAST DEBACLE

The next morning, Legless and Grimy awoke early, both slightly grumpy. This was mainly due to the fact that there had been nothing left to drink after the Ruminates and Blahguards had guzzled most of it before the two of them had got there. So they walked through the city, towards The Houses of Squealing, having been informed of the visiting hours and wishing to see their good friends the Halfbits, who were also, coincidentally, the only ones in Minus Thrifty with weed.

On their way, they met Himhadrill. Legless acknowledged the strain of lower class Elven ancestry, yet admitted it gave The Lords of Dolt Amlost a one-up in the dating game. 'It is obvious that not all the people of Nymphroving left Dolt Amlost. Oh, by the way, are there any good inns on route?' he asked hopefully.

'Yes,' answered the Prince. 'I am descended from Missfellas, maid of Nymphroving. She is also the first Barmaid of the dockyard public house, The Swan and Ship, from which we take our Battle Banner. So, where are you going?'

'To the Houses of Squealing,' replied Legless.

'I'll take you there, as I'm booked in for a colonic irrigation,' said Himhadrill.

'It will have to wait; Paragon is holding a combat convention and has asked me to convey to you and Earmore that you come at your convenience. The Grand Alf is already there, now that it is safe to leave the city,' said Legless.

They parted company and headed for their separate locations. Upon arrival at their destination, they found Pipsqueak and Messy doing a bit of weeding in the garden. After attempting to talk for a while about their adventures whilst still in the upright position, they noticed that the only one who had managed to do so was Legless.

He was standing by the battlements, doing some bird watching (of the feathered type, that is). He suddenly shouted, 'Look, look: seagulls. Quick, bring me my bow of Breaking Hold; bring me my Arrows of Retire. If we don't shoot them, we'll have an

229

infestation on our hands. I have an Elf-friend, called Kram, who lived in the Wood of Fleet, and he told me of the mounds of droppings they leave behind, and how they destroy the bags of man-made black fibre which the cheapskate Council of Addled issue for the discarding of rubbish. I think these birds must have followed the ships up from Halflong.'

Legless by now had received his bow, and was just about to draw it, when one of the gulls loosed its bowels on his head. The Elf stood transfixed, in a kind of mesmerised state that was usually associated with his having drunk something potent. Now, this state was known amongst the Elves as The Temptation of the Telewiri, and dated back to the time when they had awoken, at Kurantvinedistilin. It was at that time that O'roamin had first appeared to them, singing and dancing, whilst drinking some dark brew and telling them fantastic tales of The Uncrying Lands. He had brought DVDs to show the Elves the properties that were available to buy or rent there, for The Powers had been building them in preparation for the day that the Children of Ill-farter came into being, and The Powers wished to be very rich property magnates. The Peroxide Blonde Bimbo wives of The Vainyar had dragged their spouses to the front of the queue, wishing to get all the best houses. First in the queue was their leader Ginwe, who wasn't too happy at being pulled out of the local inn. Next came The No-older, led by Finewine, who upset The Powers by building their own houses. Then, dragging their heels, came The Telewiri, led by The Bickering Brothers, Oddwe and Eludwe. They had soon grown bored with the videos and had dropped off the property ladder, and ended up living in caves when they eventually got to The Uncrying Lands. So it was foretold that any of The Telewiri who smelled anything of the sea would be overwhelmed with a longing for scuba diving, surfing, fishing and sailing.

Legless, whose grandfather Soporific, and father Thatfool, were both of The Telewiri, had started thinking about the next booze cruise and talking about booking his ticket. For some reason, Legless picked this moment to tell the others about this.

Grimy didn't much like the sound of that: it would leave him with no one to jibe at and, furthermore, the Elf was about the only way he could get to meet the lovely Gadabout again. 'Oh, don't be hasty, friend Legless; there is lots we can do here in

Muddy Earth.'

'Like what?' asked Legless, suspiciously.

'Well, I thought we could go into business as landscape gardeners. I could do the rockeries and you could plant the trees and flowers; maybe even a small vegetable patch.'

At the mention of edibles, the Halfbits' ears pricked up. 'We could be quality controllers; chief tasters for you,' they said in unison.

'Not bloody likely,' came the reply, also in unison.

A dejected Pipsqueak decided to try again later. In the meantime, he asked the Elf and Dwarf about their journey to Minus Thrifty. Grimy became very quiet and withdrawn, so Legless explained that the Dwarf had wet himself and couldn't tell anything of that journey because he'd had his eyes closed for most of their time spent on The Road of the Dead-heads.

'What sort of numbskull would make a path out of heads? Wasn't it uneven? Surely leg bones would have been straighter; then it would have been The Road of the Dead-legs. Come on Grimy, tell us what you saw,' said Pipsqueak.

'Not bloody likely,' replied Grimy, as he glanced from side to side worriedly.

Legless, meanwhile, had taken one of the sheets off a bed and was creeping up behind the Dwarf. Wearing it, he started to make loud 'Woooo' noises, like a ghost. Grimy shot under the bed and started to shake.

The Elf roared with laughter, until he collapsed on top of the bed. When he eventually stopped, he turned to the halfbits and said, 'I'll tell you the story, because I wasn't scared of the bogeymen.' He told of the road to Hedwreck and then on to Pellagra. 'Behind us came a shambling host, and from every burial mound and silent grave crawled more. When we came to Lamexcuse, they wished to push on, for these wasting-warriors were hungry for what they called The Bite-fight; yet Paragon held them back, telling them that, for them it was not yet time for dinner. The next day, we crossed the Kitch and Ringlow, and on the next day we came to Lingerhir at the mouth of Glibbreign. And all the host of Lamexcuse that had found a reason not to go to war at Minus Thrifty, found in the end that it had come to them, for they battled with the men of Harass and Umbrage. Now, when those who battled saw the shambling host of The

King-shorn of The Dead-heads, they all ran away, crying for their mummies. Only Angbak, Lord of Lamexcuse, stood his ground. For Angbak was a horror film fan and recognised his hero, The King-shorn of the Dead-heads, and wished for his autograph. After having their photograph taken together and Angbak getting a few more autographs, one for his son and the other to sell on Ye Olde Ebay Shoppe, Paragon informed him of the cost for these: he and his people were to follow on behind, hanging back from the army of Dead-heads. We chased the army of Morbid over The Glibreign, and they ran like Dwarves from a bathhouse. We headed then for Pellagra, for there lay the fleet of The Corps of Umbrage.'

At the mention of that name, Messy asked who they were.

'The original Corps of Umbrage are also called The Slack Neomanoreans, and are descended from those Neomanoreans who decided life was a bit to dull on Neomanor, so they started to hang out at Sourone's. Later, during the King-swipe, Castimout took Umbrage and raised the New Corps of Umbrage. His descendants were defeated by Telumall Umbragekilla. However, Umbrage was soon lost again to the men of Harass, who are now passing themselves off as The Corps of Umbrage,' explained Legless.

'What's a King's wipe? Is it a large size toilet roll?' asked Pipsqueak.

Legless gave the halfwit Halfbit a whack on the head with the end of his bow. 'The King-swipe was a fight between Vanacar's son, Weldacar, and Castimout over who should be king. Castimout killed Weldacar's son, Ornamental, but Weldacar eventually won.' Then, returning to the story of their journey and their encounter with the Corps of Umbrage, Legless continued. 'When we arrived at Pellagra, we cornered the men of Harass. With nowhere left to run, they turned and made a pretence of bravery by pushing the weaker and older ones amongst them to the frontline. Then they shouted rude names at Paragon from the back. Losing patience, Paragon loosed the shambling host.

'They advanced as one great tide of decay and with many mumbling voices. Rusty, bent and blunt blades clanged against the armour of the men of the south. In every corner of the port city, the Dead-heads of Dunharrowing harassed the Harassdim. The Dead-heads turned then to the ships, and on each ship the mariners fell into the sea, to their deaths, with Dead-heads eating their fast diminishing extremities. They died armless and unable to swim. The Dead-heads, who had no need to breathe, walked along the seabed and climbed the anchor chains of those ships not in port. Again these ships were soon unmanned and overrun by the Dead-heads. The fleet was now in the hands of Paragon, who was desperately trying to find an admiral, ship's captain, or even a cabin boy who could steer a ship. He was just beginning to wish he'd saved some of The Corps of Umbrage when we discovered that most of the ships had slaves on them. The slaves were needed to turn the big wheels on either side of the ship. This was done by pedal-power. Some of these newly freed slaves came forward to inform Paragon that they had served aboard fishing vessels, so he placed them in charge of the rudders. Before we left, Paragon called for all the Dead-heads to gather together. With the rotten army stood before him, Paragon called out in a loud voice, "Hear the Heir of Evenduller. I deem that the completion of our contract is confirmed". A Dead-head at the back cupped his hands to where his ears once were and shouted, "Speak up — it's hard to hear at the back". "Hear, hear," shouted another in agreement. "Where? I lost mine yesterday" said the first, as he staggered over. Paragon continued by saying, "Decay, be in pieces and let your weapons fall to rust". At that, a low moaning was heard as the Dead-heads disintegrated. They sang as they fell apart:

'PACK UP YOUR INNARDS IN YOUR OLD KITBAG
AND SMELL, SMELL, SMELL.'

We then boarded the ships and, as told, we coerced the freed slaves and arrived in time to beat the Morbid Army and win the day.'

'But you arrived at the end of the battle. You can't say you won it by being there only at the end. It was Messy who killed the Witchy-king,' said Pipsqueak.

'I heard it was Earwax,' said Legless.

'I heard it was both of them,' said Grimy, emerging from under the bed.

'I didn't realise there were two Witchy-kings,' said Pipsqueak.
While they chased the stupid Halfbit around the room, the

war council was meeting, and The Grand Alf was informing them of the last mad utterings of Denizen.

'You may try thumping on the Pell-mell Fields today, but your army must gain power-ups or this will be a sick story. Do not despair as I did, trying to find any meaning in this drivel. Denizen was driven mad by the twisted visions sent by Sourone on the Seeing Phone. The last scenes he saw were from a film by Jack Peterson; he became confused and didn't know reality from lies. But Sourone, in using The Seeing Phone, could not wholly hide the truth; he could only poorly edit what was already a stretching of reality and double the effect of misunderstanding. Our one hope is that he will not be around to see the end of this sorry tale. We have only beaten the first wave of woe; there will be a second and a third, until we are beaten down.'

'We can always run away and hide: there are many tunnels and caverns in The Airhead Loony and The Blew Mountains, as you call them,' said Grimy.

'We can't do that,' said Legless. 'We would bang our heads continually inside your tiny hovels. I don't want to end up stunted with a bad back. I have a better idea: we could issue you all with our excellent camouflage gear, then you could hide away in the forest and never be seen, like we Elves.'

'You can't see each other because you're blind drunk most of the time.'

'No, I think our best bet, as Stan would say, is to try and trick Sourone. One of us must dress up as a Halfbit, put a ring around his neck and pretend to be The Ringbreaker. Funnily enough, I have the perfect candidate in mind,' said The Grand Alf, thinking of Pipsqueak.

'I have a better idea: I will pretend that I have the Ring. I will use my Seeing Phone and taunt Sourone. He will think I've gotten too big for my boots,' said Paragon.

'Don't you mean Borrowit's boots,' muttered the Dwarf.

'Yes, I see your point Paragon. He will be thinking how a great army was beaten by such a hopeless horde of hoi polloi, and how his great captain's chief weapon of fear has been neutralised. He will be looking to see which one of us has been promoted, or won employee of the month,' said The Grand Alf.

'I always thought that The Witchy-king's chief weapon was surprise,' said Grimy.

234

'And I always thought it was a fanatical devotion to The Dank Lord,' said Legless.

'I heard that he was roofless in a fishing sea, though I've never understood what that means,' said Himhadrill.

'OK, OK, I didn't expect this to spawn issues in quintessence,' said The Grand Alf.

'So, what do we do then? We can't run and hide forever. We can't stay here either; the gates are gone,' proclaimed Earmore.

'Then we go to Morbid and picket his gates until he pays compensation. That will hopefully keep him and his army of Dorks, Thralls, Ring-cyclists and litigation lawyers, busy while Foodo and Stan sneak in through Sourone's back passage,' said The Grand Alf.

'I can see only pain and discomfort in this,' replied Paragon.

'My brother and I have come south for such a fight, and are looking forward to giving Sourone a kick up the rear also,' said Ellovaman.

'The Lord Paragon is my Leech-lord of Gondour,' said Himhadrill. 'As far as I am concerned, where he goes I go. However, there is no Stalwart so, if he wants someone wise and strong, with an upper class chin, to stay behind and mind his house, he need look no further; I volunteer.'

'I haven't a clue what the hell you're all talking about, but count me in. It sounds like fun to me,' said Earmore.

'Right then, how many have we got?' asked The Grand Alf.

This led to lots of fingers being counted, heads being scratched and general looks of bemusement. At the end, working together, and using their toes, they figured they had about seven thousand. Further to this, Paragon told the council of the new recruits coming from the south, led by Angbak the Foeless. He also told of the army of part-timers he would be sending to destroy the Dork ambush at Stoned-way Valley from behind. He placed Effinghel in charge of the charge.

So it was decided that this motley crew of horsemen, foot soldiers, three inebriated Elves, a dishevelled Dwarf, a seriously dodgy, doddering old wiztari, all led by a semi-king on probation, who hadn't as yet filled in the application form — oh, and not forgetting one Halfbit who had decided to tag along, only because several inn-keepers were owed more money than he would ever earn — would all be going to The Back Gates of Morbid.

OPERATION BACK GATE

Two days later, Messy stood on the battlements watching the army march off. Beerguild was with him, being careful to stand upwind of the smelly Halfbit. 'I wish I was going with them, but they have put me in charge of the city's Biological Warfare Unit. All I have to do now is find the rest of the unit.'

'You are the unit; they don't need anyone else,' replied Beerguild.

They stood then in silence, watching the army disappear into the distance, marching through Ohgivusalaugh, on the road which led to The Tower of the Gloom, that was also called Minus Mucus.

The army stayed on this road until it reached The Cross-roads of The Crap-roads. There, they set aright the dark work of the Dork artist, Damanit Hurts. As they did this they shouted bravely, 'The Lah-de-Dah's of Gondour are here,' knowing that all the Dorks were now miles away, behind The Back Gates.

Himhadrill said nervously, 'Don't mention us Lah-de-Dah's; just mention The Lesser King, for The Enemy may be content to blame only him for this.'

They set out again, until they came to the place where Faraway and his Piffling Strangers had sneakily ambushed the men of Harass. Here, they were also ambushed by Dorks and Eagerlings; however, that ambush was itself ambushed by Madlunge, who had been hiding in the bushes. This victory wasn't celebrated, mainly because Paragon was holding back the mead until they got to The Back Gates, for it was there that he deemed that false courage would be needed most.

So at last, and after the fourth day of moaning and marching from the Cross-roads of The Crap-roads, they approached The Nigh of Sourone. As they stood looking at The Mushlands to the north and The Deserted Deserts of Death, many men who had only a few nights before sung songs of bravado and claimed they would follow Paragon to The Dank Tower itself, wet themselves and cried. Seeing this, Paragon's thoughts turned to the battle ahead. Not wanting these mummy's boys to flee in panic, he told them he needed volunteers to go and attack The Cairn and Rose. This they didn't need to be asked twice.

So as they marched away, heads held high, one soldier, wiping his brow, said to his friend, 'Phew! That was a lucky escape.'

'Yes, but now we won't get the bottle of battle-booze,' replied his friend.

'But if we hurry, the Dorks won't have drunk The Cairn and Rose dry.'

Then, at last, the army of the Lesser King came to The Back Gates and The Blight of Morbid. The gates were closed and nothing moved.

As they stood and stared at the massive doors, Pipsqueak asked, 'Well, isn't somebody going to knock on them and see if anyone is in?'

'Of course they are in. Where else would they be?' growled The Grand Alf.

'They could have gone shopping; or to see the latest Potty Harry movie; you know, the one about how that evil wizard, Fooldemorph, turned into a giant rubber duck and drowned Potty in the swimming baths at Hogwash. It's called Potty Harry and The Deadly Shallows.'

'Don't be so bloody stupid! Sourone can't easily leave his tower, and his eye is stuck on us.'

'Is it?' said Pipsqueak, who then proceeded to do a jig and make rude gestures towards The Dank Tower, at times adding, 'Do you think he can see me?' His pantomime was stopped by the back of The Grand Alf's hand. 'Ok then, can I go and ring the bell?' said the Halfbit, as he picked himself off the floor.

'No, we are going to draw straws for it.'

'But I haven't brought my pencil.'

Ignoring the stupid Halfbit, Paragon said, 'We are all going in that way. He will probably take more notice if lots of us are at his door.'

'Why are we all going to ring the bell? Won't the constant ringing annoy him more?' asked Pipsqueak.

'Will you please shut up?' roared The Grand Alf.

They all rode forward to the gates, halted and, in their most important-sounding voices The Grand Alf and Paragon shouted,

'Let the Lord of the Bleak Land come forth.'

'Why won't Sourone be coming first, and which three do you think will be coming out before him?' said Pipsqueak.

Grimy didn't answer, for he was concentrating on holding onto the bull, which Legless was purposely prodding with his heels. Nothing much was happening at the gates and most thought that, being stuck to his telescope, Sourone wouldn't be coming out anyway. Just as they were giving up hope, the gates creaked slowly open.

Through them came The Dank Lord's Chief Propaganda Minister, The Mouthpiece of Sourone. He approached them and said smugly, 'Well you all obviously know who I am.'

'I don't. Are you one of the first three?' said Pipsqueak, from his hiding place behind Paragon.

'Ah, The Dunce and Footsore King,' said the mouthy one, ignoring the pipsqueak.

Paragon just stared back and, with one hand resting on the hilt of Andrex, he made slicing motions across his throat with the other.

The Mouthpiece squirmed and said, 'By The Green-elves Convention, you are not allowed to touch me. I am protected by those.' He pointed to the Sourone.com security cameras, and then to a dirty white rag at the end of a pole, that was being held upright by one of his minions. His skull-like face contorted into a grimace that may have passed for a grin.

'Yes, that may be true; however, I seem to remember your lot never got around to signing that treaty, so you and all of Sourone's slaves are in deep crap,' replied The Grand Alf.

'Aha, I wondered how long it would take before your mouth started to flap, oh great boring one. We in Morbid have heard of your wily ways, wandering around Muddy Earth ranting and foaming at the mouth, talking a good fight from a very safe distance, sticking your rather large hooked nose into other people's business and causing troubles wherever you turn up. Well, you have chosen the wrong door to knock upon this time, Mr Grand Alf. You will see what becomes of those who disturb the peace of Sourone the Grouch. Oh, and by the way, would you like to see my collection of Elven artifacts?' sneered The Mouthpiece, holding up Foodo's cloak and Knitsteel corset in one hand; in the other hand, he held a rusty steak-knife that had belonged to Stan.

Pipsqueak emerged from his hiding place behind Paragon and asked, 'Yeah, but where is Stink?'

The Mouthpiece took one look at the Halfbit and laughed; it was a horrible, gruesome sound. 'What is this halfwit talking about? Why they were ever allowed to come into existence is a mystery to me. What use they are is also beyond me. and as for letting them wander around free, that is surely a mistake. Yet, the most stupid thing of all though, is to send them on an errand to the shops, for verily they will end up lost, and may even end up wandering around Morbid. Well, at least this one did, the old fool. He proved in the end to be a great entertainment for my master. I can still smell the burning of curly foot-hair. Isn't it amazing how much pain they can suffer just for the promise of some food? Yet, this will be nothing compared to the roasting he will receive in the ovens of the Dorks, if you don't sign away all your rights to the rule of Gondour: all your fishing rights, your vehicle parking zone franchises, and your bus passes.'

'Can we think about it for a few days? After all, you've only got one stupid Halfbit, and he's not worth that much,' replied The Grand Alf.

'Yes, but which one has he got?' piped up Pipsqueak from the back, just before he was re-introduced to the butt of the wizard's staff.

'How do we know he is alive?' asked The Grand Alf. 'They have to be fed on a regular basis or they tend to fall down, stunned. What's the chance of seeing him or even speaking to him on the telling-phone?'

'If my master allows it, we will let him give you a ring,' said The Mouthpiece.

Pipsqueak, who by now was staggering around at the back somewhere, said, 'Why, haven't you taken it off him yet?'

At that moment, Grimy fell off his bull and squashed the little Halfbit.

As the Mouthpiece stared incredulously at the antics of this sorry band of morons, The Grand Alf pulled his flash-in-the-pan trick, startling The Mouthpiece, thus enabling The Wiztari to snatch back the Elvish items from under his the nose. 'I'll sell these at Ye Olde Ebay Shoppe and split the money between his friends. As for you, I think it would be a good idea to scarper, for if we find you after winning the battle, we are going to tie you to a chair and dental floss you with this.' He held up a piece of bicycle chain they had found after the demise of the Ring Cyclists at the ford.

The Mouthpiece stared in horror, knowing the chain for what it was. Seeing now that the old Wiztari was grinning at him, he was for once lost for words. He turned on his ass and disappeared as quickly as he could back through the gates. Out of those gates came thousands of Dorks and their allies. The petty little army of The Semi-king of Gondour was dwarfed, leaving only Grimy comfortable with their predicament.

Pipsqueak suddenly realised that facing a few dozen innkeepers might have been the better option. 'I wish Messy was here,' he whimpered.

'What good would one more Halfbit be? Surely we could do with a battalion of Elven archers or Dwarven axe-grinders,' replied The Grand Alf.

'No, I wish he was here instead of me.'

But, even as he spoke, the first wave of maddened, drooling Dorks ploughed into them. With them came Kill-thralls, great lumbering beasts of destruction, crashing and bashing through anything in their way. Some of the more mindless Thralls headed back to the gates, kicking Dorks in the air like footballs. One had gotten a bit close to Beerygrog and bashed him on the head a few times, so that he was staggering around worse than he had after his last pub-crawl. The Thrall was just about to strike the stunned man again when Pipsqueak employed his ancient steak knife in a spot of gender re-assignment. The Thrall howled in a strange, squeaky sort of way, tottered around, and fell over onto both man and Halfbit, squashing them in the process.

As Pipsqueak lost consciousness, he heard the wizard shouting, 'The Regals are coming! The Regals are coming!' Pipsqueak said in a weak voice, 'The wizard's gone daft. He thinks he's in another story,' and then went silent without even having to be hit to make him so.

THE TOWER OF CRITTER UNGODLY

Stan, who had decided to rescue his master, but only for the sake of winning his bet, was now in a quandary. Because he had dithered and lagged behind, he had desperately tried to drag his fat, lazy body onwards in an attempt to catch up with the Dorks, only to have the gates shut in his fat face. Now he was stuck. He couldn't go on and certainly didn't want to go back through Sheblob's Larder, no matter how badly the big spidey-widey was injured. So Stan decided to look around, hoping to find a hole in the wall, or a maintenance ladder left behind by some careless worker Dork.

He then imagined, instead of a ladder, that maybe a trampoline had been left out. However, he soon calculated the odds against that. His musing was disturbed by the sounds of fighting above him. He hoped that all the Dorks were busy squabbling in some public house or other. In fact, most of them were watching the local football match between Liverpullers and Maneater United. The thought that Foodo could get caught up in all the fighting afterwards upset him slightly, so he ran on for a couple of yards until, puffing and panting, he came to a stop in front of a road sign that read:

MORBID CAN SERIOUSLY DAMAGE YOUR LIVER
(ESPECIALLY WHEN COOKED WITH ONIONS)

Stan thought that he should slow down a bit. Thankful for the excuse to walk, he made his way slowly from boulder to boulder, trying to find ones that would hide his large belly. Bit by bit, and with plenty of rests, he found himself on a ridge staring at Horridruin, the Mountain of Gloom.

The crown of the mountain was topped by an inky vortex of utter darkness that swirled up from some hidden depth. Stan hoped the strange light from The File of Gadabout would be strong enough to cut through that dismal darkness. However, he had other things to worry about first: how to get through the big gate to his left without being seen or heard, or his stomach rumbling and giving him away. He thought of using The Nose Ring again; this seemed at first a good idea, and he was prompted by images of himself as Stan the String-vested General Manager of Gamble's Greenhouses and Gardening Merchandise Inc. Everywhere he looked, he saw a potential potato paradise.

He pulled out The Nose Ring, and was just about to put it on when he suddenly stopped and thought twice about it. It would be a lot of work digging away in all that soil. So he put it away again and said to himself, 'Umm, maybe some other time.' With that, he set off for the tower gate.

As he approached it, he once again heard the sounds of fighting, which by now had grown into a major Dork ding-dong.

The football match was now over and Growbag's Mankies and Shagbag's Scourgers were beating the living daylights out of each other. As he stood watching, the two Dorks dashed out the gate. They got about a hundred yards up the road before Stan heard the sounds of a catapult being released, followed by a thud, as a large latrine landed on the heads of the fleeing Dorks. The replica shirts they were wearing turned green with their blood.

Stan was feeling very uneasy about his meal ticket being caught up in all this, so he crept up to the gate and tried to sneak through. It was at that point that he froze in fear, for on either side of the gate was the great one-eyed Silly Soundless Whatsits of the See-see T.V. He grabbed The File to see what it said about avoiding surveillance. Suddenly, he felt a tingling sensation in his hands and a super-charged bolt of electrickery shot out towards the one-eyed monstrosities, blasting them to smoky ruins. This had the knock-on effect of setting off all the alarms in the control room at the top of the tower. With a speed that would have shocked The Grafter, Stan legged it through the gateway and into a concealed doorway.

He peered out upon the carnage littered around the courtyard. Dead dorks, some wearing red, and others white replica football shirts, lay scattered all about. 'Phew, that's against all the odds. Looks like they've done all the work for me,' said Stan to himself.

Turning back into the doorway, he saw that he was in fact at the bottom floor of a spiral staircase. A sign had been posted beside it, reading, "To the Torture Chamber". He decided to go up, in search of Foodo, despite his body being in some pain after his enforced dash across the courtyard. Halfway up the stairs, he heard feet coming down towards him. Damn! I'm not going all the way down and up again; too much bother, he thought. So he took off his hooded cape, stuck the hilt of Stink into the hood and held it aloft, above his head. With his other hand, he pulled the front of the cape around his face, leaving a gap for one eye.

When the Dork came into view, Stan's knees were already shaking. However, the Dork stopped in its tracks and, on account of the dim light, which made it seem as if something that towered high above him, and which smelt like death warmed up, was coming up the stairs, it fled back from whence it came. Stan's shouted after it, in a shaky voice, 'You can run but you can't hide. I'm the Great Elf-surgeon, and I'm going to practice skin grafting on you.' With that, he ran up after the Dork.

For Stan, the next twenty steps of jogging seemed the most painful he had ever taken. Soon he had slowed to a fast-walk, and dragged himself up this stairway that seemed to go on forever. He tried counting the steps, but gave up after twenty, as he had run out of fingers and toes to add with. The betting odds in The Snore were capped at 20-1 for that very reason.

Eventually, after many rests, he arrived at the top of the stairs. Facing him was a door. He opened it and peeked inside. What he saw was a small five-a-side football pitch with two teams of dead Dorks littered all over it. Just then, the voice of Shagbag shattered the eerie silence.   'You'll do as you're told, Snotta Big-nose, or I'll throttle you with my own hands, just as I did Ridbug Toad-tongue. Then Sheblob will have second helpings.'

'I'm not leaving here until another patrol calls,' snivelled Snotta.

'I'm in charge here; get down those stairs!'

'No! Growbag's lot are down there, and they've dished the dirt on Legded and Muztdash.'

'Someone must report to Slugbash or we'll all be for it; especially you, for disobeying orders.'

'Not me. You and Growbag are going to be fed to The Nasal when they find out what you two have been up to.'

Growbag and Shagbag were partners with one of Sourman's Dorks in a smuggling ring, and their most lucrative contraband was a weed called Largebottom Leaf. 'You snivelling snitch, Snotta. I'm gonna gut you.'

'You'll have to catch me first,' shouted Snotta, as he leapt past the fatter, slower Dork.

'You worthless scum. I'll go myself, you coward.'

'Best of luck, Shagbag. Oh, and watch out for the Elf-surgeon on the stairs,' shouted Snotta, as he scuttled off somewhere.

Shagbag started limping towards the door, which Stan was hiding behind. Good, he must have been injured in the fight with the barmy army, thought Stan. With the Dork approaching, and nowhere to run and hide, he decided to try the shock tactic of surprise. He jumped out, growling and snarling, as if someone had just stolen the last piece of cake at his birthday party.

It was Stan who got the surprise though, for he hadn't seen the large, black bin bag that the Dork was carrying. He did get a very close-up view of it now, as Shagbag smacked it cleanly into the Halfbit's face.

As he did this, the Dork said, 'Get out of my way, maggot; I haven't got the time or energy for you. I have to save myself for the fight with the Great Elf-surgeon.' He then disappeared down the stairs, leaving Stanwitless witless.

Stan rose reluctantly from what nearly became forty winks and headed in the direction that Snotta had gone, leading to the furthest tower of the keep. He was dismayed to find another set of stairs leading upward. Between the sharp sabres, the dreadful Dorks and the bad CO_2 emissions Stan was growing tired of it all. He looked at the stairs and said, 'This place will be the death of me,' and staggered up them.

On arrival at the top, he found a short corridor with lots of doors along it. He began trying all of the handles and tapping at the walls, looking for hidden trapdoors and false sections, of the kind he'd seen in the film Hinder Anna Bones and the Traders of the Lost Mark. After two laps of the corridor and finding all the doors locked, Stan collapsed, panting and sweating. A strange thing happened to him as he sat there, breathing heavily: he noticed how the acoustics of the passage were quite echoic, much like his rarely-used bathroom at home. Now Stan considered himself quite the Pub Idol, and at times a struggle would ensue when trying to retrieve the microphone from him at the King's Head Karaoke Contest. He thought of his favourite Country and Western ballad, and began to belt it out, listening appreciatively to the echo:

'IN WESTERN SONGS, THERE IS NO FUN.
AND IT SEEMS SO STRANGE A THING,
SO MANY DIE WITHOUT A GUN,
THAT THEY FORGOT TO BRING.
THEY GET INTO A STUPID FIGHT,
IN THE TAVERN OR A BAR.
THEY ARGUE OVER WHO IS RIGHT,
AND WHO HAS THE LONGEST SCAR.

NOW THOUGH, IT IS THAT ONE MUST DIE,
AND TAKE ETERNAL SLEEP,
TO LEAVE A MOTHER WITH NEED TO BUY,
A COFFIN AND TO WEEP.
HE'LL LEAVE BEHIND A BABY SON,
A DOG THAT'S NEVER WELL,
A HORSE, WHOSE DAYS ARE LONG SINCE DONE,
AND A WIFE TO ROT IN HELL.'

From somewhere up above, a voice wailed thinly in answer: 'Enough! No more torture. I give in.'

It was a sound Stan had grown used to back in The Snore, for in truth he didn't know many songs and he'd worn this one out a long time ago. As if in answer to his warbling, came the sound of a door opening and Snotta unfolding a stepladder. The Dork placed this under a section of the ceiling with the words, BEWARE! HEAVY TRAP DOOR written upon it. Hiding in the shadows, Stan thought it was a clever idea for the Dorks to have concealed it so, and then remembered that this tower had been built by Evenduller and the Dulledain, and was suddenly more confused than normal. He gave up attempting to think about that and watched Snotta struggling to position the stepladder properly.

The ladder seemed to have been damaged at some time in the not too distant past, so Snotta was getting quite irate with it. At one point, the Dork caught his thumb in the locking mechanism and proceeded to throw the ladder from one side of the corridor to the other, and jump upon it as if it were alive and could feel this abuse. Stan wondered if maybe this was how the ladder got damaged in the first place. Snotta calmed a little, picked it up again and managed to set it up properly. The Dork climbed up and pushed the heavy trapdoor open, the effort of which made the ladder wobble and then topple. Snotta fell with a heavy thud on top of it, and leapt quickly up again, foaming at the mouth and cursing. He threatened every type of ill-treatment to Foodo for disturbing him in the first place. Once again the Dork managed to set the ladder upright and climbed up through the now open trapdoor.

After a moment Stan heard Foodo's distraught voice calling out, 'Please stop. I can't stand anymore.'

Many things passed through Stan's mind as he hurried up the ladder to the defence of his master. At the top, a strange sight met his eyes. The Dorks, having had Grumble to play with before, it seemed had invented a unique way of torturing these Halfbits with large feet. Snotta was crouched over Foodo, with a large feather in his claw-like hand, stroking the soles of his leathery feet. Foodo was tied down and struggling. Half-mad with delirium, he had lost control of his bodily functions and was convulsing as if he were having a fit.

The sight of his master in such a state sent Stan into a rage, knowing that, at some stage, it would be him having to do the laundry. He flew at the Dork with such speed that his flapping feet caught in his cloak and he tripped. The added momentum caused Stan to accidentally slice off Snotta's leg with Stink. If the Dork had been angry with Foodo, he was hopping mad now. On his remaining leg, howling from a combination of pain and rage, he hurled himself at Stan, intent on doing some real damage. Unfortunately for him, the feather, which he was still gripping, brushed along Foodo's furry toes as the Dork pulled himself up. It was so ticklish that it caused the half-dazed Halfbit to kick out, catching Snotta on his leg. The Dork lost his balance and fell through the open trapdoor, squealing.

Stan moved over to Foodo and started to cut the ropes binding him. 'It's all right now, Mr Foodo, I'm here. I've come to save you.'

'Stan, is that you? Where the hell have you been? You took your time, didn't you? Well, you got here in the end I suppose, but I bet it wouldn't have taken you this long to get to the betting shop.'

'So that's the thanks I get. When you get out of here, you'll see there are hundreds of dead Dorks. I reckon the odds were really big against me making it at all. I've fought to get here this quick,' said Stan sulkily. He didn't mention how much he'd fought to catch his breath on the stairs on his way up.

'Well, I'm sorry Stan; it's just that it's been a nightmare here. I've been drugged I think,' said Foodo.

'Oh, that'll be from Sheblob's poison. I heard the Dorks talking about it before they dragged you away,' replied Stan, trying to be clever.

'You're telling me that you let them take me away, torture me, pilfer all my possessions, everything I own, without even a fight? Surely it would have saved time and the bother of fighting all those Dorks you told me about to get here, if you hadn't let them take me in the first place.'

'Well ... ahem ... uh, well ... I only actually killed one of them,' replied Stan looking through the trapdoor at Snotta, whose nose was now firmly stuck in his own rectum.

'You can't count him; we both killed that Dork. And furthermore, it was an accident.'

'Well anyway, I have some good news though.'

'Go on, give it to me,' replied Foodo suspiciously.

'They didn't take all of your stuff. I have something of yours that means the world to you,' answered Stan triumphantly.

'You mean you've got it here, now? Then I must have it. I need it. Give it to me, now!' exclaimed Foodo.

'I have to tell you that I have used it a little,' said Stan looking sheepish.

At that, Foodo began to snarl. 'You dirty, thieving ration-stealer; give me what's left of it then,' he screamed, foaming at the mouth.

'But ... but ... it's all here,' replied Stan, bottom lip all aquiver. With that, he held up the Nose-ring of Sourone.

Foodo snatched it. 'You stupid fool; I thought you were talking about the Alembas from my backpack.'

'Oh, I saved the pack, because the temptation to eat your share became too much. I didn't give in; I only ate my half.'

'That's only because you don't know the combination for the travel lock I use on my bag. And have you given any thought to what you're going to eat now you've finished all your food?'

Stan looked longingly at the pack as he handed it over to his master.

Foodo held up the Nose-ring in disgust, looking at Stan in mild displeasure, and said, 'You've made a right mess of this, Stan. I thought they had taken it and we could go home, giving up on this mad quest, with a perfectly good excuse. I'd even begun to think about my apology note to Elbow and the Elves. How does, "Sorry, tried my best. See you around" sound?'

'It's a bit long, Mr Foodo. I would just write, "Sorry",' replied Stan.

'That's probably because I'm more educated than an ignorant spud-planter.'

'Does that mean that I'm more educated than a nignorant?'

'Only just,' replied Foodo, trying to be kind. 'And what's a nignorant? On second thoughts, Master Stanwitless Gamble, don't answer. Just go and find me something to wear; and don't bring me back any sportswear! We don't want to be attacked by any football hooligans on our travels.'

Stan went on his mission, returning sometime later with a sack of clothing.

As he opened it, Foodo realised that the stench that emanated from it was almost as bad as Messy's clothes on his yearly laundry day. He pulled out something resembling a pair of brown trousers; these, in fact, turned out to be a pair of dirty boxer shorts from a rather tall Morbid Dork. Next came a short body-warmer, full of strands of hair that seemed to have been doubling as bedding for the wag-dens. Next came a metal helmet that smelt like it had been used as a chamber pot, and last came a shirt made from stolen chains that had once graced the public conveniences of Ohgivusalaugh. His new garb was held together by a leather belt with a small scabbard. In this was a nasty, curved meat hook. When he was dressed, Foodo looked a right Dork, which was just as well, because Stan's attempt had amounted to making a cloak out of an old bin-liner, and a small, metal wastepaper bin for a helmet that he had poked holes in with Stink.

Eventually they set out for the gate of The Silly Soundless Whatsits. The See-see T.V cameras were still smouldering and giving off a few odd sparks as they passed them. One exploded and fell with a clang behind them. From somewhere nearby came the shrieking, attention-seeking mating call of the female Terrorblacktail. They ran for their lives.

248

'Run, Mr Foodo. Run!' cried Stan, as he jogged beside his master. 'No, not that way; this way,' Stan urged, as he proceeded to instruct Foodo in the way of The Halfbit Harriers — a very small group of rotund runners who were considered to be slightly mad, and who competed in the Barmyforlong Marathon each year. Surprisingly, Stan's uncle, Halfded of Overill, had been a champion. Stan was pumping his arms and legs so much that his elbows were knocking against his knees. His face was red and he was puffing and panting, his every movement an over-exaggeration of exertion.

'Strange technique, Stan. Where did you learn that one?' asked Foodo as he jogged past the sweating Halfbit.

'My uncle Halfded lent me a book called, "Training to Run".'

'Did you ever read it?' asked Foodo, who had now stopped running.

'Only the first chapter, called "Running on the Spot".'

'Well, see that spot at the end of the road? That's where you want to be running to,' shouted Foodo, as he shoved Stan in the back.

They reached a bend in the path and saw, just a short distance away, a bridge. After a brief rest they made for it, even though it looked very far away. Once there, they crossed it and flopped down by the side of the road, gasping. No sooner had they settled than the tower's fire alarm fell silent. This meant that one of the Nasal had found the trip-switch. They heard the sound of a horse-drawn fire engine and the heavy thud of boots belonging to Dork attendants. The fire crew had probably set off when Stan had first blasted The Silly Soundless Whatsits.

'What are we going to do now, Mr Foodo? We're caught between the two and I can't run anymore.'

'We are going to have to jump off this bridge Stan.'

'But that would be like suicide.'

'Well, it's either that or be a stew instead. Come on; jump, Stan!'

'Only if you go first.'

'Ok then, we'll go together,' said Foodo as he jumped, dragging Stan with him. The fall lasted less than two seconds, but that was long enough way for an overweight Halfbit. However, Stan's strangled scream lasted longer and sounded like the fire alarm had restarted, until that itself was silenced by Foodo's hand. Luckily for the Halfbits, there was plenty of barbed wire hanging down from the sides of the bridge. Although now rusty, this remnant of The Battle of the Last Abeyance had snagged and caught hold of the two of them in its long barbs.

They hung around for a while, until all sounds of activity had passed.

Then Stan said, 'We can't stay here for the rest of our lives. We are going to have to climb back up, or someone will notice us.' Stan though, didn't have the strength to carry both packs and his master, and soon started to slide further down, dropping Foodo a good few feet.

In the gloom and shadow of the bridge, Foodo dangled at the very end of the wire shouting things at Stan that are better not repeated. On closer inspection, Foodo saw that all was not as bad as it seemed. 'Hang on a moment longer, Stan; I think I can see the bottom from here.'

'I bet you can. This damn stuff has ripped the seat out of my trousers.'

'No Stan, I can see the valley floor. We are only a couple of feet away.'

So they climbed slowly down, and Foodo learned some new expletives from Stan that could only have been learned by someone who regularly stuck a pitchfork into his foot. At the end of their descent, they looked a right mess which, lucky for them, only added to their disguise. Once they had collected their belongings and thoughts, and had a little rest, they set off again towards their destination.

They travelled for a few days, not knowing if it was day or night, and not caring, as long as lunch and dinner followed breakfast. At some point they came to a path. Foodo asked Stan's opinion as to whether they should take it as a shortcut or not. Stan said he'd rather not get cut, or shorter. Foodo had only asked out of kindness and wasn't actually listening for any reply;

he was mulling over in his mind whether they should take this convenient path that appeared to lead towards the inky black of Mount Gloom, or head toward the strange light coming from the west.

Stan took this as Foodo wavering, so he gripped him firmly by the arm and marched him towards the darkness. 'I may not know much about these great things, but I believe this is the way.'

'I know that, Stan; look at the signpost,' said Foodo, as Stan scratched his head, trying to work out what it meant.

By the roadside was a large boulder, and on it was carved the writing which Foodo read out:

'WEST - BACK GATE-WAY OUT
EAST - DARKNESS, DEVASTATION, DEATH
BY DANK LORD'

'Looks like we may have a bit of trouble, we'll have to avoid that Dank fellow. Who is he anyway again, Mr Foodo?' asked Stan.

'The Dank Lord is Sourone, Stan, and it's his Nose-ring I have in my pocket. If I am to get rid of it, then we must avoid going anywhere near Sourone and his Bad-odour. Luckily for us, Horridruin is closer to us than The Dank Tower,' informed Foodo, as they once again set off down the Dork path.

The next few days were ones of hunger, thirst, hunger, blisters and more hunger. Eventually they came within close sight of The Mountain of Gloom and the swirling black clouds that crowned its heights. Beyond, they were able to just about glimpse the metal and glass of the uppermost point of Bad-odour. What caught their attention most though, was the army of tents in-between them and their destination.

'Seems like we've turned up in the middle of some camping convention. I wonder if we can buy a small tent for the journey back,' said Stan.

'Do you have to be so stupid all the time, Stan? They're not selling tents; that is an army ready for war.'

'Well, I wonder if they would miss one if we stole it.'

'That's even more stupid. What if we got caught? Remember the trouble Grumble got us into with The Piffling Strangers,' said Foodo.

'Hey, they may have man-food. There are some men down there from Far Harass, and even some Eagerlings by the looks of things. See, you can tell by their curly-up toes and the turbines on their heads.'

'I'd like some more of that exotic food I had at Hotness Anneal,' replied Foodo, longinly.

'You mean you had rude food in Piffling?' said Stan, blushing.

'No Stan, I said exotic. Anyway, you can forget about going down there for food, unless you want to have a swim in that large cooking pot.' He pointed at a pot, which was bubbling away over a large fire.

'Well, how are we going to get past that lot anyway?'

'I have been thinking about that since we saw them. If you'd stop talking about food, I may be able to concentrate.'

'What if I go to the top of that ridge and shout EXTRA RATIONS? They might all fight to get there first,' said Stan, trying to be helpful, yet still forgetting to keep quiet about food.

'I don't think that will work Stan.'

'Why not?'

Foodo looked pensive and offered, 'I really can't see you climbing up there and out-running a horde of screaming Dorks who are intent on having a quarter-pounder for a snack. There is nothing for it but to go around this lot.'

'But that will take us even longer and we are running out of food,' moaned Stan.

Foodo looked at Stan and his large belly and said, 'I suppose eating less hasn't come to mind?'

'I'll be eating my fingers next; they're beginning to remind me of sausages,' he whined.

'They have always looked like that to me!'

They decided on going the long way round, to avoid being Dork food. They travelled all night, until the morning half-light brought them within sight of a road that led from Castle Rudethang, in the Dale of Undone.

'That's handy: another road,' said Stan.

'A little too handy. We'll be in trouble if we get caught on it,' replied Foodo.

'Yeah, but I bet the congestion charge is costly. That's probably why the road is empty,'

'They eat you, and there is an indigestion surcharge, which is waived only on regurgitation.'

'Is there any other way?' Stan asked Foodo, hopefully.

'I don't see one, other than across that desert,' Foodo pointed at the bone-laden Gorygorge (The Land Which Eats). 'If we use that road, we'll have to move as fast as we can.'

Stan didn't like the sound of that at all, for the word fast was unpleasant to all Halfbit ears, and was in fact banned in some parts of The Snore for it's double-meaning. Stan, whose normal movement settings were slow and snooze, said, 'We'll have to rest first. All this dashing and running will get me a bad reputation back home. I don't want you telling stories and me getting a terrible nickname, like Flash or the like.'

'There is absolutely no way you'd be called that,' laughed Foodo.

Stan took the first watch and, as Foodo slept, he decided to scout around in the vain hope of finding anything else alive to eat, in this desolate place. But even the cockroaches had an inbuilt self-preservation instinct, which told them that Dorks would eat anything. What Stan did find was lead pipeline leading up to the tower. With his sword, he made a small hole in the metal and allowed a trickle of the substance inside it to fall into his sweaty palm. He examined it rather dubiously, then stuck the tip of his tongue into it. The fact that it tasted slightly salty could have simply been down to Stan's bad hygiene. He filled his water bottle and took two mighty swigs, not caring now about the taste, and then re-filled it. Unbeknownst to Stan, this pipe was in fact used to carry the old eyewash of Sourone to Rudethang for refining.

As he finished filling the bottle a second time, he looked up and caught sight of Grumble homing in on Foodo. He could hear him mumbling something like, 'I remember this when it was all fields. I blame global warming and carbon emissions.' Stan started toward the small camp and must have alerted Grumble with his puffing and panting for, when he got back, there was no sight of the wretch. He sat down beside Foodo and waited for as long as he could, trying to stay awake by thinking of all his favourite things and what order he would put them in his top ten. At first it was sleeping, eating and drinking. Sleeping had to be best, because you didn't work whilst asleep, but then he remembered that one couldn't eat during sleep. So then he decided on:

1. Eating.
2. Drinking.
3. Sleeping.
4. More sleeping,
5. And eating more.
6. My spade.
7. My wheelbarrow.
8. The Grafter.
9. Foodo.
10. Dozy Hot-one.

He thought for a moment, and changed 9 and 10 around, in case people got the wrong idea. Then he suddenly realised he'd forgotten to put in gambling, so he inserted that as 6a, creating the world's first Top Eleven. After half an hour, and now very pleased with himself, he woke Foodo. 'I'm very sorry, Mr Foodo; I was going to let you sleep a few hours more, but I can't keep awake anymore.'

'It feels like only minutes ago that I closed my eyes. How long have I been asleep?' asked Foodo.

'Oh, a fair time, Mr Foodo. I'd say a few hours at the most,' replied Stan. As Stan's head hit his makeshift pillow, he said, 'Oh, Mr Foodo, watch out: Grumble's about.' He pointed in some indiscriminate direction. 'Also, there's some water in that bottle. But be careful; it's a bit tangy. Drink it too quick and it'll make your eyes water.'

After many hours of sleep, Stan woke to find the exhausted Foodo slumped against the rocks, snoring his head off. Grumble had stayed hidden and watched from a distance, thinking that he wouldn't get caught out twice by the trick of the stupid, lazy Halfbits pretending to be asleep.

'We're lucky to be alive, Mr Foodo,' said Stan, roughly shaking his master awake.

Foodo, who was still drowsy, looked to his left and saw desert and rock. He looked to his right and saw rocks and desert. Looking straight ahead of him, he saw the large, round, and simple face of Stan Gamble. With the dawning realisation of the predicament he was in, and who with, he said, 'You call this lucky?'

'Well, at least we've both had a good long sleep now,' replied Stan.

'I thought you said I'd slept for a fair few hours before anyway.'

'Well, ahem ... yes, you did sir, and I hope you feel more refreshed than your poor servant,' said Stan, without much shame.

Still, Foodo felt a bit guilty, and said, 'Oh well, at least we can jog a bit down that road now.' He hoped that, by changing the subject, he would take Stan's mind off things. He need not have worried, for Stan was already thinking of what and when to eat next.

The time came to resume their journey and they set off with a vigour that surprised even them. It wouldn't have surprised anyone else who saw them stumbling down the steep slope which led to the road at the bottom, however. After a few miles on this road, they noticed there was no way off it. On one side was a sheer drop, and on the other, rising high above them, was the massive wall of the mountain. This wall was interspersed with locked iron gates which led down tunnels to The Dork Orphanages, places where the most seriously mutated dorks were put as children. Even Dorks got upset and scared looking at one-eyed, three-headed, slavering monsters, for it reminded them of their origins and the frailty of their gene pool. It was from one of these tunnels that a pack of mutants limped, hopped and crawled, led by a big, one-eyed, shortsighted and one-armed Dork, who was wearing spectacles.

'It looks like our luck has run out, Stan. If we lie on the side of the road and look dead, maybe that big, ugly-looking brute will look the other way through his looking glasses,' said Foodo.

'There's lots of look in there,' replied a confused Stan.

'Lie still and see if we can get more than luck,' whispered Foodo.

Stan looked and couldn't find anything but bad looks.

The big brute had a large stick which he was beating the mutants with and, as they drew close to the Halfbits, it flew out of his hand, and landed on Stan. The brute came to retrieve it and noticed the shapes lying by the roadside. Moving his spectacles, which were bi-focal, from side to side over his one eye, he prodded Foodo first, who remained as limp as a fried lettuce. He then prodded Stan, who began to giggle like a little girl.

'Stop, stop; it tickles!'

The brute roared and began to kick what he thought was two small, mutant Dorks. 'Get up, get up; you're not getting out of this war. We're all going, every single last one of us. Orders from Slugbooze. Even the mad, the maimed and the mediocre are to go. The Boss wants a show of force, and when the enemy does a headcount, some of us count as double. So get up and join the rest, even though you both count as one.'

They climbed to their feet, holding on to each other and limping, pretending to be mutants. Stan nearly gave the game away by doing the dance routine from a Jack Michaelson video towards the back of the troop. 'Hey, hey, get to the front you two. I can keep a good eye on you up there,' shouted the brutish Dork leader, blinking at them.

They set off then at a greater pace than was normally possible for a Halfbit. If it wasn't for the mutants pushing and shoving them they wouldn't have even managed to stumble half the way there. Luckily, they didn't have to go that far, as the next scheduled rest stop was only a few miles down the road.

Rest stops were for the overseer to do a count of those who hadn't died from exhaustion or desertion. This was hard enough with all the heads bobbing about, and was made harder by the fact he only had five fingers to count with. On his third attempt, a group of injured Dorks on crutches and with war wounds on their little fingers, crashed into the mutants. Immediately, the injured leader and his crew, from Bad-odour, who were part of The First Battalion of Minging Malingerers, proceeded to forget their imagined injuries and began to beat the mutants mercilessly. Foodo and Stan were the first to catch it and were thrown bodily over the side of the road. As they rolled down the side, they thought their time was surely up. Fortunately, as their troop had been stumbling along the road, they had also been heading downhill. They found that they were now much lower than they had been when they had first been drafted in to the mutant army. Foodo and Stan found this out as they hit a drainage ditch and body surfed before coming to a halt some fair distance from the fight. After lying still until all hints of movement and bone crunching had died down, they stood up and tried to scrape off as much effluence as they could, then decided it was time for another nap.

MOUNT GLOOM

Long after the sound of heads being cracked together had finished, and the moans of the dying had given way to the sounds of a party of vultures being sick, Stan was still snoring loudly and Foodo was looking for the largest and heaviest thing to throw at his head; only, he quickly realised that Stan's head was the largest and heaviest thing for miles around. Eventually, Foodo drifted off into troubled sleep again. When Stan awoke, he looked at Foodo and thought of waking him, for he was sure that he'd had more than enough sleep than he needed. Luckily for Foodo, Stan looked across Gorygorge at Mount Gloom and, thinking about how far was still left to go before the completion of his bet with the Elves, he convinced himself that it would be better to let him rest and have more energy for the run-in. Hopefully, that way, he would need less food to eat.

As morning came, Stan saw that he was standing on a vast expanse of craters. Some distance off, a flag was unfurled and stiff, even though there was a slight breeze. On the flag was the sign of a big, red, watering eye. He strolled over to have a closer look at it, and stared in disbelief at a small plaque at the base of the pole, upon which was written:

FIRST MOON LANDING.
DORKS BEAT THE ELVES HERE.

So the rumours had been true: it was a hoax, perpetrated by Sourone Inc. TV. The Dorks had never set foot on the moon. Forget the lack of breathing equipment, the photos with another moon in the background and the head of the director peering over a crater; here was real proof. Stan prised the plaque from its place and chuckled, I bet this is worth a fortune, he thought.

He went back to where Foodo lay sleeping and sat for a while, eating the bigger half of his share of the breakfast. He then dished out the last of the rations that Faraway had given them. In amongst this was a pile of small, hard biscuits, which were

258

supposed to be submerged in liquid to bloat their size and create a kind of mushy gruel. 'One for you, two for me, two for you, three for me,' intoned Stan to himself, until they had all gone and he had already eaten half of his own. At that point he shook Foodo awake; they ate what remained of their breakfast together and drank half of their water. The food inside Stan started to swell and eased the emptiness in his gut. This caused a release of toxic air from both ends of the fat Halfbit; it sounded like he was going to explode. With a final expulsion of air from both ends, Stan stood up, and put on his backpack. 'I've found a good way to continue It's across that cratered desert.'

Foodo looked across The Gorygorge. 'Somehow, that looks a bit familiar.'

'I bet it does,' replied Stan, as they set off.

Days later, Stan was wishing that he was on the moon. He had heard that everything was lighter there. He was also beginning to regret taking that heavy plaque. That thought soon disappeared though, when he imagined the money he would make from selling the story to The Daily Snore. It wasn't the heavy pack that was on his mind as they drew closer to Mount Gloom because, as their journey progressed, Foodo had continually moaned about the weight he was carrying. He didn't have any pack or sword anymore; just his shirt, trousers and The Nose-ring; now he was complaining about how heavy that was. At one point Stan said, 'I suppose you want me to carry that as well then.' Foodo had a complete hissy-fit and stopped talking to him. Instead he started muttering under his breath about wannabes and scene-stealers. So Stan decided to lighten his own load of some of the junk he'd collected on his journey. It went down a deep crevasse with some regret. He actually cried when his eating utensils went down the hole as he thought of the real food he'd eaten with them. He cried even more when he turned around and found Foodo guzzling what remained of the water. 'Hey, that's the last of it,' said Stan reproachfully.

'That's all right; I'm not so thirsty now. I'm going to have a nap. Be a good chap and see if you can find some more water. It's been ages since I last had a wash,' replied Foodo.

Stan had a quick look around, then settled down, deciding a bit of shuteye for himself was more important. During his sleep, he dreamt of bathing and having a shower. He even dreamt of splashing water on his face. When he woke, he realised he'd wet himself. 'Oh no! You stupid fool, Stan Gamble. You threw all your spare Dork clothing down that hole yesterday, and you can't even steal Mr Foodo's, because he's wearing them.' He woke Foodo and said, through cracked lips, and with a dry throat, 'Time to go. Not much further now.'

Foodo just lay there for a moment, in a daze. When he tried to stand, his legs gave way from exhaustion, and he cried out, 'I can't go on; it's too far to walk.'

'Typical soft upbringing and pampered life of the upper middle classes,' he muttered to himself. 'He gives up on me now, within spitting distance of our destination. Well, he won't cheat me out of my winnings.' He grabbed Foodo like he was a sack of potatoes and slung him over his shoulder. 'I'm carrying everything else; I might as well carry you.'

Sometime later, staggering around, he found himself on the slopes of Mount Gloom. As he approached the mountain, everything had gradually become darker. The ground was vibrating slightly, and it felt like the air was being sucked out of his lungs. He looked skywards at the mountaintop and the inky black clouds swirling around it like water going down a plughole. He plodded on, head down. Halfway there, he looked up again. In the dim light, he saw a grey path made of crazy paving. 'Oh, that's nice. I'll try that when I get home. Maybe it will catch on. I'll start a new business, called Stan's Smashing Surfaces,' he said to himself.

What Stan was looking at was Sourone's Road. Along it, long ages ago, The Dank Lord had come to The Sanctum Noir and emerged again, his nose pierced with a ring. He had dressed all in black, for his desire had always been to front a Heavy Metal Goth band, which he would call Dank Lordy. Now though, Stan was beginning to think he would have to carry Foodo all the way to the top. The problem was, if he took the road directly, it would bring him in sight of The Dank Tower. The path wound helter-skelter around the mountain, so he decided to climb the slope, then use the road to the rear and chance to luck on the shortest part of it, which faced Bad-odour. He told Foodo that he would have to put him down again for a while and rest. Within minutes, he felt himself slipping off to sleep.

He awoke later to see flashing lights in the sky. From Bad-odour came the hot glare of The Stare of Sourone. It was looking beyond The Back Gates, to a point where The Retinue of the King were doing rehearsals for the forthcoming film, based on the war to be called Carrion Ringing. The lights were flashing and illuminating the entire western sky. Stan thought their best chance was to move now. 'Come on, Mr Foodo, let's move while we can.'

They set off towards the path. Foodo didn't get far before he stumbled to his knees, so once again Stan had to carry his master. They were so close now that Stan could almost feel the money he would make from winning the first part of the bet with the Elves. Staggering upwards, he got to the road, and with each step he drew closer to the big doorway leading into The Sanctum Noir. The doorway was ornate and carved with the large, ugly, squinting heads of the Dork slaves who had built the road, doorway and Sanctum. In the dim light, Stan could have sworn he had seen the eyes move on one of the heads, and even blinked. He tried to ignore what he thought must be paranoia, and plodded on, his burden getting heavier with each step.

Within a few feet of the great doorway, a shadow detached itself from the rest and leapt onto the two Halfbits. Stan's already tired legs buckled, but he found renewed strength when he heard the sound he hated most in the world; well, the second most hated actually — the first being when a horse fell at the first fence. This sound though, was the whining voice of Smear-gob Grumble.

'The public transport system here is rubbish; give us a lift. Four little Halfbits all on their own should be travelling together.'

'Shut up, stupid; these two are planning to destroy our present,' hissed Grumble.

'No, no; if they don't want it, I'll have it,' whimpered Smear-gob.

'No you won't! It was you who lost it last time. I'll never let you wear it again. I blame society,' screamed Grumble.

Stan had heard enough. He threw off his pack, along with Foodo and Grumble, who were both still clinging to it, and drew Stink. Foodo and Grumble grappled with each other like wrestlers trying to win Come Dancing. They moved back and forth in front of Stan until Foodo, with more modern training methods, and more protein intake, threw down his older opponent. Standing over Grumble, Foodo punched the air and chanted, 'Champion, Champion.'

Grumble, full of hurt pride, lifted himself from the ground, and snarled, 'Best out of three,' and then leapt at Foodo, only to find the vast bulk of Stan Gamble blocking his path. 'Hey! Not fair. Not fair at all. Two against one,' whined Grumble.

'I thought you said there were two of you,' sneered Stan.

'There is, but Smear-gob is unconscious,' moaned Grumble.

'No, I'm not; I'm here,' whimpered Smear-gob.

'Shut up! Shut up! You always ruin everything,' screamed Grumble.

Stan advanced, sword in hand, just as Grumble smashed Smear-gob on the jaw. The scrawny creature was now sprawled in the dirt. Stan stood over him, ready to dispatch him to wherever his overdue, rotten soul would go.

Grumble looked up at Stan and, in his best imitation voice, grovelled like Smear-gob. 'Don't kill nice Smear-gob, kind and good Mr Stan. Grumble won't be any more trouble. He's died from starvation and exertion. Poor Smear-gob nearly died as well; Grumble put him on The Ratkins Diet.'

Stan stayed his hand for, as he looked down at the starving, scrawny scoundrel, pity welled unexpectedly in his heart. He thought of how this creature had eaten nothing but rodents for the last few weeks, with maybe the odd Muckdorkald's Burger. He decided that, if he didn't kill him shortly, then he wouldn't have long to live on that type of food intake anyway. Besides, he didn't want to cause a stink with Stink. Someone might be nearby and hear the old wretch shrieking, so he told him to scarper before he changed his mind.

'I'd have changed that useless thing a long time ago, you stupid Halfbit,' came the snide reply, as the old wretch turned to leave.

Stan held his temper and said through clenched teeth, 'You just can't help yourself, can you?' With that, he landed his huge foot squarely on Grumble's rear, sending him rolling down the hill. Pleased with himself, he turned back to Foodo. 'Well, looks like we've seen the end of him.' However, he discovered that his master had gone into The Sanctum Noir.

Stan set off after him and, once inside, was engulfed in darkness. Fumbling in his pack, he drew out The File of Gadabout, though it was of little use, as he hadn't recharged it since his battle with Sheblob. With no sunlight, the solar panel on the front wasn't much help either. However, there was just enough power left in it for a dim light to help guide him on his way. He edged his way along the tunnel. As he approached the end of it, he saw a white light flashing intermittently ahead of him. He emerged into a huge central chamber, and there stood Foodo, illuminated by haphazard streaks of lightning that seemed to be originating from deep down in the heart of the mountain.

Foodo was holding the ring aloft and staring at it. Seeing Stan, he said, 'How much do you think The Olde Ebay Shoppe would give me for this? It must be worth more than what the Elves are going to pay me. Maybe if I just tell them I got rid of it, I'll get twice as much.'

While Stan could see the proceeds of his bet going down the pan, Foodo did the strangest thing: he opened the clasp and placed the Nose-ring on his ear. As he did this, he said, 'Or maybe I'll keep it for myself. Funny though; as a piece of jewellery, it's useless.'

Just then, the lights went out, and Stanwitless really was left in the dark. In the gloom, he just about made out a Grumble-shaped shadow; he heard him giggle with glee and say, 'You just can't help being a stupid, fat Halfbit.'

As soon as Foodo had put on the ring, a siren had sounded inside the Hubble-bubble. Sourone knew there were only two reasons for this: the first being that maybe someone was at the front door; the second possibility was that someone had opened the locking clasp on The Nose-ring and used it within his realm. As no one really visited him these days, he began to get worried. As quickly as the Thralls could toil, the great telescopic eye scanned his lands, alighting upon Horridruin. He focussed down along the tunnel and into The Sanctum Noir, and suddenly realised how the old conjuring fool known as The Grand Alf had made a fool out of him. He could just imagine the wizard laughing at him. This time, Sourone would surely be banned from the Magic Circle forever. In his anger, he forgot all about his eyepiece problem and, standing, he ripped himself free of the great telescope and made for the communications centre. Once there, he radioed new instructions to The Nasal Airways, sending them with all speed to Mount Gloom. Then he went with haste to the Dank Tower Underground Station.

In The Sanctum Noir, Stan was watching Grumble shadowboxing, jabbing at the air with his left hand. Every so often, his head jolted back, compliments of his invisible opponent, Foodo. This carried on until Foodo landed a solid right hook and Grumble went down like a sack of Stan's spuds. Stan could hear someone counting, "One, two, three." Grumble staggered up at nine and stood poised on unsteady legs. Obviously sensing that this was one fight he was going to lose, he opted to go for the foul. Leaping forward, he grabbed Foodo in a hug and bit off his earlobe and, with it, the Nose-ring of Sourone.

Coughing it up into his hand, he danced with joy and sang, 'Happy birthday to me, Happy birthday to me.'

Smear-gob laughed, saying, 'Mine, you mean.'

'No, it's mine; yours is tomorrow,' argued Grumble.

Foodo, meanwhile, grabbed Grumble by the hand, and shouted, 'It's mine.'

Stan thought that strange, as Foodo's birthday was months away. He stared at the two of them as a tugging match ensued over the ring. Moments later, a door opened in the rockface and in walked Sourone, The Dank Lord of Bad-odour, all six-foot of him in his metal platform boots.

'I think you'll find that it is mine.' With that, the tugging match became a three-way.

Stan stood and watched in wonder while the sounds of "Mine, mine, mine," echoed around the chamber, as the ring moved in a triangular motion between the three.

After some time, they started to tire. Foodo was the first to let the nose ring slip from his sweaty fingers. This caused the other two to lose their balance and their grip on the object, which flew through the air and landed close to Stan. What happened next baffled him which, in itself, wasn't hard. An orb of white light appeared and inside he saw the outline of a person resembling Tom Bombastic. However, instead of Tom, an elderly gentleman stepped out into the chamber. He was dressed in a tweed suit, and had a pipe in his mouth. He stooped, picked up the nose ring, examined it, and flicked it toward the Crack of Gloom. As he did this, he turned his face to the ceiling and, as if talking to someone not present but looking down on the scene, said, "Do get on with it, fool!" Then he walked calmly back through the doorway, which closed behind him.

The nose ring, which had flown towards the crack, was closely followed by the three eager wrestlers, and they in turn were closely followed by Stan. It bounced once, twice, then over the edge. Sourone and Grumble leapt and managed to grab it between them, even as they plummeted into the crack.

At the last moment, Stan tackled Foodo, therefore ensuring he would at least have a chance of collecting the second part of his bet. They watched as Sourone and Grumble fell into The Black Hole that raged at the heart of the mountain. Before they disappeared and the hole closed, the two Halfbits caught a glimpse of a strange world filled with tall buildings and metal beasts. Then everything imploded and the walls nearest the hole started to melt. They began to slide down into the huge hole as the chamber trembled. Massive tremors shook the floor as Stan attempted to hoist Foodo up and once again fling him over his shoulder, then attempted to do so a second time, at which point Foodo told him to forget it — he'd rather use his own legs. They scrambled clear and hurried back down the tunnel and out into The Shady Land.

As they ran along Sourone's road into the Gorygorge, the ground under their feet became like a treadmill. All the land was being pulled towards Horridruin, like mud sliding into a sinkhole. Bad-odour was reduced to a pile of rubble on it's way towards the black hole, while The Nasal Airways were being also being pulled into the inky vortex swirling above where the shattered mountain had once stood. Later, The Nasal who survived this would only be able to find work in films. Kid Caramel, The Shade of the Least, appeared as an extra in Skreem and its sequel, Skreem Again and Again. Just then, however, the flow towards the black hole seemed to be slowing, as if it had eaten enough. Stan and Foodo struggled over to a large rock formation that seemed to be just out of range of the hole's pulling power. With the world crashing down around them, the Halfbits settled down for what, it seemed, would be their final ever snooze.

THE FEED OF KORMA-NAAN

At The Back Gates, a full battle simulation was being enacted, as the powerful spotlights of Follywood lit up the battleground. The cameras rolled and the director yelled, "Cut!". All the scenes of the army had now been filmed, along with the fake heroic scenes of the principal leading peoples; these were for the special, extended, rip-off versions of the film. Now, The Back Gates were opening, and the film crews were retreating to a safe distance, to contemplate what they should call the film. One idea was Carrion Ringing.

Out of the gates emerged the hideous hordes of Morbid, screeching, hopping and leaping. All the reflectors and cameras focused on the small army. The Grand Alf turned away from the lights, which were blinding him and half the army. Turning northwards, he heard the unmistakable wokka-wokka sounds of The Regal Eagle helpicopters. In the lead came his friend Gary Weir, and along the road came his brother in a Landroving Vehiwain. Behind him came many older vehicles. The army of Morbid stopped in their tracks, looking somewhat bemused, and The Nasal Airways fled back to Morbid, having received flight-rescheduling orders from Bad-odour Brigade Headquarters. Then, lacking any direct orders, the Dorks started to think of better things to do and fled.

In the glare of the lights, all cameras panned onto The Grand Alf. Knowing that this was a historic moment, he thought of something poignant to say. However all that came out was, 'Well, that's the end of that then.' He looked beyond the collapsed Back Gates, at the devastation, and added, 'Only thing to do is pack up and go home.'

'What about Foodo and Stan?' asked Pipsqueak, who had just woken up.

'Who?' replied the Wiztari.

'My friends who took the Nose-ring to Morbid.'

'What about them?'

'Aren't we going to search for them?'

266

'What's the point? I thought you said they were disposable,' said Earmore.

'Shush,' said Paragon, ushering away the new King of the Muck from the distraught Halfbit. 'I suppose we should at least try,' he said to The Grand Alf.

'Oh, OK then. I'll get Gary and his helpicopter on the case.'

As they left, the Dorks were running for the hills, leaving the men of Rhude and Harass, along with the Eagerlings and Slothrons to face the music, or pretend to be dead; something the Dorks and Thralls helped them with as they fled in panic. Eventually, most of these men took the hint and ran for their lives, leaving the Slothrons to awake in the Gondour prison train.

In Morbid, Stan and Foodo woke to the sound of rumbling.

'Was that your stomach or mine?' asked Foodo.

'Both, I think.'

'I'm glad there is no more food left, Stan. I don't think I could eat another one of those damn Alembas ever again. With the food gone though, we won't get far.'

'Oh, I don't know Mr Foodo. If Grumble can survive on spiders and bugs, I'm sure we can.'

At the mention of spiders, Foodo was violently sick, and Stan eyed it with a greedy glint in his eye.

Foodo stood and surveyed the surrounding land. 'I suppose we had better move on a little further; you never know what we might find to eat,' he said to Stan, who was busy cleaning up after his master.

The land that Foodo now surveyed was like rivers of muddy earth that had swirled and converged towards a single point. The hills were dripping like molten chocolate. All shifting of the earth had slowed to a crawl and the vibrations had ceased. It looked like the black plughole would need more than a bent coat-hanger to clear its blockage. A few miles from what used to be Mount Gloom, the Halfbits stopped and decided to have a rest.

'Wait until we get back to The Snore; we'll be on all the news channels. I can't wait to hear the story of Old One Ear and The Chomp in Gloom,' said Stan.

They lay down yet again and slept, having not done so for at least two hours; another thing that the Halfbit metabolism couldn't cope with. Unbeknownst to them, high above, Gary

Weir was using his radar and tracking devices to direct his brother, Landroving Vehiwain, to the location of the snoring Halfbits. So tired and fatigued were Foodo and Stan that nothing short of shouting breakfast very loudly, or the rattling of pans, could have woken them. So, being dumped in the back of a land-roving certainly wasn't a problem.

Many hours and miles later, Stan woke to find himself in bed. He was temporally blinded as someone opened the curtains and the full glare of the sun fell on his face. This was, of course, made worse by the fact he hadn't seen any sun for weeks. He vaguely thought that it must be time for a holiday. Whilst shading his eyes, he became aware of a familiar smell, one that he hadn't smelt since leaving Piffling. It was curried rabbit and unleavened bread. With his eyes now growing accustomed to the light, he said, 'What a horrible nightmare: I thought I was on a diet in a land that had no food, and the only thing to eat was puke.' He turned and looked at the bed next to his and saw Foodo's bandaged head. His master looked like he had undergone brain surgery. Stan wondered if that was anything like tree surgery. That was when it dawned on him that it had all been real, and more importantly, he'd won his bet. Excitedly, he asked, 'Are we in Lostlostion?'

'No, you are in Piffling and the King has lost patience waiting for you lazy Halfbits of The Snore to waken. Therefore, I have been sent to get you up,' said The Grand Alf, stepping into the sunlight for effect. The Wiztari was dressed all in white, and his white beard hung down his front like a bib. The only stain on him was the red wine dribbling from the corner of his mouth.

'A ... a ... are y ... you The Ghost of Yuletide Past?' stammered Stan.

'No! It's me, The Grand Alf!'

'Y ... y ... you sure look like a ghost to me. Anyway, you're dead. I saw you fall down that hole when you took that Bigdog for a walk,' said Stan.

'Labdog!'

'What?'

'It's wasn't a Bigdog; it was a Labdog of Mortcough,' replied the White Wiztari.

'I'm sorry; how was I supposed to know you were on first-name terms?'

'Actually, he was my cousin twice-removed,' admitted The Grand Alf.

'Removed from what?'

'His side of the family had gone bad a long time ago. His brother was a wolf called Carcassrot, who was killed by Howler, The Hound of Vallilost. We had already disowned him before he bit off the hand of Benny Chameleon.'

'How did you escape your pet cousin then?'

'I haven't got time to tell you that story now. You'll have to wait for my biography; it will be out in a few months. It is going to be called How I Defeated Sourone, or The Dank Tower Destruction Debate,' replied the Wiztari proudly.

'Are we in it?'

'Of course you are; I couldn't think what to put on the last page. I had to give all my notes to my ghost-writer, some Narffork called U.R.R Jokin.'

'What's a Narffork?' asked Stan.

Foodo was awake now, and was listening intently to the conversation.

'A Narffork is a bit mixed up. In Spindrawlin, it means Part'yuk, like a bit of Dork and Ill-farter knows what else. Unfortunately he was the only one mad enough to do it. Anyway we haven't got time to sit around talking, the King in-waiting is waiting and he can't wait much longer, as he has an election speech to write.'

'But we haven't got any clothes,' said Foodo.

'Ah, I've taken care of that: I've had them brushed down and folded neat and tidy,' said the Wiztari, as he pulled out their Dork clothes from under the bed and presented them.

Taking them gingerly, Stan said, 'Here, these bloomin' well stink.'

'Don't worry; the Gondourians are used to smelly Halfbits. They will think it is just your natural scent.'

The Halfbits were told that, once they were dressed, a meal had been prepared for them. Twenty seconds later, Foodo was at the table with his shirt on back-to-front and Stan was hopping towards it with both feet in one trouser-leg. They had three helpings of their favourite lamb korma and naan bread, before The Grand Alf had to drag them away towards the waiting throng.

When they arrived, all the soldiers drew their swords and commenced banging on their shields: an old Zooloo anti-riot trick they had learnt in the South Havereeker Wars. For a moment, the two Halfbits shrank back, afraid. Then the singing started.

'LONG LIFE TO THE HALFBITS. PAY-RISE THEM
WITH BIG PAY-RISE.
CUISINE FOR THE PHEW TO A MAN.
AGARIC FOR THE PHEWENOUGH.
PAY-RISE THEM WITH MASSIVE PAY-RISE,
FOODO AND STANWITLESS.
DABBLE AND BABBLE,
CONNIVE AND ANNULAR ECLAIRIO.
PAY-RISE THEM.
EGREGIOUS ECLAIRIO.
A LATTÉ, A LATTÉ, AND A LATTE COFFEE FOR ME.
PAY-RISE THEM.
CORNUCOPIA OF LATTE FOR THE TARRYING MASS.
PAY-RISE THE RINGBREAKERS.
PAY-RISE THEM WITH BIG PAY-RISE.'

The Grand Alf called them forward, until they stood before three leather lounge seats. Behind the one to their left was a pole on which hung a flag. Upon this was the pub sign of The White Bull of the Ruminates. On the right-hand pole was the flag of The Swan and Ship of the Dolt Amlost Shipyards. Behind the middle chair was the newly painted sign of The Yowltide Tree. Sat on this chair was a man whose face was instantly recognisable on account of its timeless, unchanged look, preserved that way by a botox injection.

'I don't believe it; Stupor, a king!' laughed Stan.

'You had better believe it, Mr Stanwitless; and I haven't forgotten the way you spoke to me in Free. However, seeing as you have helped to fulfill the task of Ringbreaking, I'm willing to give you a pardon,' said the nearly-King, pulling out a scroll.

Stan looked upon Paragon with amazement, wondering how he could talk without moving a muscle on his face. He asked the Stranger, 'Why didn't you ask someone to tell you a joke when you had your last injection? And have you ever thought of becoming a ventriloquist?'

Paragon thrust the scroll into the Halfbit's hand. 'Don't push your luck, halfwit.' Turning to the throng, he gave his election speech, ending with, 'Pay-rise them with great pay-rise.'

With that, they all headed towards the biggest tent in the land, which had been specially reserved for VIPs.

Before they went in, Stan stopped Foodo and pointed at the VIP sign outside. 'By rights, Mr Foodo, I don't think we belong in there.'

'You're quite right, Stan. You wait here; I'll see you later,' replied Foodo, as he disappeared inside. Stan loitered outside until the long arm of The Grand Alf grabbed him and dragged him inside.

'You're important now so you had better get used to it,' said the White Wiztari.

So the Halfbits were sat at the top table, along with all those who knew how to use a knife and fork in the correct manner. Foodo, who was seated next to Stan, had been trained by Bilious for long hours in this manner, so when Stan started shovelling food into his mouth using both hands, Foodo stuck Stan's fork into his hand, therefore sticking at least one hand to the wooden table. In the other hand he placed a betting slip.

'Has anyone got a pen?' asked Stan.

It was at this point that they were reunited with some old friends in the guise of the waiters who were bringing them food. Foodo looked in amazement at the two hulking great Halfbits and their bushy green hair.

'You two look like you've lived off spinach for a year,' said Foodo.

'Oh, no. The Rents would never have allowed that; it would be practically cannibalism for them. They gave us some energy drink called Dread Barrel, which gave us a bit of a growth spurt,' said Messy.

'A bit of a spurt; you're almost as big as a Dwarf!' exclaimed Foodo.

Grimy's ears pricked up. 'Can it be bought anywhere? Where's the nearest off-licence or inn?'

'You'll need to get a better disguise and some high heels before you go anywhere near the Rents again, Stumpy,' laughed Legless.

'What's a Rent?' interjected Foodo.

'That's easy: it's what you charge me and the Grafter too much of for living in that hovel in Blagshut Row,' said Stan.

They sat and told each other their suitably embellished stories, and drank and ate all night. Afterwards, the Halfbits washed their plates in Snore fashion.

Then The Grand Alf called time on the festivities, for the licensing laws had not yet been repealed and the laws of this land were still archaic. 'It's time for bed,' he said, springing to his feet, and wobbling a little.

Legless, had once again wandered off with a bottle stashed under his cloak, singing drunkenly to himself:

'OH I DO LOVE TO BE BESHIDE THE SHEASHIDE.
OH I DO LOVE TO BE BESHIDE THE SHEA,
WHERE THE ELVES ALL COME
COZ THE INNS SELL RUM.
TIDDLY UM YUM YUM.'

The next day, and the day after, and the day after the day after, the triumphant army of the Worst re-enacted filmed battle scenes using captured Eagerlings and Slothrons dressed as Dorks. Paragon's scenes depicted him defeating hundreds on his own. Parts of this film would be used in his political campaign for his election to the kingship of Minus Thrifty. It was all typical Follywood: based very loosely on the truth. After a number of weeks, and a few deaths due to the use of real swords — this due to the extras forgetting to use the wobbly wooden ones they had been issued — the army captains decided it was time to go home, rebuild, repaint and re-mortgage Minus Thrifty. So, a few days later, The Semi-King and his retinue settled in on the fields outside the city.

THE STALWART AND THE KING

A few days after the army left Minus Thrifty with its film crew in tow, the Lady Earwax got wind that her scenes at The Back Door had been cut. When she heard this, she rolled out of her hammock and stormed off in search of her twin-set body amour. She was followed by a number of clucking mother hen-like nurses, who were unaware of the extent of Earwax's inability to hear any words any of them said to her, let alone a gaggle of them gaggling. She ran smack into The Chief Warder of The Houses of Squealing. 'I have missed my screen test, and I can lie no longer clothed in sheets,' she said.

The Warder looked at her, and tried to maintain eye contact, whilst pointing at her large body. It was then that Earwax figured out what the nurses had been trying to tell her, as they ran up with a pair of king-sized sheets to cover her.

'Lady, it is not good for you to be about,' said The Warder.

'Look, just because my hammock is made out of sails, doesn't mean I'm a boat!' shouted Earwax.

'No, Lady, you misunderstand me; you need more rest and healing,' replied The Warder, somewhat louder this time.

'Dealing? What do you mean, dealing? Ah! I see what you mean now: you want me to bribe you. I have no money, but I'm sure we can come to some arrangement.'

The Warder looked horrified, until Earwax offered him a selection of her herd of heifers. Exasperated, he shouted back through cupped hands, 'You have not finished your medication yet! Your arm is still broken, and I can only let you go on your way when it is mended!'

'I'm ok. Even with one arm I'm better than most. However, if it's in the way, cut it off. I need to get to the war or I will have to live forever with my brothers' bragging,' she replied.

'I'm afraid you're too late; by now they will be almost at The Back Gates,' replied The Warder.

'Well, if I set out now, I might get there before the end. Who's the biggest Bulls-hitter around here?'

The Warder thought of saying that she was but could only manage a shocked, 'Pardon, Lady?'

'Who's in charge around here?'

'In here, I am. Outside of this house, a martial type has been left in charge of The Riders of Ridicule, and Whozin Charge leads the men of Gondour.'

'Yes, that is what I asked: who is in charge?'

'That is his name, Lady. However, the Lord Faraway is the real Stalwart.'

'Well that's no good; I need him here in Minus Thrifty. When will he be back?' she asked.

'He is here in The Houses of Squealing.'

'I'm sure you said he was Faraway.'

'That is his name, Lady!' shouted the sore-throated Warder.

'You Mundane people have such stupid names.'

Yes, but at least we don't look it, thought the Warder.

Luckily for Earwax, Faraway was actually quite near. He was sunbathing on the lawn, when suddenly a great shadow fell over him. His heart quailed, fearing the return of The Witchy-king. Turning, he looked up at the huge bulk of Earwax, and moved back into the sunshine. 'For pity's sake, do you have to block the rays?' he moaned.

'This is the Lady Earwax, Lord,' said the Warder, who was standing beside her. 'I cannot keep her happy, so she has asked for The Stalwart.'

'I know exactly what you mean: they won't let me go, and they keep probing my mind. They think I may be touched by the same madness as my father,' replied Faraway.

'Oh, to be tied down and probed. It must be uncomfortable on your behind though. Is that why you're lying down, because of the tenderness?' said Earwax.

The Warder was standing behind Earwax, pointing at her ears and shaking his head. Faraway got the message and dismissed The Warder, thanking him sarcastically for the intrusion. Then he told Earwax of a type of speech without words — an ancient Neomanorealmen sign language — and asked her if she would like to learn it. After a few attempts, Faraway was able to get her to understand a couple of words. It's a start, he thought.

Earwax asked if they could catch the next haywain train to the front. Faraway told her that all the troops had already left and no

274

more were going. Even if she left now, she would arrive well after the battle had finished.

'Well, if there is no transport I will jog there,' said Earwax.

'The stress on your body would be too great for that,' replied Faraway.

Earwax blushed and giggled. 'No one has ever told me that I have a great body before.'

And so it was that The Lady of Bovine followed The Stalwart everywhere, copying him in his mannerisms and ways. Faraway tried hiding in the gymnasium, thinking she surely wouldn't follow him there, yet she did. She even took up his love of fat-free food and salads, and within no time at all she became half the person she had been. Faraway loved women first and war last, so it wasn't long before his eye turned towards Earwax with more than a little interest. During these times, as Faraway taught Earwax the sign language of Neomanor, their fingers entwined like the mating dance of an octopus. They eventually fell in love, especially after Faraway's job prospects fell from ruler to footstool warmer, and Earwax told him of the lands in Bovine she was due to inherit. They stood at times upon the walls, looking out, hoping the Army of the Rest would return victorious, but leaderless, minus Paragon and Earmore. The last occasion they stood there coincided with the activation and destruction on the mini-black hole of Horridruin. Within minutes the black swirling clouds had been sucked from the skies above Gondour. As Faraway mused upon this strange omen, he realised that The Ring-breaker must have made light work of his ordeal and darkened the mood of Sourone forever.

As they stood there, a helpicopter flew overhead, a song blaring from its speakers:

'SING YO, THE PEOPLE IN THE TOWER,
FOR THE DANK LORD HAS NOW LOST HIS POWER.
SO YOU NO LONGER NEED TO COWER,
IN THE TOWER OF POWER IN GONDOUR.
TURN OUT THE GUARD IN AN HOUR,
FOR THE KING HAS BEAT THE ONE WHO WAS SOUR.

SING YO, THE PEOPLE OF THE WORST.

THE DANK LORD'S BUBBLE HAS BEEN BURST.
YOU WHO WILL NEVER BE THE FIRST,
THOUGH YOU NO LONGER WILL BE SO VERY CURSED,
COZ YOUR ISLAND SOMEHOW GOT IMMERSED.
NOW YOUR FORTUNES ARE FINALLY REVERSED.'

Some time later, they received news that The Army of the Rest was approaching in ships laden with provisions. Messy couldn't wait to see his friends and the food, and so rushed off to meet them. The people of Minus Thrifty were glad to see him do so. Earwax and Faraway sulked and wouldn't come out, even when bribed with the offer of a free korma and naan. In truth, Earwax wouldn't go because Faraway wouldn't and, being so besotted with him, she would not leave his side, which made things quite interesting when he visited the latrine. Faraway tried everything he could to make her go visit her brother, just so he could get some peace, but to no avail. So they both sat and waited for the return of the Retinue of the King.

One morning, some days later, the Army of the Rest approached the city. The light that reflected off their newly tinfoil-covered armour was increased tenfold by the cameras of the paparazzi. They approached the broken gate where they were met by Faraway (who had eventually relented and decided to show face), Whozin, The Warder of the Wees, the Hygiene Minister and Effinghel. From the army, a contingent of men stepped forward, led by a man with a blank expression and what looked like the base of a broken gin bottle hanging from his neck. Behind him stood The Grand Alf, Earmore, Himhadrill and, worryingly, three Halfbits.

Faraway stepped forward. Although he recognised most of those stood before him, he decided he to be difficult. 'What have we got here then?'

'I am Paragon, son of Paramount, Chiefbrain of the Dulledain of Another, Captain of The Army of the Rest, Wearer of the Slab of the North, Welder of the Sword Reformed, The Halfstoned, a Lesser Heir of the line of Vacantdul, Evenduller's son, Everdull's son of Neomanor. Will you elect me your king?'

'Got any I.D on you? People have turned up in the past and tried to con us; one was called Afederal; maybe a relation of yours. Besides, anyone can wave a sword about that they've bought on Ye Olde Ebay Shoppe. Wasn't that one supposed to be broken? I can't see any rivets or welding marks on it,' said Faraway.

'Well, take a closer look then,' said Paragon, thrusting the blade in front of The Stalwart's face. In runes along one side of the sword was written:

ORIGINAL. NOT A NEWLIES CINEMA COPY

On the other side it read:

ANDREX NARES BORN
ADMIT BEARER TO THRONE ROOM

Faraway gulped and grovelled as he apologised. 'I'm sorry Lord, but it is my job to ask these delicate questions. We had to make sure you are who you claim to be. Is there any other way you can prove this?'

Paragon whipped out his P.A.L.hand T.V. and pressed the D.N.A button. A special recorded message from King Ernest, the previous king, played on the video screen:

'IF THIS MESSAGE YOU DO HEAR,
IT MEANS THAT ONE THING IS QUITE CLEAR.
A MAN HAS COME TO CLAIM THE CROWN.
HE MUST BE REAL AND NOT SOME CLOWN,
SO SIT HIM DOWN AND MAKE HIM ROYAL,
AND ANOINT HIS HEAD WITH COOKING OIL.'

'Ah, right. That sounds pretty conclusive, wouldn't you agree?' said Faraway, looking at the others present for encouragement. They all nodded, either in agreement, or from falling asleep listening to the lists of names given by Paragon. Faraway reached behind him and took the Crown of Gondour from Whozin, which had been found after an exhausting search. 'Would you believe it was under Denizen's bed?'

'What was it doing under there?' asked Paragon.

'All the Stalwarts kept it hidden, a few by accident. In the dark, some have even mistaken it for something else. The thing has been cleaned using the best toilet-cleaner though,' replied The Stalwart.

Paragon grabbed hold of the White Enamelled Crown of

Gondour and tugged at it. After a couple of moments, Faraway let it go with a look of envy. Paragon held up the crown and in a clear voice chanted: 'Let allhearall endoftenure utterance sonoman uturn or holdinyak tenet Iambig mettle.' Turning to Faraway, the King said, 'Pack your bags; you're moving to Armi Hemdin. You are being promoted to Prince of Piffling. I want someone with relative intelligence to watch the borders, and I also want the royal apartments back.'

So it was that Paragon became King Of Gondour, and settled down to his royal duties of womanising, getting drunk and dropping the odd goof. On one occasion, he asked one of the Dwarven ambassadors why he hadn't brought his wife along, only to be told that the person he was talking to was in fact the wife of the Dwarven ambassador from Errorbore.

On another occasion, Beerygrog was brought before the King on the charge of spilling booze in a hallowed place. Paragon rewarded him by promoting him to manager of the Waiter Company for the beer garden of Faraway's Public House in Piffling. He then awarded Faraway the franchise for a chain of inns throughout that region as a sweetener for his family's efforts at keeping the royal footstool warm. All the while, the Halfbits stayed in Minus Thrifty milking the applause, and the free food that went with it. Legless and Grimy became drinking buddies, and The Grand Alf took bookings for his Dizzy Wizzy Roadshow.

Then one day, The Grand Alf found Paragon walking up towards the higher parts of Mount Mindofruin with an antique map in his hand. The Wiztari asked the King what he was searching for.

'I don't know. I've found this map that was left with the Stalwarts for the attention of the next king. I found it under a pile of old astrology magazines. This number written on the bottom means something: 873770. Do you think it may be a grid reference?'

'No, there are no lines on the map. Maybe we should just follow the arrows,' replied The Grand Alf.

'There are no arrows on the map either.'

'I meant these ones, on the walls and floor,' said the Wiztari, pointing to a large white arrow.

They followed the arrows and eventually came to a metal door in the wall of the mountain. On it was written "SPARES", and underneath this was an electronic pad.

'What's that number again?' asked The Grand Alf. Paragon gave him the map and the Wiztari punched in the numbers. There was a sound of clicking and whirring, followed by the hissing of a released vacuum seal.

Paragon pushed the door and it opened with the screech of rusty hinges that have long been untroubled. They both peered into the room beyond. Inside were rows of shiny Yowltide trees, all identical copies of Nimbus the Fake. Paragon was amazed and exclaimed, 'Great Utilitarian, I'm rich. I think I'll start a new tradition of a Yowltide tree in every home.' So the old broken and tarnished tree was scooped out of the mouldy pond, and Paragon plugged in a new fibre-optic shiny one. Beneath it was placed a plaque reading:

BUY YOUR REPLICA TREE.
ONLY 100 COINS OF THE REALM. PLUG COMES FREE.

Sometime later, a group arrived from the north; the upper classes of Riverdwell and Lostlotion had travelled to join them after hearing reports of the grand party being held in Minus Thrifty. They were fuelled along their journey by the booze cruise ships sailing upriver from Ohgivusalaugh and The Cairn and Rose. Elbow Halfman, happy to have another excuse for a party, brought the Sceptre of Anumbass and his daughter, equally glad to be getting rid of these burdens. So Paragon The Lesser King of a Greater Realm married Olwen Undomesticated, who was of greater wealth and lesser mind.

MANY PARTIES

It wasn't long before people grew tired of the hangovers and late nights. Foodo was the first to get homesick, reminding everybody that the Halfbits had the furthest to travel. The fact that they would first refuel their vast stomachs for the journey ahead was obvious. So as to avoid going too long without food or rest, the journey home was planned with meticulous care. When the day came to leave, Earmore brought them a number of converted haywains. Some of these were for carrying the food and drink for the journey north; the last one was a stretchwain for carrying the body of King Theoflat Edskew, and a special brew of golden beer for his wake. With the Followship went Olwen and her bored brothers, Cellphone and Gadabout, plus her father, Elbow. Along also were Faraway, Himhadrill and their hangers-on.

A few weeks later they arrived at Udderas, where they held a wake for the old king, only to wake three days later with hangovers and found they had forgotten to bury him. So off they marched downhill in quick time with the body. All the previous kings had been buried in round barrows, but Theocrat the Flat needed a different shaped burial mound due to his accident with S'nomanure. This was the origin of the Long Barrow. Each mound was named after its incumbent, starting with Err the Wrong, then Braggo, older brother of Bolder; next came Fray and Fraying, followed by Oldwhine and Deodorise, Grampa and Helmet. On the other side of the road, the mounds started with Foralaf and Leevof, then Focal and Focalpoint, Funguy and Thegnguy, before at last arriving at the Long Barrow prepared for Theocrat. Having toasted each king as they passed their mounds, they now stood swaying in front of Theocrat's tomb. As one they 'Ale'd' Earmore Eadache, King of the Muck. This was a custom that most wanted abolished, for it consisted of drenching the King in beer, and was considered a waste of good beer. Afterwards they returned to the wake, only to hear the joyous news of Earwax's intended marriage to Faraway: another party to arrange. This was greeted with howls of delight and swigging of mead. Long
280

into the night they celebrated, until one by one they fell into the glorious daze of drunken sleep.

The next day, after some bother waking up the Dwarf, those who were leaving dragged their sore heads to their mounts. They were met there by those who couldn't face a further journey; or some, like Olwen, who had left the iron switched on, and so had to get home.

Earwax was now half her old self, and could hear a lot better thanks to the bang on the head she'd received from The Witchy-king, which had dislodged some of her namesake from her ears. She gave Messy an old trumpet which her father Earnaught had used as a hearing aid. 'Take this, Messy of The Snore and Mouldiwine of The Muck. With this you can eavesdrop on the plans of your enemies from a distance, and that way they won't be aware of your presence. If you have the courage to sound it, then the screech it makes could send even a tone-deaf Dwarf running for the hills; for it is made from the tooth of Scalda the Veriwarm, Firedrake of the North, whom Err the Wrong defeated, beheaded, dismembered and sold as hot steaks.'

Messy took the trumpet from the end of the pole being held out by one of her servants. After one more drink for the road (this was allowed in those days, as the animals had more sense than the riders), they set off for Oldcrank.

A few days later, they arrived at what had once been Ironhard Ring. They were met there by Treebred, who had transformed the place into some sort of garden market. Using the green wastewater for fertilizer, he had grown rows of cabbages, carrots and cauliflowers on one side; beetroot and beans on the other. Around the old walls, great thorny bushes had taken hold, and Rents patrolled the perimeter. The Grand Alf asked Treebred whether Sourman was still sulking in Oldcrank.

'I don't really know, come to think of it,' replied the Rent. 'I haven't seen him or heard his cringing pet's whiny voice for quite some time.' Turning to Bagolard, he asked, 'Have you seen that pathetic Wiztari fellow around here?'

Totally confused, Bagolard looked at The Grand Alf. 'Isn't that him?'

'No, the one we had a game of football with,' replied Treebred.

'Oh, the last time I saw him, someone had planted him in the cabbage patch to scare away his own crows.'

Looking at the cabbage patch and seeing no Sourman, Treebred asked, 'Well, it looks like he's escaped. How did that happen?'

'I saw that dog of his with a spade a few days ago,' said Bagolard.

'Ah, well I don't suppose he can do much damage now. Since losing his powers he's been unable to even bend a spoon, and his chemistry set is still up in that tower,' said Treebred, pointing at Oldcrank.

'How can you be sure of that?' asked The Grand Alf.

'We caught him sneaking out when Worntwang didn't return, after he'd been sent to steal food from the Halfbits' stash. After we'd had a game or two with him, he fled, leaving these,' he replied, holding up a bunch of keys.

Treebred handed the keys to Paragon, who hurriedly put them in his pocket for later use on the return journey, thinking that there might be some useful things up there that could be sold as souvenirs.

It was at this point that Legless and Grimy decided it was time to leave the Followship and head for their respective homes in Murkywood and Errorbore. They chose to travel together because neither could remember what the tally stood at in the their personal points scoring argument. Also, Legless needed someone to carry his replenished alcohol horde, and the Dwarf was as good a pack animal as any he'd seen. Legless had heard that, with the destruction of Gone Duller, the trade routes had opened again. He thought it might be a good idea to open a few inns along the way, and the Dwarf might be able to advise on building costs. The fact that this one knew more about pit props than doorframes didn't register in the Elf's fuddled brain. They set off together and, from a distance, could be heard arguing about maps and directions. It was said that many months later they arrived home weary, tired, and wearing Kiss-me-quick hats. It was also said that many years after, they both left Muddy Earth as stowaways aboard an Elven cruise ship.

Treebred turned to Cellphone and Gadabout and said, 'Vanish vanguard nostalgic. I am sad I will never get the chance to see the glorious trees of Lostlotion again.'

'Maybe that's a good thing, my old friend. The Gilded Wood has now become a less than shining example, and we are looking for new property,' replied Cellphone. 'The legend of Lostlotion will fade, and we will rebuild it in The Uncrying Lands.'

Gadabout added to this, 'Yet we may be together again, when you smoke the Mellow-weeds of the Tamarind-seed; then you will see many things that never were.'

Then Treebred took Messy and Pipsqueak for a few drinks. When he brought them back, they looked more than a little green. The remainder travelled on, after saying their farewells to the Rents. It wasn't long before Paragon got sick of the saddle sores and Olwen weary of applying soothing oils to them. So she suggested they set off back home, and perhaps walking for a while. The King said his goodbyes, and offered the Halfbits jobs in the new governing bodies of his far-flung realms, in regions too faraway for him to worry about. He warned them, however, that he would come and inspect their books one day, and Pipsqueak told him that the only books he had were children's books about Potty Harry. This was when the familiar stars appeared before his eyes. The not-so-little Halfbit was soon awakened from his slumber by the smell of Messy as he bent over him. The last they saw of Paragon was him disappearing into the distance, surrounded by a psychedelic glow.

The next part of their journey took them near the land of the Duncelikings, who hid from them, thinking they were a party of travelling salesmen. A few days into this land, they ran into two of the dirtiest and stupidest Duncelikings they had ever seen. These two didn't run away or hide, but stood by the roadside, gesticulating and pulling faces at them.

It was The Grand Alf who recognised them as Sourman and Worntwang. 'I see you're still not a happy-chappy, Sourman,' he laughed.

'Happy! Happy! What have I got to be happy about? No home; no change of underwear; no place to go, thanks to the ASBO from the court of Udderas, and no weed to smoke,' shouted Sourman.

'I've got some weed you can buy,' said Messy, holding up a pouch of Largebottom Leaf.

Sourman strode forward and snatched it, then suddenly dropped it like he'd been stung. 'Phew. Where the hell has that been?' He whacked Worntwang and gave him his handkerchief. 'Wrap the weed in this and give that mucky midget his smelly underwear back.'

Worntwang did as ordered, then followed his master, who by now had already set off away from the small company. He was no more than a few feet away when Sourman turned and spoke to the Halfbits, particularly focusing on Foodo. 'You little pests are in for a shock when you get back to The Snore. If it hadn't been for my old friend, Alfred Grey, the Estate Agent, I'd never have known about the property development potential of your little mud-pit. I'm so glad I bought into it through a silent partner.' He turned then and disappeared on unsteady legs into the wood, muttering about tree-sap.

'What's he talking about, Mr Foodo?' asked Stan.

'I don't know Stan, but I think The Grand Alf has some explaining to do,' replied Foodo, looking at the Wiztari with an inquiring eye.

'Ah, well, ahem. I happened to mention a farm for sale in the Southfarting, once only, during the middle of a Magic Circle Convention Party,' said The Grand Alf. 'I'd had a few too many shandies. Sourman was rather more interested in what I had to say than usual. I should have known he was up to something insidious, but I figured at the time, why would anyone be so interested in that little mud-pit?'

'I've no idea,' replied Pipsqueak.

'No change there then,' said Messy.

The band of wanderers set off for Riverdwell, leaving Gadabout and Cellphone glad that they had at last got rid of the smell and prattle of the two green-haired Halfbits. As they disappeared into the distance, the ones heading for Riverdwell could hear the joyous chant of Nomoreihere. So it was that, some time later, they approached the house of Elbow at Dimladsbliss. The first thing the Halfbits did was head for the dining room, where they ran into Bilious having his fifth breakfast. He greeted them and asked when they were leaving on their quest.

'We've already been there and now we're back again,' replied Foodo.

'Oh! Well, when are you heading home to The Snore then?' he asked, with a worried look on his face. Bilious was thinking of how much food would be left for him once this lot were done.

'We've only just got here. I want to collect my winnings and Mr Foodo needs paying,' said Stan.

'I suppose I'd better invite you to my birthday party then,' replied Bilious sulkily. The only good news was that, with each year, his cake got bigger.

For the next few weeks, they told stories of their quest to Bilious. At first he pretended to be interested, but then started pretending to be asleep, in the hope they would leave him alone. It wasn't long before the worn-out Foodo took the hint and decided it was time to go home. They told Elbow of their decision, who was delighted for all concerned, especially his Master Cook. Then he informed them that The Grand Alf would leave with them for Free.

Pipsqueak was delighted and said, 'That's jolly decent, seeing as we have no money to pay him anyway.'

They went to see Bilious before they left, and the old Halfbit gave them all farewell presents. To Foodo, he gave some old books, saying that he'd forgotten to hand them back in to the library when he left. Foodo opened the front cover of one of them and found that they belonged to the library at Riverdwell. One book was an Elven/Halfbit dictionary that Bilious had used to translate the food labels at The Elven Emporium of Elbow. To Stan was given an envelope containing a golden ticket. He was genuinely excited because he thought he'd won a trip to Wonky Willy's Chocky Blocky. When he read the ticket, he realised that it was the winnings from his bet. The ticket read:

YOU HAVE WON 1 MILLION BAGS
OF OUT OF DATE CRISPS

'What's this?' asked a visibly upset Stan.

Bilious gave Stan a little box containing The Gamble Heirloom. Inside was one of the original crop of potatoes that Masho and Bako had started growing upon arriving in The Snore. The petrified potato was wrinkled and shrunken.

'I believe you bet a million to one on that old tatty,' laughed Bilious.

'Yes, I did,' muttered Stan.

'Well, you've won a million bags of old crisps,' replied Bilious.

Stan suddenly realised he'd put his home address on the betting slip and so would be delivered to No3 Blagshut Row. He was more than a little worried about the fact that, even if the

Halfbits could read the out of date notice, they would no doubt be munching through his winnings by now. 'What flavour are they?'

'They are the last of the special edition dragon flavour; The Smog variety, I believe,' said Bilious.

Stan started to make plans for leaving Riverdwell immediately.

To the two green-haired Halfbits, Bilious gave pot-pipes carved with strange characters that only a drunken Dwarf could have made. Then he asked for his presents. Between them, they managed to scrape together a few mouldy mushrooms and a pipeful of Largebottom Leaf.

Bilious was a bit put out. 'Is this all you brought back from your travels around Muddy Earth? I brought back gold, silver, dragon-steaks and a nice. In fact, I gave you that for your birthday once, so you can give it back for mine,' he said grumpily.

'I'm sorry, uncle-cousin, but Grumble stole it from me,' replied Foodo.

'You stupid boy, how did you allow that to happen? And after all the trouble I went through to steal it in the first place,' moaned Bilious.

'Steal it?' repeated Foodo.

'Well, ahem, you know, finders keepers and all that,' he replied through clenched teeth. He was now bored with the conversation and wandered off to the corner and his favourite chair. He shifted the cat gently from his seat with his big toe, then pretended once again to fall asleep.

'Well, it doesn't look like the lazy old fellow is going to finish our story. Maybe that's because he isn't in it,' said Stan.

'I can still hear quite well though, and if you weren't such a Hardstool numbskull, I'd ask you to write your own story,' said Bilious. 'However, with Foodo being a Braggins, we'd better leave it up to him. When it's finished, I'd be more than happy to edit out the bit about how I gained Grumble's ring.' With that, he yawned and then yawned again, nodded and mumbled, 'Close the door on the way out, chaps.'

The next day, as Stan was pushing the others through the door, Elbow made an appearance, to make sure they were actually leaving. When he saw the packs on their ponies, and the determination of Stan Gamble, he let out a sigh of relief. Elbow told Foodo that there was no need to come back, as he was moving out West somewhere and taking Bilious with him. 'This time next year, watch out for us passing swiftly through The Snore. We won't be stopping long, so keep an eye open,' he added.

The Halfbits were glad to be going home. They had seen and done things that were unnatural for them. In fact, they were in danger of becoming another species, unrecognisable in Free, let alone Halfbiton. On the way to Wearytop, Foodo played up the severity of his injuries, so getting off from cooking, packing and watch-detail. They eventually reached The Prattling Parrot. The door was locked when they got there, so they banged on it loudly. After a few moments, the diminutive figure of Nod peeked through a side window and shouted something inaudible over his shoulder to Butterball, followed shortly after by the sounds of bolts being drawn from the other side of the door. It swung open and the large figure of Butterball emerged, carrying a large piece of wood with the words "YOU'RE BARRED" burned into it. Butterball took one look at them and let out a shriek, then ran back inside and they heard wood being cracked over a Halfbit's head.

Stan peered through the window and saw the large Barman struggling to catch up with the little Nod.

Eventually, the out of breath Butterball came to the door and said, 'What are you doing standing out in the rain? Why aren't you inside, by the warm fire?'

'Because you forgot about us again, Barman,' said The Grand Alf.

'Ah, ahem, I was so surprised when Nod said we had a bunch of dead people at the door, only to discover it was you lot, I'm afraid I couldn't wait to knock some sense into that dimwit Halfbit. Anyway, come in. You can stay the night. The price has gone up a bit, as I'm still trying to recuperate the losses I made from the break-in of my larder last year.' With that, he glanced at the Halfbits, who busied themselves inspecting the wooden floorboards. 'The larder is now impregnable. It has three bolts and two locks on the new metal door,' he said, watching as the Halfbits' shoulders dipped ever so slightly. 'Anyways, there's enough food for a week or so.' Looking at the Halfbits again,

288

he changed that assessment to a few days. He settled them into their rooms and told them that dinner would be in an hour's time, then ran off to the larder when he noticed his wide-eyed guests were drooling on the carpet and looking like they could eat through walls. An hour or so later, he reappeared to find the half-crazed Halfbits pacing up and down. 'You can come to the common room tonight. There's no one in. People don't go out in the dark anymore, not with them Hobo-gobbins about. We had a big piece of trouble here not long since: some people got ate, ate alive. I think them Gobby-men must have misheard their names. For instance, they ate Fat Feathertoes, the chicken farmer, Roly-poly Appledumpling, the orchard keeper and Tiny Tim Picklethorn, the vineyard worker. Then they just ate anyone in their way, like Will E Bonks and Gary Hotleaf, the dealer of Western Weed. That Bill Fony went bad and sided with the bad-uns. We had a big fight and managed to evict the trouble-causers, then put them on a banning order, so hopefully we've moved our troubles onto someone else's patch.'

'Well, we got through all right,' said Pipsqueak.

'That's because you're only Halfbits, young sir, and normally so insignificant that you may as well be invisible. Besides, they maybe thought you mad, especially since Mr Messy is wearing a dirty saucepan on his head, the smell of which would have sent most running to the hilltops. Also, begging your pardon Mr Alf, but after that pyrotechnic exploded in the crowd at your last gig here … well sir, that must have warned a few. All this trouble started when them Strangers left, telling us that trouble was afoot.'

'It must have been a big foot to have caused so much trouble,' said Pipsqueak, to the usual accompanying clip from The Grand Alf.

'Never fear Barman, the Strangers are back, and now they want paying for keeping you freeloaders in freedom,' said the Wiztari.

'Do you think they'll accept discount on their food and beer?' asked Butterball hopefully.

'Not if the King has anything to do with it. He's tasted your beer and thinks you add too much water,' replied The Grand Alf.

'King! What king? I thought we were a republic, ruled by a Tall Wart or something,' said Butterball.

'That's a Stalwart, and he abdicated when they elected Stupor as King,' said The Grand Alf.

Butterball looked shocked. 'Well, I never. I've heard of far-off places where they elect clowns to run their countries, but I've never heard of anyone inviting a Stranger to be King. Whatever next? Maybe these two will become Education and Health Secretaries,' he said, pointing at Pipsqueak and Messy. 'I hope he won't interfere with our council boundaries and move The Prattling Parrot into a higher tax band. Here, or get lots of city folk coming to buy up our country houses. There aren't enough as it is. We don't want lots of holiday homes here, thank you very much. I need regular customers.'

'Don't worry Butterball, they'll be moving into prefabs up north,' said The Grand Alf.

'Not near Madman's Hike surely. Only a fool or a drunk would go there,' said Butterball.

'The Strangers went there,' replied the Wiztari.

'Exactly.'

'No Barman, you misunderstand; it used to be part of their land and is known to them as Forlorn Erased or Noborough of the Kings. Stupor, or King Paragon, to give him his real name, has plans for a major reconstruction of the area. The place will be swarming with builders, carpenters, roofers, mortgage lenders and one estate agent, called Alfred Whitehead, and the only inn anywhere near will be The Prattling Parrot,' said The Grand Alf.

Butterball's grin stretched from ear to ear. Then he asked in a cautionary tone if any of these hard-working, thirsty builders would be Halfbits. The Wiztari fell off his stool roaring with laughter, and he was still chuckling the next day as they said farewell to Barman Butterball. The proprietor warned them, as they left, that things in The Snore had become even stranger than the normally weird things that happened amongst its dozy inhabitants.

As they made their way to The Snore, they discussed the possible nature of the troubles awaiting them at home. Messy was worried they might have installed communal baths. Pipsqueak, who had been put right a number of times about the foot thing, now worried about why The Grand Alf had said some people are just looking for trouble, and some just attract it. He was now looking from side to side occasionally, thinking that a large, angry female Halfbit would leap out of the bushes at him. Foodo told Stan that he guessed what he'd seen in Gadabout's Mirror was to blame.

That was when Stan suddenly realised he'd forgotten about Dozy Hot-one and Ed Randyman, and blurted out through clenched teeth, 'There'll be trouble in store for someone when I get back.'

'That's funny; I've never heard of a Snore store that sells trouble. Who owns it, I wonder?' said Pipsqueak.

Luckily for him, the Halfbits were thinking of other things and didn't take any notice of him. Unluckily, The Grand Alf heard him, with the result being a ringing in his large, cauliflower right ear. Messy helped his friend up from the floor, just in time for Pipsqueak to answer Stan's exclamation to The Grand Alf that, with him along, he'd deal with any of the troubles; only for the dozy Halfbit to return to the prone position after asking how many members there were in this family called Trouble.

'I'm not going to sort out any trouble,' said The Grand Alf. 'I'm off to see Bombastic. I need some R&R, and Bombastic's cakes help me relax almost as well as a bit of Old Tipsy, and I won't find much of that left in The Snore.'

The four Halfbits stood wavering for a moment, caught between home and the thought of a trip to Bombastic's house. The Grand Alf saw the look of greed on their faces and, before they knew it, the six-legged Shinyflax, with its waving Wiztari, was a mere fleck on the horizon,

'I suppose it's Muckland, first stop then,' said Messy.

THE SCOUNDREL OF THE SNORE

A few days later, they arrived at the bridge over The Bandyleg Brook. To their alarm, it had now been turned into a toll bridge, and it was raised. At the side of the bridge, a large house with a control tower had been built. In it was a dull, flickering light, so Stan banged on the door. There was no response to this, so he banged harder still. Getting angry, he picked up what he thought was a brick and banged again with all his strength, only to find that he had Pipsqueak's head in his hand.

From a window above came a voice, calling down to them, 'Are you stupid? Don't you understand plain Wyrdsome.' A hand stretched out the window, and pointed at a sign by the road that read 'NO BAD MITTENS IN THE DARK'. 'Salesmen are banned until the light of day. That way you can't sell your dodgy goods.'

Messy recognised the voice and shouted up at the window, 'We're not salesmen, Odd Headhard; it's me, Messy Brandishmuck.'

'Well bless me, the story around here was that Old Man Wilbur had gone cannibal and eaten you all for breakfast one morning. We hung him last year for the crime — something no Halfbit had done before, no matter how hungry; we've seen plenty of hangings lately, since The Thief came to Brag-end.'

'The Thief? Are you talking about Looter Sackfull-Braggins?' asked Foodo.

'Yes, I think so, though we haven't seen him lately. We just have to call him The Great Thief these days.'

'We'll sort out my errant cousin. He won't feel so great when we've finished with him,' said Foodo. 'Here, let us in.'

Whoever was inside the house wouldn't open the door however, so Messy and Stan used Pipsqueak as a battering ram. As the door shook, another one further down the building opened and out stepped a man.

'Who's making all that noise? Wait, breaking in, are we? Well, clear off until the morning or you'll be in for lots of trouble,' said the large man.

'How many are there in that Trouble family?' asked Pipsqueak, through a hazy daze.

'What's he prattling on about?' said the man, stepping forward into the light.

'Bill Fony!' said the Halfbits in unison.

Stan and Messy stepped forward, swords drawn. Bill Fony stopped in his tracks, then turned and fled. It wasn't for fear of the Halfbits or having to fight them; it was the smell emanating from the larger of the two, and the thought of blood poisoning from the dirty blade he was waving under his nose. Fony had only a metal-turning handle as a weapon, which he had grabbed on the way down, thinking he was only going to be sorting out a few moronic midgets. In his panic to get away, he flung the bar at them, catching Pipsqueak in the middle of the forehead, felling him.

'What's that for? I didn't even speak,' groaned Pipsqueak from the floor.

The other door clicked and then opened as Odd Headhard and his Toll-guard emerged to survey the scene. They had never seen one of The Chief's yobs bested and were amazed, until they got too close to Messy. With a few backwards steps, Odd said, 'Wow, phew, it is you Mr Messy,' then tripped over the prone Pipsqueak. He landed on the metal bar that Fony had flung. He grunted in pain, and picked it up. 'It's the thing-gummy-wotsit that turns the mek-and-ism thingy for the toll-bridge. That's fortunate; it could have been lost in the undergrowth.'

Pipsqueak stirred and said, 'The bells in my head are only playing one tune, not four,' before slumping back down again.

'That must be Mr Peregrinate Talk,' said Odd.

'You bet it is,' said Stan.

They carried Pipsqueak into the guardroom and plonked him on a bed, then started to discuss how much was left of their rations and how to cook them. This had the immediate effect of rousing the half-dazed Pipsqueak to his usual state of semi-awareness.

He staggered from the bed. 'Did someone mention cooking the food? I volunteer.'

This was a custom amongst Halfbits: they could argue for hours about who would cook, knowing that tasting meant filling your face. In the end, they agreed to eat the food cold and not under any circumstances share it with the half-starved guards. They stayed there that night and learned from Odd that The Thief had made up lots of new rules; firstly, that smoking was banned in all public places. This got suddenly harsher when smoking was banned altogether. This was followed by news that all the weed from Southfarting was being exported by way of Sarky Forkedway. Some of the other Halfbits started to get worried about how Odd's mouth was flapping and tried to hush him up. When they failed, they started singing at the top of their voices, trying to drown out his words until all that could be heard was a cacophony of Halfbits.

Meanwhile, a fight broke out between a Grubby and a Chubby over some half-forgotten misdeed between their great-grandfathers: this was apparently over who had eaten the last piece of cake at The Bold Talk's one hundredth birthday party. In the end, Stan, Messy and Pipsqueak broke them up.

Stan, who had a face like a bad ham because he was still unhappy about missing out on a visit to Bombastic's Pot-shed — something he hoped to make up for with some Old Tipsy, washed down with Halfbit Hooch — said, 'I'm going to bed, and if I hear one squeak out of you lot I'm going to introduce you to Mr Pain.' To accentuate the point, he waved his Tenderiser under their noses. The guards smiled nervously as they backed away into the corner of the room, where they remained until morning. To the relief of the border guard, the four left quite early, heading for Halfbiton, where they hoped to stay at The Farting Dog in Flogmoron that night.

As they drew near to the village, they came upon a hastily erected barricade that stopped anyone from going further along the road. So they headed for the field next to it, jumped over the small fence, trotted a few yards, then jumped back over onto the road behind the barricade. Facing them was the halfwit leader of the local police force, known thereabouts as The Shufflers. This was on account of them getting to most crime scenes late due to dragging their feet.

The leader — who was known as The Defective Spectator, and was looking for promotion to Chief Constumble — stepped forward and said in the most officious voice he could muster, 'Here, you can't do that. It isn't fair.'

'I told you we should have gone round the other side,' said

Pipsqueak to Messy.

Stan looked the leader in the eye. 'We just have. What are you going to do about it?'

The Defective Spectator stopped for a moment. 'Firstly, I'm going to arrest you for trespassing in that field, then for importing illegal aliens.' He pointed at Pipsqueak and Messy. 'Then I'm going to arrest you for eating more food than is allowed under present regulations.' He pointed at Stan's large stomach. 'You, I'll arrest for having the outlawed name of Braggins, Mr Foodo. Oh, and before I forget, there are several warrants outstanding for impersonating a Halfbit by the name of Mr Undersized of Stuck.'

'Is that all you can come up with?' laughed Foodo, trying to play down the serious situation they were in.

'It's enough for me to take you into custody and hand you over to the Chief's men at Passwater. They'll put you in the stockade with the rest of the rabble-rousers for sure.'

Foodo and his companions just pushed the leader to one side, and said, 'I've had enough of this stupidity. I should have by-passed this town. It's always had more than it's fair share of idiots. Most towns are content with just one. We're off to Brag-end to sort out Halfbiton. You can come with us if you can keep up,' he finished, looking at the unusually malnourished shufflers.

They set off at once, keeping the ponies at a trot. The Shufflers weren't used to breaking into a quick stride, let alone jogging, and before long they were strung out along the road. The ones at the back sagged against The Three Farting Stones, and wilted. Sometime later, they arrived at Passwater. The place was like a ghost town, and was as bare as the awards cabinet of a boy-band trying to write credible music. It wasn't until they reached The Greedy Drake that they found any signs of life. There, lounging against the porch, was a group of inbred itinerants from Ironhard. These yobs now moved to block the road off.

'Going somewhere?' said the biggest, ugliest and most stupid-looking of the lot.

'Yes, we're off to Brag-end to sort out your master,' replied Foodo.

'What's happened to the petty Shufflers? They were supposed to stop you from getting here.'

'We sorted them out without any trouble at all,' said Messy.

'Well, you won't find it that easy getting past us,' sneered the ugly yob.

'Oh, you don't think so, do you? I was involved in killing The Witchy-king of Wagner, so you with your big stick don't look so scary to me, scumbag,' replied Messy.

'Scumbag! Who are you calling a scumbag? We're gonna teach you lot of little wasters a lesson, and don't think your little master at Brag-end is gonna help you. Shaky's in charge there now, and if there's any sorting out, then he's gonna teach you little prat-folk a few lessons in obedience, like he did to Looter.'

'I think you may be mistaken, for the only person we obey is The King of Gondour. Both Bad-odour and Ironhard have been destroyed; Sourone is now with Mortcough having his butt kicked; and Sourman wanders in the wild, as potent as alcohol-free lager. Soon the King will come north to survey his kingdom,' said Foodo.

The ugly, brutish yobbo laughed mockingly at them. 'The King, come to this little mud-hole? Hah! I've heard he's just got married to some gorgeous Elven dolly bird. I also heard he's on his honeymoon, and those Elven nuptials take a long time. Meanwhile, we're gonna be the fat-cats around here, so watch your mouth, you cocky little halfwit.'

The thought of making Foodo stand in front of a mirror and attempt to see words come out of his mouth was too much for Pipsqueak to bear. He urged his pony forward, pulling out his large gleaming weapon. 'How dare you speak to The Ring-breaker like that. He is the most famous Halfbit to have ever lived. His biography will sell to millions all over the world forever. It will be the greatest book ever written, and the film of it will break all records. You are an uncouth youth and must surely be related to Hermione Sneer, the critic who writes books that no one reads.'

Stan and Messy rode forward to join their friend, with weapons in hand. The sight of the three of them made the yobs waver. Ultimately, though, it was the stench of Messy that was too much to bear. These bullies had turned out true to form, and fled like cowards the moment they met something they couldn't beat. Plus it would have been hard to fight while holding their noses.

'What now, then?' asked Stan.

'Well I suppose we'd better push on and free Looter,' replied Foodo.

'Set him free? He's the cause of all this destruction and mayhem, isn't he? Let him rot I say,' said Messy.

'It would be a few months before he smelt anywhere as bad as you,' said Pipsqueak.

'I would have bet my best dung-shovel that I wouldn't have wasted a minute of my life fighting yobbos and Dorky-men to rescue Looter Sackfull-Braggins,' said Stan.

'Yes, the fight … which reminds me, aim for the big ones. The small ones will come over to our side when we bribe them with offers of food,' said Messy.

'I bet there's lots more of them around. The football season hasn't started yet, and they haven't got anything to do. When we get to Halfbiton, it will be swarming with them, I'll wager,' said Stan.

'Then we'd better go into hiding and form a resistance,' said Pipsqueak.

'That won't be any good; all they'd have to do is follow their noses,' said Foodo, looking in Messy's direction.

Eventually, between them, they formulated a plan to band all the Snorings together, starting with Stan being sent to Old Tom Hot-ones to gather up his tribe of sons and daughters (mothered by countless women). As Stan rode off, he heard the trumpet of Bovine blowing the clear clarion call of Muckland:

'FEE FI FO FUM,
THE HALFBITS FROM ROUND HERE ALL HUM!'

Far in the distance, Stan could hear lots of noise and people complaining, "Don't you know it's against the rules about blowing a horn after 23.00 hours?" As he rode on, he could see lights on at the Hot-one farmstead. When he arrived there, he was immediately surrounded by a group of half-mad Halfbits holding heavy axes. It was led by Farmer Hot-one with Tim, Tom, Bob, Bill, Dolly, Holly, Molly, Polly, Dick, Mick, Nick, Rick and Rumplestiltskin, the adopted one. They were just about to turn him into dog food when Stan hollered, 'Stop, it's me Stan Gamble. I bet you never thought you'd see me again.'

'Oh dear, someone had better tell Dozy; she thought you'd gone for good,' said Farmer Hot-one.

'Well, we're all back: Mr Foodo, Mr Messy, Mr Pipsqueak and

me. The others are trying to wake The Snore.'

From a distance they could hear plenty of crashing, banging, the sounds of horns blaring and the beep-beep of alarm clocks that had been set for the wrong time. Farmer Hot-one was overjoyed and, turning to Tom, he told him to fetch the rest of the family. 'Oh, and don't forget Ted, Fred, Ed, Jed, Ned, and Jared, who are living in the hayloft. Also Gary, Barry, Harry and Larry, who are in the cellar.'

'What about Dozy and Mrs Hot-one?' asked Stan.

All the Hot-ones started to laugh. 'They can't come; they're pregnant,' said the farmer. 'My Nat, Mat and Pat are there. Go check on them to make sure at least one of them is awake.' With that, he headed off, accompanied by the Number One Platoon of the Hot-one private army, towards Passwater.

Stan made his way to the farm and was met there by the sight of a group of Halfbits shovelling food into their mouths. Stan's pony came to a sudden halt, which resulted in him flying over The Nag's Head, rather than drinking in it. He landed smack in the middle of a large pile of dung, making him look like a mud baby. Nat, Mat and Pat jumped to their feet and advanced with eating utensils at the ready, convinced that someone had broken through the cordon, intent on stealing their food. Now Stan knew how desperate this situation was: attempting to take food from a Halfbit whilst they had cutlery in hand was a very stupid thing to try. Although Stan was a simple spud-planter, he wasn't so dumb as to ignore Halfbit eating etiquette. He leapt up and shouted at the top of his voice, 'Gam Stamble, Blam Stangem, Stag Namble.'

The Hot-one triplets prodded him with their forks, and Nat said, 'What sort of creature do you think it is?'

'It's too small to be a yob, unless it's one of their feral kids,' replied Mat.

'Maybe it's one of those Dorks we've heard about,' said Pat.

'It sounds pretty Dorkish to me,' replied Nat.

Stan brushed and shook off the dung, clearing his eyes and mouth. 'It's me, Stan Gamble.' At that point, Dozy fainted into the arms of her mother, while the remaining Halfbits just stood and stared, mouths gaping.

'Hello Mrs Hot-one. What's wrong with Dozy then?' asked Stan.

'She's been expecting since you left. You didn't hurry back, did you?' she replied accusingly.

Stan stood counting on his fingers but, being totally clueless about the gestation period for Halfbits, he quickly gave up, much to the relief of Mrs Hot-one. Getting back to the business at hand, Stan told Nat, Mat and Pat why he was there and why they needed to mobilise the Number Two Platoon of the Hot-one army.

'Hadn't you better get back to the others then?' said Mrs Hot-one to the young Gamble, but Stan's pony wasn't happy that a stinking mass of cow dung was attempting to climb on it's back, and it took him four attempts before he could mount. The pony took off down the road, bucking and trying to dislodge the thing from its back.

Back at the farm, Dozy opened one eye and asked, 'Has he gone yet?'

'Yes dear,' replied her mother.

'Do you think we fooled him?' asked Dozy.

'Of course we did; he's a Hardstool.'

When Stan arrived back at the village, he found that the others had built a huge fire and were sitting around it, toasting various items of food that had been liberated from the yob supply in The Greedy Drake. Luckily, they had also found a stack of weapons, which they were now using to hold food near to the fire. With help from some of the lads who had already gorged themselves, Stan re-entered The Greedy Drake and found the bows that went with the arrows that were presently being used for toasting marshmallows. Gathering everything that he could, from the spit-handle to the poker, including some mops and brooms that Messy brought, he was left to make weapons in the fashion of The Ruminates. When all was done, the Halfbit army had grown somewhat and was armed to the teeth. At that point, the exhausted Shufflers appeared and Foodo invited any of them who wished to join the revolt to the party. They looked at the weapons and those who held them in one hand, with lumps of meat in the other and, without exception, they all found new strength and raced towards the food.

'Do you think we have enough to deal with the yobbo army

now?' Foodo asked Farmer Hot-one.

'At the moment we have. I don't fancy trying to separate this lot from that,' he replied, pointing at the dwindling pile of food. 'However, if the Halfbiton gang meet up with those from Largebottom, Sarky Forkedway, Wuditt Bend, Wayward Wayland and not forgetting the ones guarding the stockade at Mickle Deviance ...' he added, as he stood totting up the total on his hands and feet (a method he used for counting his sheep). '... then the yobbo army would be about two million,' he said proudly, which yielded an audible gasp from around the fire.

That was when the excuses started: 'I left my old dad in the bath; must go. See you next year,' was the first.

'I need to water my sunflower,' said another. And so on.

However, before anyone had a chance to scarper, Farmer Hot-one shouted, 'Stop! Wait! Sorry, I multiplied my big toe by my thumb.' Most of the villagers looked at him stupidly as he began to explain. 'It should have been my little toe by my index finger, and that only makes a couple of hundred.' A huge sigh of relief was followed by the sound of munching as they all went back to happily eating anything edible.

'Well, is there anywhere we could get more Halfbits with weapons?' asked Stan, not too convinced by the farmer's numerical skills.

'There is Mr Peregrinate's family. The Talkings were the only ones who stood up to the new regime. You see, when Looter made himself The Big Snoring Master, Mr Perambulate told him to wind his neck in, as there was only one Master, and he was The One. Looter got really angry and annoyed. It took two of his yobs to get the carpet out from between his teeth, they reckon. Anyway, Looter sent some of his boys round, and the Talkings sent them back in pine overcoats. So the yobs stay away from The Great Smells, and the Talkings don't come out. It's a bit of a stalemate.'

'Yes, I've got one of those,' said Pipsqueak, looking at Messy. 'I'm off to Muckborough to see if they'll join our fight,' he added, as he mounted his pony and sped off in the wrong direction. A minute later, he returned and shot through Passwater, heading towards The Grin Hills. The reason Pipsqueak for him returning so quickly wasn't because he had realized that he was heading the wrong way; the real reason became apparent almost immediately, as a large band of delinquent yobs came ambling up the road. They were chanting guttural songs and swigging from bottles of High-on-Brew which, once empty, they lobbed at the Halfbits ahead of them. At least four of them were pulling a barrow loaded with beer, with which they planned to celebrate their victory. When they reached the fire, they found only a few Halfbits toasting old bread.

'Here, that's against the rules,' said their leader.

'Why? The bread's only one day past its sell by date. We Halfbits will eat anything, apart from one of our own, of course,' said Stan, looking at the leader and licking the chicken fat from his lips. The man flinched slightly; even these morons had heard of the ferociousness of the Halfbit appetite.

Then Foodo stepped forward. 'Besides, we have decided to do away with the rules. From what I've heard, isn't beer against those rules?' At the mention of the word "beer", the murmur of a few hundred Halfbits could be heard. The red light of the fire reflected off their enamelled teeth, as they edged forward.

'Shaky is not going to be happy with you lot. Wait until he gets the whole gang together,' said the leader, looking from side to side. The ring around him was closing, along with a low murmuring chant of, "Beer, beer, beer."

Foodo said, 'Well at least we've sorted that out. You and your lot won't live to see the rest of the gang turn up. Tell him how many will be left to fight after we've finished them off, Farmer Hot-one.'

After a few minutes of digit dataflow, the old Halfbit answered, 'Seven times my big toe, minus two times my little toe, and add a thumb or two.'

The yob leader was losing his will to live, between listening to this prattle and the advancing, ravenous, half-starved Halfbits. At this point, his will did indeed snap and he began to froth at the mouth. Without warning he attacked the nearest thing to him. Having now chopped off his right leg and become hopping mad, he aimed a blow at Foodo, who evaded it by tripping over Stan's foot. Missing with his blow, the leader went spinning, lost his balance and fell face-first into the fire. He lay there thrashing for a few moments while the rest of his men looked on in horror. They decided almost immediately that they would rather not become barbecued belly-fillers for these munching midgets, and dropped their weapons and started pleading for mercy under the Green-eaves Convention. Some of them even started to ask for the toilet. What they got was a barn with a bolt on the door and a bucket in the corner. Outside, the Halfbits were swigging beer, dancing round the fire and singing, "Easy, easy, easy."

The three remaining members of The Followship, along with Farmer Hot-one, now decided on their next course of action.

'Let's march on Halfbiton,' said Stan.

'What, during the middle of the night? We'll lose half this lot before we get there,' said Messy, pointing at the drunken rabble.

'That's if we can get any of them to move,' said Foodo, pointing at the ones who were already lying flat out.

'But I wanted to get to Blagshut Road tonight to surprise The Grafter,' moaned Stan, who was thinking of his crisps.

'Oh, there isn't a Blagshut Road anymore. They've built a super-casino there. Looter put Ed Randyman in control. There are other buildings too that are not so nice. Our Dozy was working there for a short time,' said Farmer Hot-one ruefully.

Stan remembered the scenes he'd seen in The Mirror of Gadabout and tried to push them out of his crowded mind. What with the worry about The Grafter and what had become of his winnings from the Elves, Stan was almost frantic when he asked, 'What's become of my Dad?' His bottom lip trembled as he said this.

'Don't worry about him, young fellow; he's been hiding in my barn. I've ensured that he's been fed and watered,' answered the old farmer.

Tears welled in Stan's eyes. 'I can't thank you enough, Mr Hot-one. How will I ever repay you?'

'Don't worry about that either; I've something in mind you can do,' replied Farmer Hot-one, without telling Stan that The Grafter had already dug and planted three fields for him by hand.

So Stan went to the Hot-one household and, with the help of Holly and Dolly, had a bath, something to eat, and slept for a while. Later, he went to the barn to retrieve his father.

Meanwhile, Foodo learned from Farmer Hot-one what had transpired in Halfbiton since he had been away.

'The trouble started with Pompous; that's the name we gave to Looter when he moved into Brag-end. He thought he was Mr Big, splashing cash like it would never run out. Some thought

302

he'd found old Bilious Braggin's hidden treasure. Before we knew it, he'd bought most of The Snore in a land-grab frenzy. Then came the price-fixing scandal where he bought all the farms, so that all the produce was his. Suddenly, everything started to get more expensive, and Pompous knew that we'd pay, on account of our love of food. He opened an export agency and sold all the best stuff to some strange-looking southern folk. At first it was just the food, but then we found out that Pompous was behind the GM Crops Movement. Then, by some sort of foreign magic, he crossed the weed with something outlandish called Bacca. This made the leaves of the plant bigger. We weren't allowed any of this new stuff, as it would stunt our growth. They put it all into big bags with funny body-parts drawn on them, and sent them after the food. With not enough food for second or third breakfast, people started to eat anything. Some of the womenfolk got quite adventurous with the cooking. Mrs Hot-one turns out a nice dandelion-and-nettle soup, it must be said. On occasion, she even adds the odd little beastie.'

Foodo inspected the spoon, which was halfway to his mouth, for movement. Luckily there was none, but from then on he inspected every mouthful.

The farmer continued with his story. 'Then this Shaky fellow appeared; or didn't, to be more precise. He must have slunk into Brag-end overnight. We stopped hearing from Pompous almost as quickly as we started hearing about Shaky-this and Shaky-that. All the rules were changed again and Bold Bill Bigfoot, the town mayor, disappeared. As too did old Lobbit Sackfull-Braggins, when she objected to Shaky building some extension at Brag-end.'

'Why do that? There's loads of room there,' said Foodo.

'Word got round that he was using some dangerous powders, so he needed a Sigh-hens Laborrow-tree, whatever that is.'

'So who's this Shaky then? Something sounds familiar about him.'

'He's ten feet tall, with four arms and two heads, with only one eye on each. He growls like a dog and smells worse than Mr Messy; sorry sir,' squeaked little Tim Hot-one, as he scuttled under the table to hide.

'Yeah, that's him,' said one of the other Hot-ones.

'Good description,' shouted another.

'So you've seen this scoundrel then?' asked Foodo.

'Yes, of course. Well, not exactly,' replied the farmer.

'What do you mean by not exactly?'

'It's like this: my Dozy has a friend, whose mother's brother's uncle said he'd seen him through the smoky haze of his last ounce of Old Tipsy.'

'Well that answers that; we haven't got a clue what he looks like,' said Messy.

A few minutes later, Stan appeared with The Grafter in tow. When the old fellow set eyes on Foodo, he harangued him severely. 'You shouldn't have given that idiot nephew of yours Brag-end.' The Grafter hadn't changed much, but he had obviously got a bit dafter.

Foodo gave Stan a puzzled look, and he just shrugged his shoulders and tapped his head a few times. Foodo thought about it, then said, 'No worries, Hamfist; I'll send Foodo and Stan around to sort out your bit of bother.' He left with Stan through the back door, then appeared a moment later through the front door. 'Me and Stan have been sent to sort out a bit of bother.'

'Where's my Stan then?' asked The Grafter.

'I'm here, Dad,' said Stan, as he moved to stand in front of him.

'What have you done with the other Stan, him what's always covered in dung? I don't like the look of this one,' said the old fellow, eyeing Stan's tin-pot armour.

'You should have seen him a few hours ago,' said the farmer ironically.

The next morning, Pipsqueak arrived with the army from Talkland. He informed them that the yobs had been cleaned out of Muckborough by The Stain. He almost added that the stain had been cleansed from Muckborough. The bad news though, was that a band of yobs were now heading in their direction. They came up with a plan to distract these brutes, by converting one of the barns into a cinema. A sign was placed outside, by the road, reading:

POTTY HARRY AND THE DEADLY SHALLOWS.
FREE ENTRY PLUS FREE BEER.

Farmer Hot-one had volunteered to stand in front of the doors, to translate the sign for the illiterate yobs. When they arrived, he informed them of the offer. Once told, they shoved the elderly Halfbit out of the way and rushed inside. When the last of them was inside, the doors were closed and a cart was wheeled into place, locking them in. A group of Halfbits, armed with pitchforks and bows, emerged from behind the bales in the hayloft. The yobs tried climbing the ladders, which the Halfbits had forgotten to retrieve. One after the other, they came crashing down onto those waiting to climb the ladders. This is how the term 'bouncer' came about. The bales were pushed over the side, squashing many, until at last only a few of them were left standing. These ones quickly surrendered. When they had been despoiled of anything useful, they were chased from The Snore by Halfbits on ponies.

The rest of the Halfbits then marched towards Halfbiton and The Thief. When they arrived there, they were shocked at the state the town was in. Rubbish was strewn everywhere, the grass was uncut, windows were smashed and fences broken.

'They know what they can do with their council tax demand next year,' said Pipsqueak.

As they drew closer, they saw that the old mill had been replaced by a large golf ball shaped building with the words 'New Clear Power' written on it. As they approached the place that had once been Blagshut Row, they could see The Snore Syndicate, a large casino which loomed over them as they passed it on the way to Brag-end. At the main gate of the casino was the bizarre sight of Ed Randyman dressed as some foppish buffoon.

'What do you lot want at the front entrance? Halfbit help use the back door,' he said mockingly.

Stan strode forward and punched Randyman in the eye, laying him out on his back in the dirt.

The casino manager squealed and squawked before getting up and saying angrily, 'I'll make you work in the wash-house for a week to clean these clothes.' Stan went to hit him again and it dawned on Ed that this was no ordinary Halfbit. He looked at the strangely clad individual before him and choked out the words, 'S ... S ... Stan Gamble?'

'Yes! And I've come back to sort out a little problem between us, Halfbit to Halfbit.'

'You stay away, you hear? The Boss's doormen will be here soon, and you won't be so brave then,' jeered Randyman.

'If you mean some of those yobs that Pompous employed, then I'm afraid they are either dead or have been chased away,' said Foodo.

'I don't believe it,' replied Randyman, looking at Foodo as if he was a ghost.

'Well, shall we beat you up until your bully-boy friends turn up?' said Stan, with a vicious glint in his eyes.

Randyman squealed again and ran inside, tripping the security alarms. Loud sirens blared from a box on the wall. Faces appeared from behind tattered curtains and broken windows in the surrounding houses. Halfbits emerged to join the army and learnt that Foodo Braggins had come back to reclaim Brag-end.

A few minutes later, they were standing at the very doors of Brag-end. The place looked like a fly-tipping zone. Stan cried at the thought of how many trips it would take, up and down the hill with his dad's barrow, before it would be clean again.

Foodo banged on the door and called for Looter the Thief to come forth, but there was no answer. He banged again, but still there was no answer.

'Maybe we should come back tomorrow. He may be out,' said Pipsqueak, who was ignored as usual.

Foodo looked under a nearby broken paving slab, and retrieved a spare key he'd purposely forgotten to tell Lobbit Sackfull-Braggins about. They opened the door to find that many of the most expensive possessions in The Snore had been stashed inside. Only Foodo, Stan, Messy and Pipsqueak entered.

'This reminds me of Sourman's stores at Oldcrank,' said Messy.

Outside, there was a crescendo of murmuring, and a shadow fell over them as a figure appeared in the doorway.

'Did someone mention my name?'

Foodo took one look at the person who stood before him, trembling and supporting himself on a stick, and blurted out, 'Shaky (Shakilyshookbiashaker in Old Rentish).'

'Yes, that's the name the people who I brought with me from Ironhard call me now. My shakiness is on account of those damned Rents playing a few games of football with me. I thought I would give you a surprise homecoming. Judging by the stupid looks on your faces, I have succeeded not only in surprising you — you also look quite upset, you poor little fellows. The only sorrow for me is that that old fool, The Grand Alf, isn't here to see what I have done to the property prices around here. Oh, I've had such fun. I wish you'd stayed filling your faces at Riverdwell a little longer. I had such plans for The Brag-end Mining Company.'

'Mining for what?' asked Stan.

'Oh, you stupid little Halfbits; you don't even know about the huge tin deposits under this very hole,' replied Sourman.

Stan looked a bit sheepish and began to edge away.

'Stan, explain yourself,' said Foodo.

'Well, it's like this, Mr Foodo: you and Mr Bilious ate so many cans of beans that me, and The Grafter before me, didn't know what to do with them. So we started digging big holes and burying them,' replied Stan apologetically.

'Stan, they were supposed to be recycled. The Green Police could have fined us.'

'Ugh! Who'd want a cycle made out of old cans?' said Pipsqueak.

Sourman looked in horror at the Halfbits, wondering how the likes of these had managed to bring down Sourone and overseen the demise of his own ambitions.

Foodo turned to Sourman and told him that he was being moved on, and to pack his bags. 'It looks like you can forget your dreams of world domination, I can only think of one thing for you to do now: leave and find The Grand Alf if you can, for only he can help you now.'

'There are an awful lot of cans in here,' said Sourman.

'Yeah, there's a few popping out of here,' said Pipsqueak, pointing out the back window at the trampled cabbage patch.

Sourman turned and walked out through the door. He was followed by the four Halfbits and emerged into a torrent of hate and abuse from those outside.

'Hang him!'

'Shoot him!'

'Decapitate him!'

Pipsqueak got carried away with the mood and shouted, 'Decapitate him, then hang him!' This brought a stunned silence to the crowd.

Sourman continued down the lane, shaking his head in

disbelief. At the first hut, he stopped and shouted, 'Worntwang! Worntwang! Bring out my bags. It's time to beat a hasty retreat, or they may make us clear up some of this mess you've made.'

Out of the hut emerged a figure, bent double with the weight of two bags and a backpack. He was in obvious distress.

'Worntwang, let him carry his own bags. Why should you bear all the weight?' said Foodo.

'He's carrying it because he doesn't want you to see what's in that large pack on his back,' said Sourman. 'Did you not wonder why Looter is in hiding? Well, I'll tell you, it isn't by his own choice, is it Worntwang?' Worntwang groaned and sagged. 'Even more, why don't you show them what's in that large pack on your back? These nice little Halfbits should be more diligent about what they let slip through customs control.' With that, he pulled the strap on the pack and out flopped a very dead Halfbit, in the form of Looter Sackfull-Braggins. 'Oh dear, you'll have to wash your little snack now,' said Sourman sarcastically.

There was a murmur of shock from the crowd as they edged forward. Worntwang's eyes started to roll in his head. He pointed at Sourman and screamed, 'You packed your bags. I didn't put him in there. I only put this in,' he said picking up an old wooden mallet. 'I was going back to my old trade when I left you.'

Angered, Sourman grabbed Worntwang by his ragged shirt front, pulling hairs from his chest in the process. 'Leave me? Leave me? You'll never do that! You were born to be a slave, and you'll die one,' said the shaky old Wiztari.

In agony from the chest hair ordeal, Worntwang smacked the mallet against Sourman's cranium, and only stopped when his master slid to the floor. He looked down at the face of the wasted Wiztari and shrieked, then turned away and fled back into the hut. What the maddened man didn't realise was that Sourman had booby-trapped the hut to blow up into a million pieces.

With the dust settling from the explosion which the booby had set off, Pipsqueak said, 'Phew, I was going to see what had been left behind in those huts.'

'Lucky you didn't; you'd have had your brains blown out,' said Stan.

'Have you been in any exploding huts recently?' asked Messy.

'No. Why do you ask?' answered Pipsqueak.

'Just wondering what blew your brains out last time.'

308

Once the dust had fully settled, they covered the bodies of Looter and Sourman with an old sheet from Brag-end.

'Well, that's the end of that then,' said Foodo.

'We'd better start tidying up,' said Stan as he searched for any sign of his packets of crisps.

'I'm hungry. Can't we eat first?' whined Pipsqueak, only to be pelted with objects by numerous half-starved Halfbits.

The Halfbits dismantled all the buildings which had been erected by Sourman Industries. Whilst doing this, they discovered a Fracking Drill stored in one of the huts. This instrument was undoubtedly one the worst evils devised by the mad Wiztari. The poison this would have produced meant The Snore would have been blighted forever.

Most of the huts had been built using the floorboards and doors of houses along Blagshut Road. The materials recovered from Ed Randyman's Casino were used to rebuild most of the Halfbit holes to a standard surpassing what any of them had experienced before. The new buildings were built over the stream that fed the town well, so each new hole had running water. All they had to do was drop a bucket through an opening in the kitchen floor. This caused problems at first, due to misunderstandings of the instructions, with many simply losing their buckets. Later, when the spring thaws came with the resulting rush of water, many had to be fished out of the well due to not letting go of the ropes attached to their buckets. These were merely teething problems, however, and before long many of them started to think life was better now, and how it had turned out to be a good thing that Pompous had started his renewal programme.

The four Followship Halfbits freed all the prisoners from the stockade in Stuck. There they found the local chip shop attendant, Friergas Bulging, also known as Farty, due to his bad diet. Next was Lobbit Sackfull-Braggins, who had become a shadow of her former self. Too weak to fight, argue or nag, she decided instead to be a burden on her family, the Bravegirlies of Hardbooze. Also amongst the prisoners was little Kenny Prongfoot, limping as usual; yet this brave lad was the only Halfbit in The Snore to have inflicted damage on one of the bullies before the intervention of Foodo and friends. Truth be told, he'd always been warned to watch where he threw his pitchfork. Last to emerge was old Bill Bigfoot who, due to his enforced abstinence from alcohol, had lost his famous huge beer belly. He was still heavy though, so it required a group of sturdy young Halfbits to carry him to his newly opened inn to start his recuperation.

On the way there, he threw his battered top-hat to Foodo, and said, 'Take care of things for a few months. There's a good chap.'

Foodo immediately disbanded The Shufflers, and reformed them under the new name of The Polite Force, making them all do basic fitness tests and take lessons in social verbal intercourse.

One of the major problems they all had to tackle was the amount of rubbish and rotting bodies strewn about. With the warmer weather, this brought a plague of flies and insects. One day, as he got sick of swatting the flies, Stan remembered the words of Gadabout, so he searched for the little box with the GA embossed on its front. He found it stuffed under his bed, along with things that cannot be described here. He lifted the lid and once more set eyes on the strange glowing dirt. Nestled inside, like a bird's nest, was a number of large seeds. Stan planted a couple in his garden, some along the lane leading to Brag-end, and the rest around Halfbiton. When summer was at it's hottest, the infestation grew worse, yet miraculously the trees that Stan had planted bloomed. The scent of the Malathion Tree could be smelt all over The Snore, and the insects fell down as dead as headless Dorks.

The Hardfoots worked hard that year, for a change. Free of the infestation, the harvest was abundant. All of the gardens and spare ground overflowed with crops of weed. The Halfbits of The Snore smoked so much that summer that there was a bluish haze hovering above them on many days. Most of the new Halfbit holes had to have extractor fans built in.

Foodo and Stan stayed with the Hot-ones until Brag-end was clean and ready to move back into. Messy and Pipsqueak carted Foodo's furniture back from the old folks' home in Crockhollow. This gave the two big, green-haired friends the idea of setting up their own removal firm, called The Hasty Halfbits, which in itself got everyone curious as to what 'Hasty' meant.

When Foodo was eventually dragged away from Mrs Hot-one's home cooking, and moved back into Brag-end, he asked Stan if he wanted one of the spare rooms. Stan started to twiddle his fingers and count his toes, so Foodo asked him, 'Is there a problem Stan? Are you worried about The Grafter and Widow Mumble?'

'Well, it's not only that The Grafter is hard of hearing, and Widow Mumble can't be understood by anyone, but I'm more worried about Dozy; she's due to have my child.'

Foodo whistled and winked at Stan, and dug his elbow into his friend's ribs. 'You young devil; that was fast. I never realised. There's no problem; you can knock down one of the walls. That will mean there's more room for you and your small family.'

'Can I knock down three walls? Dozy wants thirteen kids,' asked Stan nervously.

'Well, ahem, yes of course; but how are you going to manage such a large family?'

'That's not a problem; it's amazing how many people have offered to help. Even Ed Randyman has volunteered.'

So, after a rushed, pitchfork wedding, it turned out Stan had married Dozy just in time, for the child was born a few days later. Stan, who was never good with words, asked Foodo if he had any ideas what to call the child, and Foodo replied, 'Why don't you do what a lot of others do and name it after some part of your life? Or someone you've met and admire.'

So Stan thought long and hard about it, and decided to call his little girl Elanbak.

Later that year, Foodo gave Old Bill Bigfoot his top-hat back, and the Mayor immediately gate-crashed every party and celebration in The Snore, which soon resulted in him regaining his magnificent portly figure. Foodo settled down to do his favourite pastime, nothing, while Stan and Dozy did all the work around Brag-end. He would from time to time lock himself away in his study, only emerging when in need of a new bottle of Old Wino. One day a slightly inebriated Foodo asked Stan if he would go away with him.

'Sorry Mr Foodo, but I don't think I'm that way inclined,' replied a worried Stan.

'No, no Stan, I didn't mean that. I want to see Bilious again. It's his one-hundred-and-somety-whatever birthday soon, and he'll be the oldest Halfbit ever, even older than The Bold Talk.'

'It's a long way to Riverdwell, Mr Foodo, and I've gotten used to used to being with Dozy, if you know what I mean,' said Stan.

But the celibate Foodo didn't, and replied, 'Well, a bit of a rest from continuously trying to fix the springs of your bed in the middle of the night will do you good. Tell Dozy she won't be on her own long.'

'What do you mean?' asked Stan, as he looked worriedly around.

The following day, Foodo gave Stan his seven keys: six for the larder and one for the front door. He also left him the Braggins family diary, complete with Foodo's deletions and exaggerated self-portrayal. The diary also contained a large section titled "Sourone and How I Defeated Him, by F. Braggins Esq.". Along the spine of the diary, written in gold felt-pen, were the words "The Rotten Book of Wastemuch". There were a few pages left at the end, which Foodo told Stan he could use for the account of his small part.

Again, Stan didn't look happy, and looked around to check that no one had heard that.

A couple of days later, Foodo and Stan set out from Brag-end, pretending to be heading for a spot of fishing. No-one noticed them leave, as it was well before ten o'clock in the morning and most of the Snorings were still doing exactly that. They travelled eastwards all day, until the light started to fade, then they dismounted from their ponies and lit a small fire. They unravelled their bedrolls, opened a bottle of the strong stuff and lit their pipes. Before long, they were singing joyously:

'UP THE ROAD AWAITS OUR FATE.
WE'D BETTER HURRY OR WE'LL BE LATE.
AND THOUGH WE'RE SOFT, WE HAVE TO TRY,
FOR HALFBITS HOBBLE AND CANNOT FLY.
AND IF YOU THINK WE'LL START TO RUN,
I'M SORRY FRIEND, YOU'RE HAVING FUN.'

From somewhere not too faraway came, in answer, the sound of drunken merriment and singing:

'O ELDERBERRY WINE FOR ALL,
A SILVER PENNY GETS YOU MIRTHFUL.
O MANY AGED ETHYL ALCOHOL.
O ELDERBERRY WINE FOR ALL.
WE CAN'T REMEMBER ENOUGH TO TELL,

Coming up the road was a troop of Elves. The first one to come into view was Giddy Inglorious who, by the look of him, was well on his way. Next came Elbow, with a bottle of lager in his hand, and its bottle-top stuck to his forehead. His blue Willy still hung from his earlobe. Gadabout came next, riding on a pallid, plastic palomino, which had been acquired from the fairground rides at Lostlotion. It was now being pulled by some rather unhappy Elves, who kept glancing back with envy at the ice-cold drink in her hand. The bottle label had a picture of the earring Nelly on it, and was accompanied by the slogan, "Get some Nelly in ya belly".

Straggling behind was Bilious, who had obviously had too many. The Elven troop stopped in front of Foodo and Stan, which caused Bilious' pony to smash into the back of Gadabout's conveyance and woke Bilious with a jolt. 'Of course I'll have another one,' he slurred. The old Halfbit looked around with bleary eyes, until they focused on the two townies from Halfbiton. 'Hey, you're that Foodo chap, aren't you? What are you doing here?'

'I have come to join you on one final journey, Uncle Bilious.'

The old Halfbit started to pinch and prod himself, before finally roaring triumphantly, 'I'm not dead yet! In fact, it's my birthday today. I've passed The Bold Talk: I'm eleventy-somety-whatever. Oh, that's right; the elves have given me a special birthday present: a trip to The Uncrying Lands.'

'It's my birthday as well,' said Foodo.

'Of course. That's why you're here. The Elves have agreed to take you with me, so I don't get bored. I don't know why they'd think that; I was never bored at Riverdwell. Oh, actually, there was one time I was, when you and your friends came back from your holidays and tried spinning some outlandish yarn to cover up why you'd lost that precious nose ring I lent you.'

'Well, never mind that now, Uncle. What about our holiday?'

'We're going to The Great Halfways and beyond, young Foodo. I hope you've packed for a long trip.'

'But I told Dozy I'd be back in a week. I can't go that far, Mr Foodo,' said Stan.

Bilious motioned for Foodo come closer and whispered in

his ear, 'What's the spud planter talking about? Haven't you told him yet?'

Foodo turned to Stan and said, 'You're not actually going on this trip. The boat is fully booked and there is no space for you. It may be some years before the next excursion, so you can have my house and all its contents, including the larder, the wine cellar and my collection of saucy postcards. At Brag-end there will be more than enough room for you and your planned tribe. In fact, I don't know how you will manage with so many, though I have no doubt you will have some help along the way.'

Stan just scratched his head and tried to remember who the neighbours were along his new road.

The band now moved off slowly towards The Great Halfways. As they rode along, singing bawdy tavern songs, they woke everyone and everything in The Snore. Some hours later, they arrived at Mirthlong where, at the gates, they were met by Sir Dan, the Shipshape. The old sea-salt looked like most aged sailors: his skin was brown and wrinkled, his beard long and white, with bits of half-eaten fish around the corners of his mouth.

'Hey, hey, me hearties,' he said, 'I'll be your Cap'n on the good ship Mare Celestial.'

Sir Dan led them to the boat and were surprised to find The Grand Alf there, waiting for them. Hanging from his ear was Nanny, which proved he wasn't an ordinary old bloke.

Stan trudged on behind the drunken troop, visibly unhappy. As they neared the quayside where the boat was docked, he heard a low whistle from behind a bush. He went to investigate, and found Messy and Pipsqueak. 'What are you two doing here?' he asked.

'The Grand Alf told us about this cruise, so we are trying to slip aboard as stowaways,' replied Messy.

Emerging suddenly from behind the two misfits, The Grand Alf pulled them up by their ears and said, 'I knew you two would try something stupid. That's the only reason I told you. Besides, three of you have a better chance of finding your way home than one. We don't want Stan to go missing, do we?'

The green-haired duo exchanged knowing glances, and thought of Dozy, all alone.

So it was that Foodo, son of Doggo Braggins and Pungent Brandishmuck, slipped aboard the cruise-ship-cum-trawler, all without so much as a backwards glance at the unlucky three who were to remain in Muddy Earth. As Foodo's feet hit the deck, he slid with increasing speed toward a large hatch, which he fell through with as much dramatics as a professional footballer who had just been tackled. He landed in a large pile of sardines and had to be hoisted out on the end of a large hook. For a long time afterwards, Foodo could not get rid of the smell of fish, and would only have some if it was the last thing left to eat. He also began to hate the songs of the sea-elves. One particular such song went like so:

SAILING SHIPS IS IN ME BLOOD,
THE SAME AS TOO MUCH GROG.
I'VE ONLY GOT ONE GOOD LEG.
T'OTHER'S MADE OF WOOD.
AT NIGHT I SLEEPS JUST LIKE A LOG,
JUST LIKE A SEA-DOG SHOULD.

SINGING: OOOOOOOO.

UP AND AWAY, HIGH AND LOW.
FALLING FAST AND RISING SLOW.
WAVE AND FOAM, THE THINGS I'VE SEEN,
THAT MAKE THE HALFBITS FACE GO GREEN.

Foodo spent many moments doing what wasn't natural for a Halfbit: emptying his stomach, rather than filling it. After many days, they arrived at the island of Sol Erzatzhere, a very old holiday resort just far enough off the coast of The Uncrying Lands. Bilious and Foodo weren't allowed to go as there was a long-standing immigration block on what were deemed as low-lifes, regardless of whether they'd saved the planet or not.

Back in Muddy Earth, Stan still stood on the quayside, looking out over the sea. He was able to see the ship for some time. This was due to the space-time continuum, which I won't bother explaining to you at this moment, as you will have forgotten it by yesterday and, if you've got this far into the story, then you're probably as daft as me. Anyway, Stan stood with a stupefied look on his face for over an hour, then let out the type of yell one does when winning a lottery. He checked his pocket thrice, just to ensure hadn't lost the keys to the Brag-end larder, then woke the two other large Halfbits up, leapt aboard his pony, and headed towards The Snore to pay his inheritance tax bill.

A few days later, they split up, as Messy and Pipsqueak merrily took the road to Muckland, and Stan headed quickly to Passwater. Some time later, The Hill and Brag-end came into view, even though all it's lights were off. Within minutes, he was standing at the front door, fumbling with the keys. He opened the door and, with delight, called out, 'I'm back, Dozy love.'

He didn't notice Ed Randyman leaping out of the back window.

THE END ...

(NEARLY)

Somewhere else, in another place, two figures stood silent and perplexed, hardly comprehending what had just happened. Then all hell broke loose. They were facing each other, and still grasping The Nose-ring. Around them were strange metal beasts, making blaring noises. Men had become somehow trapped inside them, shouting and shaking their fists angrily at the two weirdoes blocking their way. Another metal beast with flashing eyes, screaming louder than all the others, came to a stop next to them. Two men emerged from the ears of the beast and approached the combatants.

'Hello, hello, hello. What's all this then?' asked the first one.

'Looks like we have an obstruction on the highway,' said the other.

The two men then proceeded to move the obstruction out of the way.

'Unhand me, human. I am Sourone, the Dank-lord of Bad-odour.'

'I don't care what band you're in, metal-head; you're coming with us,' said the first of the men.

'And you're coming also,' said the other one grabbing hold of the scrawny old man. 'What's your name, old fellow?'

'I'm Grumble, and I've done nothing wrong. Smear-gob is to blame.'

'Who is Smear-gob, and where is he?' asked his captor.

'He is here,' said Grumble, pointing to a spot beside him.

Meanwhile The Dank-lord was pointing at the men and saying, 'I am a powerful May-I, and I'm going to blast you all to pieces.' He gesticulated, as if he was throwing a spell their way. After a few seconds of absolutely nothing happening, nothing did. Then the back-up appeared and the Muddy Earth misfits were bundled into the back of a metal beast called Broadmoor, and sent for many years of evaluation. Grumble died a few years later, leaving Smear-gob in peace, whilst Sourone went on to form a Goth-metal group called The Morbids, and dreamt once more of world domination.

And the Nose-ring? Well, let's just say it still looks nice and precious.

FIN